Praise for Rebecca R̶

'Absolutely fantastic book, had me hooked from the first page'

'I absolutely loved everything to do with this book'

'Rebecca Raisin has a way of writing that is so evocative,
it brings each and every scene to life'

'Romantic, emotional, hilarious in places,
but most of all beautiful'

'Full of anticipation, a real page-turner. Loved it!'

'A good holiday read'

'Be whisked away on a beautiful adventure
and pick up a copy today!'

REBECCA RAISIN is a true bibliophile. This love of books morphed into the desire to write them. She's been widely published in various short story anthologies, and in fiction magazines, and is now focusing on writing romance. The only downfall about writing about gorgeous men who have brains as well as brawn, is falling in love with them – just as well they're fictional! Rebecca aims to write characters you can see yourself being friends with. People with big hearts who care about relationships, and most importantly, believe in true, once-in-a-lifetime love.

Also by Rebecca Raisin

Christmas at the Gingerbread Café
Chocolate Dreams at the Gingerbread Café
The Bookshop on the Corner
Christmas Wedding at the Gingerbread Café
Secrets at Maple Syrup Farm
The Little Bookshop on the Seine
The Little Antique Shop under the Eiffel Tower
The Little Perfume shop off the Champs-Élysées
Celebrations and Confetti at Cedarwood Lodge
Brides and Bouquets at Cedarwood Lodge
Midnight and Mistletoe at Cedarwood Lodge
Christmas at Cedarwood Lodge
Rosie's Travelling Tea Shop
Aria's Travelling Book Shop
Escape to Honeysuckle Hall

Flora's Travelling Christmas Shop

REBECCA RAISIN

ONE PLACE. MANY STORIES

HQ
An imprint of HarperCollins*Publishers* Ltd
1 London Bridge Street
London SE1 9GF

www.harpercollins.co.uk

HarperCollins*Publishers*
1st Floor, Watermarque Building, Ringsend Road
Dublin 4, Ireland

This paperback edition 2021

3
First published in Great Britain by
HQ, an imprint of HarperCollins*Publishers* Ltd 2021

Copyright © Rebecca Raisin 2021

Rebecca Raisin asserts the moral right to be
identified as the author of this work.
A catalogue record for this book is
available from the British Library.

ISBN: 9780008471415

MIX
Paper from
responsible sources
FSC® C007454

This book is produced from independently certified FSC™ paper
to ensure responsible forest management.

For more information visit: www.harpercollins.co.uk/green

Printed and bound in the UK using
100% renewable electricity at CPI Group (UK) Ltd

This one is for you, Cheryl Young.
The best MTWP ever!

Chapter 1

Is it love?

I ponder the big question as I get ready for my date with Luke, while my best friend Livvie lies sprawled on my bed, nose pressed in a book, unaware that I'm in the middle of an existential crisis.

There's a certain *je ne sais quoi* about poet Luke that makes me giddy with the thought of what might be. He's so *different* to any other guy I've dated. There's no 'dinner and a movie' blandness with him. Our dates are wonderful escapades that make me feel wholly alive.

Luke and I often go bookshop-hopping, spending long lazy Sundays in lesser known shops. My favourite is a moody little place down some long-forgotten laneway, where hardback books sit in rigid piles, the sultry scent of the past heavy in the air. Our footsteps disturb the dust as an elderly gent watches us through the swirling smoke of his pipe, as if time has stopped in that fusty ancient patch of London and the rules don't apply.

I want to find that sort of paradise for myself, and maybe I'm getting there with Luke, who's taken me to poetry slams, where he swaggers on to the stage and wins against other poets, always managing to convey so much feeling with so few words.

The way he manipulates the twenty-six letters of the alphabet into something heady and wondrous quite takes my breath away.

Luke seems to take up so much space with his big ideas and brevity. It's like he pulses with life and, by osmosis, I soak up that enthusiasm, as I'm exposed to how literature can change a mood, a life, a heart.

We've snuck into art galleries, hung out in libraries, and attended women's empowerment rallies – he's a feminist. An ally! He's the real deal; *finally*, after all this time, I've found the type of man I've always dreamed of, after so many false starts with lesser men who only wanted to change me, quieten me, make me not so . . . loud, I guess.

Luke's opened my eyes up to a whole new world I didn't know existed. He's so complex in one way and so simple in another, and he's stolen a piece of my heart after a very short amount of time. But best of all, he doesn't offer any suggestions on how I'd be the perfect girl if only I altered myself to fit in, to conform.

Right now, my wayward curls refuse to be tamed – a bit like me, I suppose – so I leave them wild. I finish my make-up with a dab of glittery eyeshadow and a swipe of thick mascara. 'It's been two months, Liv. Do you think this last-minute drinks invitation means things are about to get serious with Luke?' I'm falling for the guy, truth be told, but does he feel the same way? Each and every failed relationship has made me that little bit warier about opening my heart. Every break-up, of which there have been many, has chipped away at my confidence. I'm always 'too much' for men.

She glances at me over the top of her book. 'Yeah, I'd say so. What did his text say exactly?'

'*Meet me at The Crooked Shingle for a drink. I need to see you.*'

Taking a moment to consider it, she says, 'It sounds to me like he's missing you. Aren't you supposed to be going out with him to that book launch tomorrow?'

'Yes, tomorrow night. I had to beg Magda to let me switch

with Jonah for the day shift.' I love everything about my new job at Deck the Halls Christmas Emporium, except maybe the fact that my boss is a fire-breathing dragon and my co-worker Jonah manipulates any situation to suit himself. But hey, you can't have everything and if I get paid to sing carols while I assist customers, it's a win for me. My previous career history can be summed up in one word: *disastrous*. Usually because I speak before I think. My mouth has a tendency to get me into all sorts of bother, so I'm trying really hard lately to clamp down on any idle chitchat at work and do my job to the best of my ability. I feel like I've found my home, amid the nutcrackers at Deck the Halls, somewhere that resonates with my passion for all things festive.

'So that means Luke can't wait a mere twenty-four hours to see you – he's had to demand your presence on this fine wintry eve, eh?' Livvie shrugs. 'The man is smitten and who could blame him?'

I smile. 'I hope so. We're moving in the right direction, I think. Men are just so very hard to pin down, especially men in London, but Luke doesn't fit that mould.'

She dog-ears the page of the book and I swear I hear book-worms the world over screaming. 'Do you think he's going to make it official?'

'I do. We're moving from situationship to a proper committed relationship.' I've been in countless situationships, which is really a kinder term for friends with benefits, or worse, as my American friends say – a booty call. I blame unrealistic Hollywood movies for this spate of non-committal men in big cities.

'Well, you're on the right track, Flora. He seems genuine, like he's got a decent brain in his head.'

'It's his intensity that I like most. The way he knows what he wants and he goes for it. He doesn't overthink.'

'A little like you, then? Spontaneous *is* your middle name.'

'Sort of?' We laugh. Up until this point my love life could best be described as short, sharp and chaotic. For some reason I never seem to make it to the three-month mark with men. I don't bat my lashes and pretend to be coy, or act haughty and unavailable. I'm just me, in all my technicolour glory – but that doesn't get me anywhere. I quiz men on what they want out of life, early on, which tends to frighten them. But why can't we say how we feel? And what we want? Why do we have to pretend?

I *love* love! I fall head over heels before it all fizzles out, time and time again. I'm always told I'm rushing things but is that true or just an excuse because the guys I date never want to settle down? Don't want to be tied to one woman for the rest of forever?

As I near the big three-oh, I'm keen to find true love. Who hasn't been planning their wedding since primary school? After kissing way too many frogs, I've made a checklist to save time and angst. It's long, detailed and a little whimsical but it's for the best in the long run . . .

That's why Luke is special. He hasn't blanched when I've subtly quizzed him while simultaneously ticking the boxes on that magical must-have perfect-man list.

'He must be keen to take the relationship to the next level,' Livvie says. 'And that can only be a good thing.'

I spritz on perfume. 'Yes, I suppose. That or he just wants sex.'

She laughs. 'I'm sure it's crossed his mind.'

'Only one way to find out, I guess.'

'I won't wait up.'

'I'm not sleeping at his place until it's been at least three months! It's all so juvenile with his flatmates hovering around, giving him the nudge and those sly winks. Not for me, that kind of thing.' I shake my head at the thought.

'Ignore them – they're probably jealous! Just go for it.'

'And I'm not adding casual sex into the mix until I know for sure he's the real deal.'

She makes a show of being exasperated. 'Fine, you be you, Flora, and I expect to hear all about it at breakfast tomorrow.'

'At breakfast? Are you not listening, Liv? You know I'm not a prude but I'm also not an advocate of casual sex for the sake of it. Unless the guy is Jason Momoa's single twin brother, then I'm not interested until I know for sure we're solid! But if you're asleep when I get home I'll text you a full report, don't you worry about that!'

Livvie gives me a hug and soon I'm heading out into the icy cold London night.

Chapter 2

While Luke grabs our drinks, I find a table by the window. Outside, sparkly Christmas lights reflect on the inky Thames, swirling saffron and jade like something out of a Van Gogh painting. It mesmerises me as the river laps and eddies, making the colours oscillate on the current.

Luke returns and sits across from me but I'm still half stuck in a daze with the beauty of the water. He clears his throat. 'I'm glad we could catch up. I wanted to talk to you about something.'

'So talk,' I say holding my head in my hand while imagining various scenarios. Where we'll live: probably a tiny flat in a warehouse conversion in Soho. Where we'll have our first proper holiday: New York for its literary haunts? Paris for its romance? Or perhaps Greece for the sunshine and ouzo after long languorous beach days.

'It's been fun,' he says in that silky soulful voice of his, 'these last couple of months.'

I nod, barely able to form words as my heart beats staccato. Maybe he's written a new book of poetry dedicated to us? He's going to invite me to listen, as he reads on stage for the crowd, declaring he's never felt this way before. Never really believed in true love until now.

'But . . .'

But?

'It's time we call it quits, before one of us gets hurt.'

Whoa, whoa, whoa. '*What?*'

He shrugs. 'We're not right for each other.' The words are delivered like bullets that pierce my body, *pow, pow, pow.* Is this some kind of sick prank? This is the guy who whispered sweet nothings in my ear in shadowy recesses of the library. The guy who said 'affluence is a construct' as we snuck into the gallery without paying and held hands while walking past priceless works of art.

Mortifyingly, tears sting my eyes. 'This is a . . . surprise.' One that has quite knocked my legs from under me. 'Why aren't we right for each other?' I struggle to make sense of it all. How could I have read this so wrong? *Again!*

All along I thought he was different, better than other men, but sitting opposite me now, he looks exactly like all the others. As if he's been struck with ennui, and dropped the soulful poet act. There's something downright accusatory in his eyes, even. *Is it me?* Am I the one who needs to change? The same old pattern repeats.

Luke gulps down his drink as if he's preparing to leave. He's detonated the grenade and now he's going to run for cover. 'You're just a bit much for me, Flora. You're a little too . . . how can I put it?' He rubs at his chin contemplatively as if we're not in the midst of a break-up. 'You're zany, that's the word. At first I thought it was refreshing, cute even, but now I'm not so sure.' He frowns as he surveys the mascara that I can feel streaking down my face, before hurriedly reassuring me, 'That doesn't mean you need to change for *me!* There's a guy out there who'll adore your eccentricities, but that guy is not me.'

My sadness is quickly replaced by annoyance and I resist the urge to wallop him. 'My eccentricities?'

He pulls a face that suggests I'm boring him with my questions, as if he only wanted to rip off the plaster and leave without all the angst of my emotions holding him up. 'Yeah, Flora, surely it's not the first time you've heard this sort of thing? Eccentric can be good, but it can also be a little contrived, you know?'

I don't respond, because I don't understand.

With a sigh he continues: 'You dress like it's Christmas every day . . .'

I let out a scoff. 'I work in a Christmas shop!'

Luke gives me one of those looks that says: *I'm not angry; I'm just disappointed in you.* 'Yet here we are *after hours* and you're wearing a jumper that says: Sleigh my name!'

Gah, he's the limit. 'Because it's so funny! And isn't this the very essence of Christmas? To be *merry*?'

'It's November!'

'Exactly?!' Can he not hear himself? He's not making any sense at all! How could this smooth-talking, silky-voiced magician with words have turned into . . . this, this regular run-of-the-mill, average Joe? I'm wondering if he's in his right mind, the about-face is so sudden, so wildly different to the Luke of the last eight weeks.

'You have high heels that have flashing Santas all over them.' I give him a cold, hard stare but the fool just continues, 'And your nails, are they painted in Santa jackets?'

'Yeah, they bloody well are. *Painstakingly* hand-painted by Minh, my nail technician, who is an artist in her field!' Men just don't get it, do they? 'So, it's my love of all things Christmas you find so offensive? Is that *all*?'

'Well, I also feel like you might be rushing ahead, when I just wanted something more casual. You're a beautiful girl, it's just . . .' Who is this monster? Where did my intense, *let's feel all the feelings* poet go?

Was he acting all along? The dating game in this bloody town is BROKEN.

'How was *I* rushing ahead? You're the one who wanted to get physical the very first night, or in guy speak is that *not* rushing things? Is it because I said no, and hurt your feelings? Your tiny little man ego couldn't handle me stomping on the brakes the very first night we met?'

'No, Flora, that was fine. My tiny little man ego is intact. It wasn't any of that, it was all the questions about winter wonderland wedding venues, which Christmas song you'd walk down the aisle to, that sort of thing that freaked me out. That odd question about the reindeer names?!'

OK, OK, so a few of my dating foibles may have slipped out along the way, but can you blame a person for wanting to know the answers to those pressing questions? It's not like I *proposed* to the guy! And these are all things that are on the checklist and must be addressed at some point, so why not now?

I hold up a hand, to make him shut his trap. 'Listen, you'd be lucky if I even considered marrying a guy like you, *damn* lucky, but I'll have you know those questions are purely meant to ferret out potentially incompatible husbands – for matrimony way, way down the track. If we both have different ideas about marriage, then there's no point wasting time, is there? It's not like I want to tie the knot yet, but I also don't want to waste five years with you only to hear later you want to be married in a non-festive season in Vegas by an Elvis impersonator, while I walk down the aisle to "Love Me Tender" or something equally unsuitable.'

He grimaces. 'Marriage, though, Flora? It's too soon to even *mention* the M word!'

I cross my arms, and then realise that looks defensive so I uncross them again. 'Yet you mentioned the S word in the second bloody hour we met and *that's* OK? It should have been a big red flag, a flashing fluorescent sign screaming FAKE! You're all the same around here, just out for casual flings, hotfooting it from one girl to the other. Well, I'm not interested in casual sex, and I am especially not interested in casual sex with someone who hasn't considered their own wedding venue!'

I grab my handbag – my very kitsch and cute Christmas tree

handbag – and leave in a hurry. More time wasted with yet another guy who just wants to Netflix and Chill. Seriously, where have all the good guys gone?

Back at the flat, I dramatically throw open the door and rush inside. 'Livvie! Oh my God, he broke up with me because *apparently* I'm eccentric! Is that some kind of code? The new "It's not you, it's me"?'

Livvie lifts her head off the side of the sofa, her eyes wide with shock. '*What?* How did all this come about? What did he say exactly?'

'Well . . .' I flop beside her. 'Basically that I'm too zany, but don't worry, I'm beautiful and some other man is going to snap me right up, someone who'll love my *eccentricities*, or some other bollocks. And I'm also moving too fast because a few days back I happened to ask him his feelings on certain festive wedding venues, and walk-down-the-aisle songs.'

'Oh, Flora, you didn't!'

'I did!'

She leans her head on my shoulder. 'Maybe you could leave that sort of questioning until the third month, at least?'

'No, it's best to find out who I'm dealing with straight up.'

'OK, you keep doing you, Flora, that's what I love about you. You always run your own race.'

'Oh God, you think I'm eccentric and zany and needy . . .'

'All the best people are.'

'I think I'm going to give up on men for a while. Maybe forever. Instead, I'll marry an inflatable Santa or something, like you see those people doing, getting married to their favourite bridge, or rock. Something *meaningful.*'

'That sounds very sane.'

'Urgh, well . . . at least I have my new wonderful fulfilling job at Deck the Halls, shop assistant-cashier in the most magical place on earth to distract me from yet another heartbreak. I bloody love it there and I know I'll be able to get back on my feet soon and get my life back on track. And best of all, I have you by my side when life charts off course. You're always there to right my sails . . .'

'About that . . .' Livvie says, sitting upright. 'Wait, this calls for wine.' She dashes off to the kitchen and returns bearing two wine glasses and a fancy bottle of red.

'Oh no, the fancy wine. You're dying? *I'm* dying? What's going on!' I can't help but shriek. The fancy wine only comes out when there's a disaster and we're commiserating. If we're celebrating we always, always have bubbles.

Livvie jumps back on the sofa sending me sprawling into the arm. 'No one is dying. Here, hold these.' I take the proffered glasses while Livvie opens the wine and pours a nice healthy dose.

'The suspense is killing me, Liv, get on with it.'

'OK . . .' She scrapes a lock of shiny black hair behind her ear. 'You know how I approached that company about my skincare collection?'

Livvie's an aesthetician, with her own small clinic specialising in Botox and lip fillers and that sort of thing. She caters to the upwardly mobile of London who want a little cosmetic help. At least once a week she asks me to be a guinea pig, but I can't stand the thought of needles piercing my skin and my face being frozen by some toxin, even though I can see the appeal. Livvie'll look like a stunning airbrushed twenty-something for the rest of her life, while I'll wrinkle year by year like the picture of Dorian Gray.

'Yes, I remember, those fancy LA types who were all very dreamy!' She laughs at the lovey-dovey face I pull. 'They said yes, didn't they?' Because Livvie is an overachiever, the clinic wasn't enough so she formulated this amazing skincare range that somehow manages to blur fine lines better than any make-up can. She's been looking for a company to invest in it to fund clinical trials so she can get the brand out to the world.

'They offered me a deal. It's the only way I can build the biz,

Flora. I can't do it alone and they have the funds to make it on a grand scale and then I'll be rich and famous and I will buy you any inflatable Santa husband that you want!'

'Thank you for offering to buy me a husband – that's very sweet. But that company is in LA, which means *you'll* be in LA!' I cup my face and try not to howl. 'Just how do you expect me to cope without you?' I have this overwhelming feeling it's happening again . . . my life is spiralling out of control. A break-up, and now my best friend moving continents, all in one evening! No, I will not become a negative Nelly! I am a strong, almost-thirty-year-old woman who will get her life in order!

'What if you come with me?'

'And leave all . . . this?' 'All this' is actually *all* Livvie's. 'I have my fabulous job as a cashier to consider. People *need* me. Customers depend on me and my expert opinions on all things festive.' The words fall out a little robotically as I try and hold it together for Livvie's sake. No one wants an eccentric, zany crybaby raining on their parade.

'I can see that. And I won't be gone forever. It'll be a year or so while we set things up and then I'll be back to run the London office.'

'Look at you, the *London office*. I'm dead proud of you, Liv, even if it means I'm losing you.' For the second time in one night, my eyes go glassy with tears.

'You'll never lose me.'

I sniffle and snuffle. 'When do you leave?'

'As soon as I can but it'll probably take a month or so to get the clinic sorted so I'll play it by ear and book my flight once things are tied up here. I've started advertising for a manager. I've put together a remuneration package including offering them the flat as part of the deal. Obviously you're welcome to stay too – that doesn't need to change.'

'But I don't even pay rent, since I'm only staying until I get myself sorted.' Well, that's what I said when I moved into Livvie's spare room eighteen months ago. Gosh, time flies when you're in a rut.

'Don't worry about the rent.' But I do worry. I've always promised myself I wouldn't depend on Livvie financially. I hate that sort of thing. She's let me live here rent-free, because my life is such a disaster, but staying here without her is another thing entirely. And I could never afford rent in central London, not even for a shoebox-sized room.

Deep down I think Livvie still thinks she owes me after practically growing up at Nan's place. There's always that need to 'repay' me for sharing my family, making her one of us. She never says so in as many words, but we've been friends long enough, sisters in a way, that I know her motivations without her needing to communicate them. I really wish she wouldn't think like that though. Livvie's home life was marred by her parents' toxic relationship and it's why she strives so hard – she doesn't want to be beholden to anyone. I admire her for that. More than I could ever say. To come out of a childhood like hers and be this well-rounded, considerate, compassionate go-getter is inspiring. She had that fire in her belly back when she still wore her hair in plaits.

'I'll find another place,' I say brightly, trying to fool her that worry isn't setting in. 'Somewhere smaller.' Read: cheaper. I'll have to move to the very outskirts of London to be able to afford to rent a room on my teeny wage – but at least I have a wage and that's something to be thankful for. 'I've lost my sort-of boyfriend and now my best friend all in one day. Let's hope tomorrow is better.'

'You'll be OK, and if all else fails I'll send the private jet to come fetch you.'

My mouth falls open. 'They have a private jet?'

'No, but it sounds like a very LA thing to say.'

'It does! And what about your significant other? What's he got to say about all of this?' I can't stand the guy; I can't even remember his stupid name.

She sighs. 'I haven't told him yet.' I hope for all that is holy

13

she ditches the new boyfriend and moves on. I can tell she's not that into him even if she's pretends otherwise.

We drink the bottle of red and laugh-cry our way through the evening. Losing Livvie is like losing my right arm. We've been best friends since we were little kids and she's still coming to my rescue two decades and a bit later.

Who will I be without her . . . ?

Chapter 3

The next evening when I'm supposed to be at Luke's friend's book launch, I sit in my Santa's helper PJs, nursing a cup of eggnog and wondering where it all went wrong. The eggnog helps; it's such a soothing Christmas tipple that conjures the comfort and warmth that was Christmastime at my nan's. She was a ruddy-faced, jovial woman who never had a bad word to say about anyone, but cross her and you'd soon know about it. Nan was one of those what-you-see-is-what-you-get types, who swept up the lost and broken, fed them, housed them and set them free knowing they always had her open arms to return to if needed.

My parents were different. They were more concerned about appearances, the be-quiet-the neighbours-might-hear types – as long as outwardly we looked the goods, then all was well. My parents spent the formative years of my life telling me I wasn't quite up to their standards, I wasn't trying hard enough to succeed, I didn't compare well to my siblings. Still don't, if I'm honest. My nan's was my safe harbour, the place I went to for love and acceptance.

I miss her dearly. She's the reason I adore Christmas like I do. I spent every Christmas at her place, helping knead dough for homemade fruit mince pies as we sang along to carols. She let me measure out the brandy for the dried fruit mix including a tipple for her, '*to make sure it's not poisonous, my darling*'. The scent of cinnamon and nutmeg still sends me back to that small, tidy kitchen and the image of my cheerful, apron-clad nan cackling away after two small nips, her ruddy cheeks somehow redder, her eyes watery as she claimed, '*I love you, you know, my precious Flora. You're different to the others and mark my words, you're going to show them all. You're a late bloomer, that's all, my dear, and you know what's so extraordinary about being a late bloomer?*'

'What?' I'd ask, feeling a frisson of delight that Nan could see something special in me, something no one else could. Me, the average student, the girl who spent too long daydreaming, the sibling who paled in comparison. The daughter who Just. Wouldn't. Listen.

'*Late bloomers know instinctively they have to wait for the magic to happen. And a magical life takes time. You can't rush magic now, can you? So you let nature take its course and ignore those who try and dull your sparkle . . .*'

I don't know how many times we had the exact same conversation. It's as though Nan knew I'd need reminders as I crept towards thirty, still not having 'bloomed'. When I think of her, I'm transported back to her aga-warmed kitchen, cocooned by her love, the scent of Christmas spices peppering the air. She'd delight in wrapping presents, sitting at the island bench, while I stirred myriad pots and pans and she waxed lyrical about what she'd bought for whom and why. She made gift-giving an art form, that woman. And then there'd been the decorating of the cottage on the 1st of December every year.

Livvie and I would race to Nan's place after school, and we'd spend the evening putting up trees. She had twelve in total, one for every nook and cranny, ranging from large to small and everything in between. We'd tape tinsel like bunting across the ceiling. Ornaments were delicately prised from their tissue-paper-filled boxes, polished and put on display wherever we could find room.

And taking pride of place was the lighted grotto that Nan adored. I've still got that buried away in a box. I've got most of her decorations, and my very own collection that I've built up over my lifetime. Every year, Nan bought me an ornament to add to my stash, and I also invested in some more expensive ranges like Swarovski and Hallmark. Some girls invest in designer shoes, I invest in Christmas decorations! If only Nan was still here, she'd prop me up with a warm mug of cocoa and tell me my time was coming and all these bumps along the way were part of the plan . . .

The front door opens with a whoosh of air, snatching me from my walk down memory lane. It's freezing for November, and I wonder if it means we'll have an early spell of snow.

'Am I glad to be home!' Livvie says. 'What a *day*.'

'Wait . . .' I go to the kitchen and pour Livvie an eggnog before bustling back into the cosy front room. 'What happened?'

'Ooh, thanks.' She sips the creamy drink and falls into the armchair by the gas fire, pulling a throw across her lap. 'Urgh, just one drama after another. It's like the more I try to cross off my to-do list, the more things keep being added. Anyway, it doesn't matter, not really, it just seems endless with so much to do before I go. How was your day?'

'Pretty good, all things considered. If not for Deck the Halls, I'd have been at home bingeing Hallmark Christmas movies and wondering why it always works out for the lovable but misguided heroine and never for me.'

'Why does it always work out so easily for them?' she laments.

'I probably need to move to a small town and fall in love with the geeky librarian who is surprisingly hot when he takes his glasses off and parts his hair on the other side.'

'Ooh, yes. Like Karl out of *Love Actually*. Although, he wasn't a librarian and he was hot *with* the glasses.'

'Super hot. Anyway, you *do* have a boyfriend even if he doesn't quite meet the Hallmark standards.' Livvie's new boyfriend is a total plonker but she gets a little upset when I blurt that out.

'Yeah,' she sighs. 'Anyway, enough about all that. I dragged myself kicking and screaming from the clinic because I thought we could decorate for the holidays. What do you think? A sure-fire way to cheer up our festive Flora, right?'

'But you're leaving in three weeks. Is there any point in putting everything up only to take it down again so soon?' My throat tightens just thinking about Livvie leaving and me treading water while I figure out where I'm going to live. And how I'm going to function without my sounding board and the sensible one in this duo.

'Is there any point!' she says in a way that implies there certainly is.

'True!' I say, grinning. 'Let's do it! Let's celebrate a pre-Christmas Christmas before you go.'

'Fabulous idea!'

I consider where to start. 'How about I make us a festive feast tomorrow night?' She blanches and tries to quickly recover but I'm not fooled. 'I'll cook the turkey all the way through this time, I promise.' That's one Christmas lunch we'll never forget.

'As tempting as that sounds, you're working tomorrow so how about I pick up some bits and pieces on the way home instead? Harrods have some delicious little Christmas morsels on offer already.'

'Ooh Harrods, dead fancy. You get the food and I'll grab the bubbles.'

'Deal.'

'Let's decorate!'

We go to my room and unearth my collection from under the dusty recesses of the bed.

'What's with all the Quality Street tins? Are they filled with baubles or something?' she asks.

I blush. 'No, they're empty. I like to eat away the heartache when I have a break-up – you know how it is.'

'Going by the number of tins, that's a lot of break-ups. Are you including first and only dates in these . . . break-ups?'

'Of course! It's another reason to sit with my feelings.'

'Right.'

'It always pays to reflect.'

'I'm sure it does.'

'OK, so let's put up the tree first.'

We spend the next hour drinking eggnog, decorating the tree and swapping memories about growing up together. Soon talk swings back to my nan, who loved Livvie like a granddaughter too.

'I miss her,' she says, holding a mini picture frame ornament in the palm of her hand. The photograph housed inside is of me, Nan and Livvie, faces squished together, laughter in our eyes. 'Christmas has never been the same since, has it?' Her voice breaks.

I pretend to study my nails as if they're fascinating, not wanting to give in to tears but knowing it's inevitable. 'We've made the best of every Christmas since, Liv, haven't we? But you're right, it's not the same and I don't think it ever will be.' Despite my many years of tutelage in Nan's kitchen, I can't re-create any of the food she made without poisoning people. We can sit around a warm oven, laugh and joke and sing, but there's still that key element missing – Nan. But while it makes me sad, I always feel grateful too. Not everyone gets to have a nan as loving as mine had been, and I'm glad I got to have as much time with her as I did. I have a heart full of memories and so does Livvie, and we try and follow all those traditions she left us with.

'Here's to Nan,' Livvie says, holding her mug of eggnog aloft.

'To the best woman to have walked this earth.' We tap mugs and say 'cheers'.

'You're like her, you know.'

'I'm nothing like her,' I say. 'She was formidable and gregarious and had that ability to make you feel safe and loved and like the most important person on the planet.'

Livvie pauses and gives me such a look that suggests I'm not listening. 'You do that to people too, Flora. You just don't see it. You always think you're sticking your foot in your mouth, but it's usually when you're standing up for others who can't or don't know how to. Your nan would be so proud of you for that.'

'Now you're just trying to make me cry.'

She gives me a loose hug. 'Let's finish off this tree, eh?'

Chapter 4

The phone rings and rings – where *is* he? As far as work colleagues go Jonah is the one I'm closest to, but that privilege also comes with its own problems. Jonah does what's best for Jonah, always. He's just as likely to throw me under the bus as he is to switch a shift or lie for me in case of emergency, like the one I'm currently facing. But I don't have much choice, so I continue racing through the city and willing him to answer his mobile.

'. . . 'lo?'

'Jonah, *finally*, I'm running late! Cover for me with Magda please?' I dash across the icy London street, my velvet reindeer slippers no match for the puddles. The slippers are part of our uniform but I don't usually wear them walking to work for this very reason! In my frantic state this morning, I couldn't find my trainers, and all my other shoes are far too fancy for the daytime streets of London. Alas, there's no time to tiptoe around the many pockets of dirty water so I splish-splash through them with a gasp. I'm cold right down to my very soul. 'Tell her I'm . . . I'm in the storeroom sorting breakages.'

'Who is this?' he drawls lazily.

Cue my eyeroll. 'Very funny. It's Flora and you know it!'

'Late again, eh, Flora?' He draws each syllable out as if I'm not smack bang in the middle of a potential job-threatening disaster. Why does everything I try backfire on me?

'It's not my fault! I had a wardrobe malfunction, Rudolph's little red nose—'

'A wardrobe malfunction? Is that what you call it these days? That guy is no good for you, darling.' He laughs that infuriating cackle of his – I can't *think* why I tried to get Jonah on side. He does tend to delight in other people's misfortunes and use it in his favour.

I push the traffic crossing buzzer with a 'Come on, come on,' and rue the fact it's taking so long to turn green. I don't have the heart to tell Jonah that Luke has gone the way of all my past boyfriends. South. We hadn't even made it to the Facebook official stage! 'Look, just tell Magda I'm out the back, sorting erm . . . all the things that need . . . sorting, OK?'

'I don't know, Flora. *Rules are rules*. Plus, she'll just look on CCTV for you. Wait, I've got a customer.' The crossing signal finally goes green so I shuffle as best I can in my sopping slippers and try not to think of Magda catching me out.

Truthfully, I'm late again because inspiration hit after we decorated the flat so I stayed up to the wee hours planning a Christmas display extravaganza that I plan on presenting to Magda later today. I'm a little nervous about it because for someone who owns a Christmas shop, she certainly isn't all that joyful. However, Magda is driven by sales, so if I pitch it right I just might convince her. It's not so much a job to me, rather something I hope to make a career out of, even though I'm still considered the new girl after being here three months. The hours are long and the remuneration lacklustre, but that doesn't matter to me. What matters is, I've finally found a job that suits me, one that I enjoy most of the time.

I heard about the position through a friend of a friend, who put in a good word for me with Magda. Not that Magda really cares what anyone thinks. I'm sure she invented resting bitch face, she's so damn good at it, but I don't take it to heart. We can't all be merry and bright. I'm still a little puffy-eyed after the break-up and the bombshell about Livvie jetting off to LA. The only thing I've got left is my job, so I want to make sure Magda knows how invested I am. And like an idiot, I forgot to set my bloody alarm this morning after staying up so late trying to make my presentation shine.

We have plenty of displays in the shop but nothing spectacular, none that would get any write-ups in the press. My dream is to build a wonderland for children so they *really* believe in the magic of Christmas! And if Magda thinks it's all a driver for sales, then so be it. But for me, it's all about making fairy-tale memories for young and old.

I round the corner and Deck the Halls Christmas Emporium comes into sight. I can almost taste freedom! Well, not freedom, more like captivity but in the best possible place. A Christmas shop filled with every imaginable trinket for the festive season from simple baubles right up to imported glittering gold sleighs and everything in between. There's matching festive loungewear for family selfies, Yuletide bedding and just about every electronic Santa you can imagine.

'*She's here!*' Jonah hisses.

'So am I!' I end the call, whip off my jacket and scarf, and peek inside the double doors. No sign of Magda so I throw my drenched clothing under a table to retrieve later. I run a hand through my hair, hoping to disguise how wet it is, and apologise as I scoot past customers to get to the staffroom. I'm sure that my toes are wrinkled like prunes by now. I need to assess the damage to my slippers. I'm hoping they make it through the day but I don't like my chances from the squelching noises they make.

Shoot – I spot Magda wearing that supercilious look of hers. She resembles the Terminator, scanning faces in a robotic way, no doubt searching out mine. I dart behind a Christmas tree before she catches sight of me. I need to offload my handbag so she doesn't know I've only just got in.

I want to give Magda the benefit of the doubt, and believe that deep down she's a good person with a sweet heart, but so far that doesn't appear to be the case. It's as though she delights in tormenting her staff until they quit or she can fire them for some minor misdemeanour. It's scary how much she seems to enjoy it. Part of me wonders if too many people have done the wrong thing by her, so she's always on guard. Always ready to pounce. I hope to show her that not all employees are alike, and that once she sees I'm committing a lot of time and effort *unpaid* after work, she'll mellow out and soften towards me. My goal is to go from cashier to floor supervisor, and slowly work my way up the ladder to stock purchaser! All I have to remember is to keep my head down and my mouth closed – I've lost too many jobs by blurting out what I *really* think.

As I peer around the Christmas tree, someone taps my shoulder and I swear my soul leaves my body. 'What are you *doing*?' Jonah says loudly enough to draw attention from customers.

'Shush, I'm hiding from Magda!' I thrust my handbag at him and whisper urgently, 'Put this in my locker!' He takes it from my hands and holds it aloft as if it's offensive to him.

'What do I get out of it if I do?' He raises a smarmy brow. I'll grudgingly admit Jonah is a good friend as far as work colleagues go but he's one of those people who always *expects* something. I can't count the number of times I've covered a shift for him in return for his secrecy about a folly I've committed. 'You're on bins and bathrooms all of today, and . . .' He taps his chin not because he's contemplating but because Jonah loves drawing out his bribes.

I hide a smile. 'I won't be doing bins today, or anything else, since it's your turn.'

'You want the handbag in the locker or not?' He twirls the strap on his index finger.

'You'll do it or I'll tell Magda about Tuesday night.' I lift a brow. He gasps. 'How do you know about that?'

24

Game, set, match! 'You're not the only one with spies around here, you know.' I copy his stare-down tactic but it probably looks more like I've got something in my eye.

After an eternity he says, 'Well played, Flora, well played.' He spins on his heel before flinging my bag over his shoulder like he's a catwalk model strutting down a runway.

I don't have spies but he doesn't need to know that. Jonah does and he uses them to get out of work by sheer manipulation alone. Last Tuesday evening I'd forgotten my house keys, a usual occurrence for me, and came back to the shop at fifteen minutes before closing time only to find it locked up tight. A sackable offence. I know he had a date with a cute bar guy in Covent Garden, but still . . . *Rules are rules.*

Thrilled I've pulled one over the master manipulator himself, I straighten my Rudolph outfit, snatch a second pair of reindeer slippers off the rack and get to work. Deck the Halls Christmas Emporium might just be a Christmas shop to some, but to me it represents so much more. It's a place for people to seek refuge, to recall fond memories of Christmas past as they wander the aisles. For children, it's where dreams are made. I adore seeing their eyes light up as if they've discovered Narnia. And I love watching families wander in and plan their Christmas décor right down to the colour of napkins.

An almost palpable *merriness* radiates off shoppers and that sort of excitement is contagious. Already I've seen friendships begin in store over strangers sharing their Christmas Day traditions. I've watched when the very last high-ticket toy in town was picked up simultaneously by two mums, who then played rock, paper, scissors to determine who'd get the coveted toy. Of course, it's not all glitter and good tidings, there's plenty of drama too, but I choose not to dwell on those moments.

Livvie says I'm a Christmas tragic. And I proudly wear that badge. It's the time of year where people stop and think of others. From lovingly thought-out gifts to meticulously planning the

Christmas feast they'll share across the table. Or even something as simple as sending a Christmas card. It's all about the small details for me.

For those who celebrate Christmas or Hanukkah or any seasonal occasion at this time of year, it's as though the world pauses for that infinitesimal amount of time – smiles get wider, hope abounds and joy is found in the simplest of things, like listening to carols, or popping a cracker and donning a paper crown. It's an enchanting time of year and working in a Christmas shop only increases the fun.

Today customers bustle in as they unwind scarves, eyes wide as they take in our sparkly Christmas display at the entrance: a re-creation of Lapland's Santa's village complete with tiny cabins, faux snow, and glittering Christmas trees. I begged Magda to let me try to re-create the aurora borealis, but she refused, saying she didn't want shoppers to be looking up, but rather down, where the stock sits. It would have been wondrous, pink and green swirls on the ceiling above, snatching customers from London and transporting them to Lapland, but hey, you can't win every battle . . . I've been obsessed with Lapland ever since I can remember. After all, it's the *real* home of Santa Claus! I'll get there one day, but for now it's back to work.

Humming along to carols, I right a few fallen decorations, make sure the nutcrackers are lined up straight, and head to the counter to help serve the queue who zigzag around a gingerbread house. Before I get there, I see a young girl of about seven or eight, bottom lip wobbling as she cradles a red Christmas bauble.

There's nothing worse than tears during the festive season. Perhaps she's overwhelmed with the noise and the throngs of people who push past her tiny frame.

Well, not on my watch. I drop to my knees so I'm eye level and give her my cheeriest smile. 'Are you OK, lovely? It's a bit busy in here because Christmas is creeping closer every day.'

It seems since November has rolled around the shop has gone from quiet to chaotic all in the space of a few days.

The little girl's big blue eyes are shiny with tears as she gives me the barest of nods. Where are her parents? I glance around but don't see anyone hovering close who looks the part. 'Is Mummy or Daddy here with you?'

'Daddy's outside, on his phone.'

She slides her gaze away. 'Oh, are you shopping for a surprise for Mummy?'

At the mention of her mother, tears streak down the little girl's face. Oh dear. Whatever could be the matter?

She sniffs and snuffles. 'I wanted to get her this bauble, with her name on it, but I've only got five pounds.'

I look at the display and see to have it personalised would cost another three quid.

'Perhaps when Daddy is off the phone . . .'

She cuts me off. 'He said no. He says it's easier not to talk about it or he gets too sad. Granny said Mummy had the cancer and she's with the angels now.' More tears trail down her cherubic cheeks and I'm quite lost for words. 'It will be our first Christmas without Mummy. I want to hang this on the front of the tree so I know she's still with us.'

I can actually hear my heart shatter with grief for the little girl. She needs this bauble – no two ways about it. 'Why don't I personalise it, make up the three-pound difference and that can be my Christmas present to you?'

Her little face lights up with joy. 'Really?'

'It would be my pleasure. Would you like me to write Mummy or . . . ?'

She shakes her head. 'Her name was Grace.'

'I love that name! "Amazing Grace" is one of my favourite carols.'

She grins and her red-rimmed eyes light up. 'It was Mummy's favourite too! Can you write Amazing Grace on it for her?'

'I sure can.' I get to work, making sure it's perfect for my young customer, and then jump the queue and take her to the front of the counter. 'Coming through with a VIP customer,' I say, trying to make the moment special. I wrap the delicate bauble in tissue paper, and place it in a fancy gift box before tying it all up with a thick red ribbon. I'm not supposed to use the luxe gift boxes for purchases under a hundred pounds, but this sale warrants it. I imagine the little girl making a ceremony of opening the gift box every year, unwrapping the precious keepsake and having a silent chat with her mum as she places it front and centre on the Christmas tree.

The little girl hands over a wrinkled five-pound note, and I pop it in the till along with some coins from my Rudolph pocket to make up the shortfall. I need to pay for my replacement slippers too but it'll have to wait until I can get to my purse. Her big wobbly smile makes my heart lurch and I send a silent prayer up to her mum, amazing Grace. 'You come back and see me next year and we'll do one for you and your daddy too, OK?'

'I will. Thank you so much!' She blows me kisses across the counter, her tears forgotten, then is off and running like all her Christmases have come at once.

'Right, who was next?' I say, feeling the joy of Christmas deep in my soul. The next customer averts her eyes, and subtly points behind me. There's a distinct chill in the air, which can only mean one thing: Magda!

Pasting on a nutcracker smile, I turn and hope to all that is holy she didn't see my last transaction. 'Oh, Magda, didn't see you er, standing on the back of my ankles there. Tight squeeze, isn't it?' She makes breathing down one's neck an art form. I try to inch sideways to put some distance between us.

Magda's glare is so sharp it could crack chestnuts and it's pointed directly at me. This doesn't bode well. 'Is there something wrong?' Her face has turned candy-cane-red and shakes slightly as if she's holding herself tightly coiled but is about to explode.

Maybe she's having a moment, a hot flush, a midlife crisis? It might not have a *thing* to do with me.

She takes one of my Rudolph antlers and pulls me close. It's quite violent in a way and I am about to tell her so, when she says, 'Did you just have your *hands* in the till?' Her voice is downright *venomous*.

The customers are frozen to the spot, almost as if they're holding their breath. I rush to reassure them with a twinkly little laugh as if my boss pulls at my antlers every day, and it's just our way of communicating. 'Well, of course I had my hands in the till. I'm a cashier!' I give the crowd an *are you hearing this rubbish* look.

She shakes her head. 'I didn't mean like that.'

'Well, what *did* you mean?' I pull my head back in the hopes of dislodging the antler from her fist. I tug and tug before it finally gives way and my neck snaps backwards. Sheesh.

'That child didn't have enough money, did she?'

Oh jingle bells. 'She was a tad short, but I covered it.' Now we've drawn the attention of the entire floor and I want nothing more than to hide behind a snowman and wait for Magda to hightail it back to her office where she can watch me on CCTV rather than slink up behind.

'What did I tell you about doing that?' she hisses and I'm sure steam comes out of her nose.

I take a deep breath and repeat her last reprimand verbatim. *'I'm not to make up the shortfall no matter what their hard luck stories are.'* I don't see what the problem is when it's my own money. It's not like I'm letting them away without paying.

'And yet you did it again. Not only that, you put a five-pound bauble in a box meant for purchases over a hundred quid. Can you tell me why?'

'Well, it was eight pounds all up.'

'The bauble was five.'

'OK, yes you've got me on a technicality there.' *And it's still not a hundred quid, Flora!*

'Then why, Flora, why did you go against company policy *again*?'

She's going to feel like a right twit when I tell her the story. So I explain in detail, appealing to her (perhaps non-existent) maternal nature, putting a lot of emphasis on how each year that little girl will remember this very shop and the kindness shown and one day when she's a rich and happy mother herself she'll come back and spend a tonne of money, just like you see on those heart-warming Christmas adverts every year.

Magda rolls her eyes and looks distinctly Grinch-like. 'You're a sucker, Flora. The girl's mother is probably out the front. Did you ever think about that?'

She can't be serious! 'So you think a mother told her daughter to come in here and cry delicate tears while telling a shop assistant her mother *died*, all to save three quid? Who would do that to their own child, Magda!?' Honestly, have her brains left the building?

Her face goes from red to purple and I'm quite concerned for her blood pressure. That can't be healthy, can it? 'And what about yesterday's incident, when you caught that shoplifter?' Her voice is like steel and I'm beginning to wonder if I've pushed old Magda too far. That's my problem, I speak up when I should shut up. It gets me in trouble all the bloody time.

I close my eyes, remembering Rupert, the rosy-faced fellow from the previous day. Such an amiable chap, who's had a run of bad luck, that's all. 'Well, I thought that he'd learn from his mistakes and helping out the back would be repayment, rather than calling the police and ruining his life . . .'

'You let a *criminal* out the back with nary a word to me.'

'Not exactly a criminal, Magda.' I try with all my might to hold my eyes front and centre so they don't roll back into my brain. 'He popped a kid's Santa sack in his jacket because he's been out of work. The guy only wanted to make his little lad's Christmas a good one. I'm sure it's not his fault that he can't find a job despite desperately searching for months on end! I thought that if he had some work experience here, his luck might change . . .' Rupert really took to it. He unloaded boxes like they weighed next to nothing, then unpacked them with gentle hands. He even swept up before he left (glitter is a real problem in a Christmas shop). It's not like he ran off with the life-size gold reindeer or anything.

'That's just it, Flora.' She tuts. 'You think you can save everyone but the problem is, this isn't *your* business. You're on the bottom rung of the ladder, yet you're making decisions like you own the place.' She glances to my feet and her eyes widen. 'New slippers?'

How could she possibly know? She was on the floor when I yanked them off the rack. I surreptitiously glance at my feet and see the bloody price tag hanging over the side.

'I was going to pay for them at lunchtime.' I slump and speak in a rush because I have a feeling Magda is about to crack it with me and that usually means sweeping out the storeroom and cleaning the bathrooms, both Jonah's jobs today. 'And it's not that I think I *own* the place, it's that I can see all some people need is a helping hand, especially at this time of year and—'

'You're right, people do need a helping hand this time of year.'

I'm right? I give her one of my sparkliest smiles, usually reserved for Santa himself. She's finally coming around! Maybe I can broach my idea about toy donations for the women's and children's shelter? Customers can choose a toy and leave it under the Christmas tree and we can deliver them all on Christmas Eve. Most people love the idea of random acts of kindness; they just don't know how to go about it. Then there's my Christmas display extravaganza presentation to discuss . . . This might just be the making of me!

She crosses her arms and looks imperiously down her nose. 'With your specialised skill set and desire to give your own money away, you probably *should* be working elsewhere, perhaps a charity or something. That way you can help out until your heart is content. Why don't you take your things and go? Deck the Halls wishes you well in all your future endeavours.'

Hang on, what? 'Are you serious?' The air in my lungs leaves

31

in a rush. 'You're *sacking* me?' This has only happened five or six times before.

I'm so shocked I can't form words but my body shudders as if the Ghost of Christmases Past has briefly taken over. Being a shop assistant at Deck the Halls is my dream job. I get to live Christmas all year round, and for a festive fanatic it's a joy that's out of this world, despite my fire-breathing boss. 'I can't be sacked for this, surely?'

'OUT!' she says, loud enough to startle a handful of children who run to their parents crying. Magda has that effect on small children. Teens. And about eighty per cent of the population. Abject fear in her presence, that is.

Before long, my exit is accompanied by stern words as shoppers berate Magda for her treatment of me and parents demand to know why she's being so cruel in front of children.

I hate any scene unless it's 'Away in a Manger' so I hurry to reassure everyone. 'It's fine, it's all completely *fine*. I'm sure we'll sort this out,' I say, as if we've just had a slight disagreement and I'll leave until things cool down. I don't want to ruin their Christmas shopping!

But I know hell would freeze over before Magda has me back. She's been trying to get rid of me since I started, but luckily I've had Jonah covering for me most of the time so she's never had a valid reason to fire me.

Customers give me supportive smiles as if they want to rally for my cause, I reassure them it's all OK, because I know there's no point. And I don't want them barred over it. While Magda is a witch, Deck the Halls is the best Christmas shop there is – trust me, I've been to them all – so I don't want them losing out on account of me. 'Merry Christmas, everyone. If you head over to the lolly station Elf Bethany has candy canes for one and all!'

Before my tears morph into a fully-fledged ugly cry, I shuffle off to get my handbag and run into Jonah. 'What's with the tears, Rudolph?'

'Magda fired me.'

His eyebrows shoot up. 'For being late?'

'No, for making up the shortfall for a little girl.' I briefly explain the exchange. 'Also I gave her one of the luxe gift boxes. And I suppose for not paying for my slippers, though I had every intention of doing so at lunchtime.'

'She's bloody well Ebenezer Scrooge!'

Cor, even Jonah thinks so and that's really saying something.

'How am I going to survive here without you?' he laments as his face pales. Knowing Jonah he'll be moaning about the fact he'll be stuck with clean-up duty until he finds a more malleable cashier to do the dirty work for him and is less upset about losing me as a work friend.

'You'll survive.'

He grimaces. 'Barely. So what will you do?'

My eyes well up at the thought of missing the Christmas rush and all that goes with it at this time of year. Despite my surly boss, I'd felt that I'd found my calling but yet again I've managed to put my foot in my mouth. There's no way I could have ignored that little girl, though. And I'm only glad she wasn't there to witness the wrath of Magda. 'I honestly don't know, Jonah. What else is there for me?'

Retail isn't my thing unless it's Christmas-related and there's no other shop quite like this one so close to where I live. I can't catch a break, and the only common denominator I see is . . . me.

Over the loudspeaker I hear my name. 'Flora Westwood, security is coming to escort you out of the shop.'

'She's watching us on the bloody cameras again,' Jonah says under his breath and pretends to be busy.

'I better go.' I pull things from my locker and stash them in my bag. Mainly candy canes if I'm honest. Who doesn't like the simple minty sweet treat that on looks alone conjures up Christmas?

'Keep in touch, Flora, you were one of the coolest.'

'Super cool, that's me.'

'Don't ruin it.'

Somehow I manage a half-laugh. 'You better get out there.'

Jonah gives me a quick peck on the cheek before heading back into the throng.

I shut my locker and head back to the floor to get my jacket and scarf, where security guard Simon finds me and escorts me out like some kind of criminal. 'Sorry,' he whispers under his breath. 'I've got to make it look real – she's watching.'

'It's OK. I understand.'

'Good luck, Flora,' he says and deposits me on the kerb.

Outside, the pulsing Christmas lights reflect on my face and the enormity of this crisis hits. I've gone and lost my much-longed-for job right before the season of giving! Just how am I supposed to survive? Mince pies aren't cheap, are they?

There are no savings to fall back on, and no one's knocking at my door with job offers either. But if I'm realistic, Magda was always going to fire me; it would have only been a matter of time. Jonah's the only employee who's lasted longer than six months and that's because he's got something over Magda – or at least that's what he alludes to.

Still, it's such a blow. For the first time in as long as I can remember, I actually enjoyed going to work. The thought of being suddenly aimless tomorrow brings a fresh bout of tears so I hurry back to Liv's to hide myself away.

My nan's old saying springs to mind: bad things come in threes. I've become hopelessly single, soon-to-be homeless and now jobless all in the space of a few days! What am I doing wrong for disaster to shadow me like this? Just how late will I bloom . . . ?

Chapter 5

I get many a second glance as I race through the streets of London dressed as a reindeer, with my blotchy face and red-rimmed eyes. I gulp away the remaining tears and give myself a pep talk: *You are fabulous, Flora, and don't let anyone tell you otherwise!*

But if I was so fabulous would I keep getting fired? Would I still be 'borrowing' my best friend's spare room? Still be resolutely single? At the ripe old age of twenty-nine when most of my friends are married and popping out kids, as if they're solely in charge of populating the planet, I'm still in the I-wonder-what-I'll-be-when-I-grow-up stage.

If I'm not careful, I'll be back living with my parents and will be forced to listen to their many, *many* recriminations and throwaway comments along the lines of: *why can't you be more like your siblings?* Why can't I be a facsimile of my older sister Melody with her adorable cherubs with their impeccable manners, their love of live theatre even though they're barely knee-high.

Or more like my younger brother, hotshot lawyer Teddy who is married to Camilla, an art gallery curator who speaks the Queen's English even though she's actually a Scouser. I'm the anomaly in the family, the one who just can't get her life together, and to be honest, if having it together means being like Melody and Teddy then I want no part in it. To me their lives are so hemmed in, so pre-planned and sedate I'd bore myself to tears. Give me bright lights, adventure, the possibilities of what's to come . . .

Back at the apartment I'm relieved to see Livvie's pushbike chained to the front gate. She must be home for an early lunch.

'Livvie!' I call and fling my handbag on the couch, followed closely by my body. Where is she? 'LIVVIE! Emergency! Bring the gingerbread biscuits, stat!'

There's some rustling and low-key murmuring. Oh God, she's not alone. That's the problem with living in your best friend's flat. It's bloody tiny and the walls are paper-thin. A bit of an issue when she's suddenly romantically involved and you're the third wheel.

Livvie's dishevelled head appears, her hair's a bird's nest, her usually meticulous make-up smudged. 'Wow, you look . . .'

'I didn't know you'd be home so early.' She darts a glance over her shoulder and soon another head appears. Her new boyfriend Larry, or Garry, or Harry. I never can remember. Between us, I don't like the guy but Livvie thinks he's the bee's knees. I get the distinct impression he's a sponge. Soaks up whatever he can from her. He's the 'doesn't work, wannabe singer' type. He needs a bloody good bath and a scrub-a-dub, if you ask me. Seattle called and they want their dirty-jean-wearing, holey T-shirt grunge vibe back.

'Oh, hey Larry.'

'It's Garry.'

'Right. No work today?' I ask him.

'I don't subscribe to your version of bourgeois society.' He shoots me a condescending look.

'No, you only subscribe to Spotify, which Livvie pays for. Am I right?'

Urgh, the guy is such a pretentious phony. She deserves so much better but is blinded inside her little love bubble. He's taking her for a ride, no two ways about it.

'Flora . . .' Livvie starts and I know I'm in for another lecture.

'I'm going,' Garry says.

I drop my bottom lip as if I'm saddened by such a thing, but Livvie catches me and I grin. I can't help it – he brings out the worst in me.

They go outside and say goodbye, kissing away for a good ten minutes while I wait patiently for her to come to her senses.

When she returns, her face is dark. 'What was all that about? You can't keep putting him down like that.'

I shrug. 'He's a melon head.'

'Flora!'

'Well, he is!'

She sighs and flings herself on the sofa next to me. 'He's a bit of a melon head but he's so good in bed! Honestly, I've never had any one like that who . . .'

I put my hands over my ears. Honestly, do I have to be subjected to sex talk every five seconds? 'Make it stop!'

'OK, OK, God you're the limit, Flora.'

'*I'm* the limit? Sheesh, I'm just trying to protect you here. Next minute Barry'll have you under some kind of weird sex mind control and then where will I be?'

'You know his name is Garry.'

'Whatever.'

'So why are you home?'

'Fired.'

'*Again?*'

'I know! You'd think it was my fault or something, the way this keeps happening.'

'Right?'

I tell Livvie all about the morning from hell and she makes all the right noises.

'Magda is the worst.'

'The very worst. And now I'll be alone and broke at Christmas.'

'I could lend you the money for the cruise . . .'

My parents have booked a family holiday cruising the

Caribbean, siblings, partners, kids, the whole shebang. They offered to pay for my ticket but I know that will come at a high price. I'll have Dad outlining all the ways I've failed in my life and Mum telling me it's my loud mouth that drives men away and I really ought to change. They'll compare me to Melody and Teddy and I'll spend every night crying into my pillow and wondering why I can't just change who I am and fit into the same mould as my siblings.

'Thanks, Livvie, but I'll take a hard pass on that. I think what little is left of my confidence might not last three weeks under the Caribbean sun, somehow. If I have to hear once more about Melody taking her Cabernet and Canvas classes, I'll scream. Or how fabulous Teddy's Camilla looks in her size six Louboutins as if my size eight feet are woefully inadequate in comparison. They're feet-shaming me!'

'Is that like fat-shaming but for feet?'

'YES!'

'I'll never understand the family dynamics and why they pick on you so much. But the *Caribbean*, Flora! Can you imagine? You could find yourself a nice cabana boy . . .'

'A cabana boy on a cruise?'

'Why not? I'm picturing a hot, sun-kissed, well-muscled guy who brings you cocktails and whispers delightful secrets in your ear.'

'You watch too many movies.'

'Maybe.'

'You have to admit, my life is going nowhere fast. Just what am I doing wrong?'

She sighs. 'That's the thing, Flora. You're not doing anything wrong. I mean, who gets fired for helping a little girl buy a bauble in memory of her deceased mum for crying out loud? But it's like trouble just follows in your wake.'

'I'm a trouble magnet. Can't hold down a job, forget about love . . .'

'Have you heard from Luke?'

'Nope. Not once. And I don't want to. Honestly, he was a bit too intense for me anyway. And a bit too *small*. I never felt right eating pasta in front of him, when he kept ordering niçoise salads . . . ! Who orders salads in winter anyway?'

'People with an agenda, that's who.'

'Exactly! It was all a front for something.'

'Small man syndrome?'

'Maybe.'

'So what now?'

I shrug. 'I need a job, and fast or the festive season will be decidedly *un*festive.'

'Yes, and we can't have that. Festive Flora needs her sparkle back.'

'I can't help but think I'm just going from one dead end to the next in this merry-go-round of failure. From getting evicted for having those foster cats, losing jobs every five seconds, and scaring away men by being too upfront. Also, I've noticed if there's one lonely puddle in a ten-kilometre radius, *I'm* the one who steps in it – what's with that?'

'I don't think the universe is conspiring against you with the puddle thing, so let that one go . . .'

'I'm not ready to let that go. I think it's all connected.'

She laughs. 'OK, well let's put that to one side for a moment. I wouldn't call it a merry-go-round of failure. Yes, you've had some ups and downs, but hasn't everyone? You just haven't found your true calling yet, that's all. You tend to get caught up in the minutiae of those around you, like the foster cats – by saving them from being euthanised you lost your super-affordable apartment because technically you broke the lease agreement. And you go through jobs because you speak your mind, usually in someone else's defence, where most people would bite their tongue and debrief after work with their friends. The boyfriend thing, well, I personally think it's because you haven't found the right guy yet. Your quirks make you, you. None of this is your fault, Flora.

Most of it stems from you trying to help people and it backfiring on you.'

'So you think a personality overhaul is not necessary?'

'Nope, not necessary at all. It's not you, it's that those around you just can't see what I see.'

'You're giving me the best friend pep talk and it helps, but I'm still sitting here with absolutely nothing going for me. Sometimes I wonder if it's this town. It's out to get me, I'm sure.' I kick my bag off the sofa and my presentation falls out. Urgh, hours of my life I won't get back.

Livvie picks it up. 'What's this?'

I groan. 'A thing I spent an inordinate amount of time making for Magda so she could wow her customers – a winter wonderland for the emporium. I thought it might attract some attention in the press and she'd be inundated. Didn't get a chance to show her in the end.'

'With the employment side of things it seems to me the problem stems around having a boss, right? You were fired for dating the boss's son at that boutique – tell me again what you said to her? Something like she was "an overbearing helicopter mother whose rotors needed taking out", yeah?'

I grimace, remembering the confrontation. 'Yeah, well the guy was thirty, and still tied to his mum's apron strings. It's only that he had so much potential, but she kept popping into our lives. Remember when he whisked me away for that romantic weekend only for us to arrive and find her waiting for us in the bloody lobby of the hotel!' I'd nearly crumpled in shock but mamma's boy clapped and cheered as if it was the best surprise ever. My employment *and* relationship ended swiftly soon after.

'It would have always been you in the middle.'

'I never learn.'

'And then there was the fire at the ice cream shop where you mentioned that none of it would have happened if they allowed employees to take cigarette breaks.'

40

I slap my forehead. 'Look, I'm not an advocate for smoking, but I felt like it could have been avoided if only they listened to what their employees wanted. If they weren't sneaking ciggies in such a rush that bin never would have gone up like it did.'

'And then there's—'

I hold up a hand. 'I get it. I'm just unlucky, and I've had more than my fair share of horrible, ghastly bosses. Maybe my next boss will be amazing, supportive, caring . . . ?'

'No, you're not following, Flora. I think *you* need to be your next boss.'

'Whaaat?'

'Yes, the common denominator is you. So why let this pattern repeat? You need to start up a business and put all your energy and enthusiasm into it. I know you're capable. You have amazing ideas; you always try and think of ways to improve other people's businesses but they never listen. Why not do it for yourself and reap the rewards?'

'I like your train of thought. Only one problem. I'm poor. Soon I'll be dead broke.'

'Yes, valid point. But let's think of a business and worry about the fine print later.' She takes up my presentation again. Really it looks so silly – a hand-drawn picture of the display of my dreams, a mega Christmas extravaganza that will never see the light of day. 'This is really something, Flora.'

'You're just being nice because I got fired.'

'I'm not. Your talent was wasted at Deck the Halls. If only you could open up your own . . .'

'. . . Christmas shop!'

'They say you should always follow your passion and you're passionate about Christmas.'

'They don't call me festive Flora for nothing.'

She laughs. 'Yes. And a Christmas shop would be ideal. I'm no finance expert but I have a feeling the costs of such an under-taking would be a little excessive, a little more than you could afford, but there must be a way to do what you love. We just need to think harder.'

We put our thinking harder faces on. For Livvie, it's eyes squinted, looking off into the distance; for me, it's a blank stare as I think about all the ways I've failed and keep failing. What am I doing wrong, time and again?

It's not just about holding down a job, it's that my whole life keeps imploding at every turn. My parents think I'm on a desolate road to nowheresville. And really, all of that doesn't bother me as much as the fact that I'm bored, and unfulfilled. Without the Christmas shop to look forward to and Livvie here, my life will become downright *meaningless*.

Livvie is silent. I know from experience it means she's brewing up an idea in that clever head of hers. 'Flora . . .' Her voice rises in excitement. 'I've had the best idea! What about a van, a Christmas van, like a pop-up shop? I met these girls last year, Rosie and Aria, and they had these cute-as-a-button van shops that they travelled around the countryside in! You could pop up at all the London Christmas markets and fairs, that sort of thing.'

The air in the room leaves with a whoosh. 'A pop-up Christmas van?!' My breath catches as I picture such a thing. It's perfect, it's fabulous, it's . . . wait. 'I don't have any money for a van. Dammit all to hell and back, why am I such a spendthrift?' But even as doubt comes calling, the idea takes shape. I'd never be able to afford a real shop, but a mini shop would be more feasible, and not only feasible but fun too. I'd call the shots! I'd pick and choose my very own stock.

'You give most of your money away, Flora! It's not like you spend it on yourself. There's a solution but you're not going to like it.'

'No, I will not do bar work ever again. I still can't stand the smell of—'

'No, it's not bar work.'

It dawns on me, exactly what she's implying. 'No, I could never!'

She grins. I slump. 'You *could*, Flora! You could sell your lifelong collection of Christmas decorations if it gave you the freedom to rule your own life!'

'My Swarovski collection, my Hallmark ornaments, my Christmas décor . . . *Nan's*?' My chest constricts at the thought. It's taken me a lifetime, all of my twenty-nine years to amass such a sparkly rare haul. It's my pride and joy and I delight in taking each piece out every Christmas and lovingly displaying them. Most special are the ones handed down to me by Nan.

'Not Nan's. They hold far too much sentimental value. But the rest – the crystals, the gold plate, the rare collections . . .'

'All the expensive bits, then?'

She lifts a palm. 'Or I could lend you the money?'

'No, no handouts.' That's where I draw the line. Friendships can so easily be ruined by borrowing or loaning money and I'd never risk it. Yeah, sure I live rent-free at the moment but Livvie and I have always had that back and forth, putting each other up when times were tough financially for one of us, like when she studied or I lost yet another job.

I picture my cherishables. Could I sell my collection if it meant I'd finally be free and potentially find some meaning in my life? By holding on to those beauties will I be holding myself back . . . ?

'Anyway, it's something to think about, yeah?' Livvie says. 'We've got our pre-Christmas Christmas to celebrate, don't forget. And I'll be home about six today with some overpriced goodies from Harrods.' She gives me a peck on the cheek. 'Cheer up, Flora. Think of it like this: if you were the heroine in a Hallmark Christmas movie, what would you do?'

My eyes widen. *The heroine in a Hallmark Christmas movie . . . ?* Instead of berating myself for every misstep, I could start over knowing that a new beginning might just be the answer if only I'm brave enough to take that leap, just like they do in the movies.

Chapter 6

A couple of days later, I make hot cocoa and dollop a few fluffy white marshmallows in the mugs as I wait for Livvie to come home from the clinic. She's training the new manager and is working even longer hours than before. She rushes inside, and whips off her jacket, bringing the dank earthy scent of the London streets inside.

'Evening,' she says, hanging her jacket and slipping off her gloves.

'I've been dying for you to get home,' I say and hand over the mug of cocoa, itching to tell her my new plan. I mute *Home Alone* on the TV.

'Wow, boredom has set in already!' She motions to Kevin McCallister.

'Hush your mouth. I'm watching it during the day because you think it's infantile. Sometimes, I wonder about you, you know.'

'The kid is a precocious brat.' I gasp as she grins.

'I'm going to pretend you didn't say that about sweet, precious little Kevin.'

'Pretend away, but deep down you know it's true. You'll make a fine wife one day,' she says, raising the mug.

I let out a very unwifely grunt. 'If you're happy with hot

cocoa and mac and cheese, then yes. That's about the limit of my repertoire.'

'That's most of the food groups, isn't it?' She laughs.

'Enough for me, at any rate.' Livvie is one of those green-juice-loving hipsters. Probably a side effect of her job, where she needs all those vitamins so her skin looks good or something. I don't recall her ever eating my congealed mac and cheese, but I haven't given up hope.

Livvie takes her usual seat in front of the fire where our Christmas stockings hang on the mantel and kicks off her boots.

'So, I did some research today . . .'

Her eyes light up. 'And?'

'Lapland!'

'Lapland?' She frowns.

Why is she frowning? 'Yes, Lapland! The place I've always dreamed of visiting! If I set up a Christmas shop in the little van, I can hire an allotment at this magical Christmas market that runs until Christmas Eve. Lapland is the home of Santa Claus so it's clearly the best place for me to go. What do you think?' I've been fantasising about visiting Lapland my entire life. And the added element of the aurora borealis makes it a real-life place of miracles . . .

'You'd *leave*? In the van?'

'Well . . . yes,' I say confused. 'Isn't that what you meant when you suggested it?'

'I . . . I meant stay here in London. Pop up around town, that kind of thing.'

'Oh, but you said you met those girls, Rosie and Aria, who travelled around.' A frown appears so I hurry to explain the idea. 'I've researched this whole Van Life movement. It's gaining in popularity as people realise they can live life on their own terms, their own schedule. There're various circuits a Van Lifer can choose, depending on what they sell, or where they can afford to go. Maybe they're doing it to travel the world, or just to exist outside the norms of regular society. Lapland makes sense as it's the most festive place on the planet, and a good jumping-off point for me.'

She gives me a wide smile. 'Right, yes, it's an incredible idea! As long as you come back! I don't want to return from LA and have all these amazing stories to tell and no one to tell them to!'

I raise a brow. 'What if you fall in love with some bronzed, buff Los Angeleno? Once you get a taste for all that sunshine and sushi you might never come back. You'll be sending me selfies of you and some sex god at Malibu beach saying wish you were here!' *And in a perfect world Garry would be a thing of the past.*

Having been best friends since we were kids, we have the type of friendship that's weathered every storm and come out stronger for it. But being in different countries will really be a challenge. Livvie's my sounding board, my shoulder to cry on and everything in between – but I know I rely too heavily on her, and I need to change that. I need to become my own person, someone who solves my own problems.

'Sunshine and sushi sounds good! But maybe not the falling in love part. I'd hate to fall for a guy and then have to leave and try long distance.' She shakes her head. 'What about you, though? What if you love Van Life so much you never come back? Then what will I do?'

'Of course I'll come back! And we'll talk every day. It won't be forever. From what I gather these nomads go from place to place, depending on the season. So, I'll probably only go to Lapland for winter, and see if I can make a decent wage living on the road, bank some money then explore a bit. You gave me the idea, Liv. When you told me to imagine myself as the heroine in my very own Hallmark Christmas movie, I realised that's exactly what I need to do! I need to flip the script and start rewriting my life.'

Livvie cocks her head and narrows her eyes as if she's confused. 'Flip the script?'

'Yes! I need to *bloom*, Livvie, like a red rose. And the only way that's going to happen is if I damn well make it happen. The heroines in Hallmark movies always make some grand gesture, right? They move out of the big city, or change their lives in some dramatic way, and then slowly but surely they bloom into the women they were always meant to be . . .'

'Which is fabulous, Flora, truly, but Hallmark movies are *fictional*.' She speaks slowly as if she's talking to a child, as if she thinks maybe I've lost my mind.

'They may be fictional, but if you look past that, you'll see the plots are actually a blueprint, and if I *follow* that blueprint, my life will start to make sense.'

She scrubs her face, smudging her make-up. 'OK, so what about your love interest? After all, that's what Hallmark movies are all about – love.'

'Yes! So I know after Luke I swore off men and decided on an inflatable Santa husband, but now I see it clearly. The man of my dreams is out there, somewhere in Lapland. I just need to find him. He will be a small but essential piece of the puzzle.'

Her gaze drops to the table. 'Have you been indulging in the mulled wine?'

'No! Well, a little bit, but I promise you I've thought this through. And I bet you, when I find the one I'll know him on sight, just like in the movies.'

'O-K.'

'I probably sound unhinged, but what if we *all* lived as though our life were a Hallmark movie? What if we took chances, and said what we thought, and believed that true love would find a way, no matter what? What if we were honest about our feelings, knowing that it would all work out in the end? Then the world would be a better place!'

'I mean it sounds ideal on paper . . .'

'Trust me, Livvie, it's like a fog has lifted and I know this is the right course for me. Wait until you see the other vans at the market. It's going to be such an adventure!' I take out my phone and show her. 'There's Naughty and Nice ski lodge, a pop-up van that has decorative skis strung to the side of the van and an outdoor bar made from wooden logs. They sell all sorts of drinks, like *gløgge* which is mulled wine. *Gløgge*, doesn't that sound so exotic? And they have hot chocolate with brandy!'

Livvie flicks through the photos, amazement reflected in her eyes. 'So exotic! Wow, they've really made it look like a ski lodge.'

I lean over her. 'Ooh, check out this one – a pop-up igloo that sells all sorts of Christmas snacks and they offer board games with a Christmas twist.'

She shakes her head in awe. 'You'll be in Christmas *heaven*, Flora. What will you sell, then?'

'I'll stick with what I know and sell Christmas decorations and gifts. From what I've read, the whole Van Life movement is really inclusive and everyone looks out for one another. It's a really supportive atmosphere, so even though I'll have no idea what I'm doing, I'll have plenty of people to ask.'

'I'm tempted to join you,' she says, her voice wistful.

I know she's joking but my heart leaps at the idea. The Livvie and Flora show could continue! 'People still need to look after their skin in frozen temperatures, you know.'

She laughs and waves me away. 'I wish. So it's decided then? You'll sell your Christmas collection, except Nan's precious hand-me-downs, to fund a van and pop-up business?'

I nod, feeling a rush of emotions. On one hand I'll be devastated to part with my treasures, but on another – looking at these happy, smiley adventurers – I know my real life could begin in earnest if only I risk the safety of leaving all I know in London town. Which, to be honest, hasn't been the making of me. I haven't bloomed so much as wilted.

'I've already found a van I'm interested in checking out in Stockholm. It's all decked out for Van Life.' I show her the pic, the shiny scarlet van that screams Christmas. Inside, it has everything I need from a tiny bedroom to a little kitchenette and dining table. Everything is minuscule, but at least it's there. I can be fully independent in such a vehicle. 'If it's as nice as it appears in the pictures, then I'm all set.'

'So you'll fly to Stockholm buy the van and then what . . . drive to Lapland from there?'

According to Google Maps, it's about a sixteen-hour drive. I figure I can do that over two days. 'That's the plan. I've registered for a car boot sale tomorrow to sell all my worldly goods and I'll need to borrow your car for that too, if that's OK.'

'You may. And I'll help – and when I say help, I mean I'll go with you and then leave you alone while I go and shop for bargains.'

'You're a doll.'

'And what about stock for the van? Where will you get it from?'

'I found a Christmas decorations and gifts supplier just out of Lapland; they sell exquisite pieces, works of art, really. I've contacted them and made enquiries, they're happy to sell in bulk wholesale to me, so I can start with that and see how I go.'

'Let's think of van names!' she says.

'Van names?'

'Yeah, you know they all have names for their businesses like The Little Bookshop of Happy Ever After, and Coco's Champagne Cart, or my personal favourite: The Taco Taxi.'

'Ooh yes, we'll need a snappy name for the biz!'

'The Christmas Caravan?'

'But it's not going to be a caravan per se, is it?'

She scrunches her nose. 'No, that's true. Santa's Little Helper? Or Elf Yourself?'

I laugh. 'I need to get Elf Yourself tees made for sure. Keep going . . .'

She taps her chin. 'Got it! Flora's Travelling Christmas Shop?'

I consider it. 'That's the one! Simple and festive. Everyone will know instantly what I'm selling. *Flora's Travelling Christmas Shop!* Could there be a more perfect name?'

'Next will be booking the flight.'

'Then it looks like I'm one step closer to this grand escapade.'

She raises a brow. 'This is the Flora I know. The go-getter who won't let anyone kill her dreams.' She pretends to wipe a stray tear. 'They grow up so fast . . .'

I lob a fluffy cushion at her. 'Could it be so easy?' Every part of Operation New, Festive and Fabulous Life has clicked into place so easily, as if it's meant to be.

'Why not? Why do things have to be hard in order for them to be right? The hard part will be saying goodbye to your best friend, but we won't think of that for now.'

'Yeah, Barry is really going to be hard to say goodbye to. We've been through a lot, he and I.'

She lobs the cushion back at me. 'You idiot.'

'Maybe things will progress with me out of the way.'

'Maybe not. I broke up with him.'

I pretend to be sad. 'I'm inconsolable.'

'I bet.'

'What made you ditch Larry though? Was it the fact he ate beans directly from the can?'

'No, it wasn't but that was pretty gross. Who eats cold beans?'

'Melon heads.'

'Melon heads, for sure. No, it was the fact that I was blithely walking along Oxford Street when I happened upon old Barry/Larry/Harry/Garry locked in the embrace of another.'

My jaw drops. 'Someone else? Another *human*?'

'Another human. A female human.'

'That utter swine!'

'Right?'

'Did you wallop him with your designer purse?'

'No way, the leather on that baby is delicate and I didn't want it tarnished with his lying face print, did I?'

'Good point.'

She lets out a long sigh. 'I tapped him on the shoulder and told him that I thought his singing was rubbish and his guitar playing sounded like a small child screaming.'

'All of that is true. Surely he can't be surprised?'

'He didn't take it well. He told me I was jealous.'

'Of what?' He's bloody lucky the likes of Livvie even looked in his direction! And to think there's another female who's been wooed by him . . . !

'Who knows?'

'What was the girl like?'

'Urgh, a carbon copy of me. In fact, I'm sure she's a client, I remember her glabellar lines, they were pretty severe before I fixed them.'

'Well I hope her glabellar lines, whatever the heck they are, go back to the way they were before you worked your magic!'

'Yeah, but in fairness she probably didn't know about me, either. Men like him think it's OK to have a girl on every corner. You were right about him.'

I'd never utter an *I told you so* when it comes to love – and anyway, who am I to judge anyone? 'I'm glad he's gone for good. You deserve so much better than the likes of him.'

She gives me a small smile and I know despite her outwardly jokey demeanour, she's still hurt. 'He's a vague memory. We'd never have lasted long distance anyway, so easy come, easy go . . .'

'Good. But if you're sad, then I'm sad and we should do something to cheer you up.'

'I'm not too sad, honestly, but a night out would work wonders.'

'Does this mean I have to change out of my Christmas jammies?'

'It does.'

'The things I do for you.'

'I'm honoured. Get your dancing shoes on.'

We spend the rest of the night in a fancy little bar in Shoreditch, drinking overpriced cocktails and dancing up a storm. I know I should be saving money, not spending it like the ship is going down, but I figure when there's a break-up involved it has to be done. Surely it's part of the BFF code, or something?

Livvie soon forgets about Barry when a cute bespectacled guy wearing a button-up blazer and light blue jeans approaches her. When she looks over his shoulder at me, I give her a thumbs-up. You can't judge men on sartorial choices alone, but from eavesdropping I get the distinct impression this guy has got the goods. He's quizzing her about her life, not the usual what do you do and where are you from sort, but more interesting things like: 'What do you wish you had more time to do?' and 'What's your take on this whole QAnon thing?'

I can tell by the way she leans close to him that she feels safe and secure so best friend duties done, I go back to the dance floor, blow off some steam and think of all the ways in which our lives are going to change in the coming weeks . . .

Chapter 7

Before the sun is up we pack Livvie's car with my precious Christmas collection and head towards the park for the car boot sale.

'Whose idea was it to have so many cocktails?' Livvie asks, squinting as she clutches her head with one hand and the steering wheel with the other.

'It was mine, but it's nothing a good breakfast bap won't fix.'

At the park we gently unwrap Christmas decorations and line them up on the table.

A middle-aged lady wearing tweed comes over. She looks like a minor royal, which means she'll have money to burn! Nerves make me hesitate and I get muddled and blurt out, 'Gello.' A mix of good morning and hello. *Gah!* The late night is playing havoc with my brain.

The woman doesn't respond, and just picks up each Hallmark figurine, studies it and then puts it down again before moving on to the Swarovskis. I try not to bristle at all the touching of my cherishables but I suppose it can't be helped. Why can't she bend at the waist and peer at them? I'll be polishing away her fingerprints for days if she's just window shopping . . . !

Sensing my anxiety, Livvie takes my hand and gives it a squeeze as if to say *relax*. The woman finally speaks: 'How much for the Swarovski collection?'

My pride and joy. My one true love. My . . .

Livvie elbows me in the ribs.

'Erm, umm . . .' *I don't want to part with them!* 'They're not for—'

Livvie bellows out a number and follows up with: 'A rare collection, highly sought after and as you can see in pristine condition.'

The woman puckers her mouth in the way a tweed-wearer would. 'Cut that price in half and you've got yourself a deal.'

Is she *crazy*? I'm about to give her a piece of my mind when Livvie wrenches my arm almost out of its socket. 'Ow!' She stomps on my foot for good measure.

'How about we split the difference once more?' Livvie says. *That traitor!*

'What!' They manage to ignore me, despite the clear elevation in my voice.

'Fine, you drive a hard bargain but I'll take them.' A hard bargain – she can't be for real!

I struggle with the idea of letting them go for a song, mentally calculating how much each piece cost brand new while Livvie starts bundling them up in their original boxes with the original Swarovski tissue paper.

'Here, wrap this one and I'll start on the next,' Livvie orders as if I'm a mere shop assistant and not someone whose heart is breaking. Embarrassingly, I find myself fighting tears as I go to hand the box over. The woman takes it but I can't quite let go. It's as though it's glued to the palm of my hands. There's a tug-of-war as she tries to pry the box from my hands and I pull it back.

Livvie looks over and sighs, before snatching the box and handing it over carefree as anything. The turncoat. The terrible friend who thinks trampling over my emotions is OK. The heartless . . .

'Flora,' she hisses. 'Help me pack these up before she changes her mind with you acting so strangely!'

'But—'

'No buts. Pull yourself together before I take away the wine for the rest of the week!' Somehow she manages to spit the words out in a whisper and pull me into line, all while giving the woman a wide smile. She'll make a fabulous mother one day.

I comply but give Livvie plenty of glaring side-eye so she knows I'm absolutely furious. I know I need to sell these babies to fund my life – that doesn't mean I have to be sensible about it! Silently, I say goodbye to each piece, remembering its origins, and all the memories attached.

The woman offers up a stack of cash, which Livvie counts. 'It was a pleasure doing business with you.'

As she carts the many, *many* boxes away in her portable shopping cart, I turn to Livvie. '*How could you!*'

'How could I what? That was a great price for those and you know it. You wouldn't have sold them at all if I hadn't been here.'

'Exactly!'

She makes a moue with her lips. 'Who needs to be brave like a Hallmark heroine now, eh?' Damn it, she's got me there. 'No change can happen without some sacrifice; this is the *bridge* to Van Life, and you have to cross it.'

I use my best whiney voice to get through to her, 'Yeah, I know I just don't like rich, minor royals buying my stuff, my babies, my precious—'

'Excuses won't wash with me.' She clamps a hand over my mouth. 'But you're right, Flora. It's just "*stuff*". Beautiful, sparkly dead weights, that are sinking you. You've still got all your cherishables from Nan, and that's all that matters.'

'I hate when you speak like this!'

'Like what?'

'Sensibly! It's infuriating!'

She grins. 'In a few weeks when you're having the time of your life, you'll remember this moment and be glad you set yourself free.'

'It's just . . .' But the words vanish. She's right and I know she's right. If I want to make this work I need to flip my way of thinking. No more excuses. No clinging to the past. 'I'm going to need sugar to calm me down.'

'Makes sense. Allow me.' She flounces off and I'm left to my own devices, trying to push away the ache when I see the vacant spot on the table.

A young dad wearing a baby in a sling says hello. The baby coos away happily and he makes baby talk back to her as he surveys the table. When he asks the price for my reindeer collection, I debate whether or not I really want to sell them. I mean he seems nice and all . . . but so are my reindeer.

I cross my arms. 'Before I give you a price, can you tell me the names of each of Santa's reindeer?'

If he knows them all it's a sign, and then I shall sell him my menagerie of hoofed animals. This is the plucky sort of questioning a confident, Hallmark heroine would subscribe to, right?

'You want me to tell you their names? *All* of them?'

'There are only *nine* of them. It's not that hard a task, is it?' By the look of genuine surprise on his face you'd think I'd asked him to recite the lyrics of 'God Save the Queen' verbatim or something.

Confusion dashes across his face but he says, 'Erm, Rudolph. Dasher, Dancer, Prancer, Comet, Donner . . . ? How many is that?' *Amateur.*

'Not enough.'

He scratches the back of his neck. 'Comet?'

'You already said Comet.' I stare him down.

Livvie returns and hands me a raspberry cronut. 'Hey, what an adorable cherub you've got there,' she says to the guy, and makes that scrunched-up *aww* face people always do when there are babies around. 'Can I help?'

'Do you know all the names of Santa's reindeer?'

She shoots me a glare. 'Not this again?'

'What? It's only fair if he wants to own such a magnificent coterie that he knows their bloody names.' In my view, it's quite reasonable that he knows what he's buying!

'Dasher, Dancer, Prancer, Vixen, Comet, Cupid, Donner, Blitzen and Rudolph,' she says and beams at the man. 'Now you know them all. Shall I wrap them for you?'

'What are they worth?'

'Whatever you think is fair.'

I gasp so hard I think I'm going to pass out. They make a deal and the man wanders off with his booty. 'You're . . . you're fired!'

She rolls her eyes. 'Oh shush you. Honestly, did my little pep talk go completely in one ear and out the other? I trusted you to make some more sales, and you did that thing you do with potential boyfriends when you ask them if they know all nine reindeer names! It's a bloody miracle any man goes out with you, when that's the first question you lob at them. Now you're doing the same bloody thing with a new dad at a car boot sale. It beggars belief!'

'Well, ex*cuuuu*se me, Miss Dating Deity. My specifications for the perfect man may differ from yours, but I need to know early on if we're compatible or not. As far as first questions go it's a bloody good one if you ask me.'

She huffs. 'I'm not having this "first question" argument again. Do you or do you not want money for your travels? Because if you don't I'd rather be horizontal on the sofa nursing my hangover than here. Are you just dilly-dallying over doing this thing for real or not?'

I take a bite out of my cronut so she can damn well wait for a reply. And also because I can't actually think of one.

'Well?'

I wipe crumbs away. 'I'm a twit. I really mean it this time.'

'You *are* a twit.'

'Only, it's hard to let go. With anything else I wouldn't care one iota but these are my sweet precious babies, and I don't see what's wrong with quizzing people to make sure they're going to the right homes.'

Livvie sits beside me and sips a coffee. 'OK, fine I get that. Quiz away, but try not to do that intimidating stare-down tactic; it's actually frightening, like you're trying to hypnotise them or something. And make your questioning a little subtler.'

'Duly noted. I'll work on my delivery.'

That's what I love most about Livvie; we can bicker and argue like sisters but we make up pretty fast when one of us realises we're in the wrong – usually me.

If I'm really going to make a go of it, I'll have to sell as much as I can, including the entire household's worth of shabby second-hand furniture I've got in storage so I have enough money to last if the Christmas market at Lapland isn't as profitable as I hope.

Chapter 8

Mid-November rolls around so fast; I haven't had a moment to second-guess myself until now. My whole life is packed up into one human-sized backpack. I feel freer, lighter, having sold virtually everything else that I own, including all my belongings that have been in storage for far too long. It goes to show, I don't need that 'stuff', not really – I only hope I don't regret it later. I try not to imagine disaster, like me coming home in a month, tail between my legs, knocking on my parents' door asking for help. Just when I'm feeling overwhelmed I hear Nan's voice inside my head: *You're fabulous, Flora, and it's going to work out.* I send a silent thank you up to the heavens. Nan's watching over me, I know she is. I can do this and I will do this!

I haul on the backpack and tumble forward as the floor comes screaming into view. 'Arghhhh!'

Livvie races from her bedroom. 'Seriously, Flora! What have you got in there? It looks like you're about to trek the Himalayas for the best part of a year or something. Leave some stuff here. I can put it in storage with my gear.'

'But I *need* it all.'

'You packed the summer clothes, didn't you? Even after you promised you wouldn't.'

'So what if I did?'

'Why will you need *summer* clothes in *Lapland* in *winter*?'

I sigh with frustration. 'That's an excessive amount of emphasising, Liv. What if I meet some billionaire jetsetters who think I'm the life of the party and offer to fly me to their private yacht for a long weekend in the Bahamas and then I'm stuck because I only have winter woollies? You can't exactly wear a Puffa jacket in the Bahamas, can you? There's a real threat I'll take flight off the deck and die some tragic horrific death in the Atlantic Ocean and you won't find my body and you'll always wonder what happened. I'll try and send a message beyond the grave, like writing on a steamy bathroom window, but you being such a neat freak won't even read it; you'll just Windex it away . . .'

'If some billionaire jetsetters invite you anywhere, you'll say no because that's not your thing.'

'Well, what if—'

'Open the backpack.'

I grunt and open the damn bag. Livvie snatches out summer clothing and says, 'No, no, no, definitely not, no, yes, no. What the hell?' She unwraps my craftily hidden glassware inside a T-shirt. 'Why do you need champagne glasses?'

I roll my eyes as if she's the densest person on the planet. 'To toast my new life when I arrive, of course!'

She does a dramatic huffy-puffy charade. 'You'll only smash these en route. If not before, the way you're going.'

'OK, fine, I'll leave them here. But it's *super* annoying when you're constantly right about things.'

Livvie doesn't speak, but continues going through my things as if searching for contraband or something. When I notice a slight shake in her shoulders I realise she's crying.

'Oh, Liv, don't start all that, else we'll never stop!' I bend to hug her and she swipes at her eyes.

'I know, it's silly, it just seems so big, us both going off like this. And you potentially continuing your nomadic wandering for years! I'll never forgive myself for suggesting the van if you do.'

I wipe at my own face. 'As if that will happen. We can't be the terrible two if there's only one of us.'

'I know. It'll just be so weird without you by my side. There won't be any dirty dishes left lying around. No one will steal my clothes. Ridicule new boyfriends. And who'll keep me up at all hours playing Christmas carols? No one, that's who.'

'When you say it like that, I can see my leaving is going to be devastating for you.' We both double over laugh-crying.

'It sure will be . . . different.'

'If this were a Hallmark movie, this is where the photo montage would start with that horrifically sad music where we reminisce about just how far we've come.'

'From pigtails, to braces, to boys, to taking the reins of our adult lives, and now we come to a fork in the road, where we say goodbye and go our own ways.'

'Only for a bit.' I rest my head against her shoulder. We've been side by side for every one of life's ups and downs and without Livvie, I don't know who I'll be as a person. We've shaped each other by always being the one constant that we could count on after Nan died. But I know I need to do something before my life grinds to a halt and I never get out of this rut. I need to prove to myself that I can do it on my own, that I am capable, as much as I'll miss Livvie in the process. I'm sure she feels the same.

Livvie folds my clothes into a neat pile. 'This is going to be the making of you, Flora. I can't wait to see where this adventure takes you.'

'Lapland, the place I've always dreamed of, seems a fitting choice to start this epic adventure. How can it not be perfect under the sparkle of the northern lights?' I think of that shimmering magical sky and I know if I take a leap of faith, I'll surely be rewarded with a new outlook on life, and some goals of my own to aim for. 'And you, taking over the world with your genius skincare range and amazing work ethic.' I can see Livvie in LA, somehow. Drinking those skinny green juices and sunning herself on Malibu beach.

'We're lucky, Flora, to be able to test the waters in another country, live a whole new life – we just have to remember that when we're homesick and missing one another. Come on,' she says. 'Let's repack half of this and then you'd better get going.'

My flight to Stockholm leaves in four hours. Time has raced away these last few days as I've made my way down my to-do list written by Livvie. She still has more to do at the clinic before she jets off to LA so she's not at panic stations yet, and in fact, probably won't ever be. She's too organised for all that and even an international move won't ruffle her feathers.

I heave a sigh, hating the drawn-out goodbye. 'OK. I've left my bedroom a bit of a mess so you can pretend I'm still here. There's some dirty cups and plates and some empty crisp packets shoved behind the bed, that kind of thing. No need for thanks.'

'You're a real sweetheart to think of me like that.' She shakes her head. 'And I'm sure the new clinic manager, Marion, will adore finding all your rubbish hidden about the flat.'

'It will be like a rite of passage for her.'

Thirty minutes later, I'm all packed up and ready to go, with a glass of bubbles in hand as we toast my trip. 'Remember to be you, Flora. You're perfect as you are, eccentricities and all, and Mr Hallmark will find you and love will bloom!'

'Thanks, Livvie. I'll be unapologetically me! And my hero, well he'll be hiding in plain sight, probably a baker, or a café owner who's been waiting for a burnt-out, big-city woman to come to her senses and move to a small town.'

'I bet he owns a Christmas tree farm! The rugged local who has sworn off love . . .'

'Yes! Secret billionaire?'

'Or enemies to lovers! Or close proximity? Maybe he's got the cute little coffee van next door?'

'I'd better steel myself for all these misunderstandings since he's swamped with women making goo-goo eyes at him. I'll probably want to give up, until one day he surprises me with . . . ?'

She holds up a finger. 'He dedicates a coffee named Flora Flat White to you . . . wait.'

I laugh. 'OK, maybe not but we're on the right track.'

'For sure.' There's a beep. 'That's your Uber.'

'Thank you for paying for it.'

'You're welcome. I couldn't bear the thought of you on the Tube with this great appendage.' She points to my bag. 'Go before the tears start again. I can't have puffy eyes at the clinic, or else no one will believe I'm twenty.'

'You're nearly thirty.'

'Says who?'

I give her one last hug, as we both burst into tears. 'Love you.'

'Love you too, fabulous Flora. Go find that rugged Christmas tree farm owner.'

I laugh. 'I will.'

Chapter 9

When I arrive in Stockholm, the backpack feels heavier than ever as I make my way around the busy terminal and head outside.

The air is brisk, so I hurry to find my free airport transfer. Livvie booked me a hotel as a goodbye present – I can't wait to see it. I've left her a care package on her bed as a surprise. A box full of Christmas goodies so she can eat her feelings if she's sad. I check the paperwork and ask for directions to the bus, and am told it's a five-minute ride and to alight at Jumbo stop.

'Jumbo stop,' the bus driver announces in English.

I look out the window and see a Boeing 747 jumbo jet parked up. This is not your average plane. *It's a hotel!* I thank the bus driver and jump from the bus, excited to see just what Livvie's surprise has in store for me.

I find the check-in station and am greeted by a receptionist who informs me Livvie has booked the cockpit suite. 'Allow me to show you.'

The room is amazing; all the instruments are at the foot of the bed and there's a flatscreen TV attached to the ceiling. 'I love it.'

The receptionist tells me about the café and licensed bar and the seating area on the wing of the plane, which I'd seen from the tarmac. It's such a quirky place to stay and right up my alley.

After she leaves, I find my phone and shoot off a text to Livvie.

This is the coolest hotel ever! Thank you for spoiling me. I miss you already. Xxx

Then I send one to Mikael, the Van Lifer selling the rosy red van who I've been emailing with, discussing a possible purchase if it runs as well as it looks.

Hey, I've made it to Stockholm. I'm at the Jumbo Stay in Arlanda if you're still keen to drive the van here for me to take a look? Thanks, Flora.

While I wait for a reply, I explore the rest of the plane.

Outside, on the platform, three guys sit at a table, laptops open in front of them, cold beers close to hand.

'Hello, I'm Erik, this is Hans and Tino. This hotel is something different, eh?'

I give the trio a wave. 'Nice to meet you all. I'm Flora. Yeah, the Jumbo Stay has definitely got the wow factor. What about you guys, where are you staying in the plane?'

'We're in a dorm.' He points to the far end. 'It suits our budget. We're digital nomads.'

'What's a digital nomad?'

'We work online, funding our travel as we go. Hans and I do website design and IT. Tino does translation work, and copy-writing. We work remotely as long as there's adequate Wi-Fi and we travel as we go.'

'Wow, that sounds incredible.' Another way to survive outside the ordinary. It feels like there's this whole world out there that I never knew existed. 'How long have you been travelling together?'

'We've been on the hoof for about six months already, but have plans to do this for a year or as long as the money lasts.'

Will I make such great friends along the way, like these guys? They seem so carefree and happy together.

'What about you?' Tino says, in what sounds like an Italian accent.

'I'm here to buy a van and then head to Lapland and set up my travelling Christmas shop at the big market.'

'Ooh,' Tino says. 'A Van Lifer.'

I grin. 'Soon, I hope.'

My phone beeps with a text so I say goodbye to the guys who invite me to meet up again at dinner. 'Sure, I'd love that.' I head back to the cockpit and check the message.

Hello Flora, I can bring the van now for you to see? I'll be there in about an hour . . .

A wave of excitement rushes over me. I'm going to be meeting some awe-inspiring people along the way, and the van is going to help facilitate those friendships.

Sure, I'll meet you on the tarmac.

Darkness falls as the evening creeps closer. I head down to meet Mikael. As I make my way down the stairs I see a red campervan pull into the car park. It's definitely not as candy-cane red as it appeared on the photos but I suppose that doesn't really matter.

When I get closer I see it's actually quite rough around the edges, as though it's been used as a bumper car; there's dings and scratches along the side and a crack in the windscreen. This does not look *anything* like the pictures, and I begin to wonder if it's the same van at all. It doesn't look like it will last the month, let alone the winter.

'Hey, Mikael,' I say and my breath comes out like fog.

He gives me wide grin and holds out a hand to shake. 'Flora, so nice to meet you! Did you want to take her for a ride?'

'In a minute. So can you tell me about the history of the van?' The closer I look, the more damage I see. This guy is trying to sell me a lemon. I can smell dishonesty on him.

'Oh, she's had a long and fruitful life so far.' His voice is sugary sweet while he paints me a dream. 'Regularly serviced, no engine or gearbox trouble. Runs well. Now it's time for me to sell because I have to leave, a family . . . erm member isn't well. It's a desperate situation.'

A scam alert is going off inside my head.

'Right. Let's see inside then.'

He opens the door and inside is worse. The vinyl seating is ripped and shredded, and tufts of foam lie scattered about. The carpet is stained. Overhead, cupboard doors are ajar as if warped by water and too swollen to close. The bedding area is pungent. If this is what the interior and exterior are like how bad would the mechanical side of things be?

'Mikael, this doesn't look like any of the photos online.' My hackles are up – this is a monumental waste of my time. There's no way I can buy a van like this. Now what? Panic begins to mount. I made plans and now I won't have a van!

'It just needs a lady's touch.'

I bristle. *A lady's touch*. 'I don't think so.'

'Let me start her up.'

How on earth could that possibly help? He starts the van, which instantly backfires and spits. Soon I'm covered in a cloud of fumes. My trip might be over before it's even begun!

'What do you think? It's a good price, yeah?'

'No, it's not for me.'

'But you said you'd buy it. I've come all the way here just for you.' His voice rises.

'I never said I'd buy it, I said I'd take a look at it and you've turned up with this . . . this scrappy thing with some phony story about getting home for an emergency. Don't think I haven't read travel blogs about exactly this kind of scam.'

'I'll give you a hundred kronor off.'

I roll my eyes. 'No thanks.' I go to walk away and he grabs my arm.

'I need this money, Flora. You promised.'

'Get your hands off me.' Alarm bells ring and unease prickles my skin. I wrench my arm away as I hear footsteps on the stairs.

'You OK, Flora?' Erik takes the stairs two at a time and before long he's in between me and Mikael.

I shoot him a grateful look. 'Yeah, I was just telling Mikael I'm not interested in his van but he's having trouble hearing me.'

'You heard her, she's not interested.'

'This has nothing to do with you! She told me she wanted the van, and here I am. All it needs is some cosmetic work.' His eyes shine with malice.

'It's *not* the same van,' I say but know it's no use arguing with him – the guy thought he had the chance to make a buck selling a newbie a lemon and he's not happy I've scuppered his plan.

'You've wasted my time!' Mikael slams the door of the van so hard that part of the rubber moulding falls to the ground.

'Likewise.' The guy must have bananas for brains to think he could fool me.

Erik shrugs, not ruffled at all by Mikael's performance. Will I always have to be a bit wary on this journey? 'It's time for dinner, Flora. I'll walk you up, yeah?'

'Yes, please.' As the adrenaline abates, I feel all the energy leave my body and it's replaced with a frisson of worry at the thought I'll need to be on constant alert.

At the top of the stairs Erik says, 'I heard the van pull up and had a bad feeling that was going to happen. Are you OK?'

'Yeah, I'm OK,' I say and give him a half-smile. 'I'm disappointed the van was no good. Now what will I do? I'm only booked here for two nights.'

'The dorm rooms are much cheaper than the cockpit, so you'll move if you need to.' I love the way Erik speaks of everything so simply; there's no drama, there's no angst. Just solve the problem and move on.

I nod. 'These things to tend to happen for a reason, right? Maybe there's a better van out there and I just have to find it.' I thank my lucky stars I met these guys. Without them, I don't think I'd be in such a positive frame of mind after the van debacle.

'That's the spirit. We'll put up some posts on social media and see what's out there. That's the beauty of this journey – while one ends another begins so there'll be plenty of vans for sale. And always remember, the journey will provide . . .'

'The journey will provide . . . is that a mantra for when things go wrong?'

He laughs. 'That's exactly what it is. And it'll always work out, so don't panic.'

'OK, that I can do.' Panic be gone! I wanted to flip the script, didn't I? Things might go awry from time to time. I have to learn to let it slide.

I follow Erik to the café bar and we're soon surrounded by other hotel guests having dinner. There's a warm buzz of friendship and I know that these little bumps in the road are going to happen and I'll have to learn to accept them as part of this audacious plan to live life on the road . . .

After dinner we hang out in the bar area, and before long it's filled to bursting with other guests. I chat to so many people I'm dizzy, so I take a stool at the bar and start up a conversation with Gigi the barmaid. We make small talk and I tell her about my earlier experience trying to buy a van while part of me begins to doubt myself again. Was I wrong to think I could get this right? I struggle to stay afloat at the best of times and now I've transported myself to a foreign place hoping that a change of scene would fix me. Am I mad?

'A campervan?' Gigi breaks my silent panicking.

'Yeah,' I say. 'My plan is to head to Lapland, but things didn't quite work out today.'

'My sister is selling her campervan. She wanted to travel around Sweden but she got offered a job in France so her trip has been cancelled.'

'What kind of van is it?'

Gigi finds her phone underneath the bar and swipes through some photographs, before handing it over to me. 'Check those out. I have no idea what sort of campervan it is, but I know she had it mechanically checked over just recently.'

'It's lovely!' I say as I flick through the pictures. The design has been well thought out, and inside there's a bed with green velvet bedding and plush pillows and throws. It looks as though it's been decorated by someone who knows what they're doing and for whom money was no object. But the candy-cane-red van also looked like that, so I try not to get ahead of myself.

'What sort of price is she looking for?'

Gigi rattles off a figure that is in line with most of the other vans I've seen but that didn't have all the new interior bits and bobs. 'That seems more than fair. When can I take a look at it?'

'Would tomorrow work? It's at my parents' place.' It's a beauty and I only hope it's just like the photos. We tee up a time to look at it and the trio of guys offer to come with me.

The next day we meet Gigi's mum and see the emerald-green van. The guys check the engine and boring technical things, like if the wipers work – necessary but dull – while I go check out the inside. It's even better than the photos!

There are nooks for storage in every place imaginable, which could house extra stock for the pop-up shop. The window treatments match the green velvet cushions and give the van a distinctly luxe vibe.

Above a seating area there's a fold-down shelf that opens up to the outside. I could use it as a place to serve customers and display my range of smaller Christmas decorations and gifts.

I go back outside and check the body of the van, which is as immaculate as inside. The guys huddle around me and speak in low tones. 'Engine looks good, clean and well maintained,' Erik says. 'I'm not a mechanic, but it looks like it's had a good life.'

'Thanks, Erik. That's great news.'

'The mileage is relatively low for its age, and the body of the van doesn't have any rust, or damage that I can see,' Tino says. 'As far as campervans go, you'd do a lot worse than this one.'

Erik leans closer and whispers, 'We know this is a great van, and it comes with everything you could possibly need, but we still think you should negotiate.'

I go to protest but he holds up a hand and says, 'You have to. They'll be expecting it and they're motivated to sell.'

I wring my hands. 'But it's so lovely and I don't want them to say no!'

'Be brave,' Erik says. 'Think of how many days you can survive on a bit of extra money when times get tight.'

I sigh – he has a point. 'OK.'

I approach Gigi's mum, Kaia. 'I love it,' I say, and the guys surreptitiously shake their heads at me. 'I mean, it's nice and all but I'm not quite sure . . . about the price.' I'm sure my face flames but I need to learn the art of negotiation to get ahead in this new life.

Kaia nods. 'I understand. So what price did you have in mind?'

I mention a figure. Without a pause, Kaia counters. Behind her, the guys shake their heads again. With a warm smile, I give her my final offer and only hope she accepts it

Kaia holds up a finger as if to say *wait*, and goes to confer with her husband. After a minute of ultra-fast talking she returns wearing a wide smile. 'If you'll take it today we have a deal.'

'I can take it today, and I'll transfer the money to you now.' *Being brave is working!*

'Then it looks like you're the new owner of Noël.'

'Noël?'

'Yes, that's what she named the van. I'm not sure why it's masculine, but that's my daughters for you, guy-mad!'

I laugh but secretly I'm thrilled – a link to Christmas, which I figure is a sure-fire sign I'm on the right track. 'Well, I love the name, and I think Noël and I are going to have some fun adventures together.'

We sort the payment and paperwork, which is confusing in another language, and soon enough, the trio is reduced to two as Erik and Hans squeeze in the front of the van with me, and Tino catches the bus back to the Jumbo because he wants to stop in town to run some errands.

As I drive, bouncing high along the road, I grip the steering wheel until my knuckles go white. I haven't driven a vehicle this big before and I have never driven on the right side of the road either! Clenching my jaw, I use every ounce of concentration to keep on the road. I didn't think of this part, did I? As I come to a bend, I fight the urge to squeeze my eyes closed. This feels so unnatural!

'What's wrong?' Erik asks, as he sees my pinched expression and deer-in-headlights eyes.

I try and smile to reassure him but it's as though my face is frozen – I'm concentrating on the road and not on life-or-death things like facial expressions! 'Why do they drive on the wrong side of the road? This is harder than I imagined! Don't worry, I'll get us all there alive!'

'OK, OK, you're doing great.' Erik pales as I hit the kerb and bounce off. At least I think he does, from what I can see out of the corner of my eye, but I don't dare turn my head to double-check. 'It's UK drivers who are on the wrong side of the road. This way just makes sense. It's called the *right* side for a reason.' He laughs.

The next morning, there's a flurry of goodbyes, as I leave the Jumbo and head down the steps with my human-sized backpack, which I'm eager to never use ever again.

I'm left with the trio, who stand around and kick at the ground, goodbyes awkward in the early morning light. Except for Erik who always manages to make things easy as he pulls me in a bear hug, squashing the air from my lungs. 'We'll miss you, festive Flora,' he says with his lopsided grin. They've been like protective younger brothers, and I can't imagine waking up tomorrow and not seeing their smiley faces. It seems incredible that we've only known each other for two days. 'I'll miss you guys too.'

I give them one last wave and jump into the cab of the van.

'Drive safe! Stay on the right!' Erik says and taps the side of the van as I leave.

Chapter 10

Once I'm out of the city and on a longer stretch of road with fewer cars, I call Livvie on the hands-free.

'FLORA!' she yells so loudly I nearly veer off the road. 'You're alive!'

'Well, of course I'm alive!' I haven't sent Livvie a text since my thank you on arrival. Time has flown! 'Sorry I didn't get in touch, I'm a terrible friend who just took advantage of your generosity and forgot all about you.'

'You terrible, terrible friend! Thanks for my Christmas goodie box. I basically ate everything in one sitting. How was the Jumbo?'

'That's the spirit.' The scenery slips past in a snowy white blur. 'The Jumbo was the best! You should have seen the cockpit suite! If only there'd been a swoon-worthy man to invite back – I could have made *so* many leery cockpit jokes. It's a shame I wasted that particular opportunity.'

'A crying shame! Oh, well, maybe on the way back you'll have another chance?'

'Maybe.'

I go on to tell Livvie all about the trio and Gigi and her mum.

'They sound so lovely and supportive! So none of the trio were Hallmark hero candidates? Not even cockpit fling worthy?'

'Nope, they were like three younger brothers with my best interests at heart. Cute computer geeks with muscles.'

'How wholesome.'

I laugh. 'Very. I found it so hard to say goodbye and isn't that crazy? I'd known them barely forty-eight hours and there I was about to ugly cry.'

'Aww, that's a good thing though, right?'

'Yeah, it is. I guess I didn't think I'd get attached to people so quickly and easily. If I have to keep saying goodbye like that I'm going to have to invest in some waterproof mascara.'

'I'll send you some. So what happened with the other van you were all set to buy?'

'Oh . . .' I sigh. 'Stumbled onto my first con artist. The guy tried to sell me a bomb of a van and got quite uppity when I refused. Did the whole grab-my-arm and hiss into my face thing to try and intimidate me.' Livvie gasps. 'Erik had to come to my rescue. But it all worked out in the end because this van is perfect and do you know how I know that for sure?'

'Because it runs like a dream?'

'Nope, because it was already named Noël and I love him with every piece of me.'

She giggles. 'Fate has intervened once more. Who would have thought you first great love would have been a vehicle? Maybe this is your Hallmark moment, you and Noël?'

'Me and Noël! Instead of marrying a rock or a tree or an inflatable Santa I'll marry a machine – I'm sure Noël feels the same way about me! Erik told me if I'm open to it *the journey will provide*, and I know that sounds like some hippy nomad jargon, but I've experienced it with myself and now I'm a believer.'

'Aww, Flora, you're trying new things and it's all working out for you. I'm so bloody jealous I can hardly form words. What's the plan now? Are you on the way to Lapland already?'

The traffic on the road starts to thicken once more. Clearly real people are going about their everyday lives, heading off to work as rush hour creeps closer. 'Yep, checked out of the Jumbo and I'm on my way. I'll do about eight hours of driving today. I don't want to be driving on these icy roads in the dark, not to mention on the wrong side of the road. So I'll stop whenever I feel tired and park up, I guess. I don't need a hotel; that's the beauty of the van.'

'OK, but maybe you should find a proper holiday park so you're safe.'

'Good idea. When I stop for lunch I'll have a look on my phone and determine how far I'll be able to get before it's too dark.'

'OK, or let me know and I'll research for you.'

'You make an excellent PA.'

'I aim to please. Make sure you stop and have coffee to revive yourself.'

'Yes, Mum.'

'And make sure you let some cool air in so you don't get sleepy.'

'OK.'

'And make sure—'

'Stop nagging, Mum!'

'OK, OK, sorry! I shouldn't have had that marathon horror movie sesh last night. It's got me on edge.'

'You hate horror movies.'

'I know. I found them in your room and I thought hey, why not?'

'I couldn't *give* those things away, hence why they were still in my room. Go put them in a charity bin or you'll end up hiding under your bed every bloody night.'

'No way, under the bed is where the bad guys lie in wait!'

I cluck my tongue. 'See, you've started already, and I'm not there to make sure the front door is locked for you all eighty-seven times.'

'I know.' She laughs. 'It took me thirty minutes to get the courage to leave the sofa and check the doors were truly, definitely, unequivocally locked last night. And it was a mad dash too. Lesson learned. Anyway, just be careful, be safe. I'm picturing you pulled alongside some long lonely deserted road . . .'

'You're creeping me out. If I park up it will be beside a police station or a place where there's lots of people and bright lights. I won't be tucking myself away anywhere dark and deserted, *that's for sure.*' I don't even know the legalities of where campervans can park and what most Van Lifers do. This is what happens when you're a little spontaneous. Why didn't I do my due diligence? I add that to my Hallmark movie heroine self-improvement list.

'Safety first!'

'Yes, I'm going to get that tattooed on my hand so I remember. What's been happening with you? How's it going with that cute bespectacled guy from Shoreditch? Jasper, was it?'

'Jasper?' She groans. 'It's going too well. He's bloody lovely, which makes me suspicious.'

'Suspicious, why?'

'Oh, he's in publishing, loves British history and taking mini breaks staying at little B&Bs and searching out all those fascinating castles and such. Doesn't that just sound frightfully wonderful? What's the catch?'

'Oh, Liv, there's no catch! He's perfect for you.' Livvie adores British history; in fact at one point she considered going back to study full-time, but her clinic took off so it's more like a hobby to her now.

'He ticks all the boxes and to me that rings alarm bells.'

'Jeez, Livvie, it's almost like you *want* to self-sabotage. Just give it a go, won't you? You're happy to go out with the bad boys, ones who say things like *you're so bourgeois*, and yet you dilly-dally with a guy like Jasper?'

'Yeah, I am self-sabotaging! The thing is, I felt . . . so *seen* chatting away to him, in a way I've never felt before. I could go under with a guy like that.'

I shake my head. 'So what's wrong with that? Go tumbling down the rabbit hole and see what's there!'

'It's scary, as if I won't have any control. And I'm leaving so what's the point? I can't see a guy waiting around for a year, can you?'

'If he's The One, he'll wait a year. It's nothing in the scheme of things, is it? Remember the Hallmark movie, Liv. Be brave!'

She groans. 'It's bad timing, it'll never work and all this thinking hurts my poor overworked brain. He invited me to the Museum of London.'

'Two British history geeks – what are the chances?'

'I know, it's crazy. Yesterday we spent five hours on the phone talking about all the castles we've seen and all those we haven't. And the history books we've read about them and those we're yet to read.'

'Riveting.' I yawn.

'Shush, you. History *is* riveting. I might just be falling a teeny tiny little bit for him. He took me out for brunch yesterday and he was so animated his eggs went cold. Don't you love that? He talked so much he forgot to eat!'

'*So animated his eggs went cold*? Cold eggs, *yech*.' I slow down as I come to traffic lights. 'But I can understand it, Liv. He stared into those deep green eyes of yours and he was lost. It's how all good love stories start. Unless he's just one of those over-talkers; he's not an over-talker, is he?'

The light goes green and I remind myself to stay on the correct side of the road. For some reason when I stop my first instinct is to veer back to the left. I really hope this new road navigation clicks in soon.

'No, he's not an over-talker. He asks me a lot of questions.' I had one disaster of a boyfriend who would just talk right over me. It quite riled me up, never being able to get a word in. We didn't last long. He's in politics now.

'Jasper is a keeper. I can tell already.'

'I've told him I leave for LA soon, and he seems to want to continue . . . whatever this is. But isn't that crazy? Long-distance relationships are fraught with drama at the best of times and we've known each other five minutes!'

'How is it crazy? Seems to me he's feeling the same vibe as you and is happy to pursue it no matter where you are. Sounds bloody dreamy to me. You can take your time and get to know each other properly with no pressure.'

When I fall for a guy, I fall head over heels, and start envisaging our fabulous, wondrous future together. In my brief history of love, not many men have responded well to first-date questions like: *What do you think of Kew Gardens as a wedding venue? How do you feel about raising gender-neutral children?* Livvie would die of old age before she quizzed a guy about what matters to her. We're so different!

'I don't know; a year is a long time. What if he wants to fly out and visit?'

Livvie tends to focus on every possible reason that it might not work. The only men Livvie lets in are the bad ones, like musician wannabe Larry. She knows they're no good for her and therefore they can't break her heart because she's not truly invested in them. It's a protective behaviour that I'm sure stems back to her childhood and that desire not to need anyone. But I wish she'd give real love a red-hot go.

'Wouldn't that be a good thing if he wanted to come all that way and visit? Wouldn't it show he's committed to you?'

'Maybe. What's that sound?' Livvie asks.

'What . . . oh.' There's a hissing noise like the sound of a thousand cobras ready to strike. I grip the steering wheel tighter in order to think.

'What *is* that sound?' I say. 'Oh my God, the cab is filling with smoke!'

'Smoke?'

'Toxic deadly smoke!'

'It can't be!'

'It bloody well is! Am I going to die before I've seen the northern lights? Or met my Hallmark hero? Had my adorable babies?! This is grossly unfair!'

'No, you're not going to die. Is something really on fire?'

'I don't know! But as the saying goes where there's smoke there's fire. Could something be on fire, like the engine? The . . . undercarriage?' I glance around, looking for an obvious clue, like flames but see nothing.

'Surely not!'

It gets thicker and I cough. What do I do? 'I don't want to die before I get to Lapland! Wouldn't that be just my luck? Be a mere day away from my dream destination, and end up being burned alive?!' My voice rises hysterically as I picture myself as some kind of flaming effigy. I'm so distracted by it I don't think of doing anything sensible, like pulling over.

'Take a breath, don't panic.'

I panic more. 'Too late. What if this is carbon monoxide and I—?'

'Pull over, *pull over* as soon as it's safe. Are you sure it's smoke? Can you smell anything burning? It can't be carbon monoxide because you can't see or smell that.'

'How do we know for sure, Liv? What if this is some other mechanical type of gas with the same lethal qualities! You hear about these things all the time. Spies use it! How long does a deadly gas take to kill a person? How long has it been?' I pump the brakes hard and pull onto an empty stretch of white next to the road. In my haste I forget about the icy conditions and Noël slips and slides. 'ARGH!' The van finally comes to a stop, right about the time my heart does too. If it's not one thing that's going to kill me, it's another! I grab my mobile and slide out of the door, my legs like jelly.

'This is prematurely ageing me, Liv! I should have accepted the Botox so I leave behind a youthful-looking corpse. Who'd have thought I'd die by misadventure, inhaling toxic fumes and letting my life slowly ebb away before I've even had a relationship go the distance!'

'OK, I admit this isn't ideal but come on, Flora, this is exactly what would happen to a Hallmark heroine. She needs some kind of obstacle in her path or else how would we know her mettle? This is all part of the blueprint!'

I focus on catching my breath before I say, 'OK, OK, you're right, I guess. It's only that it doesn't feel all that fun when it's happening in the real world is all. I'm in the middle of nowhere and it's bloody freezing and Noël, my one true love, is already letting me down, just like all the real men in my life have.' But I pull my shoulders back. I will not be defeated by . . . whatever is trying to defeat me, dammit!

'Let me call my mechanic Donny. He'll know what to do. Are you OK? Where you are? It's not on fire or anything, is it? Can you see flames?'

'No flames, no fire.'

'Can you pop the bonnet and check the engine while I call him?'

'The engine is under the seat!'

'The engine is what . . . Why?'

'Because whoever designed this vehicle thought that was a better spot for it.'

'Wow, that's so weird. I didn't know that. Does it get hot under your *derriere*?'

'Not hot, a touch warm . . . but back to the urgent matter at hand, Liv. I really don't think we have time to discuss the benefits of under-seat engines when my life hangs in the balance, do we? Can you call Donny now, and make sure this isn't toxic? What if I pass out and you can't reach me? What if it's some kind of smoke signal and this was all an elaborate plan to get me to buy the van, only to snatch it back once I'm unconscious? *Oh my God*, what if this some kind of ploy to *kidnap* me like you see on the movies?'

'Kidnap you, no. I'll call Donny now but don't panic, darling. I'm sure they didn't hatch some zany plot to steal the van back or snatch you, but maybe you *have* ingested something the way you're carrying on! Inhale the fresh air just in case.'

'Yes, then that will reverse the effects of the toxic gas!'

'I'll call you right back!'

Surely it's not an elaborate plan to steal the van back? Gigi's family was too nice for that. Could they have wanted to kidnap me? You hear about that kind of thing all the time – hold me in a basement to wash their dishes, fold their laundry that kind of thing. They don't know I'm not a domestic goddess.

My phone rings. 'What did he say?'

'Most likely scenario is the radiator hose has slipped off, or it's the radiator itself. If it's just the hose, it's no big deal.'

'The radiator hose, eh? So maybe . . . I will survive?'

'Possibly.'

'You're meant to be reassuring me, you awful person.'

'You've got this, Flora!' she says in a sugary sweet voice tinged with laughter. 'You're as mechanically minded as they come.'

'That's a lie.'

'Hey, you said to reassure you, did you not? And who can put flatpack furniture together like a pro? YOU can, Flora. If you can do that, you can do anything!'

'OK, you're right. If I can put flatpack Scandinavian furniture together with those useless instructions of theirs then I can probably fix this. How hard can it be, it's a *hose*! Riddle me this, where does one find the radiator hose?'

'My uneducated guess is near the radiator. And he said check that the clamps are on tight once you secure the hose. But you'll have to let it all cool down first. Shouldn't take too long in those cold temperatures.'

I peek inside the cab trying to remember how to lift the seat to expose the engine and find said radiator hose. 'OK, well that sounds easy enough. I can do this. I don't need help. It's a simple radiator hose and some simple clips and that's that. Simple, eh?'

'Super simple.'

Chapter 11

'*Curse you and all of your friends, you stupid piece of plastic!*' I wipe sweat from my brow, even though it's about three degrees. How can one teeny tiny little hose be so damn difficult to put on? There must be some sort of mastery to it because for the life of me, I cannot make it work. I do what any sensible adult would do, I throw it, I stamp on it, I bend over and scream at it.

'Why won't you do your bloody job and just go where you bloody well BELONG!'

In my perspiring, anxiety-induced rage, I notice a small car has stealthily pulled up behind me and some Norse god alights from it. The car looks downright minuscule near such a man. Whoa. He struts over all powerful and broody as if he's just come from saving the universe. He stands in front of me, giving me one of those looks usually reserved for escaped criminals. 'Are you . . . OK?' he asks warily.

He's like the god of thunder or something, big and burly with bulging muscles, highlighted by the fact his jacket is too small, or maybe they don't make jackets in Norse god size? I really don't know about these things as all my boyfriends have been on the smaller side, which I've never really liked, being curvaceous myself. He's tall and athletic like he runs with reindeer or something; maybe he owns a reindeer farm or something equally Christmassy in which case . . . could he be the Hallmark movie hero! 'Do you know all of Santa's reindeer's names?'

He ignores me for some inexplicable reason but looks on edge. The man mountain leans over and inspects the front of the van. 'Did you hit something?' He runs a hand along the bumper as if checking for dents while surprise knocks me sideways that he has an Irish accent. 'Like your head, for example?'

'What, no?' *Hit my head*? The guys *thinks* I'm batty! But his Irish lilt throws me; it doesn't sound exactly Norse god like, but I still can't help thinking of him this way. 'My heart pumps fast as I lock eyes with him, because I have this unshakable knowing: *he's the one for me*. I feel it in my soul! We'd have a winter wonderland wedding in Lapland. Santa's village would be ideal, but do they do that sort of thing?

But why is he looking at me like that? Doesn't he recognise true love when he sees it? Another thought hits: is this heaven? Am I dead? They *were* toxic fumes! He's an angel come to guide me on in the afterlife . . . Well thank you, Jesus!

He bends to pick up the offending piece of rubber that up until now was the bane of my existence – right up until he came along, that is.

'Is this a radiator hose?'

Mechanically minded too, tick!

'It is.'

'Were you yelling at a radiator hose?' He frowns as if he can't quite make sense of the situation. What's so alarming about me yelling in frustration at a piece of plastic? He gives me a look that suggests he thinks I'm unhinged. This can't be heaven, angels would surely be more amenable, more friendly – this guy looks like he's one step away from running. But why?

I cough into my hand. 'Well, you see, I had a spot of van trouble, which I managed to self-diagnose, being a calm, capable woman who doesn't need a man to rescue her. I was trying to put the hose back on and I'm not sure what happened but this hose has clearly shrunk and no matter what I do it simply will not fit. Which makes me wonder if perhaps, it's not the right size hose and that's why it slipped off in the first place?' Look at me sounding like an engineer!

'Hmm,' he says.

Hmm? Is that it? Is he not feeling what I'm feeling? That there's the distinct possibility of love in air, once we get past our first disastrous meet-cute, just like in the movies except this knucklehead doesn't seem to get that. 'What did you think I was doing?'

'I thought you were . . .'

Being strong, independent, taking the reins of your own life. The type of woman who doesn't *need* a man, but can pick and choose if she *wants* one. And I choose him!

'. . . murdering someone. You were *incandescent* with rage.'

My jaw hits the floor. Wait . . . what? 'You thought I was in the midst of *murder*?' Am I hearing him correctly? I slap an ear to make sure I haven't damaged it somehow.

He shrugs as if he's just mentioned it's cold today, and not insinuated that clearly innocent *moi* is capable of manslaughter. 'There's a small rise there; all I could see was you screaming and stomping and kicking away at something. While you're a small woman, I thought that level of rage might have been aimed at a person. You hear strange things about the power of fury when adrenaline is pumping. People have been known to lift cars and all sorts of things.'

I don't know whether to be insulted or not. On one hand he stopped to save a mythical person being beaten to death by me; on the other he thinks I'm capable of homicide, even though I'm 'a small woman'. Do they breed them bigger where he's from or something?

'I wasn't assassinating anyone; I was merely taking my frustrations out on the hose that's had me stuck here for the last couple of hours when I've got places to be. I'm not sure I like your accusations otherwise.' My hackles rise. He's *still* staring guardedly at me like I'm demented. The love at first sight bubble pops, until I make eye contact again. He's so bloody good-looking it should be illegal. True to form with most men on the devastatingly attractive scale, he lacks the ability to have a reasonable conversation, dammit.

'Would you like me to put the hose on for you?'

I cross my arms. 'I don't care either way.'

'You don't care?'

'No, I do not.'

'It's getting colder and you'll need to get going before the snow starts in earnest. How about I fix it and then we go our separate ways?'

'Well, we haven't exactly planned to go in convoy, have we?' *The ego on him!*

'No, I meant . . . never mind. Give me a minute.' He leans inside the cab near the engine. I creep closer to see if he can fit the bloody hose on because some part of me hopes he fails too, just so I can show him it's not as easy as it looks – even though I know that means I'll be stuck here all night. 'You should think of an electric car – so much better for the environment. These old vans are a menace with terrible fuel economy and higher emissions.'

'Can't exactly live in an electric car, now can I? Bit squishy.' Is he some kind of eco-warrior? 'But thanks for the tip. I'll make sure I plant some extra trees to reverse my carbon footprint.'

'Right.'

While I've got him in such an amiable mood, I take the tyre iron from the pocket in the door, hoping he can tighten one of the lug nuts that has come loose too. He's not the nicest guy I've ever come across, but he's clearly got enough muscles to make sure my wheels won't fall off. I peek over his shoulder to see how he's going with the hose – he turns suddenly and holds up his hands. 'Whoa, whoa, whoa. Put it down and walk away. I don't want to disarm you, but I will if I have to.'

Disarm me? 'What?' His gaze drops to the tyre iron. 'Oh, for crying out loud, I'm not a murderer! I was going to ask you to tighten my nuts!'

A small smirk appears – so he's not made of stone? 'Tighten your nuts?'

'Yes my nuts, my lug nuts or whatever they're called. But you seem intent on thinking I'm some kind of creepy killer, sneaking up with a weapon in hand. And I'll tell you something, if I *was* going to attempt to kill you, it wouldn't be with a tyre iron! I'm sure this alloy isn't strong enough for the likes of you; it would probably *bend* against your rippling mass of muscles.'

'So you have thought about it?' The doubt creeps back into his voice and I struggle to see how I even remotely resemble a psychopath. Is it the messy hair? So, I haven't been taking the usual care with my appearance. I figured while I'm on the road, I'm wild and free and so are my long curly locks.

'For one brief second I might have thought about it . . . wait, no not like that. I'm just saying . . .'

'How about you stand on the other side of the van, and I'll stand here while I fix the hose and your . . . nuts.'

'Fine.' This is an unmitigated disaster! Why would the universe send me my dream man only to have it play out like this? But I suppose my dream man wouldn't be so surly or suspicious and even though he's come to the rescue of an invisible victim, it doesn't mean he's a good guy. It just means he wanted to be the hero. He probably drives up and down this road looking for people to help. Hero complex for sure. It radiates off him. My own Hallmark movie hero hopes are dashed.

Infuriatingly he gets the hose to slip on as easily as Cinderella does her slipper. Internally I fume. He tightens the lug nuts on the front wheel and then checks the others as if he's a perfect gentleman. 'What's your name?' he yells – he's yelling because he's made me stand on the other side so he'll have more warning of a surprise attack.

'I don't give my name to strangers,' I say. 'You could be anyone. You could be dangerous.'

He laughs, a deep throaty sound that manages to make my legs buckle a bit, damn him. 'That's rich, coming from you.'

'Can you *see* any dead bodies?'

'I'm not game enough to look in the van.'

'You big tough Norse god, you.'

'What?'

Internally, I cringe. 'Look, once you fix those nuts I'll be on my way, and hopefully, you'll be going in the other direction. Which way *are* you going?'

'I don't tell strangers where I'm going,' he says. 'You could be anyone. You could be dangerous.'

Touché. 'Probably safer,' I say, coming around the van and giving him my best maniacal smile. If he wants crazed, crazed he will get.

He dusts his hands on his jeans and hands me the tyre iron. 'Now I'm trusting you with this. Don't bonk me over the head when I turn my back.'

'Well, you'd better walk fast, is all I'm saying.'

'This has been fun,' he says, deadpan. 'Now get on the road.'

And he leaves as quick as he arrived, giving me a wave from the safety of his electric car. What an enigma. I slump, as if he's sapped all my energy. A man like that could never work for me. He's too big for a start; the earth literally darkens when he's around. Too many muscles, too surly. He'd have women falling all over him and who wants that kind of pressure? Not me.

I'm freezing half to death so I jump back in the cab of the van. He's gone, he's out of my life for good, but still, it irks me for some reason.

There's nothing left to do except have a quick chat with Noël and reassure him that this was a small blip, and then get going. I won't make it quite as far as I'd hoped today, but life on the road is never going to go exactly to plan and I remind myself that's the beauty of it. No monotonous days here, no sirree.

Once I'm back into the swing of it, I call Livvie. 'Well, that was a little more dramatic than I figured, but the hose is on and we're back in business. And I met a Norse god and I can confirm he's all looks and no personality and as a potential father to my children, that's no good, so he's off the list. Plus he thinks I'm a murderer, so there's also that.'

'Hang on . . . what? Bloody hell, Flora, this life on the road caper is a laugh a minute. Who is this Norse god you speak of and why does he think you're a murderer? You're not, are you? It would explain a lot actually.'

'The only murdering I've done is of Galileo the goldfish and I've told you *numerous* times that he made that face like he was starving. Can it be called murder if it was a mercy thing? I know what it's like to be hungry all the time and if anything, he died happy.'

'Well, he died grossly overweight, but OK.' Who knew such a thing was possible?

'He was big-boned! Even the vet said so.'

She giggles. 'We're getting off track.'

I laugh – even though I still miss Galileo and losing him has given me trust issues around pet ownership – then proceed to tell her about my brush with the Viking wannabe who witnessed the attempted murdering of my radiator hose. I don't get right into the nitty-gritty of the whole encounter because Livvie is laughing so hard she can't hear me.

'It's not that funny!'

'Stop, you're *killing* me here.'

'Oh, don't you start!'

Chapter 12

The next morning, I awake in the van shivering, teeth chattering with the knowledge I've never been so bloody cold in all my life. I'll need to buy some thermal clothing, and wear double layers to help ease the chill, which seems to creep up under the bed as though I'm sleeping on a solid block of ice.

Blowing into my hands, I stumble into the 'kitchen' – a sink and shelving area – and flick on the kettle and make a giant pot of tea. Cradling the mug to warm my hands, I look at the snowy view outside and know that moments like these are why people choose Van Life. There's no one about, just me and the snowy cotton-ball landscape. I reflect on my first day on the road; it was a success despite the obstacles I faced. I'm alive, Noël is running like a dream, all is well.

Still there's pressure to get to Lapland tonight and get to the supplier so I can set up my shop, so I get dressed in my favourite Santa onesie then hit the road, crank the carols and put the heater on Hades. I soon take off with a bag of marshmallows for breakfast. Needs must and all that . . .

After a full day of blissfully uneventful driving, I make it to the supplier late evening, to collect my order. I park the van and jump from the cab, my legs buckling from staying in one position so long. Note to self: take more rest breaks. Losing so many hours yesterday made me hesitate to stop when I probably should have been jumping out and stretching the legs while imbibing coffee to help me focus. But it's done now, and if all goes well here I'll be at the market soon and then I can fall into bed in a heap and snooze, knowing I have others around me and I'm not going to run into any other men with hero complexes – I hope.

I knock on the door of the warehouse and am greeted by a woman who looks suspiciously like Mrs Claus. 'Flora?' she asks.

'Yes, hi, you must be Hanne? Thanks for opening up late for me.'

'Yes, I am, and no problem. Welcome to Lapland. Come in, come in out of the cold.' She ushers me inside and I'm disappointed to find it a sterile warehouse full of boxes. What did I expect – a taste of Santa's village? 'I've got your order ready. I've popped in some string lights for the awning of your van and a few other bits and pieces to help you out.'

I'm surprised by her generosity. 'That's really lovely of you, Hanne.'

She waves me away. 'I'm quite taken by the idea of Van Life and all it entails. It's an amazing way to live, forgoing conventional work and doing it your own way on your own terms. What made you decide to take such a leap?'

I give her smile, wondering if I should make my tale a little more exciting than the sad truth but then figure it's not worth lying about. Plus, I'm a hopeless liar. 'Well, the truth is I'm a self-confessed Christmas tragic and if I could live like it's Christmas all year round, then I would. Despite my sparkly demeanour I couldn't manage to hold down a job for any length of time. And don't even get me started on my love life. So after being fired from my dream job at Deck the Hall Christmas Emporium, it was decided over too many mugs of hot cocoa that I'd give this a try and see what happens. There's almost no chance I'll get fired since I'm the boss, so that gives me hope. I'm going to attempt to live my life as though I'm a Hallmark Christmas heroine and hope that by following that blueprint I too will find my very own happy ever after.'

She lets out a barrel of laughter. 'Well, you've come to the right place – Finnish men are the best in the world.'

I waggle my eyebrows. 'I'll have to take your word on that.'

'You can trust me,' she says with a grin. 'The great thing about getting a place at the Christmas market is you won't need to move your van each night. The vendors all stay put for the season, hence why some set up extravagant outdoor areas for customers. You might want to consider that yourself. Something that you can manoeuvre around when you do want to take some day trips.'

I hadn't thought of that. I'd definitely still need to move my van from time to time to buy supplies and do a bit of sightseeing when the markets are closed, but I could set up an outdoor Christmas display where customers can hang out and warm up over a hot drink. 'Thank you, that's a great idea. I'll assess the area once I arrive and let you know what else I need. A Christmas tree is a must . . .'

She grins. 'I have a life-size gingerbread house with seats inside. Would you like to see it?'

Can I afford such a thing? 'Let's have a look.'

Hanne takes me to another room with a range of oversized Christmas decorations. There are inflatable Santas, reindeer, shiny red sleighs, and so much more. I want it all! Off to the side is a gingerbread house that looks exactly like the real thing only it's twenty times larger. It's a showstopper, cosy and quirky and just like something out of *Hansel and Gretel*. 'It's gorgeous, Hanne . . .' I say, wondering how I can explain politely that while I might look like this grand adventurer I'm not flush with cash. 'But I'm not sure I have enough in the coffers for it just yet.'

She waves me away. 'You don't need to buy it; it's not like you can cart it home with you. You can rent it for . . .' She shoots off a figure that is very affordable for someone like me just starting out. 'I'd rather it be used and enjoyed than sit in a warehouse gathering dust all winter.'

I grin. 'In that case, I'd love to rent it. I wonder if I need permission to sell hot drinks?' I think back to the many emails I sent to pitch my pop-up shop and get various approvals. There'd been a lengthy application process and I had to outline my merchandise and make sure it didn't impinge on any current vendors. But surely offering hot drinks wouldn't step on too many toes, and a seating area would be beneficial for market-goers. Somewhere for them to rest their legs and revive so they can spend longer looking at all the other vendors. But it will also be good for me; I can make a decent profit on hot drinks without much extra fuss or work.

'I don't see it being an issue. Connor is the man in charge of the markets. He's a nomad himself – this is his first season, and while he's on the quiet side everyone seems to respect him and trust his judgement. You've probably spoken to him for your place there?'

I think back. 'Yes, I think that's who I've been emailing with. He's been great, very professional and helpful. I can't see it being an issue and if he says I can't sell hot drinks for health and safety reasons then I'll use the gingerbread house as simply another place to display stock that will keep it all safe and out of the elements.'

'Perfect. I'll arrange for my husband Juho to deliver the gingerbread house to you in a couple of days once we catch up on our orders.'

'You're very kind, thank you!'

Hanne helps me cart boxes of decorations to the van and the anticipation of what's to come builds. I'm the epitome of a kid on Christmas morning because I can't wait to set up my little business and meet all the other vendors. And the cherry on top is having an outdoor area that will surely pull more shoppers in my direction . . .

Chapter 13

The sky is inky black by the time I arrive at the Lapland Christmas market and there's no sign of the northern lights. I'll see it when the time is right – of that I'm certain.

Eventually, I find the market and pull up next to the gate attendant. 'Hello, where is 49B, please?' I pull out my paperwork and show him my allotment and hope he speaks English. I really need to invest in a translation app so I can learn the language as I go.

'Go around to the back lane.' He points to the way I've just come from. 'Then head north, veer east and you'll see another gate. You can get in that way. You're beside the admin office so if Connor isn't there, check in with him tomorrow morning.'

'Thanks.' Head north? Veer east! Why can't people talk in terms of left or right? I have no idea which way north might be but I head out and towards the back lane, hoping there's a sign or something to lead the way.

I drive the wrong way down the street, and only realise when I see headlights coming towards me on the same side of the road. 'ARGH!' I hastily screech to a stop as the other driver does the same mere inches from me. My pulse gallops at such a near miss on a darkened laneway. I give the blonde female driver a wave as if to apologise but she only stares contemptuously at me before gesticulating wildly, making her oversized Christmas earrings swish and sway so that I worry her ears might be clean wrenched off. Something tells me she's spitting expletives at me. 'Sorry!' I mouth with a shrug. The blonde gives me the finger. Charming. Interesting to know the gesture isn't limited to the UK.

I turn to the right side of the road, and creep past her car. The witch doesn't move at all to let me past, but instead rolls her window down and shouts more abuse in Finnish at me.

I give her a minute to calm down but she continues, her face reddening. I roll down my window. 'It was an accident, cabbage head! That's why it's called an accident, not an "on purpose"!' I yell. There's being quite rightly upset at the near miss, and then there's being a bully and blondie here has crossed the line. Like the consummate together person I am, I don't resort to giving her my own gesture in return but drive away and hope to all that is joyful and bright that I never see her again.

My heart rate slows down and I put the other driver out of my mind. She was probably speeding and just as much at fault as me. I find the second gate and the numbered sign for my allotment, which thankfully has a large empty space next to it, so there's room to do about a four-hundred-point turn to park in exactly the right spot. I'm not used to driving such a big rig. I'm not really used to driving at all. Since moving to London it has always been easier to use public transport.

By the time I alight from Noël, a small crowd has formed, most of them laughing into their gloved hands. Are they laughing *at* me? So my parking methods are a little rusty – is it really that funny? Or is it my Christmas onesie and furry boots? 'Show's over, folks,' I say trying to remain jovial but instead it comes out a little wooden. With a sigh, I head to the office to see if anyone is there. It's locked up tight, so I head back to the van.

There's nothing left to do except get ready. Now I'm here I'm suddenly wide awake so I crank up the Christmas carols and begin displaying my loot. There aren't many market-goers left but I want to make a start while I've got my second wind. I'm singing away to 'Last Christmas' when the small bit of light I'm working under fades to black. What on earth . . .

I turn and see a six-foot-something hulk standing there, hands on his hips, giving off a distinct surly vibe. I can't see his face, but I *feel* his presence somehow. I turn on my colourful string lights and his face comes into view. You have to be *kidding* me!

'How did you find me?' I bark. I bet he's stalked me on social media! Or maybe he followed me here! Standing there is none other than the Norse god himself with that same infuriating, suspicious gaze of his.

'Find you? How did you find *me*?'

I scoff. 'I bloody well did no such thing! I'm here for business thank you very much, and I won't have you ruining this for me. I'll call security. I'll call—'

He shakes his head, ruffling his woolly mane of hair. 'There have been complaints about the volume of your music.'

'What?' He's trying to bamboozle me. I can see straight through him.

'Your music, it's too loud.' He enunciates slowly as if he's speaking to a child.

I cross my arms. 'And what's it to you? Don't think I'm going to overlook the fact you've followed me here! Did you put some sort of tracker on my van?'

Is *that* what he was doing the whole time he was pretending to tighten my nuts?

Confusion dashes across his face. 'What do you mean followed you here?'

I grunt. 'Don't play coy with me, Mister. Are you or are you not standing in front of me right now?'

He bites down on his lip and I don't know if it's to stop the smirk on his smirky face or what, but it distracts me for a moment. It's just his lips are pretty sexy as far as lips go and . . . *Don't be fooled, that's what he wants!*

'Yes, I'm standing in front of you because I *work* here. And I'm telling you to turn your music down because there've been some complaints. You've been here all of five minutes and *already* you've alienated other vendors. Can't say I'm surprised.'

Baby Jesus weeps. He *works* here! What are the bloody chances? Trouble creeps up and taps me on the shoulder. Still, I can't let him know he's thrown me off balance. 'I wouldn't say I've alienated people! It's a bloody Christmas market and if that doesn't call for a bit of Wham then what does? Alienate is a very strong word.' Not surprised he's using it though, he's a bit of an alienator himself.

'Turn it down, or I'll turn it off.'

I shoot him daggers but he doesn't seem to fathom a thing I say or do. Is the man a robot? A machine? He's an empty vessel. Yeah sure he's gorgeous but that's about all he's got going for him and – news flash – looks fade.

'Is that so? And just who do *you* think you are? You think you can come waltzing up here and threaten me like this? Try and intimidate me? Well, it's not going to wash with me! I'm going to put a formal complaint in to Connor about you!'

His eyes widen. Probably in fear.

I stare him down and get ready for him to hightail it. For some reason he does not. He gawps at me like I'm speaking another language. 'Not so tough now, are you?' I can't help but give him a triumphant smile. Connor will know on sight alone this . . . this *nefarious* character has trouble written all over him like the tattoos I can see snaking under his shirt, of all the clichés.

He crosses his arms, making his muscles bulge so much I fear his jacket is going to explode. 'Is that so?' Can the guy not find clothing in his actual size, or something? '*I'm* Connor.'

Plot twist!

Why oh why, universe, do you hate me so? What have I done to deserve this foot-in-mouth *disease*?

Did I not just have a lengthy conversation about how I couldn't get fired, since I would now be my own boss? Didn't think of this particular scenario, did I? Why does this keep happening to me? How to backtrack and not make it obvious . . . ?

'Connor . . . *in the flesh!* Wow, it's so lovely to meet you. I'm Flora from London. What nice eyes you have! Could I interest you in a cup of eggnog – it won't take me a minute to whip up. I won't put poison in it, promise.' I let out a tinkling little laugh that I hope accentuates my sweet and innocent nature. 'I have these delightful Christmas-themed straws if you'd prefer a milkshake?'

'Single-use plastic straws! Really, Flora?'

'Ah . . . well, we can wash them after if you like?' I'm all for saving the environment as much as the next person, but paper straws have a habit of turning into papier-mâché and that's not exactly appetising. 'I'll repurpose these!'

'Turn the music down.' His Viking eyes flash like he's in a super-hero movie. 'I don't want to hear another complaint about you.'

'Consider it done!' My cheeks burn and I'm sure my complexion is now Santa-suit red.

Though I wonder if now is the time to broach getting approval to sell hot drinks in the gingerbread house. Probably not, going by the dark look on his face.

He wanders away and I want to cup my face and wail. Once again there's a group of other vendors standing nearby laughing. *Really?* Just what have I walked into here? That they went to Connor to complain about my music without approaching me first says a lot. Is it because they just want to be in Connor's spotlight because he's this big, tough, hulking mass of electricity? I'd have hoped Van Lifers were a bit beyond that kind of behaviour. Sparks literally fly off the guy as he snakes in and out of groups of Van Lifers who huddle around drum fires. Where's the peace, love and all that stuff?

'Can I help you?' I say archly when I'm left with a huddle of women who continue to stand there, whispering and pointing. They soon walk off giggling. I turn the music down and shut the awning. Whatever customers I hoped to see tonight will have to wait. I'm not feeling merry, not even close.

Where's the Van Life camaraderie I've heard so much about? I call Livvie; she'll know what to do . . .

'Flora! Tell me you made it there alive and this isn't the kidnapper calling for ransom?'

'Very funny. And if you get a finger in the post please sell up the biz and pay whatever they demand. Don't waste time getting the police involved, we all know that doesn't work.'

'Not that you're dramatic or anything but consider it done. So how is Lapland? Is it everything you imagined it would be and more, or too soon to tell?'

Where to start? I find my emergency bottle of wine and go to flop on the sofa only to discover it's not really the size for flopping. Let's just say I could either flop on the top end or the bottom end but not both. I press the speaker button, find a wine glass and head to the bedroom. The bed specifically.

'Let me pour this emergency bucket of wine and then I'll tell you.'

'Oh dear. I'm bracing. Brace position!' she yells as if we're on a plane and it's going down. I hope that's not a sign of things to come.

I tell Livvie the whole sorry story, including the part about threatening to report Connor, to Connor.

She does this high-pitched screech thing that has me scrunching my eyes closed. 'Jesus, Liv. You've bloody deafened me and I'm the dramatic one?'

'Oh come on, Flora! Surely you see what's going on?'

'Yeah, how can I not?! I escaped the confines of London and blamed it for screwing my life up, only to come here and realise it's THE BLOODY SAME!'

She laughs. How can she laugh at such a thing? 'You idiot! You're living in a Hallmark movie – the blueprint is *real!*'

'What?' Has she not listened to a word I've said?

She lets out a frustrated groan. 'Flora, you and Connor had the meet-cute, yeah? The whole you're a bloody vicious brutal murdering sociopath thing was the set-up.'

'I'm listening,' I say as I chug back wine.

'Then you skipped straight to making a bad first impression, like you totally nailed that part. *Threatening him with himself* and all.'

I slap my own head. 'Yeah, how unlike me. But I don't think you're really understanding what this guy is like. He's a six-foot-something bossy britches with a bad attitude. Like, this guy cannot be redeemed. The blueprint is a lie!'

'*Of course he can!*'

'You know I love you, Liv, right?'

'Yes.'

'So this comes from a place of love.'

'OK . . . ?'

'Please stop drinking my share of the bottle of red. You're . . . you're better than that.'

There's a pause and then she bursts out laughing. 'I'm not drunk, you fool! I'm excited! I always knew there'd be sparks when you found the guy who was perfect for you. You're that type of girl, Flora, one who goes along setting the world on fire by just being you. And it looks like you've met your match but you haven't recognised that yet – *just like in the Hallmark movies!*'

I see her point, I do, but she hasn't met the groaning, face-rubbing, rule-following, long sigher that I have. I don't think I've set anything on fire for Connor except maybe some of his endless rules by ignoring them. 'Thank you, darling, for your enthusiasm; it's wonderful, especially if you're truly sober, but that guy is best matched with a bucket of rocks, and that's offensive to the rocks. *And* the bucket.'

She laughs and laughs and I cannot for the life of me think why . . .

Chapter 14

The next morning, I awake energised, the previous night almost forgotten. So the Van Lifers didn't welcome me with a loving embrace. Fine. No big deal. And yes, I got off on the wrong foot with Connor. And poor Livvie's hitting the bottle a bit hard, but I've made a note of it and I plan on sending her supportive links and articles along the lines of: Why alcohol is not your friend. Because clearly she was not listening – implying Connor is the hero to my heroine is BONKERS.

But I feel like things can only improve from here. Onwards and upwards! They can't exactly get worse anyway. That group of Van Lifers enjoyed pointing and laughing but that says more about them than it does about me. People misjudge me all the time and I don't normally shut down and hide so I'm not going to start now.

I make myself some eggs on toast and slam down some coffee, hoping the caffeine boost will help my peaky complexion. It doesn't. So I slap on some make-up and spritz on perfume. Then I crank the carols, but at a more acceptable daytime level and open my awning ready for business. There's not a single person about.

Outside is totally silent. I check the time, it's well after ten. Do they not open this early? I wander outside and see gentle snow falling. It truly is a winter wonderland with all the vans decorated in Christmas colours.

I go to the office to see about officially checking in, knowing I'll probably have to face Connor again. I knock and a gruff, 'Come in,' follows. Can he not be cheery?

'Good morning,' I say, smiling sweetly.

'Flora. Checking in?'

'Yes please and I also wanted to ask permission to set up an outdoor area, I wanted to offer customers refreshments, hot cocoa, eggnog that sort of thing.'

'No can do.' He takes down a file and flips it open.

'What, why? Can't you at least consider it?'

There's a moment of silence before he says in a gruff way, 'Nope, there's rules in place and I need to stick to those. Remember your approvals process? You never mentioned it then.'

I frown. 'But . . . but I didn't know I would find a life-size gingerbread house then! This is ridiculous; at least let me outline my idea and then you can decide.'

'Doesn't work that way.' Connor continues to file papers as if he's only half paying attention.

Steam comes out of my ears, I'm sure of it.

He continues speaking blithely, as if he's not ruining my day, *yet again*. The man sure does love office work. 'I've got some paperwork here for you to sign, including your first noise warning.'

'What? First noise warning?' That implies there might be a second and third noise warning and that doesn't sound good.

'Yeah, three strikes and you're out, I'm afraid.' He gives me a rueful smile. A smile, of all things, while dropping a bomb like that!

'But you can't do that! It's not my fault the other vendors are so pernickety.' I try not to sound whiny, I really do but that man brings out the worst in me. This is not going to plan at all!

'Pernickety?'

'Yeah, I mean, how can it be Christmas without carols?'

101

He leans back in his chair, finally giving me his full attention. 'I understand your point of view, I do; it's just that there are other vans here with music, and yours drowned them all out.'

'So why do they get to play theirs so loud?' There's a pecking order and I'm clearly at the bottom.

'Well, one's a jazz bar, and the other is a concerto singer who does performances on the hour.'

Damn it. 'Well, I can see how that makes sense but shouldn't I have had a warning that there'd *be* a warning?'

His eyebrows pull together. 'But . . . this is a warning?' Connor waves his hands about as if it all makes perfect sense.

I struggle to remain calm. 'Yeah but I mean a pre-warning warning. It's hardly fair I get threatened with that piece of paper and have to sign it like I'm some sort of naughty kid when I didn't even *know* there was a warning system. And I dread to think how many trees had to give up their lives in order for you to print all these warnings. Haven't you ever thought about digital warnings? You disappoint me, Connor.'

'It's recycled paper, which is in turn recycled again. We provide specific receptacles for this very purpose. You're not going to break the rules again, are you?'

'No.'

'Then it doesn't matter, does it?' He draws his chair closer to his desk as if he's ready to dismiss me and get back to pulling paperwork out of one file and placing it another. Is he fake working? Trying to appear busy? I wouldn't put it past him! I know I should let this warning go but I can't. This very well might be the root of all my troubles.

'Well, Connor, it kind of *does* matter. You'd have thought any one of my van neighbours might have come and had a quiet word with me before flouncing off to find you!'

I recall them standing around whispering and giggling behind their hands the previous night. Their very un-Christmas-like spirits were such a marked difference from the camaraderie I found on the Jumbo with the trio of travellers and the other hotel guests; even busy executives on work assignments for one night had joined in and swapped stories and laughed around the table. It was welcoming and inclusive, not like here!

'It's not their job though, is it? It's *my* job, and I don't make the rules, I just follow them and you'll do better if you do too.'

'The rules are lame.'

'Do you always have to have the last word?'

'Always.'

A smile plays at his lips. 'Sign here, here and here.'

What exactly am I signing? 'Wait a minute. Where is this rule book that we all have to follow?'

He heaves a sigh. 'Why?'

'Well, I can't sign a first warning when I haven't read the rules, can I? How can one avoid breaking the rules, when one doesn't know what the rules are?' When I get agitated I speak in third person. I can't help it.

'You're not going to sign this, are you?'

'No, I'm not, for the *very valid* reasons I've already stated.'

He sighs and rubs a big man-sized hand over his face. Everything about him is larger than life, he makes the office chair seem like something out of a doll's house with his huge, athletic frame swamping it. 'Fine.' He opens a drawer and takes out a worryingly large hardback book. 'Here are the rules – go wild.'

I flick open the cover, my forehead furrowing. 'But this is written in Finnish?'

'Which is why you haven't read it.'

I look back at him. 'So you're telling me I have to abide by an abnormally large set of rules, which I cannot read, yet somehow must follow and that's OK? This is an abomination!'

He groans. 'No one else has had a problem with it since I've been here and now you come along and suddenly it's an issue.'

'It's a bloody travesty – that's what it is!'

'Flora, are you always like this?'

'Like what?'

'Argumentative.'

'Why, is that against the rules too? Do you now deign what sort of personalities can work here? Because if so, I've got some complaints of my own.' I shoot him a glare for good measure.

He blows out a breath as if he's exhausted. 'Fine, fine, forget the warning. But please try and fit in, OK? No loud music, close up at midnight at the latest. Pick up rubbish around your allotment and that's about all you need to know.'

'I'll be taking this with me,' I say. I'll bloody well learn Finnish if I have to.

He goes to protest but I'm out the door in a flash in case he changes his mind about the warning. I feel strangely triumphant. So it hasn't been the best start but I'm not going to let that put me off. I take out my phone to call Hanne and cancel the gingerbread house, but I'm distracted by the surprisingly long queue of people lined up outside my van, waiting for me to open. Maybe the day won't be all bad . . .

I'm awoken the following day by the screech of wheels, and I fling myself out of bed to see what could be making such a noise at this hour. I peep out of the green velvet curtain and see a flatbed truck with a life-size gingerbread house sitting atop the tray. *Shoot!* After being caught up in the rush of the market day I forgot to cancel the delivery. Connor's head is going to explode if he sees it and will think I purposely went against his drill sergeant orders.

Throwing on a jacket and boots, I head outside to greet Hanne's husband Juho and give him the bad news. I gasp as the cold air hits me when I step down from the van.

'Hello, Juho!' I wave to the elderly man who doesn't look half as sprightly as his wife. He's stooped over as if he's spent too long lifting heavy things and still bears the weight on his shoulders. Juho gives me a warm smile that makes his eyes crinkle like stars.

It's going to be a wrench telling this poor man to turn around back the way he came with his treasure on board.

'You must be the Flora I've heard so much about! Hanne made me get out of bed early and get this all loaded up for you so you'd have it early enough for the crowds to enjoy today.'

I try to smile, while I die a little inside. 'Ah . . . yes, lovely. I'm so sorry you lost sleep over this just for me. The only problem is—'

'Oh, it's no problem, Flora. I can sleep in next month or the month after. As you can imagine this is our busiest time of year so each day gets that little bit more hectic. By the end of the day, I'm zapped. Asleep on the sofa before dinner! Speaking of, I'd better get this unhitched otherwise I'll never get back to the warehouse on time for all the other orders I've got to catch up on.'

'Yes, it's just that . . .'

Juho unties ropes and throws them over the gingerbread house, dashing to the other side to do the same. He runs with a limp and my heart constricts as he puffs and pants in exertion. *Damn it all to hell and back!* There's no way I can waste this man's precious time after he's gone to so much effort at the busiest time of year for their business. It would be the height of rudeness and add extra work to his already hectic schedule. Internally I berate myself for not remembering to cancel yesterday. *You twit, Flora!*

'Can I help?' I say, guiltily glancing over my shoulder expecting to see Connor march out at any second and ask what I'm playing at.

'I'm all good for now, Flora. But when I winch it off, if you can keep an eye out to make sure I don't plonk it down on anyone that would be great.'

I picture two legs poking out of the gingerbread house – like the Wicked Witch of the East is dead – and gulp. No one will die on my watch! Some Van Lifers wander over so I push them back and throw them a smile. 'Don't get too close, folks.'

'I didn't know we were allowed to have structures this big,' says a guy with a Scottish accent.

'Oh? It's a very short-term thing. Pretend it's not here.' I am in *so* much trouble!

Another voice pipes up. 'My outdoor area proposal was rejected because of health and safety concerns, yet this passed? Why's that?'

I close my eyes. I'm about to alienate more Van Lifers because they'll think I've been showed some kind of favouritism. Little do they know I've just caused yet another major problem. 'It's all fine,' I hurriedly reassure them as the gingerbread house is winched into the sky, like something out of *The Wizard of Oz.* 'Back up, back up.'

My chest tightens and I wonder how I'm going to get out of this predicament. It's not like Connor won't notice the gigantic, brightly coloured structure. And that's if there aren't a hundred fists pounding on his office door demanding to know why I've been granted permission and they haven't. Fiasco Flora should be my new name!

The gingerbread house is safely lowered to the ground. 'Isn't it gorgeous?' I can't help but adore it, sitting there as magical as anything. May as well soak up the moment before it all comes crashing down around me.

'I'll be speaking to Connor about this!' a blonde beauty says, creeping up behind me and making me jump in fright. 'Our outdoor areas are held to strict standards and sizing, so how is this monstrosity is allowed?'

I reel as if slapped. 'Monstrosity? That's a bit harsh!'

The blonde smirks like she relishes the challenge. 'It's tacky.'

'It's Christmassy.' There's something familiar about her.

'It's ugly.'

'Well, aren't you a barrel of laughs?' Then I realise, she's the driver I almost took out on the first night I arrived, the one with the oversized earrings and bad attitude. 'Cabbage head, is that you?'

Her eyes widen in recognition. 'That *is* what you called me! I should tell Connor about your bullying too.'

'*My* bullying? You're the one who flipped the bird and cursed me in Finnish! Who wouldn't let me safely past!'

'You tried to kill me! You're a danger to society.' Not this again. If she hears about the other murder rumours things might really spiral out of control.

'I'm anything but!'

She rolls her eyes and stomps away. I've ruffled a few feathers without really meaning to. Again. Is it me?

Juho doesn't seem to hear and double-checks the structure and tightens up a few bolts here and there, slaps the side to make sure it's immovable, then says, 'There you go, Flora. Any problems, let me know. I'd better push on.' He proffers a gloved hand to shake and I only hope I'm not calling him within the hour to come back and pick it up. I will never live that down, if so.

'Hey, new girl.'

I spin to face a tall woman wearing a Puffa jacket. It's hard to discern if she was one of the group who pointed and laughed on my first night, because everyone wears the same sort of Puffa jacket here. 'Hey, I'm Flora.'

'Raakel.'

'Would you like a hot drink?' Anything to delay heading to Connor's office to own up to my mistake.

'Sure.'

'Come on in.'

I make a pot of gingerbread coffee adding an extra dash of cream, and we sit at the table, where I open a tin of Christmas biscuits. 'I could get used to this, Flora.'

I laugh. 'You're welcome any time. So where's your van? What do you sell?'

'I'm further up on the other side. I have the candy-cane-coloured van – Santa's Toy Factory – and I sell all sorts of toys and gadgets. I'm a big kid at heart so it suits me to the ground.'

'I need to come and visit you.'

'You do. I also have the Christmas carousel next to my van.'

107

'A Christmas carousel. How have I not seen that!'

She tilts her head. 'Have you actually had a wander around yet? Word is, you've stuck to your van and haven't explored much yet.'

I sigh. There hasn't been time. 'Word gets around fast, I'm guessing.'

She shrugs. 'It's like a petri dish here – lots of culture and things have a tendency to develop quickly.'

I laugh at the explanation and feel that it's a cloaked warning of sorts. 'O-K . . . so you're saying there's certain people I should avoid?' As if I haven't felt a chilly vibe from a number of people already.

'You learn quick.' I think back to the fun and ease of the Jumbo and wonder why it's not the same here.

I'm guessing the finger-giving blonde beauty is some kind of alpha female who wants to be at the top of the pecking order. Why, who can tell? But this sort of thing bothers me because I know from experience my jaw has a tendency to flap away of its own accord and get me into trouble. 'From all the Van Life blogs I've read, I expected to be welcomed with open arms. You read about how kind everyone is, and how you'll be part of this bigger picture, bonding over the little things . . . So that's not the case?' I can't help but deflate at the thought of going from one place I didn't fit in, to another.

Raakel takes a sip of her gingerbread coffee and smiles. 'This is amazing, thanks. As for your question, it is and it isn't. Because we're all living in close confines things have a habit of spiralling fast. There are lots of lovely nomads here; it's just a matter of finding the right ones and avoiding the others.'

'Thanks for the heads-up.'

'You're welcome. There's always this sort of new person hazing, where they feel you out before you're taken into the fold. I don't know why; it's just a thing here. But don't worry, it'll soon be over and you'll be just like everyone else.'

'Yeah, it's started already. Connor attempted to give me my

first noise warning yesterday. There were complaints about me apparently.'

'Someone complained without talking with you first?'

I nod. 'Yep.'

'That's tough. Although, I can guess who it was.' She lifts a brow. 'Aine. The blonde who had a few words with you before I wandered over. Did you really try to kill her?'

I gasp and then laughter gets the better of me. It's all so ridiculous it's funny. 'No, not at all! I'd been driving all day and half the night and lost my focus for a minute, that's all. I veered into the left lane by mistake as she came towards me. Somehow she's turned my lapse in concentration into attempted murder.'

'She does that. Always goes to Connor with some complaint – just so she can go to Connor.'

'Ah, I see.' I knew he'd have that kind of pull with people. And now I've made an enemy of her.

'This is Connor's first season as manager and he's a stickler for the rules. The actual rules and then his environmental ones. I mean, yeah we should all be doing more, but if he had his way there'd be no cars, no plastics, and we'd all be living in a tepee in the woods living off the land.'

'Yeah, he wasn't happy I had plastic straws.'

'And plastic bags are outlawed too.'

'Noted,' I say. 'The man used the word *receptacles* for crying out loud.'

She laughs. 'He is *big* on recycling. A real save the planet type.'

'I can see that. Well, I suppose it's important here where there's so much waste. So how long has the market been up and running?'

'The market itself has been running ever since I was a little girl, so Connor's got big shoes to fill. It's a drawcard for tourists and the income they provide tides a lot of locals over until the next year.'

'So he moved here for the management job? Everyone seems to know him so well already.'

'No, he was here before, picking up work on farms and guest houses, that kind of thing. He got involved with the town, helping them launch a recycling project, and one thing led to another and here he is. He's good at keeping everyone in line and things running smoothly. The manager last year wasn't as good, so while Connor's strict, it's worth it in the long run. But do be careful of getting on his bad side, especially breaking the rules.'

I gulp as I think of the life-size gingerbread house sitting a few feet away! 'I've got things to learn about not upsetting the apple cart. I'm sure I'll fit in once the hazing is done and everyone gets to know me. Oh, and Connor gave me a copy of the rule book so I'll study it so I'm prepared for next time.' If there is a next time. I'm going to have to really convince him it was an oversight.

'The rule book?' Raakel cocks her head. 'First I've heard of that.'

'Really? Let me grab it, you might be able to help me translate.'

I find the weighty tome on the bookshelf.

'Here,' I say, passing it to Raakel. 'From the size of it there seems to be a heck of a lot of rules to follow. I mean, it's not like we're astronauts and lives are hanging in the balance, is it?'

She takes one look and doubles over laughing.

'What?'

'This isn't a rule book!'

I search her face for a clue and find none as she's still cackling. 'What is it?'

Raakel takes a moment to compose herself. 'It's a safety manual about the correct way to install and maintain port-a-loos and how to lessen the impact on the environment.'

I snatch the book back and flick through it. How did I not see that with the many diagrams of toilets! 'Oh, he is the limit!' That man! 'What's he playing at?'

She lifts a palm. 'Who knows with Connor? Everyone loves him though – not hard to see why, is it?'

Norse god, intense good looks, thinks I'm a murderer. 'Well, on the surface, yeah, but underneath all that I'm not so sure.'

'Yeah, he keeps to himself. Doesn't socialise with any of the Van Lifers. I guess he draws a definite line between work and play.'

Call the fun police! 'Isn't he missing out on so much by being like that though?'

'I don't think Connor cares about that.'

'Yeah, too busy making up rules for us to follow. We had a bit of a run-in before I arrived so I think I made a bad impression and that's ruined it for me here already.' I fill Raakel in on the radiator hose fiasco.

'Wow,' she says, laughing. 'So now the rule book makes sense. Maybe he thought you needed to know you'd be watched or something so you don't resort to taking your enemies out one at a time? And how funny that Aine is also saying you tried to kill her. Things are not going to be dull with you around, Flora!'

'If she's not a radiator hose then she's perfectly safe.'

'Ah, you're gold.'

'Bad impression aside, I'm not going to let Connor get away with giving me a book on portable toilets.'

'So what are you going to do?'

'I'm going to tell him exactly what I think of his rules!' I stand up, ready to face my antagonist, before I remember the unapproved gingerbread structure. 'Wait. I didn't get permission for the gingerbread house. How strict is he, with this sort of thing? I mean, is there any chance he'll put it down to a simple misunderstanding and let me keep it?' I ask, knowing full well he'll blow a radiator hose of his own when I tell him.

Her eyes widen. 'You didn't get permission?'

'Well, I asked and he said no. I *meant* to cancel the delivery yesterday but then I got busy with customers and distracted by the whole craziness of the day and it slipped my mind completely! When I heard the truck this morning, I thought I'd just turn Juho back around with a million apologies but he'd made such a huge effort and even went without sleep to get it here early so I just couldn't.'

111

'Oh, Flora you're a firecracker. He's going to go *ballistic*, but it's done now so stand your ground. You'll have to think of a sure-fire way to convince him not to have it removed after Hanne and Juho have gone to so much trouble.'

'That's it. I'll use Juho as my excuse.'

'Yikes. You'd better get this sorted before he revokes your lot.'

Revokes my lot! What have I done! My usual idiotic react first, think later! I hear my nan again: *You're a Hallmark movie heroine, Flora, and you won't take no for an answer!* 'OK, I'd better go before I lose my nerve.'

'Good luck.'

I take the book and head to Connor's office. The wind follows me and the door slams against the wall, making him look up in shock.

His face falls when he sees me. Not a good start then. 'You again.'

So that was a dramatic entrance, with my wild hair flowing out behind me, but it can't be helped now. Probably best to act angry and then slip in the mention of the gingerbread house when he's apologising for the faux 'rule book'.

'A book on port-a-loos, Connor! Really? Can you explain this?' I throw the book on his desk, which lands with a bang. Again, not ideal. Why is everything I do around this man dramatic?

'It's all I had to hand and you kept *on* and *on* about reading the rules so I passed it over, not thinking you'd *actually* take it once you saw it was written in a language you don't speak.'

'A book on toilets!? I mean, that's just crap.'

He lets out a belly laugh. 'Exactly!'

I frown. 'You think this is funny?' So the man can smile?

'It's a little funny.'

'It's really not. But I *do* have a funny story.' How's that for a subtle segue?!

He knits his fingertips and leans back in his chair, as if to say *here we go again*. 'Oh yeah?'

I can feel blood rush to my face. Why does he intimidate me

so? I scratch the back of my neck and try and work out a way to drop the gingerbread bombshell. Probably because he seems so black and white when it comes to the rules – it's his way or no way.

'Yes, it's funny, silly really. An oversight on my part that I hope you'll understand. An error. A mistake even, but in the scheme of things it's not like the sky is falling down. It's not like—'

'Get to the point.'

Sheesh. Not one for small talk, is he? 'Well, after our chat yesterday I went back to Noël, all ready to phone Hanne and cancel the delivery of the gingerbread house, because *rules are rules*—' Jonah from Deck the Halls would have a field day here '—and I respect that. So imagine my utter surprise when I returned to find a crowd had formed to buy all my lovely trinkets, and sparkly baubles!'

He shakes his head. 'And . . . ?'

Here we go! My heart thunders in my chest – it actually *thunders* – and I wonder if I'm about to suffer a heart attack. 'And one thing led to another and the day escaped me. I've never been so tired. I mean my *back* ached. I can't remember my back ever aching before and not to mention my *legs*, my *feet*, my *soles* – I mean maybe it's the new boots, who knows, but the point is—'

'What is the point, Flora?'

'The point. The point. The point is thegingerbreadhousegotdeliveredbecauseIforgottocancelit.'

The finger tepee sharpens. 'Say again, slowly for me.'

I drop my voice. 'The gingerbread house got delivered because I forgot to cancel it. OK, so now that's cleared up I have to go. Got Santas that need selling and . . .' I spin on my heel and reach for the door handle.

'Stop!'

Noooo. I stop.

'Turn around.'

'I don't want to.'

He sighs. 'Flora, turn around.'

'Fine.' I turn around and flash him daggers. 'I'm not intimidated by you.'

'Good to know. Get the gingerbread house picked up. It can't stay.' He speaks in a calm, moderated voice but that doesn't fool me one iota.

'Excuse me?'

'You heard. The rules are made for everyone. Not everyone except Flora. Get it gone.'

'Get it gone?! It's a bloody hundred-kilo piece of . . . fabulous, festive fun. Juho went out of his way, and he's *old*, he's *stooped*, he's bloody *tired*! I can't make him go back and forth like that. Yes, it is an issue and I'm sorry, sorrier than you will ever know, but it's not that old man's fault and I cannot in good conscience make his workday any longer. What if he falls asleep at the wheel? What if his foot gets jammed on the accelerator? What if he chokes on his sandwich while he's driving because he's got no time to stop and have a proper lunch break? All because of you!'

'*You* are exhausting.'

I narrow my eyes. 'That's not very nice. Anyway, it *looks magnificent*. I'm sure it'll be a drawcard for market-goers and—'

'This goes against all our health and safety rules, Flora. A structure that size needs to be inspected to make sure it's safe. There's a whole host of boxes that need to be checked in order for it to be approved. It's not a simple matter and yet here you are, stomping over the rules again. You have to send it back.'

'But—'

'No buts.'

'Hear me out.' I hold up a palm. 'What if I pay for it to be inspected as a matter of urgency? Surely we can solve this problem together.'

'*You* are the problem, Flora. You've completely disregarded what I told you. Again.'

'I'm the problem?'

114

He sighs. 'Can't you see my predicament here? Can you try and see it from my point of view? If I change the rules for you, then I have to change them for everyone. We have these rules for a reason. The health and safety of everyone here is paramount.'

'And yet there's a carousel.' *Sorry, Raakel! I'm only using you as an example . . .*

'Yes, a carousel that Raakel had approved by doing the lengthy amount of paperwork that goes with it, so that it was fully checked and deemed safe.'

Time to change tack. 'I won't do it again but please let me keep it. It's one of those things that brings Christmas to life. It'll be a joy for everyone who sees it. And isn't that what we're here for? To live in the moment, make amazing memories with like-minded souls?'

Connor shakes his head, and his unruly mane of blond hair shimmers under the fluorescent light. 'I don't subscribe to all that Van Life mumbo jumbo, that whole heart of the wanderer dream that you all have, searching for this nebulous *thing* that is always just out of reach because it doesn't exist.'

I clutch my chest. 'How can you *say* such a thing?' The man doesn't have a heart! 'People go on these types of wanderings to look outside themselves for meaning, for truth, for something bigger than they are and you've boiled it all down to three words: *it doesn't exist*? Why, because it's not tangible?'

'Exactly, it's not tangible because it doesn't exist. It's like believing in Santa Claus and the whole fallacy of Christmas.'

I gasp. I feel dizzy. I *reel*. 'Did you just say . . .' The words freeze on my tongue momentarily. 'The whole fallacy of Christmas?' Now we're really going to have a problem. How can this man loftily sit there and not believe in such a thing? He runs a *Christmas* market. As a festive fanatic, this is blasphemy!

'Yeah, I did say that, Flora. Why? Does it bother you?'

'It most certainly does! How can you not believe?'

He scoffs. 'Believe in a marketing ploy? Take a look around you,' he says, gesturing to the cold, sterile portable office. It's decidedly un-festive. 'Do you see anything magical here?'

I go to answer but he continues: 'All I see is the nuts and bolts of consumerism at its worst. People selling overpriced plastic junk for a profit, all built on the lie about a big man in a red suit. A marketing gimmick gone global. What's magical about two people fighting over the last box of Christmas crackers? Or people spending money they don't have – so their kids have the latest technology they don't need? Forcing families to be together when they're better off apart? Do you know how bad all this plastic junk is for the environment? People don't think about their carbon footprints, don't think about single-use plastics. Landfills are full of Christmas rubbish.'

'Wow, Connor, why don't you tell me how you really feel?' The air has been sucked from the room by this stealer of joy, this fun sucker, this dream crusher! My head is about to explode! 'So what you're saying is . . .' I take a solid breath in. 'You think Christmas is a con?'

He folds his arms across his wide, *wide* chest and I can't help notice the definition of every muscle on his traitorous forearms. The man probably lifts too many weights as some kind of penance against his cold, steely heart.

'It's a con of epic proportions.'

'Who hurt you, Connor?' Maybe his parents told him Santa wasn't real or some other tragedy that made him into this . . . this monster.

'I'm just being honest, Flora.'

'I need to put some distance between us. I don't want any of this negativity rubbing off on me!'

'Don't think I've forgotten about the gingerbread house, Flora! You're not to use it!'

With that I exit the dingy office and the door slams behind me. I need to call Livvie and let her know the universe is clearly still conspiring against me . . .

Chapter 15

'He said the whole fallacy of Christmas and all the rest of it?' Livvie asks, the doubt clear in her voice through the screen, and making her eyebrows shoot up.

'Word for word.'

She shakes her head and pulls the edge of her beanie down. 'He thinks Christmas is a con, yet he runs a Christmas market? It doesn't make sense!'

I swipe hair from my face and set the phone on the shelf so I can pull a blanket over my lap. I'm never truly warm here no matter how many layers I wear. 'Right? He went on about it being all about consumerism and materialism and all the *isms*. I honestly couldn't catch my breath – I was so shocked and the worst thing is he's so attractive! For some reason, my pulse thrums in his presence even though our history is already fraught with drama and it's like he meets the whole broody, chip on shoulder, misunderstood criteria of the perfect Hallmark hero, and yet, when you're really living it, it's actually infuriating and I don't want a bar of him!'

'This is wild, Flora. *Wild!* I can't believe he uttered the words "Van Life mumbo jumbo." He's surrounded by Van Lifers and Christmas, yet he doesn't believe in either of them? The man is a walking, talking hypocrite.'

'Wait until I tell you about the port-a-loo book.' I take great pains to rehash the incident and Livvie howls with laughter.

'This guy can't be for real!'

'He's larger than life, a real running up mountains for fun, save the earth, abolish single-use plastics sort but he has *so* many flaws, I need to stay well away from him.' I wait for Livvie to agree. She's the sensible one, who always steers me true.

There's a pause before she says, 'No, that's not the answer, darling. That's running away from problems and the Flora *I* know doesn't run away from problems.'

'Aren't I running away right now because my life in London was an epic fail on every level?'

'No, you're simply spreading your wings, taking flight. Getting ready to bloom, as it were.'

'Right,' I say but I'm not convinced Livvie really understands my predicament here.

'I have an idea . . .'

I squint. 'Sounds ominous.'

'You need to stage an intervention.'

'With who?'

'With who!? With who do you think! With *Connor*, of course. You need to make him believe! You need to stage a *Christmas* intervention!' Her face shines with excitement as the idea takes shape.

My mouth opens and closes but no sound comes out. While I'm all for making people believe in the magic of the season, Livvie hasn't met Connor. 'Darling,' I say gently. 'This guy thinks fun is a sin, I'm sure of it. There's just no way to make such a misery guts believe. I mean, I love a challenge as much as the next person, but this guy could have Santa Claus himself appear and he'd give ol' Saint Nic a serve about the amount of methane emissions his reindeer produce.'

'Exactly! He's the perfect candidate for this! Think back to our marathon binge sessions of *Dr Phil* – he didn't stage an intervention on a willing participant, did he? He saved interventions for the people who *needed* the most help but couldn't see it at the time.'

I frown. She's right, I guess. 'The thing is, Liv, Connor doesn't like me. In fact, I think he finds me downright quarrelsome so how do I get him to agree to an intervention to begin with? Sure, I want to make his sad life happy. Who wouldn't? But I can't see a way. Not with this guy. He's a loner, he doesn't mingle, he doesn't seem to want to form friendships. Part of me thinks he's possibly a Russian spy or in the witness protection program or something. Actually, that would make sense . . .'

'Now you're going off on a tangent. He's not in witness protection.'

'How do you know that for sure?'

'Because this isn't a Hollywood movie.'

'Or is it?'

She laughs. 'Look, you can't stage an actual intervention, like dragging him to therapy, but there must be another way to tackle this, if only you agree to put some time into it. You could make a believer out of him.'

I consider it. If the intervention succeeded then it would be worth it, right? And I'm not considering this because he's a bit of all right – that doesn't matter one iota to me – it's because of how hollow his life must be, not believing in the magic of Christmas! How sad and lonely! He's a shell of a man and he doesn't even realise. And if the magic worked, then surely he'd let me keep the gingerbread house for my customers! It's a win-win.

'So what do I do? Just how does one stage an intervention of this type? I mean he's bloody surrounded by Christmas here.'

'You need to think big.'

'OK. Big. Got it.'

We stare at one another through the screen. I close one eye and open the other, notice the latter eye has clearer sight than the former. I really must get my eyes tested. My body is already falling apart and I'm still single. Don't even get me started on the aches and pains I wake up with after sleeping on the campervan mattress.

'Are you even thinking, Flora?'

'Sorry, I'll start now.'

I muse on what might make Connor open up and actually try to enjoy a Christmas moment. 'I think I'm going to have to make up a lie of some sort. If I said, *oh let's go chop down a tree and decorate it,* he'd bloody go off about global warming or something and how I'm solely to blame for the hole in the ozone layer.'

'OK, good point. So why not turn the tables? Someone complained about you, so you go to him with a complaint . . .'

I pick up her train of thought with my own idea. 'But really I woo him with a feast. The man is hulk-sized – I bet he loves food. A festive food extravaganza. I'll decorate the table, cook all the delicious morsels . . .'

She blanches. 'What's that look for?' I ask. 'Honestly, I've been cooking for *years* since that last food poisoning debacle. I've got Nan's recipe book. How hard can it be? Men are simple creatures, you know.'

'Yeah, I guess . . .' Her voice is heavy with doubt. 'But have you cooked in your little kitchen much? Aside from packet noodles?'

'Yes, I've cooked a range of festive fare, including—'

'Hot chocolate doesn't count.'

Damn. 'It should.'

'OK, Flora, try not to kill the guy, yeah?'

'Wouldn't that be ironic?'

She makes a silly face. 'You're going to change the poor fool's life.'

'I hope so. Operation-Make-Him-Believe is a go!'

The next day, during the lull between breakfast and lunch there's a knock at the door and Raakel bustles in. 'Let's go for a wander, Flora. Have you tried Christmas bread yet?'

I zip up my Puffa jacket and find my gloves, thrilled to be invited out. 'Christmas bread?'

'Proper Finnish Christmas bread, tastes like oranges and caraway seeds, and is the prefect pick-me-up for the busy day ahead.'

We head outside and I bury my hands deep in my jacket pocket.

'Just up here.' She points to a sparkly gold van across the lane and further down. 'Tuomo sells the most amazing bread and coffee.'

Raakel introduces me to the twenty-something Van Lifer, whose grin is infectious. He gives us two huge serves of round bread that look more like cake, along with two takeaway coffees. 'On the house,' Tuomo says. 'I've heard about you, Flora. I like that you don't back down.' He winks. Oh dear. Sounds like my name's gone down the grapevine.

'Thanks for the bread. Oh, yeah? My mouth has a life of its own and tends to run off at times.'

He laughs. 'Don't catch it too soon, will you? You're just the shake-up this place needs.'

Raakel goes behind the counter and gives him a hug. 'Thanks, Tuomo. I'll get dinner later, yeah?'

'Sure,' he says and gives her a wink too.

I give him a wave and tuck into the bread. 'Oh wow, this is amazing. It doesn't look like much but it tastes incredible.' So many spices and flavours that burst in every bite. The food here is packed with flavour; even simple things are somehow elevated to extraordinary.

'Now you can see why Finland is the happiest country in the world, right?'

I grin through mouthfuls. 'I've heard about this! The "World Happiest Report" chose Finland quite a few years running or something. But why? Aside from the beauty, the amazing food and culture, what else gives it that accolade?'

Raakel sips her coffee. 'Where to begin. Free education,

including university level. Free healthcare. We believe in cooperation rather than competition. There's the northern lights, of course. But it's more than that; we're all about enjoying life. Did you know there are more saunas here than cars? We call it the poor man's pharmacy – having a bad day? Throw yourself in a sauna; that'll fix it. Or go on a hike, or go swimming. This Nordic utopia is called the home of a thousand lakes for good reason.'

'I really need to do some exploring.' I want to see more of this Nordic utopia. I want to throw myself in a sauna and make a bad day good.

'Have you heard about our annual wife-carrying competition?'

I search her face to see if she's joking, but her expression is serene as if she's already had her sauna time today or something. 'No, tell me that's not true.' Is she having a laugh?

She grins. 'Ooh, it's true all right. Every July there's a big *Eukonkanto* competition. Men compete against one another carrying their wives over their shoulders through an obstacle course.'

I try to envisage it. 'But . . . why?'

With a shrug she says, 'Why not? It's a lot of fun and everyone wants to win the prize.'

A million euro? Two million euro! 'Money?'

She shakes her head. 'The winner receives their wife's weight in beer!'

I burst out laughing. 'This I have to see.'

'You'll have to come back in July. I can't wait to get married so I can compete,' she says, her voice wistful. We continue along, passing van after van. Raakel waves to them all and they holler hellos back.

'I've heard a lot of reasons why people want to find a husband, but I've never heard one quite like that before.' And the eccentric part of me loves it. No wonder it's the happiest country on the planet – they don't take life too seriously. It's all about fun.

'Shame Connor isn't married,' I say. 'He's got the shoulders of a winner.'

'Right? He'd win it for sure. Shame he hides away in his office all the time.'

I go to tell her about the Christmas intervention but stop short. What if she convinces me otherwise? I keep the news to myself for now.

'It's a waste,' she says. 'He's got love written all over him for the perfect woman.'

'What?'

'Oh, don't give me that look, Flora. You know as well as I do, there's a spark between you two. And I notice your gingerbread house is still there. I swear that if it was anyone else he'd have had that hauled away already by now.'

A tingle races the length of me but I can't discern why. 'Well, I don't know about that. The man won't let me use it still. He's told me to get rid of it!' We find a bin and throw in our empty coffee cups. 'We should buy keep cups,' I muse.

'See, he's already getting to you!'

'What, no!' I laugh. 'I just want to reduce my carbon footprint, is all.'

She waggles her brows. 'I bet.'

'Well, I noticed a thing between you and Tuomo.' I give her a 'take that' look.

With a grin, she says, 'Yeah, it's a casual fling. It'll be over when the season ends.'

'You won't stay together?'

She shakes her head. 'Probably not. These Van Life romances never seem to last the distance.'

Part of me deflates. I wonder why they don't last. People moving on, or going back to the real world once the money runs out and the adventure pales? It's hard to know, being so new to this.

We come to an outdoor area full of inflatable igloos, which I remember seeing pictures of back in London. 'Hey,' Raakel says to a bunch of people crammed inside. 'This is Flora, the new kid.'

One by one they shake my hand and introduce themselves. There are so many names to remember that I instantly forget most of them. 'I'm Eevi. So you're the one who tried to kill Aine? Is that right?' Eevi asks but there's laughter in her voice as though she knows I did no such thing.

'Yes, that's me!'

'Welcome, welcome. Sit down. Can I get you some *gløgge*?'

I hesitate, wondering about the time, whether I should be getting back to my van in case there's customers about. But then I remember this is an adventure, a journey, and I am supposed to enjoy it. 'Sure, I'd love that. Next time I'll bring the Christmas biscuits.'

We sit inside the cosiness of the igloo and chat for hours. Board games and cards are pulled out, and Eevi gives them a Christmas spin. Instead of calling out 'UNO!' Eevi makes us say 'JINGLE BELLS!' until we're in fits of laughter.

Their stories are incredible, the places they've seen, the experiences they've had. There's no nine-to-five, daily grind complaints here. They've lived in vans, in tents, in garages. Some have zigzagged across the globe on a wing and a prayer, hoping they'd find jobs at the other end; some have made their way around every corner of Finland. Their happy-go-lucky natures reminds me of the guys from the Jumbo, and the idea that the journey will provide. I see now that you have to be open, have to make friends, share your spoils when you're up and not be afraid to ask for help when you're down.

'So who's up for a sauna tomorrow?' I say. If this is the happiest country on the planet then I'm going to follow their lead.

Eevi nods. 'Sure, there's one in town. We'll go after breakfast tomorrow.'

'I'm busy tomorrow,' Raakel says, 'but I'll show Flora where your van is, Eevi, so she can meet you there in the morning.'

* * *

The sauna is located in an unassuming wooden building in town. Inside are small sauna rooms that resemble log cabins. We're shown to a locker room where we take a quick shower before putting our clothing away.

I wrap the tiny white towel tightly around me. Why are they so small! I slide my feet into the white slippers provided and look to Eevi for further instructions.

'Ready?' she says.

I nod. 'Sure am. One thing I'm curious about, why are saunas so popular here? Is it because of the arctic temperatures? A way to warm up?'

'Yes, that I suppose but it's mainly for the health benefits. For general wellbeing. If the sauna can't cure you, nothing can. I use it for detoxing, anti-ageing, to speed up my metabolism. Back in the day, my grandmother gave birth to all her babies in saunas, as did many in her generation, thinking it was the safest, most sterile place for such a thing. Every single member of my family has a sauna at home – they use the sauna, then swim in the icy cold lake and head back into the sauna. It's invigorating, makes you feel alive! It's just one of those things that's ingrained in us.'

Golly, I've lived a sheltered life. 'OK, well I can definitely use some detoxing.'

She smiles. 'We're in the communal sauna. Number seven.' She points to a door further down the hall. 'It's bigger.'

'OK.' I can do communal. Aren't I here for these life-changing experiences, after all? I tug the towel a little tighter around my bust. These tiny Finnish towels are not made for curvy women like me.

I push open the door and am enveloped by steam. I breathe it deep into my lungs and feel the warmth all the way through me. There's no one else in the room, so I find a spot to sit on one of the terraced benches.

'Oops,' Eevi says. 'No towels, Flora. You use it to sit on, not have wrapped around you.'

My heart stops. 'What?'

'You must be naked, like in the shower.'

I'm sure my eyes are as wide as golf balls. They feel as though they're about to pop out of my head, *ping, ping*. 'Naked?' I stall for time.

'Naked.'

I suppose no one is here. I slowly slip the towel off and place it underneath me. Eevi throws hers down and walks around free as a bird, naked as the day she was born. I don't know where to look. She uses a ladle to add water to the hot stones and the air goes thick with steam.

'Amazing, right?'

'Ah . . . amazing.' I'm stiff as a nutcracker. My British sensibilities don't extend to being naked in public.

'Are you not hot enough?' She adds more water and the steam is so thick I can hardly see her.

'That's better,' I say while internally wondering how long I'm supposed to sit here. Naked.

'I'll be right back. I forgot to hide my money tin. I'll phone Raakel and ask her to keep it safe.'

'No, don't go!'

But she's already out the door, and just as it swings out, it soon swings back in and I see the shape of a man. A very tall man.

What's the etiquette here? Surely we cover up! When the steam dissipates I see his face. Oh my God, no! How does Connor seem to catch me out unawares every damn time?!

I cross my arms over my chest and one leg over the other to hide as much of my lady bits as I can. The man will cop an eyeful and he's never even bought me so much as a glass of wine. That can't be right?

'Flora, didn't expect to find you here.' I can't look. I don't know where to look. He sits back, muscly arms wide on the wooden bench behind him. I don't dare look any lower than that. Call me old-school but I believe seeing a man's penis should be reserved for the one he loves.

Now I can't think of anything other than his penis.

Penis.

Where's Eevi? But then another thought hits: three of us naked is even worse than two of us naked! What's the protocol here and why can't we use our towels?!

'I've never seen you this quiet. Makes me worry you're plotting something.'

'Death in a sauna,' I croak. 'Plenty of ways to do it in here.' *Do it?* Will he think I mean do it, as in sex? The steam is making me crazy – I can't think straight in here! 'Commit murder, that is.'

'Why does that not surprise me?'

The steam is clearing too fast and his body is mere steps from mine.

'Would you mind throwing some water on the stones?' I say. I need that steam thicker, dammit, much thicker.

'Can I trust you with my back turned?'

I gulp. I'm going to get a full view of his butt. 'Yes,' I squeak.

He stands, and I can't help but take in the whole spectacle that is Connor's body. PHWOAR. Every muscle is defined; tattoos snake across his body. His abs are not just a mere six-pack, but hard defined ridges that I'd love to run my hand across. Then my turncoat eyes drop and *holy moly* it can't be real.

It's all too much. I snatch my towel up and shove past him, my pulse thrumming in my ears as I go.

'Something I said, Flora?'

I'm never going to be able to look the man in the eyes again!

Chapter 16

The next afternoon I'm inundated with customers who stock up on a range of decorations. I quietly tell them about the ginger-bread house and suggest they use it to warm up with a hot drink and rest their tired legs. 'Oh, we can use it?' one of them asks. 'What about the tape?'

'The tape?'

'The caution tape. The entrance is covered with it and there's a sign saying "Out of Order" so we presumed it was closed.'

That man! 'Oh, yes, closed for the cleaners. Sorry, I forgot about that. Maybe next visit, it'll be ready to go.'

'Sure, we'll come back another day.'

A cluster of teens approach the van and speak so fast in Finnish I can only guess what they're saying by their facial expressions.

'Aren't they cute?' I say and point to the stackable snowman candles they're looking at. Then I say it again in their language. Well, I try to. They give me those polite smiles that manage to convey they have absolutely no idea what I've said but they'll tolerate me talking to them in halting Finnish because at least I'm giving it a go. The teens buy a few sparkly trinkets before they're off to the next van.

The youth here seem so self-assured, confident in a way I certainly never felt at that age. I'm still not all that comfortable in my own skin and you'd think by now with the big three-oh looming I'd be resigned to it at least, but I'm not. I'm never going to be one of those haughty have-it-together types. I'm too awkward for all of that.

Still, even though I can't quite communicate fluently with words, gestures seem to help for the most part and all of my customers have been lovely. Most of my customers speak English but I think it's just good manners to try and learn the native language when you're a guest in a new country.

And sales are proving that a little bit of effort goes a long way. I've sold out of a number of lines already, so I'm thrilled to find this just might be viable.

Once I get a break in the queue, I send Hanne a text:

Hello Hanne, things are going well here! I'll need to order another box of wreaths and also twenty more DIY make-at-home gingerbread house kits. Let me know when the order is ready and I'll swing past, otherwise come to the market for a drink! Flora xx

A family dressed in bright yellow jackets and matching beanies peruse a stand of decorations set up by my little fire pit out the front. They buy candy-filled stockings and I'm only glad Connor isn't here to see how much plastic is used to wrap each and every sweet. Maybe I should be looking at more eco-friendly options? When I think of Connor my traitorous mind goes straight to the naked visual I've stored and my cheeks flame. I do my best to put it out of mind. Think, think, think. What was I . . . oh, right, eco-friendly options.

I make a mental note to ask Hanne about products with more sustainable packaging. But I won't let Connor know that.

A queue forms, so I handle it by pointing and gesticulating that I won't be long as we try and navigate our two languages. There's a lot of laughter and mirth as we converse as best we can. Over much giggling I sell a pinecone and berry wreath and some handmade knitted stockings for the mantelpiece – at least I think that's what they were asking for. Once I've caught up and the remaining customers say they're happy browsing, I head back outside to see the snow that's just started to fall.

Flakes swing lazily down so I fling my arms out, throw my head back and stick my tongue out to catch snowflakes, just as Connor comes along and whispers in my ear, 'You're not planning on eating your customers too, are you?'

How does the damn man have such impeccable timing!

I snap my mouth closed and glare at Connor. 'Excuse me?'

'Just curious . . .'

'I was catching *snowflakes*, if you must know! The whole I'm a murderer thing is getting pretty old.' He's managed to unsettle me, somehow. My heart races, and I feel hot all of a sudden. *Don't think of him naked.* Too late!

'That's exactly what a murderer would say.'

I huff and take a step closer so any market-goers walking past don't hear me. 'Well, if I was going to eat anyone, it would be you first.' I hold his arm and take a soft bite, until I catch myself. What the hell am I *doing*? I drop his arm and let out an awkward giggle, which I hope masks my mortification. *You bloody idiot, Flora!* God, he smells good and even worse he *tastes* good! He probably uses some fair-trade, organic body wash made from fresh strawberries hand-picked by vegans or something.

'Do you always act first and think later?' He lets out a strangled chuckle – perhaps I've crossed a line.

'Always, it's something I pride myself on.'

'I see.'

Time to get my head back in the game. I need this market to work for me. I need the funds so I can take a long adventure in the country of a thousand lakes. 'So the caution tape is overkill, don't you think? Quite the eyesore.'

'It is. And I've had a record number of complaints about why you were approved and others weren't. Lucky I love conflict, eh?'

Is that sarcasm? 'Well, you could approve it, and really stir the pot. In for a penny, in for a pound, and all that.'

130

'Unlikely.'

'You're quite the stickler.'

'I've been called worse.'

'I bet.'

'Anyway, sparkly conversation aside, I really have better things to do . . .'

I feel a blush creep up my neck and I struggle to think of what to say, sure I'm going to put my foot in it again. Then I remember the Christmas intervention! The only way I'm going to get Connor to agree to my gingerbread house is by making him believe. And really, the man needs some fun in his life – that is abundantly clear. He needs to lighten up and enjoy good tidings!

'I'm glad you came along.' I cough, to clear my damn mind. 'I'd like to report a safety issue I've come across, since safety is paramount, is it not?' He loves his rules and he's obsessed with health and safety!

'Safety issue, where?'

'It's . . . well, it's a bit of a long story, and it's best if I show you, but as you can see I'm super busy right now.' I turn to point to all of my customers to find they've bloody well vanished! 'Busy inside with my very important work, so how about we meet tomorrow night and I'll show you then?' I'll cook him a delicious Christmas feast and soon enough he'll be a believer. While my cooking abilities might be lacking if I take my time I'm sure I can nail it. I have Nan's recipe book with me. How hard can it be?

The suspicious stare is back. 'If it's a safety issue, time is usually of the essence. Can't you just tell me what it is?'

'No one will die, not today at any rate.'

He makes a show of wiping his brow. 'That's a relief. Well, I'd better get this looked at.' He points to his arm, where I'm horrified to see an impression of my teeth.

'A cold compress should do the trick.'

'Right.' He wanders off, but I'm sure I catch him grinning.

* * *

The next morning, snow falls thick and fast and I know we're in for a freezing day. I've never seen such thick piles of fresh powder. It's so Christmassy I'm outside attempting to make a snowman when Raakel comes to my van for an early morning coffee. 'You don't have a carrot for a nose, do you?' I ask her.

Raakel helps me mould the snowman's head. 'We can use a stick.'

We find bits and pieces, including an old scarf and beanie to make our snowman come to life. 'It looks magnificent,' I say grinning broadly.

We go inside to warm up. While the grounds are quiet and everyone sleeps, we chat over too many sugary sweets and endless cups of coffee.

'Much on this week?' I ask.

'Actually, I've got a toy drop at the local hospital. We do one each week from now until Christmas, to help those stuck inside feel a little bit merrier.'

'Wow, that's amazing. What do you do? Donate your toys?'

'Yes, I donate and I raise money to buy gifts from other vendors. Van Lifers usually donate money when they can and I have a tin that customers throw loose change in to. We hire a *Joulupukki*, which is Santa Claus in Finnish, and an elf, and make a big thing of them wandering the corridors and visiting each ward.'

'I'd love to donate and help too.' Then another thought hits. This is exactly what I've been searching for. This is intervention dynamite! 'Raakel, I've got a crazy idea. Do you need a Santa?'

'I've hired a Santa already but I need an elf still.' Her eyes narrow. 'Why?'

'An elf could work.' I explain all about Operation-Make-Him-Believe.

She guffaws. 'And you want to do this to prove to Connor that Christmas is the best time of year and that it's not about consumerism; it's about . . . what exactly?'

I stare at her. 'It's about joy! Love! Goodwill to others. Feasting with those who make your soul feel good. Sharing the day with people who make you smile. Singing Christmas carols to make you feel festive. And about a billion other reasons, don't you think?'

'Yeah, but this is *Connor* we're talking about. There's no way he's going to believe in all of that. He doesn't care about socialising. About joy or love. At least I don't get that impression from him.'

'Exactly! Which is where we come in, Raakel! Don't you see? Imagine Connor walking the wards, dressed as an elf, and making the little faces of sick kids shine! He'll be moved to tears, won't he? That he, gruff mountain man, made someone's day brighter. Slowly but surely we'll chip away at that frosty exterior until we get to his warm soft underbelly. And then he might let me keep my gingerbread house. He'd be crazy not to.'

'*You're* crazy.'

'All the best people are!'

'OK, he can be our elf, because I'd love to see that. Just how are you going to convince him to do it?'

We spend the rest of that day formulating our devious plan . . .

Chapter 17

The evening starts with a bang. Literally. The oven goes: boom!

Why does nothing ever go according to plan! 'You stupid oven, you useless appliance, you TIME WASTER! I'm going to KILL YOU!' Just then, there's a knock on the door – of course!

I take a moment to rearrange my expression to something more serene. 'Connor, welcome, welcome.'

'Is everything OK?' He wears that same cautious look as if his life hangs in the balance.

I'm out of breath from berating the stupid oven. 'Yes, why wouldn't it be?' I smile and whip a tea towel around to circulate the air. It makes it worse somehow and soon my eyes are stinging. Livvie was right as usual; I should have tested the menu out first!

He waves away the thick smoke but I pretend this is all going according to plan. 'I'm just going to open this window here. I'm hot from all the cooking.' So far everything is stone-cold raw, but he doesn't need to know that.

'Can I offer you a drink? Wine, whisky . . . ?'

He ignores my very polite offer. 'Is the safety issue . . . you?'

That would actually make a lot of sense! I let out a tinkly little laugh. 'Of course not! The safety issue is . . . is . . . I really can't focus when I'm hungry. How about we have dinner first and then get into it? You're hungry, aren't you? A man your size needs *sustenance*, doesn't he?'

His eyebrows pull together and I realise what I've said might come across as flirtatious. I am playing this all wrong! *Think of the plan, Flora! Operation Make Him Believe!*

'I could eat.'

'Great, it won't be long so how about that drink?'

'I'll take a whisky.'

'I don't have any whisky. It just sounded like the type of thing you'd offer. Wine suffice?'

'Ah, sure.'

'It's had time to breathe and everything. I didn't have a decanter on hand but I quite dexterously unscrewed the top.'

'Great.'

I give him a stiff smile, playing it cool, all the while internally fretting about how to cook the bloody ginormous bird I stuffed in the very tiny oven that has now decided to implode. I hope it's not a sign of things to come. Little does Connor know, but I'm about to catapult him into Christmas with a feast of epic proportions just like Nan used to make, if only I can figure out what to do now . . . *Think, Flora, think!*

I have an electric frying pan.

Can one fry a turkey? Connor has no idea about Christmas feasts, does he, being an anti-believer? So it just might work.

'Drink, be merry!' I say as I bend to get the bird out of the oven. The damn thing is wedged in tight. No matter what I do, the blasted thing won't budge. I heave and ho, and ho and heave. Slide it this way and that, and that way and this. And still it's wedged.

'Do you need a hand?'

'Why, because you're a man?' I bristle.

'No, because it looks like it's stuck.'

I scoff. 'Connor, have you *ever* cooked a turkey?'

'No.'

'Well, this is all part of the process, you see. It's all about getting

135

that lovely caramelisation,' Or more truthfully charred blackened skin from the electric elements. If this were a gas oven I wouldn't have this problem. It's not my fault. It's the electric oven's fault! 'Before I pop it into a frying pan to finish off.'

'A frying pan for a bird that size?'

'Yeah, Gordon Ramsay. This is how I do it, OK?'

He holds his hands up as if in surrender while I pull and push and bend and squeeze – it's quite the workout. Internally I am screaming like a banshee. I take a deep breath and with one last heroic effort, I use every single muscle I possess and pull the bloody thing as hard as I can. It comes free but I go flying and the bird slips from my hands and is lobbed into the air above me. I fall onto my back and see the charred mess come screaming towards my face. I let out a blood-curdling wail. Death by fowl! Nooooo!

I snap my eyes closed as I hear an oomph.

I peek out of one eye and see Connor cradling the bird.

'Nice catch.'

'Thanks.'

'So where was I?' I take the turkey from his hands with a silent apology. 'I don't usually throw my food around, but hey, I'm still getting used to these small spaces.'

'I get it.'

I find the electric frying pan and plug it in, whack in the turkey – which barely fits – and put a lid on top of the bird. The lid, of course, does not fit. It teeters like it's going to fall off and Connor points, but I shoot him down with a look. 'That's how my beloved nan used to do it,' I lie.

'She really must've been ahead of her time.'

'That she was.' *Sorry, Nan!*

The pan barely sizzles but I'm sure it's just got to heat up a bit more. I don't have any other pans to cook the vegetables and really, are they any good unless they're roasted? The potatoes need to crisp in duck fat so they're ready to soak up the lashings of gravy. How did I think this would work? And the Yorkshires, they'll never rise in a frying pan, will they?

I paste on a smile and find some cheeses and various accoutrements in the fridge and make us a platter. I tie some tinsel around the board for a little merriness. So far, so good . . .

'Merry Christmas!'

'You've outdone yourself, Flora. But that bird is never going to cook, is it?'

'No, not tonight. It's slow cooking, for tomorrow.'

'I see. So was there a safety issue or did you simply want to slowly suffocate me with toxic oven smoke? Render me ill with raw food? Keep me locked in here while people enjoy your gingerbread house?'

'All of the above.'

He stares me down.

'OK. OK. The thing is . . .' Lucky I've got a cunning plan B because the Christmas feast hasn't exactly made miracles happen. Right on cue my phone beeps with a message from Raakel. 'Oh no!' I say dramatically, eyes wide, clapping a hand over my mouth. I have to really shine in my performance, otherwise it's going to be a hard sell and Connor is going to reject the idea and shut down the conversation.

'What is it?' he asks.

'Terrible news! Terrible, terrible news. Raakel was set to do a charity event, a present drop to all those sick kiddos stuck in hospital over the Christmas season, and now Santa's elf has called in sick! Can you imagine the disappointment of all those brave little kids? It's horrible to think of.'

'Can't Santa give out the presents alone? You could offer to wrap them in recycled paper, or no paper at all. The amount of waste produced at Christmastime is astonishing. And for what?'

Before he goes off on a rant about how Christmas is single-handedly destroying the planet, I bring him back to the problem at hand. But his muttering about single-use wrapping paper does give me an idea that just might sway him if this attempt fails. 'No, no Santa can't hand out the presents. Santa is the *star*. He has to jolly everyone along saying ho, ho, ho and ringing that bell of his. The elf is the *worker*, the one who does all the . . . erm heavy lifting. Raakel says they're *beside* themselves with worry. Such late notice for this to happen.'

'Yeah, stressful for her. Can't Raakel be the elf?'

'No, she handles all the behind-the-scenes stuff. Who will we find at such late notice? There must be someone around here who would make the perfect elf . . .'

I wait for him to stick his hand up.

He does not.

I tap my chin. 'There must be *someone* . . . close by.'

The man remains mute. It's like talking to a bag of hammers. I guess I'm going to have to jolly him along and point out the obvious. 'Got it! *You* can do it, Connor! You'll be the most amazing elf! And you're strong enough to lug all those presents around! If you get involved I'm sure we could mention the wrapping paper thing too.'

His eyes go wide with shock. Really, did he not get all along I meant him? Is he truly that un-Christmas-like? 'Me, Flora? In an *elf* suit?' He guffaws. OK, so he will be the world's biggest elf, but isn't that fantastic? No one will forget their brush with him, will they?

'Yes, you as an elf! It's too perfect. I bet there's an amazing brand out there that does recycled sustainable wrapping that can also be reused for kids to draw on or something so it doesn't end up in the bin.'

He simply glowers at me. Can the man not hear how hard I'm trying? I continue to rally him along. 'We'd better take your measurements so we can let out the suit a bit. Wouldn't want it ripping and you flashing all those bulging muscles, would we?' Then I think back to the sauna and blush. *Stay focused, Flora!*

'No but I never said . . .'

I cut him off and go and find my travel-sized sewing kit. I knew it would come in handy! Inside the little tin is a tape measure and before Connor can wriggle out the deal, I stand him up. 'Right, this won't take a minute. Scribe for me, will you?' I only pause when it comes time to measure his inseam. His nether regions are *right there* and it just feels a little close. A little personal. At least they're covered this time!

'Be careful down there,' he says, when I bump my head into said nether regions. Idiot!

I laugh. 'Sorry, sometimes I forget my head is joined to my body.'

'Flora, I . . .'

'You're so lovely for doing this, Connor. Truly, the world is a better place with you in it!'

He snaps his mouth closed. Now all I have to do is find a suit in his size. How hard can it be?

'Flora, how did we get here? I came over to see some sort of safety breach and now you're measuring me up for an elf suit. Your gingerbread house is still here and—'

'Shush, I'm counting.'

Connor leaves wearing a bemused expression as if he can't quite work out how he got himself tangled up in our elf scheme. But that leaves me with a bigger problem. I need an elf suit pronto and the only person I know who deals in all things Christmas is Hanne. Surely she can help?

After a steadying breath, I phone Hanne and hope she'll agree.

'Hello, Hanne!' I make small talk about this and that and then figure time is of the essence.

'You're not going to believe this. Connor thinks Christmas is a con! I mean, it's almost too horrific to say out loud, right? So with the help of my best friend Livvie we came up with a cunning plan to make him believe!' I explain all about his reasoning behind it and our operation and Raakel's charity toy drive and impending hospital visit. I still haven't told her that the poor sad gingerbread house sits outside, unused, unloved and covered with caution tape as if a murder took place . . . !

'This is a lot to process.'

'Look, there's another thing. He's not letting me use the gingerbread house.' She gasps. She gets it. 'I know, he's a beast. A stealer of joy. But don't you see – that's why we need to swing his thinking around. Once we convince him, we'll all be able to have outdoor areas, and not just those people who got approvals ages ago! You'll probably be able to rent out all those life-size Christmas decorations you've got stored away, lonely and forgotten, Hanne!'

'This is more serious than I thought. He doesn't believe in Christmas? I mean, I know he's reserved and doesn't socialise much unless it's a town meeting about plastics and recycling but he runs a Christmas market!'

'So now you see why we have to do this, Hanne, right? I can't do it alone.'

'Yes, yes, I see your point. This does call for an intervention. How can I help?'

I grin. 'I need a Connor-sized elf suit.'

'An elf suit in *his* size! That's impossible, Flora.'

'It *can't* be impossible, Hanne, and one other thing . . . I need it by tomorrow.'

'You don't ask for much, do you?' She lets out a weary sigh. 'Do you have his measurements?'

'I sure do!'

She mutters to herself about lack of sleep and near-sightedness. 'OK, send them over and I'll see what I can do. I'll deliver something to you tomorrow but it'll be whatever I can magic up so don't get too excited.'

'You're a star, Hanne.'

'Remember that when I drop it off! It's just . . . I can't wrap my head around the fact you got Connor to agree to this. Was the man drinking or something?'

'Well, he'd had a glass of wine, and I told a lot of lies so that's how I got him to agree to be an elf. Personally, I think he secretly wants to believe in Christmas and wants to celebrate with others but he just doesn't know how.'

'Adding psychology to your repertoire, Flora?'

'Why not? We're peeling the layers away like he's an onion . . .'

'What a picture. I'm as busy as a person ever was, and yet, this I've got to see. I'll be involved on one condition: I want pictures. Proof that Connor actually undertook such a thing.'

'Deal.'

'See you soon.'

I text her Connor's measurements and she sends me back a muscly emoji.

Chapter 18

After locking up the van, I wrap my scarf tight around my neck and hurry along the moonlit snowy lane, looking for something to grab for dessert to share with Raakel. I'm excited to tell her the good news about our elf and can't wait until tomorrow. I pass the most delightful pop-up shops, selling all sorts of goodies, from toboggans to ice skates. There are even festive photo booths. You could spend days here and never tire of visiting all the vans. There's a sign announcing fresh *joulutorttu*, mouth-watering pastries filled with jam and dusted with icing sugar. My mission stops in its tracks because I need these in my life, or better still in my belly. While the turkey feast didn't work out, I still managed to eat enough of the cheese platter that I'm fit to bursting, but hey, the Van Life rules are: there are no rules. Besides, I eat when I'm nervous and Connor has a way of always making me second guess myself.

'Hey! These look delicious! Can I have a box please?'

The girl behind the counter turns and gives me a slow cat-who-got-the-cream smile and doesn't rush to reply. And then I realise it's Aine. Got-it-in-for-me girl. Maybe she's softened, maybe the hazing is over and I should give her the benefit of the doubt and try and start afresh. I give her a wide smile and point to the pastries. 'A box please,' I repeat.

She takes up some tongs and throws pastries into a box – one that looks suspiciously sustainable and eco-friendly – with a distinct lack of care. Icing sugar puffs up and out like dust. I battle with whether to say something in case this isn't personal and she just doesn't give much consideration to her *joulutorttu* … but she beats me to it.

'We see what you're doing,' she says.

I glance behind me to make sure she's talking to me. 'What's that?'

'The whole coquettish thing you've got going on with Connor – it isn't going to work, you know.'

Oh Lord, I've found myself in the Lapland version of *Mean Girls*. 'Coquettish thing? I hardly think the word *coquettish* and I belong in the same sentence! If anything I've been downright hostile to the guy, and anyway what's it to you?'

She shoots me a disgusted look that's so nasty I can't begin to imagine how I've ruffled her feathers so badly to warrant such a thing. 'Just stop with the whole act you've got going on. We can see through it, you know. Stay away from him.'

'Who's we?'

'The ones who were here first.'

I feel like I've got a bit part in a soap opera. These women are definitely not subscribing to the principles of the happiest people on the planet. *Let it go, Flora.* I have a minor internal battle with myself to keep my trap shut, and walk away, but just like always the mouth wins. 'Ooh, how mysterious. Well, feel free to pass this along to the others: there's nothing going on with Connor and if there was, that would be my business, not yours. And further-more, I'll speak to who I damn well please. But thanks, I might just go keep Connor company. From the sounds of it, he could use a friend – someone who doesn't say this sort of thing behind his back. Keep your pastries; I bet they taste bitter.' I flounce off, feeling daggers pierce my back as I go.

Is Connor some sort of prize? Off limits unless you're on the roster system or something? Well, one thing I know is, I'm not afraid of conflict, and I'm not going to be told who I can and can't speak to! Aine has clearly taken a disliking to me since we nearly collided on the road.

I find myself still marching in an angry huff when I get to Raakel's van. Its pretty candy-cane stripes distract me for a moment. Outside under the awning, there's a stand with minia-ture carousel keyrings that blow about in the wind. There are tables lined with figurines and remote-controlled cars and lots of Barbie dolls on offer.

'Hey, Raakel. How are you?'

'Hey.' She motions me inside. 'Better than you by the looks of it. What's wrong?'

I let out a sigh. 'I had a run-in with Aine. And now I don't have the dessert I wanted to surprise you with. Feel like heading out? My shout?'

'Yeah, we can go out but come in first. Looks like you could use a drink. Tell me what happened inside without too many eavesdroppers about.'

'I could murder a drink.' Oops. 'I mean that sounds lovely.'

Inside is filled with Christmas-themed plush toys as far as the eye can see. 'Wow, you've managed to fit a lot in here.' Somehow Raakel has fitted upright racks along the 'hall' that hold all sorts of goods from keychains to backpacks. Bright knitted Christmas scarves and beanies sit perfectly folded in little pigeonholes. Every usable space has been transformed to hold something saleable. 'I should look at using my interior space a bit better.'

'I'll give you some pointers later. It took me a while to get the knack of making it all fit and still look neat. It's amazing what you can display if you make a plan and group things together. As long as you don't mind going without much space yourself. My bedroom is the only place off limits, and the curtain keeps all my mess hidden.'

I peek behind the curtain. 'Oh, it's not messy at all!' Raakel clearly doesn't know what messy is. My bed is already piled with discarded clothing and paperwork I'm yet to file. I really have to get organised or it'll get out of hand. 'I love the idea of having a dedicated area where no one goes.' So far customers have been welcome in my van so they can check out the more delicate stock and no one has wandered into the bedroom section but maybe I should make that more clear like Raakel has, with a rope looped across. 'If I can fit more stock inside, it'll help when the snow comes down heavier and give people a break from the weather. I've got the gingerbread house sitting there being wasted. If I got permission I'd be able to take more stock from Hanne.'

'It could happen, like winning the lottery.'

I laugh.

'So what happened with Aine?'

I let out a long sigh as Raakel opens a cupboard above my head and takes out a bottle of berry wine. 'Lingonberry OK?'

'Perfect.' The climate in Finland isn't conducive to growing wine-quality grapes so the creative Finnish use what they have on hand, resulting in lots of varieties of wines made from arctic berries. At first the flavour is quite surprising to the palette, but I've acquired a taste for the tart, sweet and sour wine now.

She pours us a glass and I take a deep sip, ruminating on Aine and why she's targeting me.

Raakel motions for me to talk. 'So, I was minding my own business, off to grab something for us for dessert when I spotted sugary sweets on offer.'

She grins.

'I stopped to put in an order and then I realised it was Aine, the girl who swears I tried to kill her! She practically throws the pastries into the box like she wants to destroy them. Then she pipes up with this whole "your coquettish thing with Connor isn't going to work". When I countered that, she said "they" can see straight though my act, *the ones who were here first*. Isn't that just the limit!?'

145

Raakel shakes her head. 'There's a group of girls here who are old enough to know better, who really like making things hard for others. I don't know what to advise you, because you're already on their radar. But seriously it's just high school behaviour. If you can ignore it, then I suggest you do that.'

'That's the problem, I'm not the ignoring sort. She told me to stay away from Connor, as if she's in charge of who he talks to!'

She arches a brow. 'So what are you going to do?'

I lean back and fiddle with the stem of the wine glass. 'What can I do? I'll stick to my end of the market and hope she stays at her end.'

Raakel swizzles her wine around in the glass before taking a sip. 'Good plan. I'm sure Connor would be surprised if he knew they spoke of him in that way, as if he's theirs and theirs alone. She's probably annoyed she hasn't managed to woo the guy.'

Relief surges through me. While Aine has the personality of a dead fish, she's beautiful and I can only imagine she turns on the charm when Connor is around. 'Is he involved with anyone?'

She stares me down. 'Are you asking for you?'

I scoff. 'Absolutely not! There's no way I could ever fall for a guy who believes Christmas is a worldwide marketing ploy! Although . . . I do have good news on that front. He agreed to be the elf for your hospital present drop!'

Her jaw drops. 'He did? Wow, I honestly didn't think he'd say yes to that! You must have turned on the charm to convince him. How did you do it?'

I laugh, remembering his face. 'I didn't let him get a word in so then he couldn't say no. I started measuring him up for the elf suit and that was that. Accidentally hit my head into his nether regions, so by then both of us were too mortified to say much. Oh, also, I forgot to tell you earlier I saw him stark naked at the sauna. He's everything you imagine him to be and more.'

'What!'

Golly, my heart races as I mentally recall the sight of him. 'I don't know how you all do it, march in there naked as the day you were born, like it's nothing. Eevi stepped out to call you, and in he walked.'

'Yes, Eevi called about her cash tin. Then what happened?'

'I copped an eyeful and then I dashed out of there as fast as I could. Don't forget I was also naked and that's a few steps too far for my British sensibilities.'

'Ah, yes, nakedness is hallowed there or something, right?'

'Yeah sort of. For a place that's freezing most of the time, I'm surprised how comfortable everyone is *sans* clothing.'

She shrugs. 'I guess we've grown up with it, so it's not an issue for us.'

'It could be liberating in the right circumstances.' But maybe not for me, who still has way too many hang-ups about my body. 'But anyway, I'm trying to push that memory far from my mind and instead try and think of him in an elf suit.'

'I can't even *picture* him in an elf suit and personally I'd stick with the naked visual.' She cackles like a witch and I cover my face with my hands.

'Hanne agreed to make the elf suit as long as I take pictures, and she'll drop it off tomorrow.'

'Everyone wants to see the Nordic god himself dressed like an elf! We've got five hospital drops to go until Christmas. Who knows, maybe he'll become our regular elf?'

'Can you imagine?'

'No, somehow I can't. I'm sure it'll be a one-off thing, I'm just glad I'll be there to see him in the flesh.'

'Me too – it should be quite the sight.' I think of the fact time is racing by at the Christmas market. While I haven't been here as long as the others, I feel a tug in my heart about the end creeping closer every day. 'What will you do after the market closes?' The last day of the market is Christmas Eve and then we each have a few days to pack up and leave.

'I'll go to my family who are close by. I'm always shattered by the time the 25th of December rolls around. Christmas for me is a full day of resting on my parents' sofa while Mum potters around making lunch and telling me it's high time I got married and had babies.'

'Urgh, the marriage and babies talk. I get that too. It's as if they think we're not serving our purpose unless there's a ring on the finger and a squalling baby balanced over our shoulder. I can't wait to have kids, but it's not like I can do it alone, is it?'

'Right? If that's your goal, then great, but it's not mine. My parents don't understand this lifestyle. They think I'm wasting time, but they don't realise it's a whole new way of life.'

'I suppose it's hard for most people to understand unless they've experienced it. I've got a lot to learn still but so far I can see the addiction. Why wouldn't a person want to live on the road, and then spend time off the beaten track? I suppose it depends on how much wanderlust runs in your veins.' She nods. 'Where will you go next?'

Raakel considers it. 'Not too far. Lugging the carousel around is costly so I stay close. But I'll take January off and go get lost somewhere. It's my favourite thing to do. Find a forgotten lake and pull up. Just me and the view. I read, I sleep, I swim.'

'Don't you get lonely?'

'After the bustle of the Christmas market I like the quiet for a while. It's almost like a reset. A reboot. Time to reflect and set some goals for the New Year.'

'Makes sense.'

'But I don't get lost until the 1st of January. So if you're free we can do some driving after Christmas? I can show you some hidden gems that only locals know about.'

I feel a frisson of happiness that I've found such a great friend in Raakel. 'I'd love that. Secrets spots are the best.'

'You're not to tell a soul.'

I mime zipping my lips and throwing away the key. 'Won't utter a word.'

Chapter 19

The next day there's a quiet knock on the door. I open it to find Hanne standing there in the fresh, icy dawn. 'Come in, come in,' I say and hand her a freshly brewed mug of coffee, expecting her early morning visit.

'You don't know how much I need this, Flora.' She accepts the cup and sips.

'I think I do know. You've been run off your feet and you've got this foreigner making it even harder for you. But don't worry, I have fresh Christmas bread for you from Tuomo, so sit for a minute and relax.'

'You know how to speak my language.'

'I'm fluent in food and coffee, you could say.' I bring over the Christmas bread and an assortment of buttery, sugary goodness. 'I got this from Tuomo at first light this morning. He's the only other crazy one up as early as me and he'd already been dog-sledding with his huskies, over to deliver some bread to the families who live in cabins in the forest. He's going to teach me how to control the dog sled myself tomorrow morning. Should I be scared?'

Hanne sits at the table, while I hastily move half-completed wreaths. 'No, it's the best fun! Just make sure you learn the commands and all will be well.'

She passes me a bag. 'Here you go – the best I could do in a hurry.'

'Thank you!' I take out the brightly coloured elf suit and double over laughing. 'He's going to look amazing in this. Oh, Hanne, you are a genius.'

'I'll take that.' She shakes her head. 'You've got a way about you, Flora. Managing to convince Connor – that's really something.'

'Not sure it was me, exactly, Hanne. I think it was the mention of kids in hospitals that appealed to him. He'll probably call himself "Recycle Elf" and lecture them all about the pitfalls of global warming.'

She laughs. 'It'd just be white noise to me anyway, seeing him dressed in that suit. I know elves are meant to be cute and Christmassy, but somehow I think our man is going to make his elf suit look . . .' She struggles to find the right word.

'Sexy?'

'I'm glad you said it! I'm too old for all this!' We fall about laughing.

Only time will tell just how Connor will look and act in the suit but I know for certain, I'm keen to see for myself too!

It's midday when Connor approaches the van. 'I don't think I've ever seen you so quiet. It can only mean bad things.'

I give him a wide smile. 'Well, that depends what you mean by bad.' Time to turn it on and make this guy believe! 'I was picturing you wearing an elf suit. It's got me musing about just how many *lives* you're going to change today. You're going to grant wishes, and make dreams come true. You're going to turn their frowns into wide smiles. That must feel pretty amazing, Connor.'

Do I detect a blush creeping up his cheeks? 'Yeah, right. A six-foot-something *grown* man wearing an elf suit. I'm probably going to traumatise those kids. They'll have nightmares for years. They'll need therapy to forget.'

I wave him away. 'I hardly think so! Raakel wouldn't have

suggested you if that were the case and if there's one thing she knows, it's elves.' He's not buying it, so I push on. 'Would you like to see your fancy new suit?'

'Not really.'

I ignore him. Poor fool doesn't know where to put himself. 'Then come with me!'

The suit hangs in all its festive glory on a coat hanger on the curtain rod. 'Oh my God, it's an assault on my eyes.'

I grin and clap my hands. 'I knew you'd love it! I particularly like the yellow tights and green jacket. It's *exactly* like Buddy from the *Elf* movie and the kids will love that won't they, Buddy?'

'What movie?' He doesn't take his eyes off the suit. The colours do look truly gaudy under this light and the material shines just like Lycra did back in the Eighties. It's a delight to behold.

'*What movie?!* Have you been living under a rock, Connor, seriously? The movie, *Elf*? Haven't you seen it?'

'Not that I recall.'

'Golly, you haven't lived if you haven't watched that movie and made pasta drowned in maple syrup.'

'Pasta with maple syrup, are you kidding?'

'No, it's simple Christmas fare, Connor, jeez.'

Confusion dashes across his features. No wonder he doesn't believe! He hasn't been exposed to the best Christmas movies – and if you don't have a festive movie marathon session every year, then is it even Christmas?

'Let's get you in this suit, eh?' I realise what I've said and want to die. 'I mean, I'm sure you can dress yourself, but shout out if you need a hand.' I turn away as the memory of him in the sauna appears at the most inopportune time. It feels improper. Why do they just waltz around naked? It's almost like the colder it is, the less clothing they wear. I'll never understand.

'I'm not putting it on here; there's no room. I'll knock out a light or something.' I realise that Connor is stooped over to fit in the van. 'I'll dress at the hospital.'

Ah! He doesn't want any Van Lifers to see him as his alter ego Buddy! 'Where's the fun in that? What if we need to make alterations? What if the tights split wide open, then what? What if . . .'

He sighs and scrubs his face. 'OK, OK, I'll get dressed here if only to save another lecture from you.'

'Yay. Go elf yourself.' I point to my bedroom. 'There's not much room in there either but you can lie on the bed and wiggle waggle the Lycra up that way. Now you'll know what it's like to be a woman who wears skinny jeans.'

He shakes his head. 'How did I let you talk me into this?'

'Think of the children. And hurry up. We have to go.'

'I'll be glad when this is over.'

'There's always next week if Elfie doesn't return.'

'I'll track down Elfie myself and make him an offer he can't refuse.'

'Leave poor sick Elfie alone, you monster,' I say, knowing there is no such elf.

With a shake of the head, he goes behind the curtain into my room. My pulse races a teeny tiny bit thinking that he's almost naked just behind that very *thin* curtain. I'm not saying I try hard for X-ray vision but I do keep my eyes glued on the thin fabric just in case.

He grunts and mumbles under his breath. 'Your room is a mess.'

'I have a big personality and a small space in which to live. Don't judge me for it.' I pray he doesn't see all my empty takeaway cups and blow a save-the-world gasket. I really must find a keep cup to invest in. The guilt is real.

'Does it fit?' I ask.

He grunts. 'I look like a fool! A gigantic, brightly coloured fool.'

'What, like a court jester? That's not good, you're supposed to look like Buddy the Elf. Let me see.' I pull the curtain back and see him in all his Buddy the elf glory. If you didn't believe in Christmas, you would after seeing this sight, a pleasure trove for the senses! How does the man make Lycra look good?

'Connor, you look amazing! The kids are going to love it.'

'I'm never going to live this down.'

'National treasure, that's you.' I take out my phone.

'No, no pictures! That's the last thing I need.'

I make a show of holding up my hands in surrender. 'But I want to "take an Elfie". Hanne wanted to see the elf suit on, the suit she went without *sleep* in order to make for you, Connor. And at the busiest time of the year too for that poor, elderly woman with arthritic hands who suffers from far-sightedness!'

'Hurry up and take the damn pic.'

I grin. 'Elves smile, Connor, they don't scowl.'

'I'm going to get you back for this.'

'Can't wait. Say cheese!' He throws me a cheese-eating grin while I snap away before sending some to Hanne – and to Livvie. 'Right, let's go. We're meeting Raakel there, so don't forget your matching Santa sack! Come on, Buddy.'

'I'm never going to live this down.'

We head outside and the Van Lifers soon catch sight of the big man himself and follow us, peppering him with questions. I expect Connor to be surly or closed off but instead he jokes with them and doesn't mind taking the mickey out of himself. When he explains it's for the hospital toy drive everyone claps and it's like I'm in the presence of someone famous. He's magnetic when he opens up to people. Even dressed as an elf, he's heart-stoppingly gorgeous – perhaps more so than normal, if I'm honest.

We meet Raakel in the hospital lobby. 'Wow, Connor, what a transformation!' She covers her face with her hands as if she can't quite believe it's him. 'You need to be on the silver screen. You've missed your calling!'

He doffs his elf cap. If I didn't know better, I'd say the man is enjoying every second of his newfound stardom. 'Thanks, Raakel. I've learned all about Buddy the Elf from Flora so I'll try and stay in character.'

Raakel gives him a big hug. 'Thanks for doing this.'

'Pleasure.'

When Santa arrives we hide behind our hands laughing. Connor dwarfs Santa, who wears a nervous expression and seems almost like a kid himself.

Raakel marches over to him. 'Are you Jessob?'

He gives her a wobbly smile. 'I am.'

'*Thirty-year-old* Jessob with five years' experience performing as Santa? Excuse me for stating the obvious but you don't look a day over twelve.'

Jessob juts his chin out. 'I'm fifteen, thank you!'

She sighs.

'I needed the money. I'll do a good job, I promise.'

Raakel throw her hands in the air. 'OK well there's not much else we can do now. You and Connor make quite the pair. Buckle up, Santa, and get ready to wow those children.'

The unassuming pair huddle together and plan their act before we get going from ward to ward.

The children's eyes light up as Connor does a fantastic job of playing his part. He gently ruffles their hair, delivers their gifts, and picks up those who hold out their little arms for a hug. Could the icy outer layer be melting? Surreptitiously, I stare at his face and see he wears a wide smile as if he's truly enjoying himself. Who wouldn't? There is so much joy in their faces, it's a sight to behold.

Connor goes from room to room, behind our mini Santa – but the children are all mesmerised by Buddy the Elf. Maybe it's his sheer size – he's like a superhero brought to life – or maybe he's feeling the magic of Christmas and the children recognise that.

'Buddy?' The Santa sack is empty and we've managed to visit every room in the small children's ward. 'Is it time for an eggnog?'

'High time,' he replies to me with a tired grin. 'Buddy needs to head back to the workshop, kiddos. My elf friends are waiting for me and we've got a lot of toys to make before Christmas Eve.'

The children wave and a little girl launches into his arms despite the IV in her arm. 'Will you come back, Buddy?' she says. It's hard not to tear up, seeing her delicate little frame, so ravaged by illness, but her pale face shines as she stares into Connor's eyes.

He waits for a beat. 'I sure will.'

'Pinkie swear?'

Connor switches her weight to one side to free up his hand and links his pinkie finger with hers. He's so gentle and loving, the whole room goes silent and stares. It's one of those moments in life where you realise what matters and it's pure and innocent encounters like this. 'Pinkie swear,' he says.

It's enough to melt the steeliest heart. I turn away because my eyes are bright with tears. Connor would make the most amazing dad.

Chapter 20

Later that night I'm back at the van and deep in conversation with Livvie over a video call. 'He's such a hot elf, Flora,' she says, flicking her hair to one side, from the comfort of a bar in Heathrow. *City of Angels, here she comes.*

'Right? He had doctors and nurses following in his wake like he was some kind of celebrity brought to life. You should have seen him with the kids though – their little faces peering up at him like he truly was a Christmas miracle. My potential baby father alert went off.'

'Whoa, the baby daddy alert? What happened?'

I sigh. 'It was like this feeling of déjà vu. Like I'd been there before and I could see Connor hoisting our own children in the air, connecting with them like the most perfect father. Like he'd blossom in fatherhood, or something.' *Listen to me!* 'He changed when he was around those children, Liv. Like he soaked up all their anxiety, all their fear and pain about being in hospital and he made it better. When he was surrounded by those little angels he wasn't gruff, rule-following, save-the-earth Connor. He was . . . happy. Truly happy to be there. *And* he's offered to go back once a week until Christmas.'

'Wow! So the big question: does he believe? Because it sounds like you witnessed yourself a Christmas miracle!'

Behind Livvie people bustle past, dragging bags, in the busy airport bar. 'That's the thing. He was all smiles and then afterwards, he reneged on the promise of sharing a medicinal eggnog and went straight back to work! *And* he reminded me to get rid of the gingerbread house! Like he flicked a switch and broody Connor returned,' I say. 'I thought the experience changed him and he could see with his own two eyes why believing is more about the magic of the season than all the consumerism he's so hung up on, but no, he still clearly doesn't believe.'

'Maybe he had to process it all. It's a big thing, making promises to sick kids, like he did. It sounds like he was really affected by it.'

I consider that. 'You could be right, Liv. That last little girl . . . she was so sick, so fragile and stared at him like he was God. It was the most beautiful thing I've ever seen.'

'That sort of thing really tugs at the heartstrings whether he's a believer or not. And I think you need to try again, try another scenario to make him believe. Interventions are never easy – that's why they're so important.'

'True. I'll have to figure out what to try next. Let me prop you up here.' I lean the phone against a shelf in the bedroom, the shelf I hit my head on every damn morning when I pop out of bed, forgetting I live in a box-sized place. 'Now do you like this Puffa jacket, or this one?' I say, brandishing both so she can see.

'They're exactly the same!'

I shake my head. 'Maybe it's the poor lighting, but they're not the same at all. One is jet-black and the other is blue-black. My question is: does the jet-black wash out my complexion?'

Her eyes narrow. 'What, why do you care so much?'

My mouth opens to protest but the words won't come. 'What do you mean? Can't I ask my very best friend for fashion and skincare advice like I've done for at least two decades now?'

She tilts her head and gives me one of those looks that sees straight through me. 'Why do you, Flora Westwood, *suddenly* care about your complexion of all things?'

'It's not because of Connor if that's what you're implying!'

'Oh yeah?'

'Yeah!'

'You're a hopeless liar but worse I think you're lying to yourself. But I guess that's all part of the Hallmark movie blueprint. The heroine can't see what's before her very eyes because she's so hung up on their differences, she forgets that their differences are what make them so special together.'

I double-blink. Could this be true? Somehow I doubt it. Connor is definitely not a Hallmark hero. He's too broody, too regimented and has far too many tattoos. 'It's not that at all! It's because the freezing temperatures here are drying out my skin and even though I've never cared about my skin before, I've since realised that when one approaches thirty, one should care about these things. If I can delay my skin resembling that of a three-week-old apple left in the sun for too long, then I will.'

'Third person, eh?'

'Eh?'

'Oh, stop and admit you like the damn guy. That your ovaries went into overdrive when you saw how amazing he was with all those kids – you said so yourself. If that's not a sign I don't know what is. Your heart recognises him; now you have to get your head to catch up.'

'My ovaries?' Can ovaries go into overdrive? Is that a thing! I blow out a breath. 'Are you even listening to me?'

She rolls her eyes. 'No, I'm reading between the lines because you're full of it. I thought you were following the blueprint, and the blueprint has Connor's name written in thick black ink!'

'Yes, I'm following the blueprint and living the dream but I've been distracted by Operation-Make-Him-Believe. They are two different storylines, in two different stories! To be honest, Connor has too many hang-ups for me.'

'This is the part where the enemies-to-lovers story comes together, and they start to fall for each other, but don't want to admit their feelings. Actually, this is probably why he hightailed it out of the hospital today – you guys shared a life-changing moment and it scared both of you! There are some intense *feelings* flying around Finland right now.'

I guffaw. 'I get what you're saying, really, but it's not like that. The guy is so frosty he could be a snowman. Seriously, all he's missing is a carrot for a nose.'

Livvie shakes her head. 'Well, you can warm him up!'

'What are you like? Now which jacket?' I try to distract her as I'm momentarily hit with a dizzy sensation. Just what exactly do I feel for Connor? Could he be my happy ever after or am I grasping at straws in the hopes of finding love? Hard to tell, since Connor is such a closed book. No one wants to be the one to speak up and be rejected. I've been there too many times, and I'm sure he doesn't even know Santa *has* reindeer, let alone all nine of their names. And that's a deal breaker, right?

'Blue-black brings out the *azure* in your eyes.' She flutters her lashes and makes quite the spectacle of herself.

'Blue-black it is. Anyway, enough about me.' I fling the jacket on the bed. 'What's happening with Jasper? Did you have a long, languorous goodbye, whisper sweet nothings to one another?'

She pulls a face that suggests she did not. 'We had a casual farewell dinner on Friday. He made all these lovely promises about waiting for me, and how we'd talk every day. But I told him I didn't know if it would work, not with me being away for so long and us being so new. Is there an "us" yet? I'm not sure since it's all so new. So I did what any modern new-age gal would do and hid my phone on Saturday night so I wouldn't drunk-dial him and tell him I adore him. I hid my phone so well, it made getting an Uber home from dinner with Rochelle a little tricky.' Rochelle is an aesthetician at Livvie's clinic.

'Bloody hell, Liv, here you are making a big deal about me and you're letting The One get away!' I don't know how to make the girl see sense. 'How will you feel if he moves on with someone else, and next minute you see pictures online of the loved-up couple staying at a cute little B&B that has some historical significance, like Jane Austen once lived there, or something . . . ?'

'Well, I wouldn't feel good.'

'So why not do something?'

'Like what? Hope the guy is the most patient man on the planet?'

'You're not going to Mars, Livvie. Aeroplanes exist, you know.'

'It's not only the distance. My whole life falls apart when he's around. I nearly injected the wrong woman last week! I had one for lip fillers and one for Botox and I got them mixed up because I was off in La-La land dreaming about wedding rings for crying out loud. When have you ever known me to dream about bloody *wedding* rings?' Her voice rises as panic mounts. 'I only have one opportunity to get this deal right and *he* is a huge distraction.'

'This woozy lovestruck haze will go away, you know. How do I fix you when you're so broken! Do you ever think maybe your psyche, your inner self *wants* to be loved up? To get married? But it's not like you need to do it all in some big rush. Just take baby steps; at least let Jasper know that you're into him. You'll be in another country for crying out loud! It's not like he's going to pop over with pizza and overstay his welcome.'

'Yeah. I guess. I'll think on it.'

'Urgh.'

'Urgh back.'

I grin. 'I miss you.'

'Miss you too. Now, go and make that Viking fall in love—'

'With Christmas.' I salute. 'Will do.'

'Bye, trouble.'

'Bye and safe travels.'

I hit the end-call button and toy with my phone for a bit. Does a good friend stay out of her best friend's life, or does she meddle, knowing her friend won't make the move even though it's in her best interests?

There's nothing wrong with looking Jasper up on social media, is there? It's not a *crime* to check out his profile. I find him on Facebook, and boy oh boy . . . he's just so obviously Livvie's perfect match. I've hit the jackpot as his page is not secured, poor fool, and I can see all of his posts. He's adorably bookish. Seems to love hiking. Enjoys sharing pictures of his food, all healthy dishes too so that will appeal to Livvie with her tragic hatred of food with no nutritional value.

I dilly-dally with what to do, knowing if I message him I'm violating the BFF code and that if it blows up in my face it'll be hard to come back from that. And whoops, my finger slips and I send him a friend request. That way I can keep an eye on both of them and give them a shove if I need to.

Chapter 21

The next morning a knock at the door wakes me from a deep slumber. I'm cosy and cocooned under so many layers, I have to force myself to get out of bed.

'Coming,' I say and wrap a robe around myself. I open the door to find Hanne there, holding a box aloft.

'Hanne, come in! Whoa, it's freezing.'

She shuffles inside, tracking snow with her. She takes off her coat and hangs it on the back of the door. 'I have more boxes in the car, including advent calendars, which you're bound to sell out of.' Hanne says that Finnish people adore their advent calendars so she's managed to source some more for the rush tonight before December begins.

'You are a lifesaver! Thanks for delivering them.'

'Oh, it's no problem. I have a big day of deliveries so I was going this way and I wanted to check in and see how you were going.'

'Coffee?'

'Would love one.' She unwinds her scarf and sits at the table. 'So the hospital trip went well?'

I bustle around, grabbing mugs and making a pot of coffee. 'It did! Did you get the pics I sent?'

'I sure did. Connor managed to pull off that outfit. How does he do it?'

'Some people have all the luck.' I sit opposite Hanne and she pours us both a mug of coffee. Steam fills the air between us.

'So what's next for the operation?'

I tap my chin. 'That's the problem. I'm fresh out of ideas. I need to step it up a notch but how?'

She sips her coffee and stares out the window as if in contemplation.

'I could try wrangle him into making candy canes with me?' I say. 'Although I'll probably end up setting something on fire and I'm not sure he trusts me when it comes to cooking.' We had that raw turkey incident . . .

She screws up her face. 'Making candy canes, no, it's not his style. Besides, you have to go bigger than that to get the man to really see the magic of Christmas. Why not try something that will appeal more to Connor's sensibilities?'

'Like what? All I know about him so far is he likes to keep his office shipshape, and he's got a real thing for rules.'

'Yes, and he's also community-minded.'

'He is?' I'm surprised to hear that.

'He's always there to lend a helping hand when needed. We had a big incident in town just after Connor first arrived, a fire at a recycling plant, and he stepped in and showed them the danger points and how to redesign the factory. He has some background in that sort of thing and could have charged a bomb for it, but he didn't. They wanted to hire him, but he refused. Didn't want to be tied down. That's why the market appealed to him, I think. He only had to commit to one season. But since he saved the day, he's been popular in town.'

So he's generous with his time if he believes in the cause. I file that away for future reference. 'What do you suggest?'

'We could have a stall wrapping presents for the locals for a gold coin donation that can go to a charity of his choice,' Hanne suggests.

'No, no he'd push back on that idea. He's got a real thing about the rubbish generated from Christmas and he'll probably tell people that the packaging their gifts are housed in will end up in landfill and that they're not helping the planet in their quest to buy presents people don't need.'

'Yes, I see your point.' She holds up a finger. 'What about something that's more a gathering of people simply celebrating the joy of the season, something like putting the star on the town Christmas tree and the official turning on of the lights?'

'Yes! That's more like it. But would he go?'

'He's got to do more than that!' Hanne says, her voice high. 'He's got to be the person who scurries up the ladder and dresses the tree, turns on the fabulous lights and so begins the symbolic start of Christmas! Tomorrow is the 1st of December and it's when we as a town gather in the main square, and wait for the annual festival to begin. You'll have to move fast if we want this to happen.'

'It's a great idea. Surely he'd feel like a superstar being the man of the hour, amid so many happy faces . . . but who would I ask? Wouldn't they already have someone lined up for that honour?'

She nods. 'They do. Me.'

'You?'

'Me. I do it every year as chairperson of the town social calendar. I'm happy to pass the baton on. To be honest, I wouldn't mind the break. I'm getting too old to climb that ladder, I swear it gets higher every year. And not only do I have to turn on the lights, I have to give an inspiring speech about Christmas and I can only rewrite the thing so many times. It's become quite the chore.'

'Connor would have to do a speech?'

Hanne lifts a palm. 'One of those rallying, inspirational types. But maybe don't mention that part. Probably better if he wings it. He seems OK with public speaking so I don't think it'll be an issue for him.'

The idea takes hold. If all else fails I can tell him it's a gathering about climate change, only a little white lie to get him there. 'I'm sure he'd love to stand on the stage and address his fellow community members.' I'm sure he'd love nothing less, but hey, miracles never come easy.

She shrugs. 'It just might tip him over the edge from nonbeliever to believer. There's something very humbling about being up there, with so many eyes on you, as everyone's energy is so high because of the coming holidays. It's quite the spectacle to be part of.'

I can't see how this could fail. 'Great, so what time and where do we meet?'

We sort out the nitty-gritty details before I help unload the boxes of stock from Hanne's car. Now I just need to work out how I'm going to tell Connor he's been bestowed such an honour and get him to agree to it . . .

There's no time to ruminate as soon enough Tuomo is at the door and I'm off for my first dog-sledding lesson.

'Now the trick is, Flora,' he says as I shiver in the thick snow in the middle of the forest, 'you have to command them. You're the boss. Make your voice strong.' He gives me an hour's worth of instructions and I try hard to follow his words. But the dogs, they're so cute!

I look at the adorable fluffy huskies and just want to snatch them up and snuggle them. 'Absolutely no hugs for the cute doggies?'

He frowns. 'They're working dogs, I already told you.'

'Boo. But they're so . . .'

'No, no hugs for the dogs, Flora. They take me from A to B.'

'Aww, OK.' I follow Tuomo's directions and stand in the little dog sled at the back of the pack. I give the command in a loud strong voice like he showed me and the dogs take off. 'ARGH!' I hold the reins tight but the rope still manages to slip through my fingers bit by bit. The huskies race through the forest like they've things to do and places to be. We snake in and out of trees, so close that when I upset branches I'm doused with fresh lumps of snow and soon I'm shivering with cold and exhilaration.

We complete a loop they know well and too soon we come flying back to where Tuomo stands. I expect them to slow down like you would when you park a car, but instead they come to an abrupt halt and I go flying off to the side, landing hard on my butt half buried in snow.

'Flora, I told you the command to stop!'

I unearth myself. 'I forgot! Let me try that again!' He laughs and when his back is turned I give the heavy-breathing huskie closest to me a little pat and I'm sure he enjoys it, working dog or not.

Chapter 22

When the day comes to a close, I find Connor in his office, poring over paperwork.

He looks up when I come in, the door banging behind me. 'One of these days, you'll work out how to open and shut it properly,' he says, trying and failing to hold back a smile. 'Come to lodge another complaint, Flora Westwood?'

'Do you associate me with such doom and gloom?'

'Usually.'

'I'm offended.'

'OK.'

'OK? And don't think I missed the fact you're suddenly spouting my last name. Been checking out my paperwork, stalking me, eh?'

'In case the police ask, I thought I'd better try and remember it.'

'The police?'

'I had yet another complaint made against one Ms Flora Westwood, would you believe?'

I fold my arms. 'By whom?'

'Would you like to know what the complaint is about first?'

'I think I can guess.'

'Humour me.'

'Fine.' He shuffles his neat stack of paperwork, even though

I'm sure he knows exactly where the written complaint is. 'Don't drag this out, Connor.'

He grins. Is he enjoying this? It doesn't look like he's written up a warning this time . . .

'Here it is. A formal complaint made about one Ms Westwood, who tried to run one Ms Aine Korhonen off the road. What do you have to say for yourself, Flora?'

I narrow my eyes. 'She's a liar and a menace! I'd like to make a complaint about Aine myself.'

'Don't worry. I looked at the dash cam footage from her van after she reported the incident and it's obvious it was just an accident and not premeditated attempted murder.'

'Not yet, anyway.' That woman! 'I'm sure she's just making up excuses to visit your office, Connor.'

'I doubt it, but nevertheless I told her to keep a wide berth from you. There's less than four weeks to go until everyone moves on, so I'm sure we can all be grown-ups until then.'

I bite my tongue, as a very un-grown-up insult threatens to burst out. He's right. There's no point going back and forth with Aine; it's only going to egg her on to continue making complaints for Connor's attention. And to make me look bad.

We lapse into silence. I take pains to rearrange my expression to something akin to angst as I remember my mission and the real reason I'm here, which is much more fun to imagine than any hostilities with Aine. 'Look, *we* do have a small problem. And I don't know who else to ask for help. There's only you.'

'*We?* Why do I get the feeling I'm not going to like this?' He runs his fingers through his hair as if his head suddenly hurts.

'Because you're cynical?'

'Maybe.'

'So Hanne just called me, *terribly* upset. Quite *hysterical* actually. In *floods* of tears.'

He sighs. 'Get to the point, Flora. Why you feel the need to overemphasise things is beyond me.'

'I'm simply painting you a picture.'

'Paint it faster.'

'OK, well, poor Hanne is in a pickle.' He makes a hand gesture telling me to speed it up. 'She's unable to put the star on the town Christmas tree this year and turn on the lights at the annual town festivities.'

'Why can't she do it?'

'It's a sad story actually. Tragic, in a way. Hanne was getting her fortnightly pedicure – you know how it is, even as crazy busy as she is she keeps up her beauty regime – and there was a bit of a glitch. I won't say they chopped her toe *clean* off, but it was pretty close, if you get my drift. Therefore, she can't climb that big old rickety ladder with it hanging in the balance like that, can she? Nor should she! The best course of action is bed rest, which I believe is what her toe surgeon has suggested.'

He rocks back in his chair, his expression unfathomable.

Can he not see where I'm heading with this? 'So, it's a big disaster for the town, is it not? Hanne's been doing the star and the lights for about a hundred years. And as she was thinking of possible replacements, your name came up as someone who is community-minded, someone who always thinks of others, someone who is so downright sparkling you're practically a star yourself, that every single other candidate fell straight out of her head. So, tell me, will you do it so I can call Hanne and put her out of her last-minute misery and so she can focus on her recovery?'

He frowns. 'There are plenty of people who'd love to showboat on stage and I am not one of them.'

'Even through her immense pain, Hanne *specifically* asked for you. This is the same Hanne who always helps with cut-price decorations for this very market every year. The same Hanne who gives generously to the *orphanage* every Christmas! The same . . .' He's not buying it. 'The same Hanne who wants to outlaw single-use plastics.'

'OK, OK, please not another monologue. But why me, really? I've lived in this town less than a year. Is this another one of your schemes?'

I'm mock outraged. 'My schemes, *schemes!*' Is he onto me? But how? I've been so crafty about it all!

He scrubs his face – he does that a lot when I'm around. 'Look, I'll place the star and turn on the lights, but I'm not standing up there doing a long, impassioned speech about the glory of Christmas or anything because you know I can't, Flora. I'll end up saying it's all a big bloody waste of time and money and we could all better use that to educate ourselves on the real meaning of giving. Like giving *back* instead of giving *things*. Plant trees instead of pulling them up for useless . . .'

I could be here all day if he starts on this line of thought. 'You're right, you're totally right, Connor. But you will say a few words, right? Give the crowd something to hang on to in these uncertain times? Rally them, if you will.'

'These uncertain times?'

'Yeah, surely you feel it? We're barely hanging on as a planet. What if our earth *is* hollow and there's a whole other civilisation living on the inside? I get chills just thinking about it. They could be our doppelgängers! Have you ever thought of that?' He remains stony-faced. 'Then there's the whole mystery surrounding cryptocurrency, like is it money or not? Is Elon the puppet master? Is Elon a robot, come to think of it? There's something decidedly mechanical about the way he moves, don't you think? So much hangs in the balance, and people need some *hope*, something to look forward to, is all I'm saying.'

He closes his eyes and lets out an inordinately long sigh. 'Flora, where have you come from?'

'London.'

'Outer space.'

'Are you saying I live on another planet? I'm from Hollow Earth? You think I'm spacey?'

170

'Hollow Earth sounds about right. Fine, I'll do it, but it's going to be brief. Very brief. And you're going to help.'

'What!' My heart stops.

'We come as a pair, Flora. I'll do it with you right beside me or I won't do it at all.'

Noooo. As scattered as I am, I note the 'we come as a pair' thing and that also sends me over the edge. Dizziness spikes. 'Why me?'

'Why not you?'

I stare him down but it doesn't do a damn thing. It's no big deal; I'll wait him out until he cracks. I press my lips together and give him my best impression of someone suffering huge anxiety. Still nothing. I will a faux tear to fall, and it does. But still zero reaction. Bloody hell this guy is good. I glare. Huff and harrumph. His expression remains neutral. 'OK, fine.' Bloody, blast!

'Great, so it's agreed, we'll do it together.' His eyes glitter with triumph. The damn crafty conniving con man! 'We can both say a few words.'

'Wait, what? Oh no, no, *no*, I'm not a public speaker! I will happily stand beside you.' Gah, this has gone from bad to worse!

'Either we do this together, or not at all.'

Damn, why do these plots keep backfiring on me? I take a deep breath because suddenly I'm as nauseous as that time I ate the turkey Christmas lunch that I made for me and Livvie. The thought of public speaking is terrifying. I'm more of an 'on the sidelines' person rather than standing in the full glare of the spotlight.

He gives me a look I can only decipher as teasing. It almost like he knows and he's turned the tables on me! 'Fine.' I huff and I puff so he knows I'm out of sorts. 'Even though I'm new here . . .'

'And I'm new myself . . .'

Dammit! 'But they love you already. So far there's two people in this small town who think I'm capable of *murder*. That does not bode well for me being centre stage and rallying the troops.'

'This is the perfect chance to show them you're as innocent as a newborn baby.'

'I don't care for you, Connor.'

'Yeah you do.'

Heat rushes to my cheeks but I put it down to him turning the tables on me. 'Fine,' I say. 'You're buying me dinner after so bring your wallet. And I'm having an entrée and a main and possibly two desserts, maybe three.'

'Deal.'

What have I done?

Chapter 23

Later that night Raakel approaches my van, the wind blowing her in a zigzag. The wild weather has scared most market-goers away. There are only a few of the brave scattered here and there, drinking mulled wine and eating warm morsels of food as they wander by. My Christmas bells have been jingling so loud my ears feel like they're about to burst, so I'm in the middle of taking them down (in case I get another noise warning!) when I see her trudging through the thick white powder.

'Raakel, come out of the snow!' I say, as she rushes in and pulls the door closed behind her. 'It's bloody freezing!'

'Isn't it? Everyone's gathered around the fire drums if you want to catch up.'

'They are?' These rugged Van Lifers don't let anything get in the way of their late-night gossip sessions. Maybe it's a Finnish thing. I really have to get accustomed to the arctic temperature. Connor and I are really the only blow-ins, along with a couple of guys from Scotland and Wales, I think. Most of the Van Lifers are Finnish or Swedish. 'Yeah, let's have a vodka first to warm up. I'll have to add on another three layers of clothing.'

'Just a heads-up: your name has been mentioned.'

I groan. 'That can't be good.'

'Aine seems to think you're all set to take the stage with Connor at the turning on of the town Christmas lights, and she's none too happy about it. Reckons that you've come in here and taken over.'

'What! How does she even know about that?'

She shrugs. 'Isn't it crazy? Says you've been demanding all of Connor's time and he's never around for anyone else.' Did she see me go to his office this afternoon? But it's not like she hasn't done that herself a few times, is it?

'It's the whole romantic dinner afterwards that's got her fired up.'

'Jeez, has she bugged his office or something?'

Raakel laughs. 'I wouldn't put it past her. More likely she sent one of her gang to listen outside his window. They used to do it as a joke and report back on whoever he was dressing down about violations.'

'She's the gift that keeps on giving.'

Raakel takes a seat at the table. I find the vodka and pour us two shots. I use vodka purely as a warming agent, not to take the edge off or anything. 'Thanks,' she says, and drinks it down in one gulp. 'Rumour has it that Connor *never* goes out to dinner. He always works late and spends his evening securing the perimeter or whatever those laps are about and now suddenly you've arrived and he's booking fancy restaurants.'

'It's fancy? Livvie made me take all my fancy clothes out of my bag! All I've got is puffy things that might make me take flight in these high winds!'

'Don't worry, I'm sure it's not your sense of style he's interested in.' She waggles her brows.

'No, no it's a disaster. A fashion disaster among so many other problems.' I figure Raakel needs to know what's really going on. 'Hanne and I had this sneaky plan to make him believe by putting the star atop the tree and turning on the town Christmas lights. Then *somehow* he bamboozled me into doing it together even though the thought of speaking on stage makes feel like death.'

'How did you get yourself caught up in that?'

'He lulled me into a false sense of security, then *bam*, surprise attack! He's quite cunning at the core.'

'So what are you nervous about? The event or the dinner?'

'Both! I had hoped the dinner would be a casual affair so I could eat my body weight in food he's paying for to make up for him roping me into this mess. But now you say the place is fancy so it'll be that minuscule food that one has to eat impossibly slowly to make it look like one knows fine dining, and I get itchy just thinking about it. I don't know all the fancy terms; I can never tell which fork is for what, even though they're all different sizes. And don't even get me started on that wine swizzle thing you're supposed to do without showering yourself in the liquid, which is always red have you noticed? It's never white wine when that happens – what's *with* that?'

She cocks her head. 'Flora, you need to take a deep breath for me. It's a fancy restaurant but it's not exactly Michelin-starred. You'll be fine. Use whatever fork you like and if they give you a second look tell them that's not how the British do it.'

'OK, OK, good plan.'

'And don't worry about swizzling the wine. Tell them you'd like the sommelier to try it, and if it's not up to standard you'll be sending it back.'

'Act haughty! I couldn't!'

'Then tell Connor to try it.'

I pull at my cheeks. 'Yes, yes, OK. And I know women say this all the time, but I don't have a thing to wear.'

'Surely you do? Let's have a look.'

We go through my cupboard, my teeny tiny rectangle bursting with puffy clothes, and I unearth a long black knit dress. 'It looks like I'm going to a funeral.'

'Put it on – let me see.'

I pull it on. It hugs my body a little too snugly. I can see a lot of lumps and bumps I don't recall being there a few weeks ago. It's all this eating to keep warm thing I'm doing.

'Turn around let me see it from the front,' Raakel says.

'I look a little too . . . curvy in this.' I turn to face her, tugging it from my hips.

'Ooh la la, Flora, you look *buxom* in that!'

'I don't want to look buxom, I want to look a little more . . . streamlined.' Practically everyone here is tall, straight up and down, like they're about to strut down a runway. It's grossly unfair, because I see them scoffing just as many sugary treats as me, if not more, and yet it doesn't touch their bodies. I only have to sniff a sweet treat and *boom* another inch on my hips.

'Are you mad?' Raakel asks. 'Flora, you have a body to die for! I would kill for your curves! Instead, I've got this . . . surfboard physique.'

I burst out laughing. Raakel does not resemble a surfboard in any shape or form but I can see it's the age-old dilemma of always wanting what we don't have. 'Well, if I could swap bodies with you I would, but we can't. So how do you suggest I dress this up a bit more?'

'Make-up, hair and jewellery. Come to my van an hour before you have to leave tomorrow and I'll help you out.'

'Thank you!'

'Right then, let's go to the fire drums and catch up with the others.'

It's like they don't feel the cold. We get to the fire drums, my teeth chattering away as if they're having their own conversation. Aine and her posse are sitting on the other side, and shoot me mean-girl glares. I give them a cheery wave. 'Hi!' But they don't respond.

Eevi calls us over. 'Hey! Sit with us.' I find a spot next to her, and Raakel moves close to Tuomo.

'How'd you enjoy the dog-sledding?' Eevi asks.

I hug myself tight to keep the heat in. 'I loved it! I want to do it again, but Tuomo said no.' I shoot him a faux-hurt look.

He rolls his eyes as if he's dealing with a disobedient teen.

'That's because she kept patting the dogs when my back was turned. Next minute she had one unharnessed and was romping around the snow with him saying, "Who's a good boy!" After I gave her strict instructions not to do that.' He shakes his head and laughs.

'And I'd do it again too.'

'They're hard to resist, those huskies,' Eevi says. 'We need to take Flora to a hot tub in the forest. She hasn't lived until she's tried that.'

I gulp. 'Is this another naked escapade, because if so I'm out. I'm too British for all this bare skin on show.'

The group laugh and Raakel hands me a cup of warm *gløgge*.

'No,' Eevi says. 'You can wear a swimming costume; in fact, I think it's a rule.'

'So where is this hot tub then?'

'Five minutes from here, if we drive. It's in the middle of the forest clearing and is one of the best places to see aurora if she comes. Better yet, there's a lake so you can try ice swimming.'

'Ice swimming – in this temperature! Why?'

'Good for your blood circulation, didn't you know?' Eevi says.

Soon enough I'm dragged into one of their vans, a borrowed swimming costume in hand and wondering just how cold is too cold for this group. If they're right though, I'm going to be the healthiest person on the planet by immersing myself in and out of hot and cold temperatures like some kind of torture device inflicted by myself!

The next day is a blur, there are so many customers I can barely keep up. I do feel strangely refreshed from the hot tub and ice swimming, although sadly there was no sign of the northern lights.

Today everyone wants to find something festive to wear for the turning on of the Christmas lights. I sell out of flashing reindeer beanies and Santa hats. The Christmas jewellery that Hanne replenished on Tuesday is gone. And all of my snowman scarves have been snapped up. Who knew that everyone was so festive in this town? Everyone except Connor, that is. I shut the van door to keep the heat in and go outside with a box of supplies to replenish the racks.

Speak of the devil. As I'm restocking the rack of Santa sacks and reusable elf shopping bags, Connor struts past, his face dark.

Is he nervous about tonight?

'Where are you off to with that brooding look on your face?' I ask as he goes to walk straight past.

'Flora, how are you?' he says, ignoring my question.

'Peachy, and you?'

He sighs. 'I'll be better when this whole mess is over. I don't know how I let you talk me into these things.'

'Well likewise. I'm not too keen on the whole speech thing either.'

'How is Hanne?'

'Fine, why?' Too late, I realise my mistake when I see his eyes cloud with suspicion. 'Except that now it looks like she might lose the toe, after all.' I cross my fingers behind my back, hoping to erase the many, many lies I've had to tell in order to do good. 'She told me to pass on her thanks to you, says you're a real lifesaver, even though we know you really aren't since you're dragging me into this with you, when the locals only want you.'

He ignores my jibes and says, 'She's going to lose her *toe*? From a pedicure?'

'Terrible set of circumstances. It just goes to show you have to be so careful about when and where you sneeze. In the blink of an eye a body part can be gone—' I click my fingers '—just like that.'

He shakes his head, his mane of hair catching the filmy sunlight. 'I should go see her. Times like this, people need their friends around. Maybe take her some flowers. Some meals. I guess she can't do much while she's recuperating.'

'No, no, no,' I squirm. 'Don't do that. She's still very sensitive about the whole fiasco. Still coming to terms what having nine toes will look like, you know? *It's too soon.*' His expressions are always so unfathomable I can't tell if he's onto me or not. It's not like the story is that unbelievable, is it? 'Poor Hanne, going through such a thing so close to Christmas! Best to give her some space and wait until she puts out a call for help.'

He tilts his head as if that will help him see through my words, and remains mute. It's quite intimidating when he doesn't talk, because I have this unhealthy need to fill the silence, which increases the risk of outing myself as a gigantic liar.

'Cold, isn't it?' When all else fails, change the subject. 'Oh look, a customer.' As I go to welcome them, I see it's Aine and her gang. Urgh.

'Oh, hey, Aine. Looking for some festive fun in your life? Can I recommend anything for you? I have some lovely earrings here . . .' I find them and hand them over. '*Bah humbug.* Cute, right?'

She rolls her eyes and speaks in rapid-fire Finnish to her friends. I can only imagine what she's saying isn't complimentary because they're soon in fits of laughter.

'I'm not here to see you, Flora. I was after Connor actually.' Like the biggest cliché going, she bats her lashes, and acts like some kind of screen siren. How do women know how to flirt like that? It's quite the performance and internally I scream. No man could resist such a beauty turning it on like that. It should be outlawed! Connor doesn't seem to change in her presence, doesn't seem to react to her love-heart eyes at him. And do I even care if he does? It's none of my business, is it? I guess it's more that I'd hate him to fall for a woman like her, one who is only outwardly beautiful but internally sour as a lemon.

I snatch the earrings back. 'These might be a little small for your ears. I'll see if I have something bigger.'

'Excuse me?' she says, her voice incredulous.

Connor stays silent through the exchange. He's probably stuck in a fantasy about Aine and her ridiculously long lashes.

I paste on a sweet smile. 'Oh, don't be upset! It's only there's a size guide for these delicate pieces, a lobe to earring ratio and from what I can see, there's a bit too much ear there. It will dwarf the jewellery and we don't want that.'

I spin the rack and find an oversized Grinch pair. 'Here we go, these should fit.'

She ignores the proffered pair of glittery green earrings and looks downright murderous.

'I don't wear cheap jewellery,' she snaps.

'Why, because it doesn't fit?'

Truthfully her ears are just as perfect as the rest of her. But I can't let her know that. She brings out the worst in me.

'Connor,' she says, looking up to him as if he's a delicious boozy Christmas pudding. 'I was hoping to get a ride with you to the town square tonight. I'm having a little trouble with my van. It won't start.'

How transparent! I can see straight through her lies.

'Can't any of your other friends take you?' I ask.

'I'm talking to Connor.'

I hold up my hands in mock surrender.

'So, Connor, what do you say? Can I ride with you?'

Urgh, somehow she *sexualises* the sentence. Is there some kind of school for this level of flirting? A book, a memo I've missed out on? Are some of us not hardwired to flirt?

Connor kicks at the ground and looks like he'd rather be anywhere but here. He's probably one of the only men I know who wouldn't want two women fighting over him. Not that I'm fighting *over* him per se, but fighting in the sense of not letting Aine close so he doesn't make any mistakes with her when it comes to affairs of the heart. So he doesn't regret it later. I'm basically doing the guy a massive favour. 'Sorry, Aine. I'm going to visit a sick friend first, and I don't know how long

180

I'll be needed there.' I cheer silently – but wait! Does he mean Hanne? I'm screwed! Can I text her and tell her to limp? To wrap her foot up and hobble? Would she go so far to save me!?

'That's OK, I can come with you. I don't mind going early.'

He digs his hands into the denim of his pockets. 'Thanks but it might be contagious. The last thing I want is you all to fall ill at this time of year.' At this time of year! Is it working? Does he have Christmas on the brain? He continues, 'It's best if I go alone and see what's what. Like Flora said, maybe one of the girls—' he points to Aine's friends, who stand just offside scowling at me '—could take you?'

Her shoulders sag but Aine manages to keep her expression serene as if she didn't just get rejected. 'Yeah. Sure. And if you're still around maybe I can catch a lift back. The girls are probably going to stay on in town and you know me, I need my beauty sleep!' She lets out a high laugh that sounds so forced it takes all my might not to scoff.

'I'm taking Flora out for a thank-you dinner afterwards.'

'Oh, how sweet. Flora's really struggled to make friends here. It's hard to fit in when you're so . . . different, I suppose. Right, Flora?'

'She sure is,' Connor says, and his voice sounds strange. 'It's that difference that is so intriguing.' He stares at me like he's lost in a bubble. I wonder if he's thinking of all the run-ins we've had but something tells me otherwise.

Take that! I want to say, and I'm sure triumph shines all over my face but I can't focus on that because I'm light-headed all of a sudden.

'Another time, then,' Aine counters with a steely smile. 'Let's go, girls.' I wait for her to do the mean-girl finger click like you see in the movies but thankfully she doesn't resort to that cliché. She saves one last withering look for me before they flounce off as quickly as they came.

The devil sneaks up and makes me spit out one last thing. 'Want me to hold the earrings for you?' She doesn't turn, choosing to ignore the jibe. I'm a horrible person. 'Guess they're not her colour?'

Connor laughs. 'Flora, the master of How to Win Friends and Influence People.'

'That's me.'

'You don't suffer fools, do you, Flora?'

'Sometimes my mouth runs off before my brain catches up. Gets me into trouble all the time.'

'Don't ever change, Flora Westwood.' He lopes away.

Don't ever change? I put a hand to my van to hold me upright as wooziness runs through me. The men who have breezed in and then quickly out of my life have all told me what I needed to do in order to be right for them, and it always included my need to improve myself in some way. To change. To fit in a box. Have I blossomed here? Are my differences really intriguing or was Connor just saying that to help me save face?

But then I remind myself, Connor isn't a boyfriend, so it doesn't matter either way. It's just a throwaway comment from a man who hates Christmas, and I'm clinging to it like it means more than it does. And yet, the feeling doesn't diminish. Things feel different for me here in snowy Finland. Part of me feels like I'm coming into my own, or maybe accepting who I am and knowing that's enough.

I spend the rest of the day floating high. Nothing can bring my mood down, even when I get a complaint about my hot cocoa being too hot, or that my English accent is impossible to understand. I smile and apologise and walk with a spring in my step. Soon enough the work day comes to an end and the crowds disperse.

Once I've showered and changed, I head to Raakel's van and hope she can work her magic on me for the town festivities and turning on the Christmas lights.

*   *   *

182

'Can you stop wiggling?' Raakel admonishes me. 'I'm going to get mascara all over your eyelid!'

'It feels like you're stabbing my eyeball!' And the nerves have kicked in and I can't stop fidgeting. I could power a town with the amount of restless energy radiating from me. How sustainable would that be?

'Have you never had your make-up done by someone else?' Raakel asks.

I try to stop rapid blinking, so I don't end up with bloodshot eyes. 'Yes, Livvie has tried on many occasions but she doesn't have the patience for it. Reckons I'm a terrible make-up subject, and I see now she might be right.'

'You're not the best model, that's for sure.' Raakel continues to stab me with the brush and I wonder if I should have done my own make-up, going for my usual sparkly Christmas look, a focus on glittery eyeshadow and lots of rouge and highlighter with lashings of thick black mascara and candy-cane-red lips usually does the trick for me. Livvie says I'm a throwback from the Nineties, which I take as quite the compliment.

'My talents lie in other areas.' Why did I think a new look would suit me? It's too late now to back out and what's the worst that can happen really? It's only make-up!

'So, what's your grand plan for this evening?' Raakel asks. 'Have Connor climb the ladder and find his Christmas spirit?'

'In a nutshell. Imagine the ceremony of the Christmas lights being switched on by the man himself, and then he turns to his adoring crowd, sees the joy in their eyes as they all hold candles aloft singing "O Little Town of Bethlehem". He climbs the ladder and puts the star on the town Christmas tree, everyone cheering him on. Back on stage, he'll rally them with some inspiring words about joy, and hope and good things to come. It'll be one of those moments. The crowd will fall silent, shed a few happy tears, which Connor will feel deep in his heart, and then *lightbulb moment*: he'll realise this is exactly what he's been missing in his life as snow drifts lazily down and the scent of gingerbread is heavy in the air. He's been missing the Christmas spirit. And you don't find that in shops, you don't buy it, you can't gift it. It's inside you and the only way to share it is moments exactly like the one he'll be living – on stage, with a crowd of other believers whose lives are brightened simply by the act of celebrating together. Really it's about togetherness.'

'Huh,' she says. 'It's almost enough to make me shed a tear, Flora. Togetherness – you're right. All the bells and whistles are nice, but it boils down to spending time with those you love. And avoiding those you don't. Right, that's your mascara done. You can open your eyes.'

I blink. *'I can see the light!'*

She laughs. 'Now, smoky eyeshadow or are we going for something modern?'

'Can we go low-key? I don't want Connor to think I've gone to any effort for his sake. That would just make it all awkward and I already feel awkward about all this public-speaking malarkey.'

'Just tell him it's for the photographers.' She shrugs as if it's nothing.

'The photographers?'

Raakel opens a compact full of brightly coloured eyeshadows. 'Yeah, the community paper does a ten-page spread every year, with all those involved. You and Connor will be on the front cover for sure, him with his stunning Norse god looks and you his beautiful sidekick.'

I gulp. 'Beautiful sidekick?' I don't want to be a sidekick! I don't want to be photographed. 'I don't want to do this!' My voice rises as panic mounts.

'Do what?' She frowns, looking at the eyeshadow palette.

'Pose for photos, be in a newspaper! It's really not my thing.' How to explain my intense fear of the limelight? People think they're terrified of such things, and rightly so, but I am *more* than terrified. I once landed a job for a jewellery store, announcing

184

their sale pieces on a microphone, and it did not go well. I lasted less than five minutes. I'm not made for the stage. I'm built for behind the scenes. Party girl, I am not. Unless it's a Christmas party and even then, I don't want to be front and centre.

'Oh, Flora embrace it! You're beautiful and funny and you're going to have a great night. Why not let them snap some pictures so you have a memento of the occasion?'

'I always seem to have my eyes closed in photos. I look *wooden*.'

She gives my shoulder a comforting squeeze. 'The trick is to widen your eyes slightly more than normal and blow out your cheeks before you smile. Then the picture will be perfect. Let me demonstrate.' Raakel demonstrates by widening her eyes and filling her cheeks with air like a puffer fish before breaking into a wide smile. 'See?'

I smother a grin. 'OK, I'll give that a try.'

'So, let's go with a gentle smoky eye, yeah?'

I'm a little dubious but I give in. 'Yeah, OK.' I'm only half-listening and I imagine everything that could go wrong, instead.

Once my make-up is done, we raid Raakel's jewellery box and find some gold bracelets and diamante earrings. 'It feels weird not to wear my Christmas jewellery.'

'Just for tonight, dress to impress.'

I lift a palm. 'I guess. What if I get to the restaurant and Connor is wearing his lumberjack jacket and I'm all sleek and sparkly?'

She shakes her head. 'It's about the photographers, remember?'

'Oh, yeah. I just feel so overdressed for a community event in winter.'

'You'll have your jacket over the top of all of this.' Raakel goes behind me and does up a thin gold necklace.

'True. OK, well, that's it then?' I feel faint from all the nervous energy, as if the adrenaline has spiked and now I'm left with the come-down.

'Ready to see the transformation?'

'Ready as I'll ever be.'

She opens a cupboard to reveal a skinny full-length mirror. The Flora who stares back wears an astonished expression. 'Wow, Raakel, wow.' Her make-up technique has brought out the blue in my eyes, and the contouring makes me look as though I've got high cheekbones, giving me a haughty look. 'This really is a Christmas miracle!'

Raakel beams. 'Who knows what the night will bring?'

'Gut-wrenching nausea probably. Why did I think forcing Connor on stage was a good idea?'

'Roll with it, Flora. You're quite the talk of the town, so use it to your advantage. It's gone down the vans like a game of ping pong, and the stories have a life of their own now. Clear up one thing for me, is it true that Connor chose you over Aine earlier today? Word is, he shut her down a few times even though she was flirting up a storm with him. Rumour has it, she made him choose and he chose you.'

I let out a frustrated sigh. The rumour mill here is something else. 'No, not true. Aine asked for a lift into town and he blew her off, that's all. Then she asked for a lift back and he told her he had dinner plans with me.'

'OK, I thought it sounded a little too *Dynasty*. One more thing, did you say she had *fat* ears?'

I bite back laughter. 'I never said she had fat ears!'

'Oh my God, Flora, you did!'

We giggle like schoolgirls. 'Look, I don't know what came over me, but she was batting her lashes like the biggest cliché.' I try to demonstrate but I probably look more like someone in the throes of a nightmare. 'And her voice was all husky and lilting, not snarky like it is when she talks to me and it just riled me up. In front of Connor she acts like this sex goddess, this coquette if you will, when really she's a nasty piece of work who bullies everyone, especially me. So I happened to mention her ears weren't delicate enough for my smaller earrings, that's all.'

'Her ears are tiny, like her mind.'

'Yes! But I didn't let her know that.'

'She's not happy with you.'

I lift a shoulder. 'So same as usual then.'

'Yeah, same as usual. And hey, you're not in charge of everyone's happiness, only your own, so go out and enjoy the night, yeah? Strut on that stage like you own it.'

What she leaves unsaid is that Aine and her gang will be watching my every move and I only get one chance to prove I deserve the honour of being invited on stage. But in reality, that makes it worse, much worse. Still, there's got to be a silver lining in all this.

Jumping out of the comfort zone. Check.

Potentially making Connor believe. Check.

Facing fears. Check.

Oh, and . . . 'I can eat until my heart is content afterwards as a reward.' Check.

'Good plan. If I don't see you in the town square beforehand, I'll see you tomorrow. I want every last detail.'

'Done.'

I give Raakel a hug and head back to my van to wait for Connor . . .

Chapter 24

Connor arrives in a cloud of aftershave, an alpine scent that makes my mouth water. Is that a normal reaction to men's perfume? I glue on a smile so he can't read my mind, and the fact I want to taste his skin. It would only spark all those worries again about me being potentially dangerous. Cannibalistic or something, yikes.

'Wow, Flora, you look stunning.'

Part of me flutters at the compliment. But he's probably just being polite. That's Connor, right? A man with manners who follows the rules. I realise I've left him hanging for too long so I hurry to think of something to say, 'Likewise. You smell so good I just want to eat you up.' I slap my head. *Twit, Flora, pull yourself together!* 'Sorry, I have this thing with perfumes; they always make me hungry. Rationally I know they're just a bunch of chemicals mixed together, but still . . . they conjure this . . . thing and I think I'll leave it at that.' I don't know what else to say and *stop talking, Flora!*

'It's OK. I get it.'

'I'm nervous, so excuse me. I'm not myself. I'm quite literally beside myself.' I feel like I'm outside of my body, standing next to this Flora who says idiotic things. On a fear scale of one to ten

I'm at a hundred for public speaking. Public viewing. But one must make these sacrifices for the greater good.

'Don't be. We'll plonk on the star, we'll flick the switch, say Happy Yuletide and get the hell out of there.'

'Well, that's reassuring and all but surely we'll need to say a bit more than that? Plonking the star on doesn't seem right. You'll have to make a real show of it, won't you? And as for the switching on of the lights, it's like a metaphor for the season. Turning on the lights signifies it's time to switch on their hearts and think of others. It's time to—'

Connor interrupts, his face impassive. 'No, no, I'm sure it's nothing of the sort. People don't care. We'll be in and out in five minutes if I have my way.'

'*People don't care!* Connor have a listen to yourself! People *do* care – that's why they take their families from warm cosy homes and head out into the arctic temperatures to celebrate with their friends. It's more than a social thing, it's a celebration of another year gone, and the anticipation of what's to come, if only you believe. You can't rush it; you can't do that to them.'

'Why drag it out? They want to see the pretty lights, mill around with their friends while eating a whole bunch of Finnish food and glugging *gløgge*. That's it.'

He *still* doesn't get it! 'Look let's just go.' I'm sure he'll be a changed man once he turns to his adoring crowd and sees the light in their eyes at the official beginning of the season. I need to be patient and wait for the miracle to happen. As much as I'd love to dash on and off stage, we can't do that. The crowd needs to be wowed, and in turn that will change Connor once and for all.

We head into town in Connor's car and park down a side street. While I'm panicking about where I left my phone, Connor comes around and opens my door like a gentleman. I thought that kind of thing only ever happened in the movies. Hallmark movies, in fact. Has he been doing some research or is that part of his impeccable manners? Either way, it's sweet.

'Thank you, you're a gentleman. And yet you don't have an ounce of Christmas spirit in you. It doesn't make sense.'

He laughs. 'We've had this talk, Flora.'

'If you don't believe you won't receive.'

He frowns. 'Receive what?'

'Presents from Santa, Connor. The goodwill of others.'

We wander into the square and find it jam-packed with wrapped-up locals. Stalls sell roasted chestnuts, and *piparkakut* a traditional Finnish gingerbread. There's a sign for the ultimate comfort food *riisipuuro* otherwise known as rice pudding, mugs of steaming hot cocoa and warm pastries. The scent of Christmas – a mix of nutmeg, vanilla, star anise – is heavy in the icy air.

'Aw, everyone is dressed up. Look.' I point to a little girl dressed as a snowman, and little boy in a gingerbread man costume. 'Look how cute they are! They make me yearn to have my own children, who I can festively dress from November onwards. They'd need matching Christmas-themed bedding and—'

'Is there such a thing as Christmas-themed bedding?'

I blush. When will I learn not to muse out loud? 'Is there . . . ? Are you a Martian or something? How do you live in this Christmas utopia and not know there's such a thing as Christmas bedding? You can even get quilt covers to match your Christmas onesie.'

'Is that the fluffy thing with a tail you were wearing when you arrived?'

'Yes. It's very comfortable for driving and it's super warm so not only does it look the part, it's practical too. You'd look good in one. Although . . .' I give him a once-over '. . . I don't know if they make them in your size.'

'Shame.'

'Yeah.'

We come to a small government-looking building and wander into the warmth inside. Connor leads us to an office with a door slightly ajar. 'We're about to meet the who's who of this so-called Christmas extravaganza. They're going to give us our instructions for the evening so I'm counting on you to remember the details. Hanne emailed them about me and since then I've been bombarded with replies. I notice you never seem to get sucked into the vortex of these things, Flora, even though you start them. Why is that?'

The who's who? My nerves ratchet up. For some reason I always feel uncomfortable around dignitaries and the like. While I'm an adult, I feel more like a teenager around those types. They spend their days making important decisions, while I spend mine wondering what Christmas outfit will most match my mood. 'Important people?' I blurt.

'If you believe in such a thing, then I guess so. But they're just people, same as you and me.' I give Connor one of my sparkiest smiles but I think it must come across maniacal because he frowns. 'Are you OK, Flora?'

I can only nod. This night just keeps getting worse. Connor senses my unease and takes my hand, leads me to the office and introduces me to the town mayor, Mr Something Something who is passionate about *something*. I'm still sizzling from Connor's touch and my nerves so I miss half the introduction and what the mayor says to me. All the words blend into one monotonous sound so I tune out as anxiety takes hold. Nothing to fear, I just smile and let out a twinkling little laugh and hope he wasn't expecting an answer. I'm met with a look of confusion, dammit, so I say. 'Yes, of course.'

And both men nod and smile. Bullet safety dodged. Is it hot in here? Their words are in slow mo. I can't make sense of a *thiiiing*.

The mayor goes over the timing or something of the evening and I soon zone out, figuring it's best to focus on breathing and staying alive as a strange fog comes over me.

'Ready?' Connor asks, jolting me from my reverie.

'For what?'

A look of disquiet passes across his features. 'For the festivities? I'll meet you on the stage and we'll turn on the lights together?'

'OK, right, yes, the festivities.' I stand rooted to the spot as if superglued.

'How about I walk you out first?' he says.

Connor places a hand at my lower back, to propel me, or to unglue me, who can tell? We walk to the stage and my legs . . . I can't feel my legs, as I see thousands of people staring up at me. I'm a goldfish in a bowl and it's downright terrifying. What if I make a mistake? What if the words freeze on my tongue when I'm mid-speech?

Connor squeezes my hand to reassure me. I get stuck staring into those mesmerising eyes of his and I must hold on too long as he slowly unlaces my grip, and my sweaty palm falls limply to my sides. 'Flora,' he leans close and whispers in my ear, his breath hot on my neck. The sensation makes me feel giddy and it's all too much. I swoon as he catches me in his arms. Is it him causing this strange sensation or the millions and trillions of people gawping at me? I can't be this close to the man; he's sending me cuckoo. 'I'll be back as quickly as I can.'

'Quicker,' I say between clenched teeth.

He pecks me on the cheek and I let out a 'Gahflark.' I try and smile at the crowd but it's more like baring my teeth, because I can't actually feel my lips anymore. Do I even have lips at this point? Maybe it's the adrenaline coursing through me, but I feel disconnected, sort of like I'm standing above myself and can only feel half of my body.

I give myself a silent pep talk: *Flora, this is about making him believe!*

With my arms wrapped tightly around myself I try to will mind, body and soul back into the moment. Connor races up the ladder like it's not at a great height, and somehow I still have the presence of mind to worry about him taking the rungs so fast. He plonks the glittery star on top, turns to the crowd and waves and is down again before I can blink but maybe that's because I can't seem to blink either. Is he a changed man? Hard to tell as I turn back to the crowd and am once again frozen. Why are they staring in my direction? If only I could make my body move and then I'd run! I'd sprint, even. But it's like my boots are glued to the stage, and I can't move my limbs.

'I'm back,' Connor says and takes my hand.

'Back.' I stare, dumbstruck, at the crowd.

'Are you OK, Flora?' He gives my cold hand a squeeze.

'No, not OK.' Not even Connor staring at me can break the spell.

'Do you want to leave?'

My brain is in a fog. 'Rally. The. Crowd.'

'OK, we can do this, eh? Remember what the mayor said about . . .'

Connor keeps talking but I feel a rush of nausea and I do all I can to stem the feeling. Swallow it down. I do not want to *consider* what such a thing might mean. Do not want to picture any projectiles from my own body. I do not feel good.

Connor's voice is white noise. A sweet droning sound.

'OK?' he asks.

'Ahem,' I manage.

His eyebrows pull together. Even his eyebrows are nice. Manly. *Get me out of here!*

Connor drags me towards the podium – it's like my legs are made from lead – and taps the microphone. 'Hello, one and all! Flora and I wanted to officially welcome Christmas with good tidings to everyone.'

Am I imagining it or are the crowd turning? I'm not seeing smiles, I'm seeing a sea of orange candlelit faces like something ghoulish out of a horror movie.

'Ready, Flora?' he asks. 'Are you still happy to do the honours?'

The honours? Maybe I should have listened to the instructions instead of whatever the hell I was doing. How hard can it be? Flick a switch and then I can get off this bloody stage!

'Yes.'

193

I look down to the podium table and see about a hundred small buttons. 'Which one?'

'The red one on the—'

I press it hard and instead of lights Christmas carols start, too loud in the still night air.

'Not that one, the—'

How many red buttons can there be? In desperation, I press another and the spotlights above us turn off and we're thrown into darkness. Panic looms. I press every goddamn button I can and bedlam breaks out. Children scream. Parents yell. There're a few sniggers.

Connor grabs my shaking hands and says, 'Stop, Flora, stop. Let me.' He holds me tight to his side while he presses a button and the spotlights come back on, the carols end.

'Sorry, folks, slight technical glitch,' he says in a very unflustered, even tone. 'Without further ado, Merry Christmas!' He presses the goddamn red button that was front and centre all along. It reads: 'Town Christmas lights'. They mercifully spring on, flashing and shining while the crowd goes wild. 'We hope you enjoy the evening and we look forward to seeing you all at the Christmas market throughout December. Oh and . . . there is no Hollow Earth civilisation. Cryptocurrency is a digital asset using a technology called blockchain. Elon is a robot and that concludes my part of the festivities. Enjoy your evening!'

He threads his fingers through mine and leads me off the stage. The town mayor is there, wearing a stupefied expression. 'Sorry,' Connor says. 'I got myself mixed up with all the excitement. It's done now and I've got to get Flora . . . home. So see you around.'

They shake hands and I give him a weak smile.

'You didn't need to lie for me, Connor, and I'm fairly certain everyone saw me stabbing buttons like the bomb was about to go off.' He shrugs as if it's nothing. 'Do you really think there's no civilisation in Hollow Earth?' He shakes his head.

'Well, there *is* a Hollow Earth and there lives my doppelgänger, Flora who has it all together. That Flora is wise, and confident and successful and knows how to wow a crowd.'

The further away we get from the crowd the more the feeling comes back to my body.

'I like this Flora just the way she is. But why didn't you tell me you had such bad stage fright? I thought you were going to pass out.' He keeps a protective arm wrapped around me and I don't fight it. I feel safe with him, like he'd be there to catch me when I fall. And I very nearly did – right off that bloody stage.

'Well, you did sort of force my hand. And I thought I could get through it. But now I know that I'm actually physically incapable of such a thing. I *actually* believed I was going to die!'

'That's unlike you. You're usually so level-headed and sensible.'

'Very funny.'

He stops and moves his hands to my shoulders. 'Jokes aside though, are you OK?'

I nod, gazing into those glittery blue pools of his eyes. He's beautiful and he quite snatches the words from my tongue. Once again, I've left the conversation in limbo for too long and hurry to think of a reply, one that makes sense. 'I'm fine but I'm never going to live this down! Everyone from the market witnessed zombie me, a catatonic mess who pressed every button except the right button! I'll be a laughing stock.'

'Not at all. Yeah, they'll have something interesting to talk about this week, but if you just laugh it off as part of the Flora charm, then what does it matter? No one has such an exciting life as you. You own it and then what can they say?'

Gorgeous and clever, what a combo. 'That's good advice.' And just what does he mean by the Flora charm? 'You're just trying to make me feel better.'

'Is it working?'

'A little.' He drops his hands from my shoulders, and slings an arm around me again, cocooning me against him. Warmth emanates from him, despite the cold. We continue down the back cobbled laneways towards his electric car.

'Is that Hanne?' He points to a woman who is definitely Hanne. A Hanne who is not limping and who looks as though she has every one of her ten toes. 'I thought you said she was bed-ridden?'

'That's not Hanne! You need your eyes tested, Connor!'

He squints as if that will make his vision clearer. 'It is, I'm sure it is. She always wears that striped Puffa jacket.'

There's nothing else for it. 'Connor.' I stop and take his face in my hands so he can only look directly at me but as I look up I see that the lampposts are decorated with branches of mistletoe. 'Look, Connor, it's mistletoe.'

He turns to check. 'So it is.'

I'm wary he's still on the lookout for Hanne so I lean on tiptoes and kiss him softly on the lips. A jolt of longing goes through me, as we pull away and stare at each other; for a moment I'm lost to him, to what could be. He doesn't speak, so I hurry to fill the silence. 'One must follow Christmas traditions.'

'Yes,' he says, his voice husky. I grasp his hand and lead him to the car in case Hanne makes another unexpected appearance. My heart, my poor heart, can't take any more excitement for one night. I brush my fingers over the place where his lips touched mine and feel that strange sense of longing again. As brief as it was, I've never felt such euphoria with a kiss in my life. Connor sure has some magic about him; if only he was the settle-down sort, which I know he isn't, nomad that he is.

He shoots me a strange look, as if he's confused. He does that a lot like he can't quite work me out. 'If you're still up to it, would you like to get dinner?' he asks eventually.

'I'd love to. Near-death experiences make me ravenous.'

'Then let's eat.'

I decide to put the disaster out of my mind, so of course it plays back reel by reel. Then I remember Raakel mentioning the town photographer. 'You didn't see anyone taking photos, did you? I hope there's no photographic proof of my fall from grace.'

'No, I didn't see anyone. I was only looking at you, Flora.'

'Oh, OK.' He was literally only looking at me because I messed up the annual tradition of turning on the town Christmas lights, because I was too distracted to listen to instructions. He wasn't looking at me for any other reason, so I need to stop that train of thought right now. *Flora! You just kissed the guy and it's not like he swept you up in his arms and deepened the kiss, is it?* Part of me wilts, at the thought that he doesn't feel the same way as me. And just how do I feel? Like he could be the man of my dreams. He behaved exactly like a Hallmark hero, so I'm bound to feel a buzz. It's not real. It's imagined. Time to distract myself and get back to the real world and the problem at hand.

'So how did that feel, being the big man on stage, the one who starts their Christmas with a . . . bang? Did you feel all their love and joy radiate?'

He laughs. 'No, all I thought about was getting you off that stage, Flora, as quickly as I could without making it look obvious that we had a problem.'

How could he feel the magic when I went and ruined it? *Again!*

Chapter 25

The idea of dining at a fancy restaurant doesn't seem so intimidating anymore. I can handle a tuxedo-wearing waiter asking me in another language what I'd like to order because it's only two eyes staring at me, and not five million.

The charming waiter points to his recommendation on the menu. 'Umm, yes, I'll have that,' I say, not sure what he's on about and whether I ordered wine or food but willing to live in the moment.

'You just ordered *mykyrokka*,' Connor says.

'Yes, been dying to try that for ages.' I thrust out my chin as if I've been fine dining in Finland my whole bloody life.

'You've been dying to try blood dumpling soup?' Connor says. 'Quite the culinary neophile, eh?'

'The what? Oh no, I don't want that! I'll have the chicken! Ah, *kana*, the *kana*!' I say desperately to the waiter. If all else fails, go for the chicken – isn't that the way of the world?

Connor laughs and orders the same. I'm strung out and a dish of *blood dumplings* might just put me over the edge.

'I basically want comfort food and lots of it,' I say. 'If you could translate that too?'

Connor finishes ordering for us both. The waiter nods, lays

our napkins over our laps and glides off. I toy with the napkin, grateful it's linen so I can't shred it in my anxious state. Before long, the waiter returns with a bottle of red and a decanter, and makes a performance of opening the bottle and filling the vessel so the wine can breathe, as if it's a living thing.

'Ooh, fancy.'

'Do you like red wine? I should have asked; it's just that I've seen you imbibing once or twice and assumed.'

'You've been stalking me again, Connor?'

Surprised laughter spills from his mouth. It's loud and draws the startled attention of the other diners. He doesn't notice or doesn't care and it makes me like him even more. This kind of environment is like any other to him, whereas I always feel like I'm not quite good enough to be in a place like this. As though they'll sense I'm a fraud and that I don't know a thing about grape varieties – all I know is there is red, white and rosé. Don't know a thing about the cutlery. How much to order and what goes with what. Give me a good old-fashioned Italian home-style trattoria any day. The kind of place that's loud with banging and crashing and laughter in the kitchen, so the diners have to yell over the din. That's where I'm most comfortable.

'I haven't been stalking you, Flora. In fact, I would go so far as to say you've been stalking me, but what would I know? I'm not a methodical homicidal maniac like you are.'

'Not yet, that is.'

He laughs. 'Yes, to the red?'

'Has it had enough time to breathe?' The waiter mentioned he'd be back to pour for us, as if our arms are useless in this situation.

He waves me away. 'Do we care?'

'No, not at all. I need that wine like I need oxygen. It'll help me forget.'

'But tomorrow it'll all come crashing back.'

'Live for today, Connor – don't you know the Van Life mantra?' He fills our wine glasses.

'Of course. Cheers.' We clink glasses. 'Congratulations for facing your fears and jumping out of your comfort zone on stage tonight.'

'Cheers, and here's to me knowing my limits and never doing that again. In future I'll stay well *within* the lines of my comfort zone, where strangely I feel *comfortable*. So why Lapland, Connor? What brought you here?'

He takes a slug of wine. A big slug. Nothing he does is small. 'I've been travelling since I was sixteen, about fifteen or so years now. I've gone from one place to another so there's nothing that mysterious about it really. I hadn't been to Lapland and it was the next place on the map.'

'Let me guess, you were looking for that nebulous thing you can't quite explain.' I can't help but tease him.

'No, looking for work.'

'That's so unromantic!' How can he not feel like this is a gift? This nomadic life where he can go anywhere, be anything? He makes it sound like a chore. Or like he's on the run from his old life, or something.

'OK, fine, you want romantic then you shall have it. I'm connected to the earth, rather than to people or ideas. I go where I know there's beautiful scenery, a place I can fall in love with. Wherever I go, I try and make each place that little bit better than it was when I arrived, by doing things like community clean-ups, in some cases educating about plastics. I know it sounds like I'm obsessed but it's all about preserving what we have; protecting ecosystems.'

So his motivation for looking after the earth stems from wanting to keep it beautiful and natural so it can be enjoyed.

He continues, 'When the place fizzles out, I move on again. I'm not searching for anything except enough work to survive and to tide me over when I want to be on the move again.'

'But isn't that just as dreamy as the whole falling for this way of life thing? I think underneath that big gruff exterior there's a soft heart. You must be searching for *something*, otherwise you'd be at home.'

'There is no home to return to, not for me, Flora.' His words are even, level, but almost emotionless, which strikes me as odd, as if he's just making small talk about insignificant things.

'What do you mean there's no home to return to? Everyone comes from somewhere. You must have a base you can return to if you needed – family, siblings?'

'No, there's none of that for me.'

I stare at him, willing him to share more. I sense this is why Connor is so reserved, strung so tight. There's a story here and I presume it's not a happy one. I place my hand over his, and am quickly distracted by how well they fit together despite the size difference. 'Why, what happened to your family, Connor?'

'It's a bit of a saga, and one I don't usually share.'

'I'd like to hear it. I want to know more about you.'

He takes an age to reply, as if he's considering whether he can trust me with such a thing. I wait him out, hoping he will. 'Things weren't great at home. My father was strict to the point of being controlling. Mum and I walked on eggshells around the guy. But it had always been that way, so we just got on with it.'

Sounds like his father had been cold. Cold and mean.

'I never saw my father smile. Not once. It was as though he didn't have feelings, or lacked emotional connection with us. It hurt when I was old enough to figure out that not all dads were like that.'

'I'm sorry, Connor. No child deserves to be frozen out like that.'

He shrugs as if it's nothing but I know there's years of pain there. 'When I was sixteen one Sunday I caught the train to the next town over, when Dad was at his "second job" and instead found him with his "second family".'

Shock knocks me sideways. 'He had a second family?'

His jaw works, so as much as he tries to play this down I know it's cut him deep. 'Yeah, they were playing football on this big

201

expanse of green, and one of the little kids tripped over the ball, and my father ran up to him and held him in his arms, smiling and encouraging him that he'd kick the next goal, not to worry, they had all day to play. I was struck in that moment, and I felt such confusion. I'd *never* seen my dad smile, not once in my life. Not on my birthday, not at Christmas, not ever, and here he was dishing out smiles to these two children and a young woman, much younger than my mum. These strangers, his second family, held his heart and got the happy version of him, and we got the bitter angry leftovers.'

Well, no wonder he doesn't believe in much. I bet everything stopped for the sixteen-year-old Connor the day his heart was shattered by the man who was supposed to love him unconditionally. 'Connor, that's heart-wrenching. Did he see you; did you talk to him that day?' My heart breaks. Who could do that? Hide behind two lives, like that? And why? Why not admit you're in love with someone else and stop ruining innocent people's lives? Two innocent people who deserved so much better.

'He saw me. I had a bit of stage fright, like you did tonight, in that I was frozen to the spot as this whole family tableau played out in front of me. I knew they were his children, because they looked exactly like me at that age. Eventually, he saw me standing at the edge of the park, and his face dropped, but he didn't come over, didn't acknowledge me at all.'

My blood boils. How could any father do such a thing? But I want to be supportive of Connor opening up to me. 'What did you do next?' I caress his hand across the table, hoping it helps him know I care. I'm right there with him in that moment, all the way back then.

'Once the shock wore off, it was quickly replaced by anger. I went home and told my mum and she cried and cried. You know, it explained a lot. He must've felt we kept him from them, so he made us suffer in silence. My mum tried to console me, but I was so mad. We'd been living under the roof of this dictator for so long when he was living this double life, a life that obviously made him happy. I knew I could never respect the man again. I could never look into his eyes and listen to him. He was the worst kind of hypocrite.'

Our entrées arrive but they remain untouched. 'What did your mum say?'

Connor averts his eyes and takes a deep breath as if to steady herself. 'I think my mum suspected all along. She must've known there was no second job and that was code for his other family but she loved him so she let it be. I couldn't though. I packed my clothes. I told her I had to leave and she said she understood. She gave me some money she had hidden away, almost like she knew this day would come, and she told me with tears in her eyes if she could give me one piece of advice it would be: "Don't do what I did – don't settle. Go and explore the world and never look back".'

'So that's why you started this?' I feel so despairing for the boy he was back then. Unmoored, alone. Broken.

'That's how it all began and I've been on the road ever since.' It explains why Connor never wants to settle. He probably doesn't ever want to fall in love either – he'd have trust issues big enough to build a wall so solid no woman could climb it.

'Did you ever see your dad again?'

'No, and I never want to.'

'Did he try?' Surely the man cared about his first son enough to try and find him and see if he was OK?

'He's tried to contact me on social media through the years, but I never respond. What's the point?'

'What does he say?'

'Things like he couldn't help how he felt, he'd fallen in love with the other woman and he knew he'd made mistakes raising me. He tried to correct those mistakes with his new kids. I hated him for that though, as if I was the practice child. My whole life had been a lie.'

'What about your mum? Do you visit her still?'

'Mum died a few months after I left. I think her heart actually broke and it killed her.'

The air in the room grows heavy. 'Connor . . .' I don't know what to say to convey all the emotions I feel for him and what he's been through.

'It's OK, Flora. Truly. It's such a depressing story – that's why I never share it with anyone, but it hasn't been as bad as it sounds. As soon as I started my travels, I discovered how free I could be, how somehow my mum knew I'd relish this new, unstructured life. I've been all over the world and each day I felt that I was growing into the person I was always meant to be, not caged, not owned.'

I take a sip of wine while I try and process everything. From what I can gather, Connor has spent the last fifteen years hopping from one place to the next and he's still alone. Everyone needs their own people; does Connor have his?

'So have you ever fallen in love? Found someone who lit up your soul? Collected friends along the way?'

'We should eat,' he says.

I take up my fork but press on. 'Connor, have you made any connections along the way?'

'Yeah, sure. I've had relationships, I've had friendships, but things never last when you're of no fixed address. You'll see that too, Flora, if you continue on your travels.'

'But if you had a strong connection with someone, surely you'd move heaven and earth to be together . . . wouldn't you?'

'No. Nothing lasts – that's what I know for sure. I wouldn't tie myself down to a feeling, an emotion, something that's guaranteed to change. What's the point?'

My heart sinks. He's so damaged he can't form attachments on the off chance he'll be hurt again. 'The point is building a rich and full life. Just because yours started off on such an unstable foundation doesn't mean you should give up. Don't you want to find love? Have children? Know your best friend will be there in a flash if your world falls apart?'

204

'No, I'd rather rely on myself. That way I can't be let down.'

I've quite lost my appetite. 'That's so sad, Connor.'

'I don't think it's sad. It's common sense.'

Connor is so lost inside the past – is it even possible to pull him back from that? It's no wonder the joy of Christmas is a mystery to him. He can't imagine the gathering of family around the dinner table, the anticipation of opening a gift that took weeks to find, the wacky matching festive jammies for the annual Christmas card, because he's never known that kind of love. All he's known is disappointment and his own father breaking his heart and teaching him no one is trustworthy.

'I'm not going to harp on about this, Connor, because I know you don't share your past with many people, and I'm honoured you chose me . . .' *Flora, think before you speak, do not ruin his decision to confide in you!* 'But you have to change! You have to fall in love. It would be a crying shame if you didn't give yourself the chance to be a father, if that's what you want, just because of the way your own father treated you. I *know* you'd raise your child the opposite way your dad raised you! You'd *smile*; you'd smile all the time. And I can see your little blond-headed lion of a boy on your big strong shoulders. Why would God give you such broad shoulders if it wasn't for carrying your children around? Have you ever thought of that?

'And what about love – maybe I'm working backwards here, but love, Connor! It will set your world on fire, and even if you have itchy feet and the desire to keep wandering the earth, the girl you love will be right there beside you, because wherever you are is home to her. Don't you see? You're wasting your life because your dad was a screw-up! He's probably languishing in family life, and you're alone and lonely and still living this solitary existence and it's just not right!' I run out of breath.

'Is that all, Flora?' He arches a brow.

Colour rushes up my cheeks. I'd been a sentence away from sticking my hand up for the position. Only to show the poor man that love exists! 'A couple more things – life is worth taking a chance on. Even the most damaged hearts can heal. Don't let him win, by living in the shadows. That's all for now.'

'I'm not that guy, Flora. I'll never be that guy.'

Oh yes, you bloody well will be if it's the last thing I do. 'OK,' I smile sweetly. 'Have you read that book about the man who circumnavigated the globe?' A subject change is in order so we can enjoy the rest of our night. As Connor talks, I'm only half listening while I think of all the ways I can make this guy believe. Not just in Christmas but in living life to the full; in taking risks with his heart . . .

Chapter 26

'His dad had two families?' Livvie screeches on screen, the next morning. I'm tired from the late night with Connor. Stupidly, I asked him to dinner this evening but he said he had other plans. That he had to catch up on work. Whatever that means. So I'm also licking my wounds in the privacy of my van.

I lean back on my pillow and expel a breath. 'His whole backstory is so sad, Liv. It's no wonder he's so closed off. It's a clear case of Damaged Past 101. It's tragic and I can see why he is the way he is. He's never learned to form attachments; in fact that's anathema to him. There's a bitterness in him that will surely turn him sour if I don't fix this.'

'Eurgh.'

'What's that supposed to mean?' I lift my head from the pillow.

She purses her lips before saying, 'Flora, I don't know. It sounds like he's been through the wringer and if he's gone *fifteen years* without making any firm friendships, or relationships, it's probably not going to happen. Maybe he's not the Hallmark hero I pegged him for. Could we have been so very wrong?'

'Are you saying give up on him?' My voice rises. Livvie is not the sort to give up.

'I'm saying the guy seems to want to be left alone. Why do you think changing him is a good idea?'

'I'm not going to *change* him; he's perfect the way he is. I'm going to get him to open up his heart. It's two different things!'

She gasps. 'Oh my God. You LOVE him!'

I don't dare tell her about the brief kiss we shared when I had to distract him from looking at Hanne. She'll see love written all across my face even if it's *not* love. It's just . . . something unexplainable. 'Don't speak in capitals to me! I do not love him, that's such a ridiculous thing to say! I'm here to SAVE him!'

'Save him from what?' she says, dubious.

I try to hide my true feelings and make a mental note to stop using video call so Livvie can't tell what I'm thinking just by looking at me. 'From himself! Oh, Liv you're usually so understanding, what aren't you getting here? Is LA changing you, *already*?'

She laughs. 'LA is not changing me, you troublemaker. I can see where you're coming from, but I feel like you need to tread carefully with Connor. His childhood sounds messed up and it's obviously shaped him into the person he is today, for very good reason. You can't just wave your magic wand, and he's suddenly fixed. That sort of stuff lasts a lifetime.'

I harrumph. 'Well, I can at least try. I want Connor to know that I care. Out of this big, wide world, there's one person who'll be patient—'

'You're not patient.'

'Right, well out of this big, wide world, there's one person who truly cares with no hidden agenda.'

'OK, but aren't *you* leaving the market in a few weeks? Then what?'

'I guess I have to make this miracle happen before I go.' The thought of leaving takes a bit of my sparkle away. Van Life is about always being on the move but I guess I'm the opposite to Connor and form attachments fast. Leaving will be a wrench. But I can't for the life of me imagine never seeing Connor again. Just the thought hurts.

'Then Operation-Make-Him-Believe needs to step up a notch. What's next?'

I let out a sigh. 'We need to work on him connecting to others, like feeling he's part of a whole, and not the outsider. Like we did for the Christmas lights, but this time, have it not end in disaster.'

'An impromptu Christmas party?'

'Yes! I'll gather together some of the Van Lifers, we'll swap stories around the campfire and . . . wait.'

'Wait? Why?'

I swipe my hair from my eyes. 'I don't know, I think he'll sneak back to this office when I take my eyes off him. He's really not a joiner.'

'OK, so why not start with a more intimate setting? Why don't you take a reindeer ride or something? Something a little more intimate, just you and him and the reindeer . . .'

'You're brilliant, Liv.'

'I know.'

'So how is life in LA? Has the sun bleached your brain yet?'

She guffaws. 'What's that supposed to mean?'

'Oh, it's a well-known phenomenon that the Malibu sun bleaches sunbakers' brains and then they never want to leave.'

'Right, well the old brain is still firing on all cylinders. The skincare line is being tested and so far the results have been positive. If all goes according to plan we'll have it out in stores within two years.'

'*Two* years!'

'I know, I know, there's a million and one safety tests to take and it goes on and on.'

'So will you stay in LA for two years now?'

There's silence.

'Liv?'

'Maybe. Maybe more like a year and a half.'

'Far out, you *have* been sunbaking!'

'In winter?'

209

'Your delicate English rose complexion can probably only handle the gentle winter sunshine.'

She laughs. 'True. Lucky I know someone with a good skin-care range. And what's six more months in the scheme of things? It's not like you're in London. You won't be missing me. I bet you keep on in that van of yours, with nary a thought for me.'

'Hardly. But I'll drag you back from La-La land if I need to. Have you heard from Jasper?'

'Sort of. But I've had virtually no free time.'

'No free time to send a few quick texts even?'

'Is there any point now, Flora? A year and a half is a long time to make him wait.'

'God you're just like Connor. How can this be?'

'Maybe we're both just practical people.'

'Not on my watch.'

'I do miss Jasper,' she admits.

'So why not say how you feel? People like you are why there are so many conflicts in rom-coms. Why it takes so long to get to the happy ever after.'

'I don't want to pressure him. Can you imagine? Hey, I miss you, but I'm half a world away and there's nothing either of us can do since we both have jobs we love and different lives, but let that sink in and then we can do absolutely nothing about it.'

I sigh. 'You can video-call, take him for a walk along Venice Beach, show him LA from your phone! You can text, email and make a date to meet for a holiday – you do take holidays in the city of angels, don't you?'

'Yeah, I guess.'

'So, are you going to be a grown-up and tell him how you're feeling?'

'Gah, maybe, but if this backfires, it's all your fault.'

'I'm fine with that.'

'I miss you, festive Flora. Life sure is different without you.'

'Same! My van is a total mess because there's no one to nag me about cleaning it up.'

'Well, you'd better get it cleaned up in case you have a man sleep over . . .'

'I hardly think so!' I say, scandalised.

'Send me a proper picture of Connor. I want to see this Nordic god myself when he's not in his Buddy the Elf costume.'

'Hang on, I'll do it now.'

'You've already got one?'

'Yeah, I stole it from the Christmas market website.'

'Why?'

I pause the photo search on my phone. I can't think why I saved it. 'As a safety precaution. He did follow me here, after all.'

'He works there!'

'That's all hearsay.'

'Is it? Flora, it looks like you need to take a bit of your own advice and admit how—'

'Stop. I have one job and one job only: to make him believe and hope to get permission to use my bloody gingerbread house before I leave the market so I can recoup at least some of the rent I bloody well paid for it.' I find the photo and hit send.

Livvie fiddles with her phone to open the photo. 'Ohhh, Flora. Whoa, he's a living, breathing Braveheart! Jesus, now all the pieces are slotting into place. Help the damn guy realise what *love* is all about because PHWOAR, he's bloody gorgeous.'

'It's his mind I like.'

'Yeah, I bet you do!'

We fall into screaming heaps of laughter.

Chapter 27

The next evening we're sitting around a campfire, enjoying the end of another long, busy day. A group of young local kids have huddled together to enact a Christmas scene. They're dressed in period costumes to look like the three wise men and King Herod.

'It's called *tiernapojat*,' Eevi says. 'Very sweet the first time you see it performed.'

I nod, listening to their sweet voices as they sing and act their parts to perfection. Once they're finished we clap and throw some coins into a hat for them as thanks.

'There she is, Freeze-up Flora!' Samuel from Scotland calls out as he comes to sit beside me.

'Is that what they're calling me?'

'Among other things.' He gives me an awkward smile.

I slap my forehead. 'It was a disaster.'

'But so funny. I've never actually seen someone react like that before. It was almost like you'd separated from your body.'

I gasp. 'It was exactly like that! I felt totally numb and like I couldn't move. I'm just glad there were no photographers to catch me in the moment.'

'Erm . . .'

I turn sharply towards him as he averts his eyes. 'Tell me there are no photos, Samuel.'

'O-K. There are no photos.'

Who should walk over swinging a newspaper in her hand at that exact moment, but Aine. I really shouldn't have made the comment about her ears – reap what you sow and all that.

'Flora's made the cover!' she says gleefully so I know it's not a flattering photo.

'Let's see.'

'You wouldn't understand it anyway, it's in Finnish. Let me read the article for everyone.'

Oh God, there's an article?

'The headline reads: Festive Fiasco!'

'I wouldn't go that far . . .' I say but all eyes are on Aine.

'There's never been an incident in the fifty-year history of Lovinskaa's annual Christmas light display until brash, bossy newcomer Flora Westwood arrived in town.'

Brash, bossy newcomer? 'They did not say that! Give me that newspaper.' She takes a step back so I can't snatch it from her.

'Ms Westwood chose not to listen to instructions so when it came time to turn on the lights, disaster struck. Not only did Flora ruin the evening, she may have just ruined Christmas as the cries from children sounded high into the frigid evening air.'

'I did no such thing! Give me that!' I snatch the paper from her but can't read the bloody Finnish words. Instead I see a hideous picture of me, mouth agape like I'm comatose, eyes wide like I've just found out Santa isn't real, and looking like I'm knock-kneed. My lovingly applied smoky eyes appear panda-like, as though I'd been rubbing at my face the whole time – which perhaps I had, now I think of it. It has a distinct look of the caricature about it. I can't believe I kissed Connor while looking like something from fright night!

'You look uh . . . amazing in that dress,' Samuel says, trying to bolster my ego. I do not look amazing in that dress, because you can't even see the bloody thing under my voluminous Puffa jacket. I look like a big, round, inflatable mass of black.

I play it cool, remembering Connor's advice to laugh it all off. 'Thanks, I especially like it how it brings out the black under my eyes.'

'Ah, yeah.'

Aine sits opposite me with a smug look on her smug face. 'So do you plan on attending more community events? If so, please let us know – we'd love to come along. Don't want to miss out on any more Flora fiascos.'

'Yeah why not, if they all end with me going out to dinner with Connor afterwards.' I'm a horrible, vengeful person and I don't even care. 'That man is worth a million bad photographs in the paper! And he sure can kiss.' I slap a hand over my mouth as if I've let a secret slip.

'Didn't stay too long though, did he? He was at my van later that night and again the next.' Challenge shines in her eyes. 'And he's coming to my van for dinner again tonight. I'm not the kind to kiss on the first date. But this being the third date, well that's another thing entirely.'

Samuel leans close to whisper, 'Don't let her get to you. That's what she wants.'

Whatever it is it hurts to hear, but I tell him, 'I know.' I face Aine. 'First date, was it? I heard someone made a complaint about you for food poisoning. So was it a date, or did Connor just come to inspect your van for . . . germs?'

'Yeah, well, some jealous soul put in a malicious complaint.' She says it in a way that suggests it was me when I did no such thing. 'Connor came and discussed it with me, long and hard.' She waggles her brows and it's all I can do not to explode. 'Obviously he checked a few things out and realised there was no reason for such a complaint. It was snowing hard outside, so he stayed and we had a few drinks to warm us up . . . He's such a kind-hearted person when you really get to know him. Quite hands-on, in his approach to things. And his tattoos, they go all the way down if you know what I mean. I've never seen such artistry until I saw Connor's . . . I love a man with tatts. He's a wild one.'

Is she lying? She must be lying. Or is Connor one of those men who have mindless one-night stands and think nothing of it? He could very well be that sort of person, if his past is anything to go by. Didn't he admit he'd had a few relationships but nothing serious? I suppose it's none of my business but it makes me want to scream. More so when I remember Connor said he had work to do and refused my invite for dinner the night after the turning on of the Christmas lights. Stupid red wine fool, asking him out again after too many drinks. Only to find he's gone to Aine's instead with the excuse he had work to catch up on.

'Hope he didn't catch anything.' There are a few gasps around the fire. 'From the food, I mean.'

I take the newspaper and wave to the group. 'I'm off to bed. See you all later.'

I stomp away, knowing Aine's got the upper hand this time. Could he really be so shallow as to have locked lips with her? Surely he's got higher standards than that. Yeah, sure she's drop-dead gorgeous, and supermodel-esque but she's got the personality of a dead rabbit.

I take the newspaper to Raakel's van and ask her to translate it for me. She quickly skims it. 'It says no such thing, Flora. It's actually very flattering! It says how lovely it is to have so many Van Lifers in our midst who all join in the fun and get behind the town to help. There's not one bad word here about you.'

'I should have known!'

'Don't let her upset you, Flora. You're playing her game.'

Is there any point continuing my mission to make Connor believe? Is he too damaged, too broken to care? Is he just going to run from one girl to the next? I hate thinking like this, and it's not like Connor and I are *anything*, anyway, but that's how it feels to me. Like he spent one night in my company, found it tedious and then went to Aine for a romp between the sheets or something.

Maybe bringing up his past has brought with it a lot of painful memories and Connor's answer to that is to avoid me.

When things get hard, I usually give up so maybe this is also a chance for me to redeem myself. For the first time ever, I will finish what I've started even if Connor feels awkward around me now after telling me about his past.

I head outside, literally *dashing through the snow*, to get to the front driver's door of the van. For some reason each door of Noël has a different key. I guess over the years, locks were changed as owners came and went. I try to open the driver's door but the key won't go in. I peer closer. Is the lock frozen?

I try and twist and shimmy the key inside but it's no good. Now what? How does one unfreeze a lock? Connor will know. I retrace my steps and barge into his office.

'Can I help you with something, Flora?'

In despair, I lock eyes with the giant who chose Aine over me. I search his face, looking for some evidence of it. Her mark over him, or something, but it's the same Connor as before. Concern in those glittering eyes of his. Those same eyes that probably slowly wandered over her body. I swallow down disappointment. There's the weight of despondency heavy on my shoulders and I can't make sense of it, or why the feeling is so strong that I'm on the brink of tears.

He's still waiting for me to talk, just like normal. I should have gone to Raakel for help and left facing Connor for another day. 'Yes, it appears that my door lock has frozen over, and I can't open the driver's door of the van.' My words come out sounding mechanical. I've never felt this way before, and it strikes me that it could be the very first stirring of real love. It must be. The sensation of falling, so that the world tips. And worse when it's not reciprocated. Stupid heart, choosing the stupid wrong person. Just how long does it take to fall *out* of love? Is it even possible?

'I'll boil the kettle.'

He brings me back to the now with a statement like that. *Boil the kettle!* As if we'll just sit down to tea and pretend nothing has happened. We'll pretend that Aine doesn't exist. 'I don't have time for tea, Connor.'

He grins. 'OK. How about I put the key into boiling hot water and then we try the lock?'

I internally face palm. 'OK, that seems like a sensible plan.'

Once the key is sufficiently boiled, Connor takes it out with a glove and we jog back to my van to try the lock. After a minute, it slips in. 'Wow, I honestly didn't think that would work.'

'Happens all the time as it gets colder.'

I want to tell him I'm onto him, that I know about Aine but I can't. I just want to talk to him, as much as I can before we all leave here. As friends, I guess. To show him that I care; that his past can be shared and the sun will still rise. Deep down, I guess I want Connor to at least try to make a friend out of me, if nothing else. 'Do you want to stay for a drink?'

He thrusts his hands into his jacket pockets. 'I'm good, Flora. I have to catch up on some work.' That old chestnut. Code for: he's got plans with Aine.

With a wave, he's gone, just like that. There's a pain in my chest that feels suspiciously like heartbreak.

I shut the van door and crank up the heat. I still need to give it one last shot with Connor, to make him believe . . . and then at least I'll know I had some impact on him. That there was a reason for us meeting. That it wasn't all for nothing. That my sadness was worth it.

Snow falls hard as Raakel and I are sorting the inside of my van, stashing things in nooks and crannies because the mess has taken over and customers can't find their way inside. We tie thick ribbon along the roof line and I hang shiny baubles along the length of it. They catch in the light and sparkle, sending prisms of colour around the van.

'That looks so pretty!'

'You'll sell more when people can see all the colours like that. What about the dining area? Should we tidy it up so you can display your Santa hats and scarves?'

I glance around. 'Yeah but where will I decorate my wreaths?'

'You can still decorate your wreaths there, but just store your art supplies in the seats when you're not using them.'

'*In* the seats?'

She lifts the top of the seat clean off and exposes a deep drawer. 'Huh, I didn't know that was storage. I can put all my art stuff in those and hide it away.'

'Where can you display the wreaths you've already decorated? They're so lovely, they need to be on show.'

We cast an eye around the space. 'I could hang them down the side of the door, so they'll be safe from the weather but still visible to those walking past.'

'Hooks! I have some gold hooks somewhere.' She checks the box of goodies she brought over. 'We can drill these into the metal.'

'Do you have a drill?'

'No, do you?'

'No, Livvie wouldn't let me bring it.'

'Connor would have one.'

'Yes, he would, but I don't really want to see him right now.'

Raakel shoves the wreaths to one side of the table and takes a seat. 'Why not?'

I sit opposite. 'Surely you've heard about the whole Aine and him thing?'

Her forehead furrows. 'Yeah, sure I've heard all about it.'

'And?'

She lifts a palm. 'And I don't believe her. She's been jealous of you ever since you arrived, Flora. And I can't see Connor and her together. I just can't. Why don't you ask him?'

I rub the back of my neck. 'Because it's none of my business and he'll probably tell me so.'

'Flora . . .' She draws my name out but stops when tears well up in my eyes.

'I need to protect my heart, Raakel. It's just so overwhelming, I thought I'd been in love before, thought I knew what it felt like. But I was wrong. What I feel for Connor . . . it's indescribable and it's also suffocating when I know he doesn't feel the same. That he's not open to a committed relationship. And then the thing with Aine just goes to show what type of man he really is. I feel foolish, thinking he's this god when really he's just like all the others, and yet my silly heart still yearns for it.'

'You really need to tell him how you feel, Flora. Why not risk it and say? What if he's feeling the same way and you let him go?'

I shake my head. 'I'll still be his friend, but that's all. I'm going to make him believe in Christmas and force him to let me have my bloody gingerbread house open to the public if it's the last thing I do. But I need a few days to compose myself before I face him.'

'OK, that's understandable. Give it a few days and maybe things will be clearer and you'll know what to say.'

'Yes, that's what I'll do.'

Raakel drums her fingers on the table. 'Do you think any of these Christmas experiences are changing him?'

I consider it. 'I think they are. After the toy drive he walked around with this dreamy expression on his face, as if he'd made miracles happen. He did the same kind of thing after the Christmas lights once our dinner was done, but maybe that was because we'd had our meal and he could finally drop fiasco Flora home.'

'He's not a very smiley person at the best of times, so you've got to ask yourself why he suddenly is around you.'

'The magic of Christmas is rubbing off on him? Or maybe it's the magic of Aine. Maybe he was so smiley because he knew he was meeting her afterwards. He'd paid his dues with me, so he was free to have fun with her.'

'Umm, no I wouldn't say that. I'd say festive Flora is making his heart beat a little faster.'

I roll my eyes. 'I don't think so. He basically told me in no uncertain terms that he doesn't believe in love or relationships that last any length of time. And then point proven, he's at Aine's as soon as he can escape me!'

'Allegedly.'

'Would Aine make up a story like that? A story any of us could check simply by asking Connor?'

She gives me a look that suggests the answer is yes. 'Have you asked Connor if it's true? No, you haven't. So I think Aine's known all along exactly how to work this to make you give up on Connor, and you're playing right into her hand.'

'It's more complicated than all that.'

'It's really not. Connor only has eyes for you. Any fool can see it. But if you won't make a move or be honest with him, then all you've got left to do is make him believe, and if you can do that, then I know there's magic in the air and that love will conquer all. What are you doing to me, Flora? You're making me into a softie with all this romance talk! I want to knock your heads together so you'll both admit to what you're feeling.'

'No, thank you! I don't want the *I'm not the stay-in-one-place sort* lecture ever again! But I will finish what I started.'

'You do that. Don't let him slip away, Flora.'

'He already has . . .'

'What's next then?' I fill her in on my magical reindeer ride plan, wondering to myself if I really do want to be pressed against him in the sleigh.

'Let's go see, eh?' she says.

'You're going to help me?'

'Of course! Carolina runs the reindeer and is a good friend of mine. Plus I want to see Aine's face when she hears about you and Connor taking a ride together.'

'How will she hear?'

'I'll tell her!'

'You're going to get me in so much trouble.' And I delight in it because I'm a horrible, jealous person and I can't help it.

'I know, isn't it fun?' Her blue eyes shine with mischief.

'Well, what are you waiting for? Let's go!'

We go and visit Carolina who loves the idea of the intervention and thinks Connor will be a changed man once he's taken a sleigh ride with her precious reindeer. 'I'll provide the fluffy throw rug, and the cute-as-a-button reindeer and you bring the champagne and the picnic . . .'

I start. 'Champagne and picnic? Isn't that a bit . . . romantic?'

Carolina and Raakel exchange a glance and if I didn't know better I'd say they have their own operation underway. 'No, everyone does that. It's all part of the ride. I am prohibited from selling alcohol because I don't have a licence; otherwise it'd be a part of the package.'

Makes sense, I suppose. 'OK. I can do that, if it's for the greater good.'

She beams at me. 'Tomorrow evening, meet me at the edge of the forest near the eastern gate.'

'Eastern?'

'Next to the toboggan track.'

'There's a toboggan track!? Why am I only hearing about this now? OK.'

'You'll find a big red sleigh sign affixed there and you'll see the reindeer. Usually, I don't leave my clients in the forest because we are in the Arctic Circle and all . . . but there is a small cabin decorated for Christmas that we use for romantic interludes.' I go to protest but she hurries on. 'Not that this is romantic or an interlude of any sort – but it's a warm, dry place to enjoy the platter of food while the reindeer run back to base and have a rest. There's Christmas lights and it's really a very merry cabin.'

'O-K, that sounds great.' I'm not convinced about being locked away in a cabin as it could be read the wrong way but I suppose

I can easily explain it if he's worried. Besides, it'll be charmingly festive in that cosy cabin so he'll see Christmas isn't just about plastic presents and credit cards, it's about reindeer whisking him into the forest so he can find joy in these moments and take the time to appreciate them. Who knows, maybe he'll whisk Aine away there next. I push the thought from my mind.

Who wouldn't love a private reindeer ride through the snowy forest of Lapland, culminating in a festive feast while we share a nice bottle of bubbles . . . ?

Chapter 28

When I'm tucked up in bed that night, I video-call Livvie.

'Hey! Don't you look cute as a button all rugged up like that?' I'm wearing my Christmas onesie, two blankets and a beanie and mittens and I'm still cold.

'Cute – yeah, that's me.'

She laughs. 'How's it going there?' She peers into the screen. 'What the bloody hell is going on? Why are your eyes so red?'

I try to control the inevitable lip wobble. I can't seem to get hold of my emotions these days. 'I'm fairly sure Connor had a one-night stand with Aine, or it could be a three-day fling, or maybe an eight-day affair, or even—'

'Stop, Flora! What happened?'

I fill Livvie on the whole sorry saga and exactly what Aine implied. 'And I know it all sounds so childish . . .'

'Not at all, darling – you're allowed to feel whatever you want!'

'But the thing is, I think I'm in love with the damn fool, and now he's gone and ruined it all.'

She gasps. 'I KNEW it! No, darling, no – it can't end like this!'

I shake my head sorrowfully. 'It has to. Connor isn't interested anyway.'

'How do you know that?'

'Oh, maybe the fact he keeps saying no when I invite him for dinner or drinks.'

'Could be a life preservation thing. Your cooking is pretty bad.'

I glare at her, and somehow manage to laugh, but I know she's right. How ironic that Aine had the complaint for food poisoning when I'm the master of such a thing.

'You don't see, do you? This is the last hurdle for our hero and heroine! This is the thing they have to work through so we, the audience, know how much they're willing to fight for each other. This is the bloody Hallmark blueprint come to life, and if you can work this out, you're destined to find your happy ever after!' She's clapping and making quite the spectacle of herself on screen.

'Liv, thanks, I get it, I do. But I can't love the guy if he had a thing with Aine. I just can't. And I know you think it's all a rom-com come to life, but Connor isn't feeling what I'm feeling, so you do have to consider that. You really do.'

'Never! Look at you, Flora. You're drop-dead gorgeous, funny and frivolous, and dare I say it, eccentric in the best way. There's no one like you, Flora. There's probably an Aine on every corner.'

'Thank you, darling, what a pep talk, what an ego boost. You're the best of the best when it comes to friends.' I sigh. 'I'm not myself and I don't know what to do. Raakel said it's like a petri dish here, and she's right! Because we're all living in each other's pockets, things tend to be intensified, and this has just got me mixed up and unsure.'

'So, why don't you ask Connor what's going on with him and Aine?'

'No, if he says he likes her or it's just sex, I will die. I will end up hating him and I don't want that.' I blow out a frustrated breath. 'I do really like the damn fool. That's just the problem Livvie, I've gone and fallen for a guy who doesn't stay in one place for long, who doesn't do commitment, or relationships. As far as flawed Hallmark heroes, he tops the list; there's no coming back from this!'

'The course of true love never did run smooth . . .'

'Shakespeare? Really, Liv?'

She gives me a sad smile. 'So you're not going to fess up. What next?'

'I can deal with the fact we're different, that he's got issues from his past, that he'll always have the heart of a nomad and will never settle in one place, but one thing I can never accept is a man who doesn't believe in Christmas. This is my last shot at making him feel the magic of the season. A reindeer ride and drinks at a cosy cabin . . .'

'You'd better make it the best sleigh ride of his life!'

'And then I'll know what to do.'

Once we've said our goodbyes, I send Connor a text:

Need your help tomorrow evening 9 p.m. Slight safety issue I've come across, want your opinion.

He shoots back: *Again???*

I smile.

Yes, and I won't be questioned like this.

The next evening, I dash to Connor's office in a faux tizzy. He takes an age, lining up his bloody wooden pens, neatening his already neat desk, looking anywhere but at me, like a man with a secret to hide.

'Come on, the desk is pristine and those pens were already straight!' I hurry him along, knowing that Carolina is waiting patiently for us and we're already ten minutes late. I only hope no one turns up for a reindeer ride and she accepts, thinking I'm a no-show.

Connor pushes his chair in just so and locks his desk drawers. He's neat to a fault, but I try not to hold that against him. I work better in chaos, but I guess not everyone is the same. How can one find *anything* when it's stacked in neat piles with military precision? It's just so austere, that kind of organisation.

'What's the rush?' he says, following me outside.

225

'I do have a life, you know. And I'd prefer to be doing something other than watching you line up your pens. Wooden pens at that.'

He grins. God, he's beautiful when he smiles like that. I go jelly-legged so I look away in case he sees it written all over my face. Why can't he be an ugly unbeliever?

'They're made from bamboo. Better for the environment. So where are we going for this safety breach this time?'

'My van.'

His brows shoot up. 'The safety issue is in your van?' Do I detect a slight look of fear? Is he worried someone will see him and report back to Aine?

'No, it's not,' I huff, offended. 'My van fully meets all the safety criteria as you know, so don't even start all that again.'

'You're so prickly.'

'Like a cactus.'

He shakes his head.

'Stay there. Don't run away.' I quickly unlock the van and grab the picnic basket. It's a bit of a giveaway, but it's all I had so I'll just have to think of some excuse to distract him.

'Here, hold this.' I hand it over and turn my back, locking up the van.

'We're going on a *picnic*?' he asks dubiously. 'You do know we're in the Arctic Circle, right?' Has he never been ice swimming?

'A picnic, in winter!?' I scoff. 'No, I just like to take snacks, it's a blood sugar thing.'

'Right.'

We trudge past other vans, heading towards Carolina's reindeer, which are at the other end of the market on the edge of the dense snowy forest. It's a quiet Monday night so we catch the eye of almost all of the Van Lifers who sit in groups around drum fires, having a drink or two to warm up in the freezing night. There's lots of laughter. These relaxed nights give everyone a chance to

226

catch up socially and put their feet up for a while and usually end in some crazy adventure where we wind up half naked and plunge ourselves into icy water for our *circulation*.

When we get close to Aine's van, I see the shutter closed and breathe a sigh of relief. A run-in with her right now would probably end me and I'd give up on the reindeer ride.

We trudge on in silence, which convinces me whatever I thought we had – that spark, that connection – was all in my mind. The man doesn't even make small talk. After what seems like days spent in uncomfortable silence, I see the sign.

'Here we are.' I pull Connor close and whisper, 'Now please don't say anything about the safety breach. I don't want to upset Carolina, but we need to take the reindeer ride in order for me to show you, OK?'

'We're going for a reindeer ride? Can't you just point the problem out?' Impatience leeches from every word. Does the man never stop to have any fun? Or is it that he doesn't want to have fun with *me*?

'No, I can't, hence why I just said what I said. Don't you *listen*, Connor?'

He shakes his head, probably realising words are futile in times like this. 'Hey, Carolina, mind if Connor and I take a ride? Drop us at the cabin for a bit?'

Carolina pretends to consider it. 'Sure, Flora. I can drop you guys there and come back to collect you in an hour or so. Would that suit?'

'Sure.' Connor goes to speak but I tug on his hand. 'Shush. You'll understand soon enough.'

Carolina gets the sleigh ready. It's so cute and cosy and so utterly Christmassy with fluffy furry rugs and gorgeous reindeer who keep turning to catch a glimpse of us! I steal a glance at Connor but he just looks bored.

'Would you like to pat them?' I ask him.

'Who, the reindeer?'

It's like pulling teeth, with this guy. 'Yeah, the reindeer – who else would you pat?'

'It's not my thing.' He's probably scared to feel a connection with them too.

Carolina sorts out some extra throw rugs and cushions for the journey while I take Connor's hand and force him to the front of the line. 'This is Rudolph,' I say, giving the amazing creature's fur a soft pat and managing to keep his beautiful antlers from poking out my eyes. 'He's the leader of the pack.' I have no idea if he's really called Rudolph but it doesn't matter. It's all about selling the Christmas miracle to Connor.

Rudolph chooses that moment to sneeze, covering Connor with wet spray. 'You never can trust Rudolph,' I say, laughing. 'Such a devil! You're lucky you weren't in the middle of a pedicure, is all I can say. Be thankful you still have ten toes.'

'Charming,' he says in a voice that implies he's not super impressed by being sneezed on.

'Ready then?' Carolina says.

'We sure are! After you,' I say to Connor. He bends his gigantic frame into the small wooden sleigh – yikes, he makes it seem almost too small and I wonder how the reindeer will cope. Carolina must sense my worry as she says, 'We've added a few extra reindeer for tonight's ride. So you'll get the full experience.'

'Can't wait!'

Carolina instructs the reindeer by saying, '*Liikkua*,' and soon we're off, being pulled through the snowy forest. Drops of cold flick up at us and I snuggle closer to Connor to escape the icy winds that blow up the side of the sleigh.

Connor pulls a throw rug over us. Ooh, chivalrous. But then he ruins it by wrinkling his nose and saying, 'Wow, they don't smell great, do they?'

I roll my eyes. 'They smell exactly like animals who are pulling a hefty sleigh along with a man of your stature.'

'Right.'

'Look at that view.'

We're going slow, rollicking low to the ground, bumping against each other as the starry night shines overhead. Still no sign of the northern lights but I can only imagine how much more spectacular that would make the sleigh ride.

Connor doesn't speak but wraps an arm around me. 'To stop us bumping back and forth into one another,' he explains.

The reindeer whinny as they trot. They're such magnificent animals up close. As we head deeper into the forest, the temperature drops again, and I'm grateful for the fur-lined rugs. I pull another one onto our laps. I'm cocooned in warmth with Connor's arm tight around me and embarrassingly I feel my eyes well up with tears. We'd be the perfect Hallmark couple, he the big tough reserved guy who is secretly sweet inside, and me the eccentric fun-lover who forces him to really live. Can't he see that?

'Are you OK?'

I can't wipe my face because I'm wearing gloves and my hands are buried under all the blankets. 'Yes, I'm great. It's just . . . this is amazing, isn't it? A reindeer ride has been on my bucket list for an eternity and I have to pinch myself to make sure it's real. The beauty of the dense white snow, the stars, the sleigh, the gorgeous animals bringing the spirit of Christmas alive – it feels magical, like all my dreams are coming true. Do you feel the same?'

'Ah, yeah . . .'

He doesn't.

'People spend their whole lives dreaming of having this kind of once-in-a-lifetime experience. And yet here we are, able to do it every single day if we wanted. How lucky are we?'

'Yeah, who wouldn't want to be outside in the elements in the snowy landscape when we could be inside by the fire?'

'Do I detect sarcasm?'

'Absolutely not!' he says. 'So I'm looking around for this so called safety breach and I can't see it.'

'Hmm,' I muse. 'Look, a deer!' I point to a tree to buy time.

'That's a tree.'

'Behind the tree, Connor. Sheesh, can you not see out of those big blue eyes of yours?'

'Clearly not.'

We continue on in silence. I want to soak this up so I'll remember it for the rest of my life. It's truly a spectacular way to see the forest.

Soon we come to a little cabin that's lit up by the soft glow of yellow lanterns and Christmas lights are strung up along the eaves. A real Christmas tree stands off to the side, decorated with silver and gold baubles that blow about in the wind. It looks just like something out of a festive fairy tale.

'Welcome to Santa's Winter Cabin,' Carolina says, alighting from the sleigh and helping us out. She opens the door to the little wooden structure and I see a fire in the hearth crackling away. There's a small table set with a red-checked tablecloth, and a sofa piled high with cushions and a thick red blanket. There's a Christmas tree in the corner with flashing snowflake lights. 'I'll be back in an hour. There's more wood under the bench if you need to stoke up the fire. Enjoy!'

'Thanks!' I say, giving her a wink when Connor's back is turned. 'Don't forget the picnic basket,' I say to Connor.

We give Carolina a wave and then settle inside. I open the basket and place cheeses, olives, berries and nuts on a plate, and then manage to completely butcher cutting up some bread with my blunt knife. I pass Connor the bottle of bubbles to open. 'Would you mind?'

He takes the bottle and pops the cork. 'Are we celebrating something?'

'Shoot, I forgot the glasses.'

He goes to a curtain and slides it open. There's a small kitchen area hidden away. Perfect! He takes two water glasses and pours the champagne. 'Well,' I say, 'it's better than drinking out of the bottle. Can I tempt you with some cheese?'

'What is all of this, Flora?'

'What?'

'This.' He waves an arm around the small cabin. And then I remember my phone. I take it from the depths of my jacket pocket and hit play on my Spotify Christmas list and let Mariah Carey sing to us about the glory of the season. Soon, he will be overwhelmed by the spirit of Christmas. I can just tell by the glint in his . . .

'There is no safety issue, is there?'

I go to protest but he holds up a hand.

'You wanted to get me away from the market, but why? Is someone breaking the rules, and you're covering for them?'

The man and his damn rules! 'No, of course not. Why would I do that? *I'm* a rule follower. You make it sound like I'm this rebel just because of one noise complaint, one unapproved gingerbread house and Aine's attempted murder appeal.'

He drinks his champagne in one gulp. Golly. I should have brought two bottles! 'So, I don't understand it, then.'

'Let me explain. From my long daily morning walks—' there's no such thing '—I thought that this little cabin wasn't up to code and I wanted to point out some of the issues to you, but now being inside, I can see my mistake.'

He gives me a look that suggests he doesn't believe a word. 'You walk all the way here in the mornings? How long does that take you in the fresh snow? Three hours, four?'

Flip. 'It's more of a run, I guess. I can be very nimble when I need to be.'

He narrows his eyes. 'Why did you think it wasn't up to code? Before each season everything is rigorously checked, and then checked again.'

'My mistake. It was more a feeling. A vibe I had. Perhaps it was the glint off the fresh white morning snow that somehow distorted my vision. I can see it's safe, safer than the average cabin. Then I wondered if it had been properly approved, unlike my poor forgotten gingerbread house that I'm paying rent for and yet can't use. So, yes, that's why I asked you here – to check it has had the tick of approval, because if so, I'd like to ask for my gingerbread house to have the tick too. There's not long to go, Connor, and you can see it's not going to fall down.'

He doesn't speak, just glances around as if he's actually looking for a safety breach. What if he finds one and then this backfires and Carolina gets a warning? I'll never forgive myself. 'Anyway, we're here now, we may as well enjoy it. Can I tempt you with some snacks?'

Connor peers at the food as if it's a science experiment and could blow at any minute. 'So the food is safe?'

'Totally safe.' I take a slice of cheese and a chunk of bread and pop into my mouth. I let a few seconds pass before I grab my throat and theatrically fall to the ground, writhing and jolting, pretending I'm in the death throes, until I *actually* start choking on the bread and grunt, 'HELP!' I gurgle. A death rattle.

Connor lifts me up with one arm and whacks my back hard. The bread dislodges and goes flying across the cabin. How attractive, half-masticated food! I'm sure my face is blood-red, from embarrassment and the lack of oxygen. I give myself a minute to revive, sucking air into my lungs, before I say, 'That backfired.'

Connor helps me to a seat and sits opposite, staring so deeply into my eyes I feel faint again. 'I don't know quite what to make of you, Flora Westwood.'

'I get that a lot.'

He continues to survey me like I'm a puzzle he can't quite solve. 'No, it's more than that. You're so unusual.'

'Yeah, I get it. Zany. Eccentric. Change the record, already.'

He laughs. 'But isn't that a good thing?'

I pause. 'Apparently not for the most part.' I just faked my own poisoning and then almost choked to death on a piece of bread, so I'm not sure if I'm thinking straight.

'You're amusing.' Am I about to be friend-zoned?

'Thanks.' I drink some more champagne to stem the burn in my throat. 'This really *is* a Christmas miracle, isn't it? You saved my life!'

He scoffs. 'I wouldn't go that far. But that performance was pretty impressive before it turned into an actual life or death situation. Things are never boring with you around.'

'Bread should be banned! It's not safe!'

'Perhaps we'll slice it a little thinner in future.'

'Good idea.'

He goes to the little kitchen space and finds a bread knife, brandishes it in the air.

'What are the chances?' I say, lifting my woefully blunt travel knife. 'This can go in the bin!'

'No, keep it, you never know when it might come in handy.' He slices the bread into whisper-sized pieces and I laugh.

'That should slip straight down,' I say.

'Good, because slapping your back is about the limit of my first aid capabilities.'

'Wait, you mean you, Mr Rule Follower Extraordinaire, don't know first aid? Hasn't done every health course known to human-kind?'

A pop of colour pinks his cheeks. 'I have a medic here for that.'

'Right.'

We share the picnic and talk, and slowly Connor opens up again. He loses that mask he wears when he's around everyone else. 'Where've you been all week?' I say, wanting answers about Aine without having to outright ask them.

'Work – you know how it is. Not long to go here so I've got a lot on in terms of preparing to close up. Plus, there's been some . . . stuff happening behind the scenes that I've had to deal with.'

Like a certain blonde perhaps? 'Oh yeah? What kind of stuff?' I steel myself for it. His face remains impassive but he lets out a small sigh.

'Stupid stuff. Bickering among Van Lifers, lots of complaints made that I had to investigate only to find out they were fake. But it creates a tonne of paperwork for me, because I have to report every incident to the powers that be and—'

I cut him off because I don't give a hoot about the intricacies of the paperwork. 'Who put in fake complaints?'

'First there was one about Aine's van, sent in by a customer saying they suffered a severe bout of food poisoning.'

I try to look sympathetic and as if I haven't heard the rumour. 'So what happened when you went to her van?'

I'm interested to see whether he admits anything or pretends his visit to Aine was all above board. Truth is what makes a relationship, so I'm on tenterhooks wondering if Connor will pass the test. But if he doesn't care for me in the way I hope, then he probably wouldn't say a word anyway.

Connor stokes the fire and returns to the table. 'There was no truth to it. None that I could see. The day in question she hadn't opened her van shop. Aine claimed someone had it in for her, someone new to the group. Someone who stirred up trouble just for trouble's sake.'

I roll my eyes dramatically. All thoughts of keeping my mouth contained fly up and out the chimney. 'It wasn't bloody well me, if that's what she's implying! If I had a complaint that would actually stick, I'd have lodged it in person with you!'

'Yeah, I know that, Flora,' he says, his voice level. 'While I might not socialise much with the Van Lifers, it doesn't mean I can't read the room and figure out what's really going on. Standing on the outside looking in, you can actually see the dynamic a lot more clearly and what I see is Aine finding her target, you, and doing her level best to ruin your time here at the market.'

'There's more, isn't there?'

He crosses his arms. 'She put in another complaint about you, but she used a fake name to lodge it.'

I knew it! 'How did you know it was her then?'

'It was the same IP address as the first complaint.'

I'm confused. 'Wait, you're saying she put in the food poisoning complaint about her *own* van herself?' Ah, and then it dawns on me. It'd be the quickest way to get Connor to her van, play the victim, the 'everyone's jealous of me' card.

'She did. She's since admitted to lodging both complaints.'

'Why would she admit that? She would out herself as a fool!'

'Because I had proof of her IP address and also the misspelling of a few words were the same in both emails. I know what game Aine is playing so it wasn't hard to work out.'

'And what game is that?'

Heat rushes to his face as he goes beetroot-red. Is he embarrassed to admit he has feelings for such a low, lying snake? 'I think you know, Flora.'

'Spell it out for me, Connor, so there's no mistake, would you?' No misunderstandings in a Hallmark world.

With a shake of the head, he lets out a groan. 'When I went to her van to investigate, she didn't seem concerned about the complaint at all. She made us drinks and I knew there was more to it . . .'

My heart plummets.

'I told her I couldn't stay for drinks, that I was working, but before I could leave she . . . kissed me.'

I feel my heart shrivel up and die a little death. 'She kissed you!'

He closes his eyes as if the memory is hard to share, and nods. 'She kissed me, unfortunately. So then I had to give her a written warning, which you can imagine was awkward for us both. But there's no kissing of the boss allowed. I'm sure Aine is a lovely person, but she's not *my* person.'

'Wait. Wait.' Laughter barrels out of me. I've never been so happy he is such a rule follower! 'You *wrote her up* for kissing you?' I want to scream and dance all at once. He is the limit!

'Yes, of course, Flora. Rules are rules – isn't that so?' A grin plays at the corners of his mouth. 'She can't go around lodging fake complaints and trying to get other Van Lifers, like you, in trouble. I can't stand liars, Flora. And I can't have someone like Aine catching me unawares and kissing me, when there was no sign from me that I'd be interested in such a thing. It came out of nowhere. I've barely talked to her so I'm still confused as to why she thought that would be a good idea.'

'But I kissed you.'

'That's different.'

'Why?'

'Do you really not know, Flora?'

'No, I really don't.'

'. . . Mistletoe.'

Is that it? 'Why've you been blowing me off all week?'

He shrugs. 'It's hard for me to make friends, Flora. I have this internal battle about whether it's worth it, and what's going to come next. Am I doing the best thing for us, when you and I go our separate ways—'

'Friends can remain friends, Connor, even if they're not in each other's daily lives. You'd give up the possibility of us sharing moments like this on the off chance things might change in the future?'

He stares into the fire as if looking for answers. 'It's hard for me, that's all. I know it's impossible to understand. But I find it easier not to rely on anyone, not to need them.'

'I do understand, Connor. I really do.' I can read between the lines; the air is electric with all the things we don't say. He's scared to reveal his heart and leave it open to be broken. I get that.

'Let's take it one day at a time, eh?' I say because I'm scared to admit how I really feel. Everything backfires, and I don't want this to.

'OK.'

'One last thing,' I say. 'So Aine alluded to the fact you'd been very hands-on, and your tattoos went all the way down, and . . .'

He throws his head back and laughs. 'Flora, you've seen me naked, right? And I've seen you naked. I know you've got a belly button piercing.' Jesus, just how close did he look! 'Everyone has seen everyone naked in Finland in a sauna, or swimming, so my tattoos aren't exactly a secret.'

The bloody saunas! Does no one have a modicum of modesty here! 'I bet.' I'm reassured and more than that, I'm hopeful. I'm going to see how the next little while plays out. 'Christmas cake?' I ask, to defuse the stare he's got going on. I feel a warmth that makes me woozy.

'Sure,' he says. 'As long as you didn't make it.'

I cut two slices. 'Hush your mouth, Connor. I'm a very good baker, I'll have you know. OK, fine, Tuomo made it. It's perfectly safe and I'm a terrible baker. It's tragic. But I'm a pretty good eater.'

'You've got a little . . .' His fingertip brushes the side of my mouth and sends a shockwave through me. The man's touch is literally electrifying. 'Crumb,' he finishes his voice husky.

'Oh, thanks.'

We eat in silence, the Christmas cake a heady mix laden with brandy. Coupled with champagne, it's enough to blur the edges and relax me.

The carols play quietly from my phone but when 'Little Drummer Boy' comes on I pull a surprised Connor up by the hand. 'Let's dance! This is one of my all-time favourites!'

'This song?'

'It's beautiful and it always make me feel the joy of Christmas right down to my very soul. I get goose bumps.'

Connor takes me in his arms and the goose bumps double. I hold his hand and loop my arm around his waist and he pulls me tight against him as we sway to the song.

I sing the lyrics, touched as always by them while Connor stares deeply into my eyes and hesitates like he wants to say something but stops. Part of me feels the same. It's on the tip of my tongue to blurt out how I'm feeling, just like I have in the past, but this is different. And for now, it's a secret I hold within me and enjoy feeling the warmth it radiates.

Being this close feels natural, like we've been slow dancing to Christmas carols all our lives so I don't overthink it. It's just enough being here with him.

When the song ends, we sit on the little couch and catch our breath.

'So, what do you think, Connor? Did that Christmas carol make you feel . . . anything?'

'It sure did, Flora. It made me feel . . . alive.'

I laugh. It's hard to tell what Connor feels when he gives answers like that.

Connor gets up and goes to the window. 'But the spell will be broken soon. Carolina is due back,' he says, peeking out into the still of night. When we get close, he does this: he pulls back, disengages, and I know it's his internal struggle, his defence mechanism. To put distance between us.

'Yeah, she should have been back a while ago.' I note the time on my phone. That hour flew past.

'Maybe she got held up?' He glances at the fire, the orange flames shrinking as the wood burns down. 'I'll stoke the fire just in case. We don't want it to go out. There's no way of lighting it again if it does.'

Worry prickles. What if she's forgotten us? I don't think Connor will take too kindly to being stuck in a little cabin in the forest overnight. *Stuck with me!* He can't exactly put distance between us then!

'Yeah, good plan.' I find the wood box and pass him some of the bigger logs. It's so cosy and warm, I kind of wish I could stay here forever. But somehow, I don't think the man mountain would feel the same. He's got paper to shuffle, pens that need lining up. Rules that need following. At least he doesn't have plans with Aine!

'Should I call Carolina?' I ask.

'Do you have reception out here?'

I look at the phone. 'No.' No way to contact anyone. No way to leave. Not enough wood to last us all night and into the morning. Worse, the champagne bottle is dry.

'Then perhaps not.'

'OK, let's not panic,' I say, panicking. What if she never comes back? What if the snowfall covers the entire cabin and they can't find us for days and we die of dehydration?

'No one is panicking,' Connor says, with a reassuring lilt to his voice.

Just how cold does it get out in the forest? What if Carolina left town and forgot to tell someone we were here? What if my blood sugar truly drops? What if we run out of cheese? 'We're going to die out here, aren't we?'

He gauges the stress in my voice and puts a comforting hand over mine. 'Why are you panicking? Is it being stuck here with me that worries you?'

'Umm ... no. It's mainly, well, what if wolverines with big sharp claws bust in and want the bread but they mistake us for food and next minute, after a scuffle we have claw marks down our faces, and on you it will look cool, like you fought this wild animal and won – you'd somehow look more rugged and appealing – but on me it would just look a mess and people would point and stare, well more than they already do and . . .' You hear about these wolverines all the time around the campfire. Van Lifers tell all sorts of stories about near misses, and the like.

Connor pulls me up and holds me tight against his chest. I can hear the steady thrum of his heart as I rest my head. God, he's tall. And he smells so good, so edible. But I'm in the midst of a crisis and I can't think of all that! 'Relax, Flora, it's going to be OK. They can't get in and I wouldn't let any animal hurt you, OK?'

OK, but that brings me to being trapped with Connor himself. I stiffen in his arms. He must notice because he takes a step back and looks into my eyes. 'You're safe, I promise.'

Can I trust Connor? I don't know him enough to know that

he'd truly think of my welfare in a crisis. I suppose he has so far, but what if that was a ploy and really he's selfish right to his core? 'What if you steal the only blanket and then I end up with frostbite and I lose all of my toes? What if you roll over and crush me and I can't breathe, and I try to tell you but you're in a deep sleep because of the champagne? And the life ebbs from my body and I'm this ghost hovering above you and you still don't know because you're sleeping peacefully, wrapped warmly in the only blanket with all your toes and—'

'OK, OK, is it normal for you to always think of the ways you're going to die?'

I whisper, tearfully, '*Yes!*'

He holds my arms and gives me a look filled with such sincerity I almost crumple. 'If, and that's a big if, we get stuck here, you can have the sofa and the blanket all to yourself, OK? That way you won't get frostbite and you won't be . . . crushed to death by me. You won't need to hover ghost-like above me because you'll be the one who's wrapped warmly in the blanket sleeping peacefully. How does that sound?'

I wipe a stray tear. 'Better.'

'Good, good. But I'm sure Carolina will come back. She probably had a couple of tourists turn up and thought she'd fit a couple of extra rides in on a slow Monday, right?'

'That makes sense.'

'So how about we enjoy what time we have left?'

'OK.'

We sit back down and I slowly let the anxiety subside. Who would have thought rugged Connor would have such a caring, soft side? But of course he does – he's shown me time and time again. With the kids in the hospital, when he saved me on stage . . . The only thing he hasn't done is given in to me with one thing.

'Connor.'

'Yes?'

'Can I open my gingerbread house for customers if we get out of here alive? Will you break a rule for me?'

'Will it make you feel better if I do?'

I nod.

'Then consider it done. I had it checked over last week and have just been waiting for the approval to come in.'

'You had it checked over for me?'

'I did.'

I swoon. The man is amazing.

Before long we hear the sounds of reindeer trotting casually along the soft snow and I let out a sigh of relief. 'This is going to sound strange after my outburst, but now I know we haven't been abandoned, I don't want to go.'

He laughs and it lights up his face. 'You're one of a kind, Flora, and I love that about you. Hey, would you like to come to my cottage tomorrow for a movie night? I managed to find a festive movie.'

My eyes widen. 'An actual Christmas movie?'

He pretends to be shocked. 'Is there any other kind?'

I stifle a grin. If I didn't know better I'd say Mr Unbeliever is beginning to believe! 'What is it? *Love Actually* or . . .'

'*Die Hard.*'

I scoff. '*Die Hard* isn't a Christmas movie!'

'Yet it's set at Christmastime.'

'So close, yet so far. OK, how about I bring a selection too?'

'Only if you promise to watch *Die Hard* first.'

I make a great show of being put out. 'Fine.'

'Great. Come to my cabin, say nine?'

We head out to the reindeer who whinny and whine as if to say hello and head back to the market. I rest my head against Connor's shoulder.

Back home in my van, I burrow under the blankets and think of the guy and what tonight meant. We might never make it past the friendship stage, so there's no point worrying. But as an honorary Hallmark movie heroine, I think I handled the situation just right. I showed *constraint*. I creep lower under the covers and switch out the bedside light, my mind firmly on the Viking and how safe he made me feel . . .

Chapter 29

Late the next afternoon, I'm trying to tidy up the front racks but I cannot focus on a single thing. All I keep seeing is Connor's face as I replay the night before. Being snug against him as we slow danced to 'Little Drummer Boy'. I'm distracted from my reverie as Raakel comes running over. 'Oh my God, I heard about you guys getting stuck together in the cabin for a few hours. Spill, did you guys fall in love and have mad, passionate—'

I clamp a hand over her very loud mouth and look around to see who's eavesdropping. The walls have ears in this place. 'Would you quieten down! No, we did no such thing!'

She reels back. 'Why not? He's an absolute demigod and everyone wants a piece of him. Why would you waste your chance!'

'I don't sleep with men until I know for certain, that's why.' But the thought of Connor makes me downright woozy and I struggle to stand. 'Raakel . . .' I tug her arm. 'I don't feel good!'

She moves forward and catches my arm. 'What's wrong? Dizzy spell?'

'I think I'm . . . *in love.*'

Clarity dawns on her features and a grin splits her face. 'Ah, I see.'

'What do I do?'

'Tell Connor how you feel?'

'That's good solid advice but I don't want to do that just yet. I need to sit down before I fall down. I'm supposed to be meeting Connor for a movie night in a few hours. A *Christmas* movie night of all the glorious things! Can you tell him that there was a slight issue with my . . . plumbing?'

'Your *plumbing*?'

'Not believable? OK, a slight problem with my blood sugar and I'm just going back to rest for a bit.'

'No, I can't. Isn't this what you've wanted all along? If you cancel he'll pop over to make sure you're all right.'

'Damn. I just need some time to think. I need Livvie. My best friend can help me make sense of the scramble that is my brain. I can't focus, I can't think straight. What on earth is happening to me? Can you put him off until tomorrow night?'

Raakel gives me a sympathetic look. 'OK, I'll tell him you've developed a headache and you just need complete silence, lights out, lie in a dark room kind of thing and you'll text him when you're feeling better and you'd like to reschedule to tomorrow night. You go talk to Livvie and then let me know how you are.'

'OK, thank you!'

Raakel gives me a hug and heads in the direction of Connor's office.

I climb into bed, and video-call Livvie. If I didn't know better I'd say this strange lethargy was some kind of mystery illness. I'm probably going to die before I tell the man how I feel!

'Livvie, oh my God, I feel sick.'

'What's the matter? Wow, you do look sick; you're pasty white. What is it?'

I gulp back panic. 'The reindeer ride. We got stuck in a cabin together. I thought we'd die and then we didn't and he was all chivalrous and caring and sweet and . . . I felt like I was literally falling, like the earth tilted on its axis and I didn't have solid ground beneath me anymore. I still feel it, a seasickness, like

244

I don't quite know where to put myself in order to feel whole again. Do you think I've developed some kind of flu, some deadly Finnish flu? I don't have health insurance . . .'

'Oh my God, Flora you're sick all right, you're lovesick!'

'I am?'

'Can you eat?' She stares me down with her doctor face on.

'No.'

'Think?'

'Definitely not.'

'Sleep?' she asks.

'Look at the bags under my eyes.'

'Wow, Flora. You've got it bad! This is a very serious case.'

'What do I do?'

'You have to go to the source, it's the only cure. So where is he?'

'Sorting his pens.'

'What?'

'His office.'

'OK, OK, make yourself a pot of strong tea.'

'That's your answer to this . . . this malady?'

'For now. We're British, it's what we do.'

'Well, it can't hurt I suppose.' I climb out of bed and flick on the kettle and get the tea things ready. 'I'm supposed to be meeting him in a few hours, but I've told Raakel to tell him I've got a migraine and I'll meet tomorrow night instead. But even then, I'm not sure I'll be ready. What if I forget how to form words? What if I want to kiss him all night? What if I want to have *sex* on the first date?' I whisper as if such a thing is scandalous. *It is for me!* I have very strict rules about this sort of thing in order to avoid situationships or worse, one-night stands.

'Flora, this is all very normal, so you just act accordingly in the moment. If he has the characteristics of a true Hallmark hero he will help you in any given situation. And my gut tells me he's been doing that all along.'

'What?'

'Can't you see, Flora? You've set up all these activities to get him to believe and every single one of them has backfired on you, he's had to come to *your* rescue every single time and he's done that without so much as an I told you so, just like a real hero would.'

I process it all. 'Oh wow, Liv, he has! He really has! How did I not see that?'

'Too caught up in the moment, which means the moments matter! They're real and they're everything!'

'He likes me?'

'He loves you!'

'Let's not get carried away. I think I'll still feign illness tonight so I can make sense of it all. I just have this horrible feeling I'm going to blurt out that I adore him, or something equally upfront and then there'll be no going back from that. I'm still not one hundred per cent sure he's on the same page, you know?'

She laughs but it sounds more like a scoff. 'You could avoid him. But it doesn't seem like a very Flora thing to do. The Flora I know tackles things head on! She doesn't bite her tongue, she definitely doesn't hide out!'

'All of that is true. But *that* Flora has never felt like *this* before!'

'What's the worst that can happen? You tell the guy how you feel and he says he doesn't feel the same? And trust me, he's not going to do that.'

'I haven't even asked him all the questions I need answers to. He could be completely unsuitable . . .'

Livvie sighs. 'Is it because none of that matters in the scheme of things? You'll eventually agree on where to hold your winter wonderland wedding if he's the right guy for you, but you won't know any of that unless you give this a chance to develop naturally. You always eject before you've given love a chance because they don't know Santa's reindeer's names or some other folly and really it's because you've known all along they haven't been the one for you . . . until now.'

'What? That's not true!'

'Yes it is. That's the reason you ask them the serious questions on the first date that you know will frighten off most men. It's a *defence mechanism*! I've only just figured that out. You bandy that about all the time, but really it's because you have one!'

'Well, thank you, but I don't agree.'

'It is! You're so frightened of actually being in love that you instantly reject men when they don't meet your criteria, but you feel differently with Connor!'

She's bloody well right. 'Oh God, so what do I do?'

'What was the next phase of the intervention?'

'There isn't a plan.' I groan. 'But he invited me over to his cabin to watch a Christmas movie. And wait for it, the *Christmas* movie is *Die Hard*.'

'*Die Hard* isn't a Christmas movie.'

'Exactly! But Connor seems to think it is.'

'Aww, see? He wants to do things you like! And to him it's a Christmas thing. That's so bloody sweet.'

'I'm sure he's doing it under sufferance. I'll be taking my own Christmas movies so we can follow up with those and then he'll really know what it's like to be with festive Flora. If he can't sit through *The Holiday* then he's not for me.'

'Good idea, so have the movie marathon tomorrow night if you really must avoid him tonight, and then see how you feel.'

'OK, OK, yes, I think that's the best plan.' I change the subject to her man so I can have a break from obsessing over mine. It's quite exhausting, this love business. 'So, how is your love life? How's LA?'

'Jasper is the cutest. I always wake up to lots of funny video messages and we're discussing the possibilities of him coming over in April for a couple of weeks, but that's still an aeon away, so we'll see. He seems far too amiable and patient so there's probably something really wrong with him . . .'

'He's really a divorced father of three?'

She laughs. 'Yeah, something like that!'

'If he drops that kind of bombshell on you, I don't think you'd care, would you?'

Livvie contemplates it. 'No, I wouldn't. Not if he was definitely untied. It's being here in LA. Taking chances and not having time to overthink things. In my downtime I want do what makes me happy and if that means I lose my mind a little with lusty thoughts while Jasper is here, then so be it.'

'Wow, this is a huge change for you, Liv.'

'If I can do it, you can too.'

Chapter 30

The next day, I open up the van and get my trinkets polished and on display. After a great night's sleep, things feel better. I'd exhausted myself from being stuck inside that love bubble so today I feel refreshed and ready to tackle the world. I set up the racks out the front, noting that for such a cold, frosty morning the sky is clear and cloudless. Raakel wanders over and catches me staring upwards.

'How're you feeling today?'

'Much better. Did Connor agree to tonight?'

She nods. 'Yeah. He was worried about you though, but I reassured him it was just a bad headache and you'd be good after some rest.'

'Thanks for doing that. I just . . . I just had a moment.'

'It happens to the best of us. We'll probably see aurora tonight.'

My breath catches. It's been weeks and no sign of the magical aurora borealis, the northern lights. 'How do you know?' As far as I can tell there's no real way to be sure when the phenomenon will happen and that's what makes it more special.

'Cloudless skies are always a sign that it might appear.'

'I hope so.'

'Me too, it has this unique ability to energise me. It probably

249

sounds crazy.' She laughs. 'But I always feel this connection of heaven to the earth, like it sends a positive charge, or something. Cleanses and heals us with its ephemeral presence.'

'I bet it's the most beautiful sight.'

'You can make a wish on it, you know, and it'll come true.'

'How do you know?'

'It happened to me.'

'What did you wish for?'

'I can't tell you that; it's between me and aurora.'

I laugh. 'OK, well let's wait and see if we're lucky enough for it to appear.'

'There are lots of superstitions about it. Some people think it's heaven and it's the souls of the dead returning to wave to us. That's why they can grant wishes. It's a way for them to connect, to show they're still around, helping us from the great beyond.'

Goose bumps break out over my skin. I think of my nan. And Connor's mum. I think of the little girl who visited Deck the Halls and her mother, amazing Grace. Are they up there, waiting for a chance to connect? To grant a wish? If anyone could connect heaven and earth to send me a sign it would be my nan and I get teary at the thought that she might be part of that swirling emerald sky.

'Wow, I didn't know that. But I love the idea.'

'Don't forget to make that wish, Flora. I'll come back later. I've got to set up the carousel.' With that, she wanders off and I continue to stare at the blue wintry skies, wondering if it's true. If it's the souls of the dead up there in some kind of starry, shimmering paradise waiting to connect. Why not, if it gives someone hope, if it makes their loss a little easier to cope with.

Morning shoppers arrive, carrying hot drinks in keep cups and with wide merry smiles. With not long to go until Christmas things are ramping up once more. I cross-check all my stock and decide to put in one last order with Hanne. I send her a text with the order and she replies that she'll have it delivered to save me time even though she doesn't have much extra herself. I've come to love Hanne like a surrogate mum.

The clear day brings lots of customers, and I take great delight in showing them into the gingerbread house and offering them a seat to enjoy their marshmallow-filled hot cocoas. Inside the gingerbread house is a table filled with all sorts of Christmas trinkets and they take their time perusing them. I think of Connor going out of his way to get permission even though I didn't follow the rules. We got there in the end . . . !

The gingerbread house attracts Van Lifers too and soon I'm sitting around a table with Raakel, Samuel, Eevi and Tuomo.

We talk about our plans for Christmas Day and I'm touched when Raakel invites me to celebrate with her family. 'Beware, Flora. They'll make a big fuss over you and they'll insist you keep eating even when you're ready to burst at the seams.'

So just like my nan then? 'That sounds perfect, Raakel. Is it really Christmas if you're not ready to burst at the seams and go into a food coma?' Not to me it isn't!

'We partake in *joulusauna* too, so there won't be time for a food coma.'

'What's that?'

'A Christmas sauna!'

'You have a word for a Christmas sauna?' This place is wild!

'Yes, it's tradition!'

'I have to be naked around your family?' There's being brave and then there's . . . that.

She shoots me a shocked look. 'No, Flora, never! In the family sauna we wear robes!' The group burst out laughing.

I laugh along with them. 'Well, that I can do.'

While I'm happy to accept the invite and relieved there'll be robes for the partaking of *joulusauna* part of me wonders what Connor will be doing that day. Will he spend it alone? Eating something decidedly un-festive, and watching mindless TV instead of sitting around a table with people who care about him? Because no matter what he thinks, there are plenty of people here who do care. Especially me.

As if sensing my thoughts, Raakel says, 'And you can always bring a plus-one.'

I send a smile her way. 'Thanks.'

Samuel knocks against me. 'I'll be heading back to Stockholm, to my girlfriend Liisa. I can't wait to see her. It'll only have been six weeks since I left her, but it's felt like forever.' Liisa is a barrister and stays in one place while he takes little adventures here and there and sells what he can on the road. I admire their relationship; they make it work even though they seem like two very different people. 'She's planned a big family feast, where I'll finally meet all her relatives, including her father. Do you think it's still the done thing, to ask his permission for her hand in marriage?'

We all gasp and jump up and hug him. Love really is in the air! Raakel says, 'I think he'd really respect that you considered him, for sure. What are the family like? Are they stuffy and haughty or relaxed and casual?'

'I don't know! I guess we'll find out. But if they're anything like Liisa, then they'll be relaxed and casual. While she has this amazing, successful career, she's a homebody at heart. I can see us growing old together on a patch of land by a lake . . .'

'Let us know what happens,' I say, and imagine my own life, a little cabin in the woods with its very own private sauna, *with robes*, and not a wolverine to be found.

Tuomo pipes up, 'I'm spending it with Raakel and then I'll be coming back here for dinner with whoever is left. There's a few of us who've made plans to each bring a dish of whatever we've got and we're going to sit around the campfire and sing songs and drink too much *gløgge*, knowing that for once we don't have to get up the next day and work.' I send Raakel a look, which she bats away. She's still insistent there's no long-term plan for them but I see the way they make eyes at each other and it doesn't seem casual to me. What was her aurora wish that came true? Was it him? Something tells me it was.

'And then we'll all have to pack up and leave,' I say, my chest tight at the thought. I've only been here five short weeks, but it feels like a lifetime already. I've made friends who will take a piece of my heart with them wherever they go.

I see Hanne in the distance carrying a stack of boxes as if they weigh nothing. Juho trails behind her, his limp more pronounced as if the season has exhausted him. I race over to take the boxes and welcome them inside the gingerbread house.

Raakel dashes inside my van to make them some cocoa and soon returns, bringing the biscuit tin with her.

'So, I see you finally got your way, Flora,' Hanne says, gesturing to the gingerbread house. 'And not before time!'

'What can I say, the guy is a softie really.' We all laugh and I offer the biscuit tin to the elderly couple. 'He's sweet, I think, or maybe I truly did wear him down like he says.'

Hanne grasps my hand and gives it a squeeze. 'Maybe a bit of both.'

I swallow a lump in my throat at the thought of leaving these two behind as my adventures continue. But then I wonder if I really do have to go so far. It's the country of a thousand lakes and I've got some exploring to do, but that doesn't mean I can't come back to Lapland from time to time to check in on them. 'I hope things are winding down for you two and you can take a bit of break after we're all gone and Christmas is finished.'

Hanne crunches on a biscuit, so Juho speaks up, 'Yeah, we're thinking of finding a manager who might eventually buy our business, Flora. We're getting too old to be ferrying out life-size Christmas displays and running up and down ladders in the factory. Wouldn't know anyone who'd fit the position, would you?'

I double blink. Could I, hopeless employee, unlucky in life, manage a business the size of theirs? How could I eventually buy it? 'Something to think about,' I say, and wonder if this is what I came here for, to stumble on an opportunity like this.

'You could manage it, and pay it off slowly with the profits. You'd still have time to travel as it's only seasonal.' It's a great deal, and I know they're being generous because they know how much I love Christmas. Owning such a business would be a dream. Every fibre of me wants to say yes.

Raakel's face shines with happiness. 'Then we wouldn't have to say goodbye for good, Flora.'

'I'd love to talk to you more about it, Hanne.' The new improved Hallmark heroine thinks before she leaps. Well, at least sometimes.

She grins. 'Plenty of time – we're in no hurry.'

I feel myself blossoming at the thought of running a business such as theirs, one I'm madly passionate about, one I know I could take to the next level.

We spent the next little while talking about our travel plans and where we hope to visit for the holidays. I feel a buoyancy, a strange euphoria as if I'm right where I'm meant to be. Is this how it feels to bloom? Could I have found my place in this big wide world? It certainly feels like I have. The only hiccough in the plan is Livvie, but I'll have plenty of time to travel back to London and visit during off season. And Livvie could spend her holidays here, in this Nordic utopia. I see why people visit and never leave, and I'm yet to explore the beautiful outer reaches of this picturesque country.

Daylight draws further away, and we soon disperse after many hugs and promises to catch up once this busy week comes to a close.

I'm packing away the cups and dishes when I sense him. I don't know why I can always tell when he's close. Maybe it's his sheer size – it changes the energy in the air. Or maybe it's his alpine scent, that rugged perfume that is so him, and quite knocks any sense from my brain.

'How are you feeling, Flora?' I turn to him and get lost in his gaze.

'Goof.' Oh God! 'I mean good, but goof is probably more accurate. I was going to say good then I was going to say fine, and my brain, well, it's not firing on all cylinders.' This is off to a good start then!

He does that same slow smile as if I could say any mumbo jumbo and he'd still find it amusing.

My pulse races. Is there something here for us both? Is the chance of love worth risking it all? It will be, I know it will be. I know I can't leave things as they are. I'll have to admit to him how I feel or I'll regret it for the rest of my life. It's Connor's reluctance to put down roots that concerns me. He's so used to dashing away when things get serious. Will he do that to me too?

'I'm glad you feel goof. Are you still keen to watch *Die Hard* later?'

I grin. 'Well, I wouldn't go so far to say I'm keen to watch *Die Hard*, but I'm keen to visit your cabin and I hope there'll be snacks.'

He laughs. 'Sure, I'll have snacks.'

Connor gives me directions to his cabin which is on the edge of the forest.

Instead of video-calling Livvie in a mad panic, I remain calm and tear my wardrobe apart searching the perfect outfit that screams casual, but also makes me look a little better than my usual market attire of jeans and Puffa jacket. All the while I curse Livvie for making me halve my clothes because all I have is denim and puff. Puff and denim. And Christmas PJs in every possible colour combination and style.

I decide to just go with what works for me and don a Christmas onesie. You can't watch festive movies in jeans, can you? That's just not Christmas.

Just before nine, I head off in Noël. Determined to stay on the right side of the road and not have any near misses. I try to remain laser-focused but something is drawing my eye.

Jingle bells! Above me the sky is shimmery emerald and pink as if an artist took a watercolour brush to the canvas of night sky and then sprinkled some glitter over it. A galaxy of stars pulsing with light as if calling for those below to look up, make that wish! Happy tears fall down the ruddy cold of my cheeks at the magnificence before me. It's a dream come true, and I'm thankful to be one of those who were here at the right time to see such a display.

The scent of jasmine permeates my van – Nan's perfume that she wore her whole life. I know that she's here, sending me a sign that I'm on the right track! I took a risk coming here, and it's paid off. Leaping from a life that wasn't working, into this new reality that albeit has had plenty of bumps along the way but bumps that I figured out how to navigate and keep going. I chat with Nan in my mind. I explain what I'm feeling and I ask her to help me make it happen. I'm sure I hear her voice: *Make that wish, my beautiful Flora! And let love bloom!*

My nan would never steer me wrong. So with all of my heart I make the wish, the only wish for the thing I want most. *If Connor is the one for me, send me a sign! Show me the way!*

I continue driving to Connor's cabin, trying to keep my eyes on the road but failing when the sky is awash with such beauty. I find his cabin. It's like something out of a fairy tale. An orange glow shines from the windows, like there's a warm fire roaring in the grate. Smoke drifts from the chimney. I park the van sideways and fall from the cabin in my haste to tell him about the northern lights.

'Connor! Connor, come quick!' I knock hard at his door, all the while looking back over my shoulder so I don't miss a thing.

'Hey,' he says. 'What's all the excitement?'

'Look at the sky!'

He walks out from the cabin, bringing a wave of warmth with him from the fire I can hear crackling. 'It never loses its magic,' he says, his voice heavy with awe. 'Sometimes I think I can never leave this place, because losing this would be like losing my heart.

When you've spent your life looking for beauty, to believe in something and then you're met with this, it's hard to argue for a reason to ever leave such a thing.'

He's looking at me, not the sky.

'It's a miracle. A natural wonder. And I'm so glad I finally got to see it.'

'You'd have always seen it, Flora, but it had to be at the right time. That's the magic of aurora.'

'The magic of aurora. You're sounding a little sentimental there, Connor, a little romantic even.'

'I can be romantic when I'm moved.'

'I like the sound of that.' I shiver in my onesie but don't want to go inside and miss a thing. Connor wraps an arm around me and we spend an eternity staring at the show in the sky and I lean into him. I want to tell him how I feel but the words won't come. Why? This is the perfect time under a dreamlike sky. Tears roll down my cheeks. I seem to have a lot of happy tears here. It's just so beautiful and I am moved beyond words.

We stay silent, but stand close, one arm looped around each other. Connor gently wipes my tears away and I let out a nervous laugh.

After an age, he says, 'You're shivering, do you want to go inside and warm up?'

My teeth chatter in response. 'Yes, we'd better even though I could stay out here all night.'

'Next time. Christmas onesies are not all that waterproof.'

I smile. 'No, it's a bit of a design fault.'

'Turn around,' he says when we get to the door of the cabin. 'Close your eyes.'

'Why?'

'It's a surprise. And before you ask no, I'm not a serial killer and no, I'm not leading you to your death.'

'I wasn't thinking that!' OK, so maybe it briefly crossed my mind but I'm not going to admit that to him.

Connor puts his hands over my eyes and the world goes black. I wonder just what I've got in store. Is his house a mess and he wants to lead me past the worst of it? No, he's too tidy for all of that. Maybe it's a surprise party of some sort? But no, he's not really a crowd person.

'Ready?' he asks.

I take a deep breath. 'Ready.'

He opens the door and warmth seeps out of the cabin. Connor moves one hand to my hip to help lead me in. 'A few more steps,' he says and then removes his other hand from my eyes and I slowly adjust to the scene before me while he closes the door behind us.

In the corner of the room is what looks like the skeleton of a tree, dried and decorated with strange baubles made from recycled milk tops. Beside the fire stand two nutcrackers, at least I think they're supposed to be nutcrackers made from odd-shaped reclaimed wood, which look like they've been painted in a hurry. By a five-year-old. In a thunderstorm. Garlands of popcorn are laced around the room.

'What is all this, Connor?' I'm so surprised I can only whisper.

'It's you, Flora. You did this to me. It's my interpretation of the true meaning of Christmas. It isn't about gaudy festoon lights, or maxed-out credit cards, the forced proximity of family members who don't get along. It's about finding someone who makes you feel like it's Christmas every day. Someone who finds joy in the simple things, like singing at full volume to corny Christmas carols, slurping gingerbread milkshakes like they're manna from heaven. A person who spreads that joy to everyone she meets, as if every day is Christmas and it should be celebrated. Just like you do, Flora.'

'I do?' I double blink and try and make sense of it all. I feel fluttery and love-struck but also still in a daze. 'What's with the erm . . . decorations?'

'I wanted to do something special for you but my eco-soul wouldn't let me purchase all that mass-produced plastic, so I used recycled materials and hoped you could just squint hard and get the same festive feeling when you looked at it.'

The nutcrackers are hands-down the ugliest thing I've ever seen, and yet after hearing his sweet explanation they feel really special. I love the sentiment behind it all. The intervention worked! It really worked!

'You did all this for me?' Everywhere I look there are more little touches. Christmas carols play softly in the background. Candy canes hang from the tree, but they look suspiciously homemade, more like candy rocks, but hey, he tried. He's even gone so far as to decorate the sofa cushions with snowflake patterns. On the mantel are two stockings, sewed together with what looks like wire. There's a C on one and a F on the other.

'Is that a wreath made from plastic straws?'

'Yes, I had to find a use for them somehow.'

I laugh. Only Connor would think of such a thing. 'I love all of this.'

'It doesn't seem like much when you've gone out of your way to try and convince me Christmas is more than consumerism . . . that's it's a *feeling*. I never thought about it like that before. I never thought it meant anything. I thought that it was all a marketing ploy but it doesn't have to be that way. It can be whatever you make it. And how could I not see when you were bent on making me believe right from the time you tried to poison me with the raw turkey, up to the sleigh ride where we got stuck in the cabin.'

'I did no such thing!' I pretend to be outraged.

'There was never a safety problem with the cabin, was there?'

'No.'

'And Hanne never had a pedicure from hell, did she?'

I make a face. 'No.'

'And the elf thing?'

'Lies, all lies.'

'All to get me to believe in the magic of the season?'

I give him a winning smile. 'Yes, because you're worth it.'

'No one has ever done anything like that for me before, and no one ever will again. It touched me, Flora. It made me realise that living in my own world wasn't really living. And you're right in thinking that when I get close to anyone, I escape. It's easier to pretend I'm more of a solitary type and that way there's no surprises. No chance of getting hurt. But it's an empty existence. Lonely as hell. And you've made me realise that I need to take a risk, to open my heart even if that means I risk it being broken.'

'I think it's a risk worth taking, don't you?'

He pulls me into his arms and we share a deep kiss. That sensation of falling returns but I'm safe in his arms, and he anchors me here.

'But you always move on. You run when things turn serious.'

'Not anymore. I'll go where you go, Flora, if that's what you want? Or I'll stay. I've never settled anywhere because there was no reason to. I always felt like I hadn't found the perfect place yet, but now I know I hadn't found the perfect *person*. And if that means I have to watch Christmas movies on a loop or sing Christmas carols all night, then that's what I'll do. I've never met anyone like you before. You speak your mind, I love the way that you dress, the way you speak fast when you're angry, how you demand to be heard and you never, ever give in. You stand up for yourself. I hope you never change.'

Again – *he hopes I never change*. My heart races at his words. He loves me just the way I am, foibles and all. 'I promise you, Connor, that I'll always be on your side. That I'll always say how I'm feeling and there'll never be any secrets between us. You can trust me with your heart.' I know Connor's heart is fragile but it won't take long for me to show him what real love is and that he can count on me.

This is my very own miracle, a real-life Christmas miracle. And I knew all I had to do was take a chance on this new life and I'd eventually find my way. I see a brand-new business in my future, to go with my brand-new man. It feels right, it feels like what a newly bloomed Hallmark heroine would do.

We kiss once more, and I wonder if I'll lose myself in this man, this Norse god who likes me just the way I am. Maybe we'll become the people we were always destined to be, just like in the movies. I know I've found my hero and I'm the heroine for him. We've saved each other, come to the rescue for one another at just the right time.

'One question, do you know Santa's reindeer's names?'

He throws his head back and laughs. 'Why, Flora? Will it bother you if I don't?'

'You can learn!' We laugh and he pulls me to the sofa where we sit wrapped in each other's arms. We kiss once more while outside the sky shimmers and swirls, granting wishes for those who believe.

Acknowledgements

Special thanks to Dushi for all your help with this one! We worked as a great team to meet those deadlines and I couldn't have done it without your professionalism, insight and enthusiasm. I've absolutely loved working with you.

To readers near and far, thank you for your constant support and social media messages which I seem to receive on days where I'm suffering imposter syndrome! They give me such a boost and make my solitary writing days not so solitary after all.

For those who've been with me since the start, I can't thank you enough, and for those just joining us, welcome! I have the best readers in the world.

Keep reading for an excerpt from
Escape to Honeysuckle Hall . . .

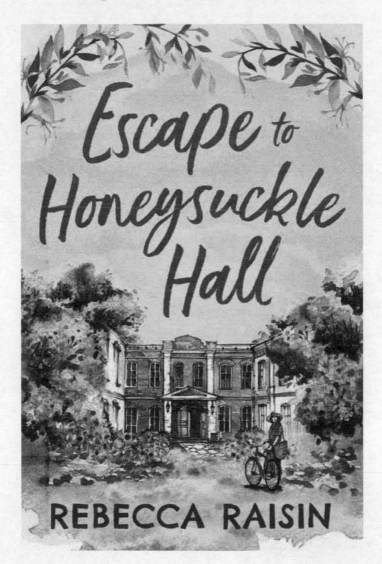

Chapter 1

Moonlight casts a pall of grey over London as late spring rain hits the office windows sideways, reminding me we should all still be tucked up in our warm beds, not here at work at such an ungodly hour. I rouse myself and try to jolly the team, even though I feel anything but jolly myself. The marriage proposal of the millennium is about to happen and we've all had to forgo sleep in order to be here because the surprise event is taking place in Tinseltown, no less.

It'll be livestreamed to cater to the happy couple's friends and fans alike. Celebrities, eh? They don't do anything by halves, which is where we come in: luxury concierge to the stars. Got a wish? We can grant it – as long as money is no object.

Excès curates exclusive, bespoke experiences for the super wealthy. Ever dreamed of having private access to the Temple of the Sun at Machu Picchu to propose to your paramour? Need front-row tickets to the Oscars but you're not in the movie biz? A wedding renewal with the Pope? Dinner for two at the Tower of London under the stars? Birthday flash mobs? The unimaginable is available for a hefty price tag. I bought a share of the luxury concierge club four years ago. Along with the other investors, we built our empire from the ground up and are still trying hard to expand the business and become the biggest name in the biz.

This darkened pre-dawn, the team gather around the table, stifling yawns, mainlining caffeine or eating their feelings with the smorgasbord of food I had delivered to bribe them all to be in attendance so bloody early. Sometimes I think the only 'refined' thing about me is my sugar habit, as I take another cinnamon doughnut and top up coffee cups. My bestie told me all about the clean-eating diet – but I lost interest when I found out it's not about consuming a family-size block of chocolate in the bath.

'It's nearly time!' I say, and dazzle everyone with one of my 'work rocks!' smiles. They're not fooled. They're just bloody tired and no amount of caffeine is going to shock them into faking it for my benefit. 'Are you ready for the proposal—'

'*Of the millennium*!' they all chorus robotically. OK, so they might have heard that one too many times. Aren't people down-right *prickly* when they lose sleep?

As far as proposals go, this one is fun and flamboyant and will be the envy of many a would-be bride. It's quite the coup for Excès because the couple themselves are famous and daily fodder for the tabloids.

Our groom-to-be, John Jones better known as JoJo, is one of the world's most bankable movie stars and, despite his advancing years, is still very much hot property. After a swift divorce from his loyal wife of twenty-five years, he hired Excès to mark this new stage with all the bells and whistles.

I'm a hopeless romantic and adore seeing love bloom for my clients, but, in this instance, part of me cringes that his ex-wife is bound to see the new lovers flaunting their romance to all and sundry. I guess I'm not the moral police; I'm just a luxury concierge doing her job as best she can. It's not my place to judge.

Still, I secretly grieve for the forgotten first wife. Will she flick on her telly later and relive her heartache once more? I shouldn't be worrying about that. But what happened to good old-fashioned romance, and making marriages go the distance? I'd probably be out of a job, that's what, so I grin and bear it, even though it nags at me from time to time.

'Is Harry going to tune in?' my assistant Victoria asks, taking the seat beside me.

My fiancé Harry is tucked away on some tropical island with music sensation Carly C. She's a new client of ours, a reality TV personality turned global superstar. A touch of pride runs through me as I remember when I announced I'd managed to get her to sign up with Excès – but she chose Harry to help with her album launch because he's so well connected in the music industry.

Carly C is a magnet for the tabloids for all the wrong reasons: boozy nights out, online spats with other celebs. You name it, Carly C has done it, although part of me admires her sassy attitude. She is a breath of fresh air in a world full of faux person-alities. What you see is what you get and she doesn't pretend for anyone. That being said, we'd thought it'd be safer with her stashed away on an island to launch her album and shoot a behind-the-scenes documentary.

Trouble is less likely to find Carly C there because she can't exactly fight with other celebrities when the internet is unreli-able! Her reputation has taken a battering in the press, so having her show her softer side and capturing the 'real' Carly had been a brainwave of Harry's. And he sold the streaming rights for the documentary for a bomb . . . !

I lift a shoulder. 'Harry'll try and tune in I guess, but the Wi-Fi on the island is patchy at best.' It feels so strange not to be able to check in with him, especially now with all this going on. 'It only works when it wants to.'

'A bit like Harry,' Victoria says and then quickly covers her mouth. 'Sorry.'

I smile. 'It's OK.' It's a running joke around the office that Harry swans in and out without doing a lot of work. But his job is to make people more *pliable*. He's our chief schmoozer and client wrangler and sadly the office staff don't really see that side. They hear about him jetting off to exotic locations almost daily to meet with managers, owners or a board of directors, to wine and dine them and grease the wheels so the impossible becomes possible. I can see why people envy him, but deep down he's lovely and I thank my lucky stars he chose me. Although he can be a bit of a diva himself, if I'm honest . . .

I'm more of a homebody when I'm not working. I hate wearing high heels and fussing over fashion. My idea of a fun day out is scouring vintage shops for my philatelic collection (stamps and postage material) then finding a cheap greasy spoon to eat at. Harry, on the other hand, prefers the finer things in life: designer labels, micro food at macro prices and being seen at all the latest hot spots. I guess the old adage is true that opposites attract. I sometimes find myself staring at him as though he's speaking another language that I can't quite decipher. I'm a small-town gal, and he's this larger than life big-city go-getter. We're like the perfect rom-com couple brought to life.

Tonight's epic proposal is Harry's baby. He was the one to secure JoJo and sell him the dream, including peddling all the rights to the media for an obscene amount of money. La-La Land, eh?

Harry vowed this would be the proposal of the *millennium*, emphasising the word until everyone obviously tired of hearing it. Soon after, he flew off to a remote island with Carly C leaving me to do the rest of his job while he's away. I'm *always* doing someone else's job; I can't seem to set myself any boundaries or say no. I suppose it's because I want Excès to be a success and if I don't take up the load, who will?

More staff rush into the room and snatch seats, mugs of coffee and buttery croissants. Their excited chatter eases the tension. Everyone is eager to see what Harry's magicked up for our celebrity couple.

'Here we go!' Louisa from marketing says.

Our movie star JoJo appears on screen, new girlfriend in tow.

She's a few decades younger than him, and I can't help but notice he's dyed his salt and pepper locks jet-black. Hand in hand they stroll down Hollywood Boulevard. Stars twinkle overhead, while the moon dips low. They're the epitome of superstardom, dressed to impress, not a hair out of place and their toned, tanned bodies glow even under moonlight. They look a million bucks and my heart just about explodes when I think of the surprises about to unfold.

When they arrive at Grauman's Chinese Theatre, JoJo stops to point out the stars lining the Hollywood walk of fame. I hold my breath, knowing what's coming is quite the achievement for a B-grade actress whose greatest claim to fame is a long-running sitcom where she plays the cliché ditzy blonde. To give her credit, the show has longevity, coming into its tenth season and she can act; in fact, I think she holds the show together. I admit I binge-watch it on occasion and am always left in stitches afterwards – she's got great comic timing and I hope JoJo with his connections will help catapult her onto the next rung of superstardom.

Hidden cameras pan in on our actress as JoJo points to the latest pink terrazzo and brass star bearing her name: *Chastity Cocker*. How on earth Harry managed such a feat is beyond me, but I'd hazard a guess a lot of money greased palms. The pink stars are supposed to be sacrosanct – but that's Harry for you. He could buy Warner Brothers itself before anyone was any the wiser.

Chastity's hands fly to her face and with a squeal she jumps up and down, which concerns me when she's wearing five-inch stilettos with an ice-pick heel. How don't they snap? If it were me, I know they'd break clean off and I'd topple into the only puddle around for miles, screaming like a banshee and making a fool of myself. Some people have all the luck.

She flings her lithe frame into JoJo's loving arms and lands a kiss on his lips. Before it can deepen, a troupe of showgirls with big feather headdresses prance down the steps of the theatre and onto the boulevard singing Etta James' 'At Last' as theatrically as it deserves.

Chastity has love hearts for eyes, and I heave a sigh of relief. As far as magical marriage proposals go, this is hitting the mark. A crowd has formed, recognising the celebs. They hold phones aloft as they follow the lovebirds down the boulevard. It strikes me they must be used to people tagging along, as if they're a tourist attraction. They don't even blink as the crowd around them thickens. I guess it's all part of being in the spotlight, but it'd be my worst nightmare. There's a lot to be said for being invisible.

JoJo eventually stops in front of the Dolby Theatre where the Academy Awards are hosted every year. The red carpet has been rolled out and he moves Chastity along it, as paparazzi scream into view and snap their pictures as if the awards *are* truly happening. It's all a farce, of course, but Chastity is lapping up all the attention as if she's won an Oscar and is about to thank the Academy itself.

'This is so sweet!' Victoria chimes. It really is, and makes me wonder if my very own fiancé is a little more romantic than I had him pegged for. I'd expected grand gestures, but I hadn't expected quite this level of starry-eyed expression of love drama, which is exactly the type of thing these cashed-up stars thrive on.

'Right?'

'He's done a great job appealing to all the things Chastity loves,' Victoria continues in awe. 'And pulled out all the stops to make sure this goes off without a hitch.'

'I didn't think he had it in him to be honest.' We laugh good-naturedly at Harry's foibles. He's usually more into the adrenaline junkie side of things – if you want to jump out of a perfectly good plane over the Grand Canyon, or zip line across Tokyo, Harry is your go-to guy.

He doesn't usually take on marriage proposals. Even ours had been very low key. He'd dropped to one knee over an Indian takeaway in our apartment. A nice surprise, but very simple, right

272

down to the plain gold band that he said suited me since I'm not flashy and didn't need diamonds to know my worth. But a girl wants a diamond at least once in her life, right? And if not at her engagement, then when? Anyway, I'd just laughed it off and said yes, thrilled to marry him, and that was that. We're engaged three years later and still haven't had time to sort our own wedding out.

The paps take their shots and then disappear to beat the pack and sell their pictures. A guy wearing a bright neon ensemble approaches, and asks Chastity the time. She takes out her phone to check, not knowing it's a cue for the flash mob who start singing and dancing to Bruno Mars's 'Marry You'.

'If that's not a clue, I don't know what is!' Victoria says, her eyes ablaze at the theatrics of it all. Flash mobs are kind of passé now, but JoJo insisted, claiming Chastity would adore it. And what's not to love about flash mobs? Passé or not, I think they're fun.

Dancers circle Chastity and she soon joins in, while JoJo stands on, smiling wide like all his Christmases have come at once. When the number is over, a limo appears and the two are whizzed away to the Hollywood sign on Mount Lee. A drone flies overhead filming their journey so we can only guess what they're talking about in the limo.

'OK,' I say, while I nervously eat a handful of sugared almonds. 'This is the big finale.' The limo pulls up and the driver helps Chastity from the car, as she sips on champagne and looks up at the bright sign that so many dreams are made of.

A close-up of their faces reveals wide eyes and beaming smiles. Chastity will die when she sees what's coming next! I only hope JoJo has remembered the ring – a huge pink diamond that cost more than a small island and was just as hard to procure.

On the lawn sits a Persian rug, Louis XVI chairs and Queen Anne tables as if they're in their own little chateau and not on the side of the Hollywood Hills. The limo driver returns with an ice bucket and obligatory bottle of Cristal and tops up their flutes before disappearing.

Camera people now close in, and Chastity laughs. 'Is this being livestreamed or something?'

'For posterity,' JoJo agrees and clinks his flute against hers. 'Pretend they're not here.'

She leans in and kisses him in such a way that I'm sure it's going to be blurred on the replay. *Holy guacamole.*

'Jeez,' Victoria says. 'She looks like she's about to eat him!'

'She does!'

They finally break apart. 'I want to find a man who looks at me the way JoJo looks at Chastity, like she's a soft juicy bao bun,' Victoria says, her voice wistful.

There are a few titters around the table and we hold our breath once more as fireworks explode from the top of the Hollywood sign. 'How did he get permission for *that*?' Bailey from HR asks.

'He's a great negotiator.' *Money, money, money.*

I hold my breath as the big reveal creeps closer. JoJo turns to Chastity and bends on one knee, before whispering, 'Look up,' just as a plane flies across the sky above the Hollywood sign. Light grid mantles under its wings illuminate the night sky and spelled out in lights is the pièce de résistance:

Will you marry me, Sarah?

It's the most beautiful thing ev— Wait.

Sarah.

SARAH!

Nooooooo!

The breath leaves my body in a whoosh. No, no, no! I close my eyes – maybe I've imagined it in my fatigued state. When I wrench my eyes open to check, I see confusion dash across Chastity's face, which is swiftly replaced by a dark cloud of anger. Her eyes flare with a rage that makes me shrink down in my seat.

'Is this some kind of sick joke?' she says in a menacingly low voice. JoJo has gone white with shock. What do I do?!

'Melanie!' I screech to our media guru and slam my hands on the table, making cupcakes launch upwards in surprise. 'Make it stop! Turn off the livestream, get those cameras out of there. Shut it down. *Shut it down now!*' Melanie hurries from the room, the others from her department follow close behind, barking orders to each other.

Onscreen, JoJo is chasing Chastity, trying to explain and letting out an expletive or two about Harry and the whole 'damn gang at Excès' – oh dear – 'who are clearly incompetent!' But she doesn't listen. Instead, she throws herself into the limo and tells the driver to make haste, but not in so many nice words. The limo skids out of the park leaving a bereft JoJo standing alone with just his long face for company. And then, praise the Lord, the screen goes black.

Chapter 2

This is a PR disaster! 'Sarah is JoJo's *ex-wife's* name! Do you think Harry just got them muddled up?' Wild thoughts swirl as I wonder how to contain this. I stand and pace around the room. 'How could this have happened?'

Victoria shakes her head. 'Harry's royally stuffed up, he has.'

'How could he make such a careless mistake . . . ?' My former sugar high is now a distinctive low.

Victoria grimaces. 'Can you imagine how Chastity feels? This epic marriage proposal, dancing girls, walk of fame star, flash mob and fireworks, with his ex-wife's name up in lights while it's being *livestreamed!*'

'None of that is good.' Faces around the table are downcast. No one knows quite how to react. It's not a good sign, not a good sign at all. 'Can you check online? See what's being reported and then we can work out how best to spin this?'

She swipes at her iPad and gets to work. 'It's *everywhere* already.'

I rub my face; this is not a good start to the day. 'OK, how can we play it? What can we do to minimise the embarrassment for JoJo and Chastity?'

Tapping her chin with a pen, she says, 'What about showing close-ups of the walk of fame star, the smile on her face, how happy she was dancing?'

'Yes,' I say. 'Tie that in with some stories about how she came from nothing and is set to be one of the world's most-loved actresses? Let's highlight her philanthropy work. If we can drown out today with all the good Chastity has done, we might swing this back around. Didn't she give a season's salary to a women's shelter last Christmas? Let's remind everyone about that.'

'This error is dynamite for every news outlet, Orly, but I'll do my best.'

'I know, the vultures!' I groan. 'Get onto to every reporter we're friendly with and let's get them sharing. Other celebs too. Who's she close to? Find out and start sending gifts and get them to tweet about how beautiful the proposal was, send them the first part of the video, minus the ending and let's get that online and boosted as much as we can.'

'Good idea.'

There's no time to ruminate; I need to start damage control with the couple themselves. I'll send flowers, I'll send money, I'll send a private jet! No, I'll send a posse of rescue pups for them to play with and make an obscenely large donation to their favourite animal shelter! I'll do whatever it takes to fix this while I wait for Harry to return from his island adventure and start the grovelling process himself. It irks me he's absent at such a crucial time. It's a pattern with Harry and the other business partners. They presume I'll fix their mistakes because I always do.

I call Harry and leave a voicemail: 'Harry I need to speak to you urgently—'

The voicemail cuts out and a recorded message tells me his mailbox is full. My head is about to explode – just what is he doing? Surely there's a Wi-Fi signal *somewhere* on the bloody island! Today of all days I'd thought he'd find a way to tune in.

The remaining staff leave the boardroom on pretences of having a busy day, and work to do. Victoria pats my shoulder and says, 'Let's move to our office.'

We spend the entire day attempting to make amends. I send

exotic fruit and expensive champagne. I hire them a suite at the Chateau Marmont and fill it with luxury gifts. But it's no good, they've gone into hiding. I call Harry and his phone is still infuriatingly off. The story is reported throughout the day on television and social media.

Reporters gleefully discuss the disaster, the juicy livestreamed 'Cocker Love Cock-up' a ratings win and a play on poor Chastity's surname – yikes. Memes start circulating. Gifs are next. I want to cup my head and cry. Nothing we do stems the tide.

Day turns into night and I field calls from JoJo's lawyers threatening to sue. I beg, cajole and bargain for more time, insisting that it was a gross error and that we're investigating it. All steps will be taken to punish the person responsible. Who knows, maybe it wasn't Harry? Maybe it was someone who has it in for JoJo or Chastity? It's too late to fix it, but I make all the enquires I can and alarmingly everything circles back to Harry.

When the airport emails me a copy the sign-off form with Harry's signature in thick cursive, I slump on my desk. It's right there in black and white: *Will you marry me, Sarah?* with Harry's approval.

It's a mistake anyone can make, of course, but it's not acceptable in our line of work. We have staff who double and triple check everything, yet Harry insists on going rogue and doing it all himself. And now look!

'You've done everything you can to mitigate the mess,' Victoria says, giving me a look usually reserved for lost puppies. 'Why don't you head out and meet Maya for dinner like you're meant to? They can still call and threaten you as you're walking, you know.'

Somehow, I laugh. 'Yes. Yes, they can.' I let out a world-weary sigh. 'I don't think there's anything else I can do now anyway. I've tried everything. It'll be up to Harry now. He's probably sunning himself on that bloody tropical island, blissfully unaware that this place is falling like a house of cards.'

'That's Harry for you.' She gives me a long look.

'Yeah.' I don't even have the energy to think of an excuse for him. 'I'm *so* late to meet Maya.' She's my best friend and we meet for dinner religiously at the same time every week.

'Go,' she says more forcefully. 'Maya won't mind. You're always late.'

'True.' I nod. 'OK, see you tomorrow?'

'It's Saturday tomorrow.'

'Right, sorry.' Suddenly, I envy her being able to have two days – forty-eight blissful hours – away from work.

'Have the weekend off, Orly. Seriously. Switch your phone off for once. Harry wouldn't think twice about ignoring calls if something like this happened to him. Why don't you try it?'

'I wish. What *does* my schedule look like for the weekend?' Everything else has quite flown out of my mind.

She sighs. 'It's bloody busy.' Swiping through her iPad she says, 'Tomorrow you're emcee for the charity luncheon at the Ritz.' Oh bollocks, I'd forgotten about that. Usually Harry emcees but I had to agree on account of him going away. Public speaking isn't my forte; I'm more of a behind-the-scenes kind of gal. 'And then you've got the industry cocktail party at Bars on Barges. The end-of-month reports are due, and Harry chalked you up for those.'

Of course he bloody well did! 'How can I hide, with all that going on?' I groan. 'The industry party will be a nightmare!' A room full of industry experts with this juicy gossip swirling about the room and still no Harry to face up to it. 'Is anyone else from Excès going?' I hope and pray.

'No, just you.'

'Waaah.'

'Don't go, Orly. You're busy with other things anyway. Just don't do it.'

'I have to go or it'll look bad for Excès.' When I give my word, I don't ever renege on it – something drilled into me by my father who said the one thing we can never break is our word. If you commit to something, you follow through. Dad died relatively young, when I was only ten, so those little adages have stayed with me. And I'd feel like I was letting my dad down if I started breaking my promises. That's something I won't do.

'See you on Monday.' I air-kiss Victoria and take my bag, then dash outside into the balmy evening air. Always running late, late, late!

I glance at my watch and continue down Brompton Road, past Harrods whose concertinaed green awnings resemble eyes half-closed for slumber in the inky night.

I walk then hobble, ruing the fact a cab would crawl even slower in this traffic. It gives me plenty of time to consider the fact my career isn't quite as gratifying as I'd once imagined it would be. In fact, it's a great big migraine-inducing nightmare.

Eventually I see the bright lights of the West End. Bars and restaurants heave. The streets of Soho are packed with late-night revellers. People clutch cigarettes and spill from pubs into alley-ways, their laughter punctuating the chilly night. Music blares from unseen speakers as I dodge tipsy executives who give me slow lazy smiles.

I turn down a cobblestoned lane and slip past a trio of friends wearing kilts who dance and sing as if all the world is a stage. Gosh, I love London. It's a melting pot and anything goes. But tonight, all I want to do is eat spicy dumplings with Maya and decompress.

'Sorry, excuse me, can I just . . . sorry.' Ever the apologetic Londoner, I slink through, imagining my first sip of wine after a very long week.

Maya is a cardiothoracic surgeon. We met by chance at a charity fundraiser a million years ago and we've been firm friends ever since. She's always around when life gets impossible or when I just need to sink a few gins and forget about the world.

As I stumble on my heels, wishing I'd changed into trainers, I finally see the little yellow lantern of the hole-in-the-wall Chinese restaurant we've been meeting at on Fridays since forever. They make the best mapo tofu dish in London. Owners Huan and Bai took us under their wing and are like surrogate parents. They always insist we eat more, fuss over us and are sweet and protective. They have a gaggle of their own children, now grown, who work at the restaurant and one who works as a neurosurgeon in the same hospital as Maya.

Bai sees me and commits to a launch hug. For a diminutive woman she packs a punch when she envelops me in her arms and squashes the air from my lungs. I make a sound like 'Ooomphfzwark . . .' before she frees me and I drag sweet precious oxygen back to its rightful organs. 'Hey, Bai, how are you?' I say, gasping.

Her eyes are wide with worry. 'Maya is crying – you have to hurry.'

'Crying?'

'Quick, quick. She needs you.'

Bai points to our usual table in the back. The flickering candle highlights Maya's face: mascara trails track down her cheeks and her exotic dark eyes are sunken. What on earth? Her earlier confirmation text message hadn't given any of this away. I flick my mobile on silent so the barrage of incoming calls buzzing away won't disturb us and then I rush over.

'Darling!' I drop my bag and move to hug her. 'What's wrong?'

She sobs, the kind of can't-catch-your-breath tears that imply she's been at this for some time. I hastily sit opposite and take Maya's hand, unsure of what to do. I can count on one hand the number of times she's cried like this and usually it revolves around losing a patient. She's more of the stiff upper lip variety, essential in her job.

'Did something happen at work?'

'He's gone.'

I rack my brain about who she could be referring to and then I realise. *Oh no!* 'Ernest?'

She gives me a trembling smile with the barest of nods.

'Oh, darling, I'm so sorry. What happened?'

She lifts a shoulder as if it's just one of those things. 'His daughter just called me to let me know . . . It was actually quite peaceful in the end. He drifted off in his sleep at home surrounded by his cats and that little barky dog of his.'

Poor Maya. 'Without you, he wouldn't have had all that extra time, but he *did* because of the excellent way you mended his broken heart.'

'I just did my job, but I love the way you romanticise heart surgery. He was the best. A true gentleman.'

Maya had been treating Ernest off and on for years. His ticker gave him trouble, then he had a stroke, but he had an indomitable spirit and never gave up in all of his ninety-plus years. They'd grown close as Maya had moved up the ranks and he'd been in and out of her care. While Maya tried to maintain a professional distance with her patients, some managed to creep into her heart, and jovial old man Ernest was one of them. Every Friday Maya regaled me with Ernest stories and I knew I would miss hearing about the incredible man.

'It's hit me so hard. I can't imagine not seeing his dashingly suited self, propped up by his cane wandering the corridors, asking if it wasn't too much trouble for a pot of tea.'

'He was lucky to have you.' I don't know many surgeons who'd scoot off and make a patient a pot of tea. In the end, Ernest would often pop in to visit Maya, making some excuse or other when he just liked having a mug of tea and some sugary biscuits with his pretty doctor who carved out a slice of time in her busy day and gave it to him.

'I was the lucky one.'

'You both were.'

She balls the napkin and averts her eyes. 'I hate that I didn't get to say goodbye.'

I squeeze her hand. 'But that's the sweetest part, darling. He didn't die after an emergency visit to hospital; he wasn't hooked up to machines and heart monitors. The last time you saw each other you shared a slice of cake and waxed lyrical about your day. And rather sweetly, he slipped off peacefully surrounded by his menagerie of fluffy critters . . . As far as deaths go, that's a pretty good one.'

'You always know what to say.' She takes a deep breath, her sobs slowly abating. 'Work will be that little bit less shiny without Ernest popping in to visit.' Maya exhales long and loud as if releasing some of her grief. 'Sometimes I wonder whether all the heartache is worth it.'

I stare her down in a maternal way and say softly, 'Darling, you're fighting the good fight. Look at how many *lives* you've saved! Your work matters.' Despite feeling low tonight, Maya loves her job. She thrives in the pressurised environment and always goes the extra mile for her patients. While days like today are impossible, she always bounces back.

'So does yours, Orly.' Maya knows I've been struggling with work lately and the lack of meaning I find in it.

It's not comparable to saving lives. Not even close.

I fidget with the paper napkin. 'Sometimes I feel I'd like to do something more meaningful. But then I think of how hard I've worked to get to where I am and I wonder if I'm having some sort of mid-life crisis. Shouldn't I be grateful? I dreamed of this high-flying London life but it all seems so . . . different to how I imagined.' I feel ridiculous moaning about such a thing after Maya's day, but here we are and I wonder if the distraction about my crazy life will help her bruised heart.

Maya nods. 'You're *right*. I can't even remember when I last enjoyed the view from my apartment. Or when I caught a show at the theatre. When I walked just for the hell of it, not because I was racing to get back to the hospital. There's never time.'

I cluck my tongue. 'We're burnt out at the ripe old age of thirty-five.'

'Looks like it. How will I ever have a baby when I'm already too tired?!' Her boyfriend Preston isn't exactly dad material either, so part of me is relieved that there's no time for making babies. He's openly bigamous and doesn't care a jot if Maya dislikes that or not. She deserves so much better than him. Conversely Maya's dream has always been to have a houseful of babies, which she's been saving for since forever. I only hope she'll move on from Preston to someone who deserves her. But then again, when would she have *time* to meet someone new? Like me, Maya works crazy long hours.

'Right?' Deep down I recognise this as a huge problem. We've spent so long striving for these lofty goals and lost ourselves along the way. We should be enjoying our youth, soaking up every ounce of pleasure in one of the most amazing cities on the planet, but there's never enough energy for all that.

'Today I went to work with two different shoes on! I had to pretend it was all a ploy to distract my patients, then I spent the rest of the day acting like some jokester so they didn't think I was losing my marbles and take my scalpel away from me!'

'Oh, Maya! You need some downtime!'

'We both do.'

'Right? Give me a bubble bath and a good book and I might last a chapter before I sink into oblivion or my phone inevitably rings and startles me back to consciousness.' For Maya, it's even more hectic. Double shifts and long surgeries in a world where time is of the essence and there's just not enough doctors to go around.

Maya flicks her glossy mane of curly black hair. 'What *would* you do though if you didn't have a share in Excès? If you could just forget everything and do what you wanted to do?'

'Retire . . . ?'

She laughs. 'At thirty-five?'

I toy with the empty wine glass in front of me. 'No, I'd be bored. But seriously, I have these wild thoughts of escaping. Throwing it all in and going back to a small town and doing something that actually *helps* people. But how? Doing what exactly? And what if I hated it?' I shrug. 'Maybe I'm just well overdue for a holiday.' But I know it's more than that. Some days I feel like I can't catch my breath and anxiety makes me dizzy.

'What does Harry think? Is he feeling the same?'

I think of my curly-haired fiancé, with his dark broody eyes. I'm still shocked he proposed; part of me always thought we'd have this fleeting passionate romance that would burn out because Harry is so fickle – always on the hunt for the next shiny bauble. But then he surprised me by proposing and making grand life plans that we've never quite got around to.

'Harry has no idea. You know what he's like; he thrives on his high-octane life. Flying here, there and everywhere, barely taking a breath. I haven't seen him for ten days now, actually. He's been on a private island with Carly C, helping meet her every whim while she's launching her album and filming a behind-the-scenes-of-fame documentary thing, sort of like Beyoncé did.'

'Celebrities.' She rolls her eyes. 'Let's hope he's not meeting her *every* whim.'

I giggle. 'She's engaged to some YouTuber, isn't she?' You'd think I'd follow the tabloids in order to keep one step ahead, but very rarely do they get it right. I've learned it's much like everything in the shallow world of celebs – a big, fat lie. Usually a marketing ploy.

'I have no clue about Carly C.' Maya laughs. 'But you should talk to Harry, tell him how you're feeling about things at work. That you feel like something is missing.'

I lift a shoulder. 'Maybe. He'll just tell me I'm being dramatic.'

'Which is ironic since he panders to people who only eat the blue M&M's.'

'Right?!'

'How are you going with your plans to buy a property in the country? Is he still keen on that idea?' Harry and I sat down a while back and had a heart-to-heart about our dreams for the future and where we saw ourselves in five, ten, fifteen years. Our plan had been to save for a sprawling country property, a place that could become a sanctuary; a wonderland where we could safely raise children and have a nest to commute from. Once again, it was all just words. Promises like vapour, diaphanous and fleeting.

You can't help who you love though, and I adore him despite our differences. It's those differences that leave me enthralled; the way Harry takes charge of a room, charms everyone – men and women alike. His utter confidence that things will always go his way. It's quite blinding being in love with such a guy, almost like staring at the sun at times.

'Time has marched on and we're still no closer to buying a place. He never commits to any viewings, and definitely never has the time to spend a weekend attending open houses . . .'

I don't tell Maya I still spend every Saturday morning scouring the internet for my dream home even though Harry's got cold feet about it. 'It's hard to explain but I can *see* myself in that new lifestyle. A big old house with high ceilings, a roaring fire, Vinnie the little rescue pup at my ankles, maybe some adorable fluffy chickens so I could forage for eggs for Sunday brunch. Time to pickle vegetables from my garden, make chutneys for grazing plates when friends from town visit, that kind of thing. A simple life, where our children can climb trees, play chase and breathe fresh country air. Wouldn't that be the perfect tonic for burnout?' But am I dreaming? Is it pure fantasy when Harry won't even attend viewings?

'It would and it sounds bloody lovely, Orly. Who wouldn't want that?'

'Maybe Harry . . . ?' I consider the day from hell, his absence. It feels as though something has shifted between us and my love for him has dimmed a little. Like staring at the sun doesn't so much blind me but instead burns. I change the subject because talking about my would-be country house causes an ache in my heart – it's like I can *feel* it's the right move and yet I can't convince Harry. 'Have you heard the latest celebrity gossip around the hospital today?' I ask, knowing she probably hasn't. Maya is old-school when it comes to technology – she rarely uses social media and spends her downtime exercising, of all things. If there's a juicy story in the press about one of our clients she'll usually hear it via the nurses who fill her in on life outside of the wards.

'No, I haven't, darling. Did something happen?' So I tell her all about the so-called proposal of the millennium and everything that followed. Her jaw drops. 'It was livestreamed? Oh God, Orly, he *didn't*!'

'He did.'

'How could he get Sarah and Chastity mixed up? That's taking distracted to a whole new level.'

I nod. 'And now he's nowhere to be found.'

She clucks her tongue. 'Just like bloody always. Darling, it's not fair that he scarpers when he sees fit and coincidentally it's always when he's made some huge cock-up. Why didn't *you* go with Carly C?'

I shrug. 'She chose him. He's such a magnet for celebs – he can talk the talk whereas I'm better in front of the computer sorting out all the headaches. I don't actually mind that though,' I say truthfully. 'I can't parade around with their entourages and take it seriously. It makes me feel all sorts of awkward; I'd feel like this gangling bird tottering behind these glamorous over-the-top characters. Harry loves that side, so it's best left to him. Anyway, let's not ruin the evening with any more talk about boring old work.'

'Darling, we can park that conversation if you want, but it sounds like you had a really stressful day. I'm worried that you're always left to fix things with very little support. I know you all have your own clients, but you all share in the successes and it's like they ride your coat-tails when it suits them and you're on your own when it doesn't.'

Bai's son pops a plate of prawn crackers down and I take one, crunching it into a million pieces over myself, while Maya delicately eats hers without a crumb in sight. 'I know, I need to get harder, tougher, but when I'm in the thick of it I'm just in problem-solving mode, you know?' What else is there to do except fix it as best I can?

She tilts her head. 'You don't need to change, Orly. They do. Especially Harry, who should be by your side when things like this happen.'

I take a bottle of wine from my bag, a freebie from the office. 'Red?' I ask, knowing Maya is right but not knowing what to do about it all.

'I'll stick with Chinese tea. I'm not feeling one hundred per cent and a wine headache will only keep me up. But I've heard—' she peers at the label '—*Congratulations Mr and Mrs Deely* is a great vintage.' She gives me a megawatt smile. Maya is one of those health-conscious types and doesn't usually partake in a lot of alcohol. Her way to deal with worry is to run, a much healthier stress reliever but not one I'd subscribe to.

'The best! Perks of planning fancy weddings at Claridge's, eh?' I laugh as I fill my glass with the exotic red, which is actually a pricey little quaffer, and top up Maya's tea. 'Here's to Ernest, one of the finest gentlemen to walk this earth.'

Maya clinks her cup alongside my glass. Her eyes fill with tears. 'May he rest in eternal peace back with his beloved Betty.' I think about the man I never met, but feel I know. He cherished his wife and talked about her every single day, even decades after she died. That's the kind of love affair I want, one that lasts a lifetime.

'Why don't we start planning *your* wedding?' Maya asks gently. 'That'll give us something fun to do, something to drag us out of this rut we're in.'

'Maybe . . .' I say, when I really mean no. The thought of my own wedding just seems so abstract; I can't picture it for some reason. I don't have time to ponder why as tiny Bai's thundering footsteps echo behind me.

Our favourite tofu dish is presented to us and I smile. Bai

determines what we need to eat and we duly comply by hoovering up every last delicious morsel. Usually, she'll feed us something *to put colour in our cheeks*, or *meat on our bones*. Wordlessly she continues placing steaming dishes in the middle of the table and then hugs Maya whose eyes pop out of her head from the pressure. 'Now eat, girls, eat, eat; you need to put some colour in your cheeks and some meat on your bones.'

Dear Reader,

Thank you for shutting out the real world and diving into the land of fiction for a while. I hope you've journeyed far and wide and had an incredible adventure from the comfort of your own home.

Without you I wouldn't be able to spend my days talking to my invisible friends who become so real to me I name-drop them in conversations with my family, who all think I'm a little batty at the best of times . . . so thanks again!

My sincerest hope is that you connected with my characters and laughed and cried and cheered them on (even the baddies who I hope redeemed themselves in the end) and that they also became your friends too.

I'd love to connect with you! Find me on Facebook @RebeccaRaisinAuthor or on Twitter @Jaxandwillsmum. I'm a bibliophile from way back, so you'll find me chatting about books and romance but I'm also obsessed with travel, wine and food!

Reviews are worth their weight in gold to authors, so if the book touched you and left you feeling 'happy ever after', please consider sharing your thoughts and I'll send you cyber hugs in return!

Love,
Rebecca x

Dear Reader,

We hope you enjoyed reading this book. If you did, we'd be so appreciative if you left a review. It really helps us and the author to bring more books like this to you.

Here at HQ Digital we are dedicated to publishing fiction that will keep you turning the pages into the early hours. Don't want to miss a thing? To find out more about our books, promotions, discover exclusive content and enter competitions you can keep in touch in the following ways:

JOIN OUR COMMUNITY:

Sign up to our new email newsletter: http://smarturl.it/SignUpHQ

Read our new blog www.hqstories.co.uk

: https://twitter.com/HQStories

: www.facebook.com/HQStories

BUDDING WRITER?

We're also looking for authors to join the HQ Digital family!
Find out more here:

https://www.hqstories.co.uk/want-to-write-for-us/

Thanks for reading, from the HQ Digital team

If you enjoyed *Flora's Travelling Christmas Shop*, then why not try another delightfully uplifting romance from HQ Digital?